EMPIRE'S *Children*

PATRICIA WEERAKOON

rhiza press

Dedication

My father was a Tea Maker in the plantations of Sri Lanka. This novel is dedicated to him, my mother Annie and my two wonderful brothers Godwin and Godfrey. Their guidance and sacrificial love made me the woman I am today.

Also to my husband Vasantha and son Kamal for their help, encouragement and patience. I could not have written this without their support.

Finally to my publisher Rochelle and editor Lynne. Thank you for bringing the Empire's Children to life.

Chapter 1

May 1957 Watakälé, Sri Lanka

Eight-year-old Shiro Rasiah skipped down the dirt path leading from her house to the tea factory.

'There once was an ugly duckling, with feathers all stubby and brown. And the other birds said in so many words – get out of town.' Her sweet, high voice spiralled into the majestic hills of central Sri Lanka, robed in the emerald green of tea bushes. The aroma of fresh picked tea leaves blended with the fragrance of fermenting tea wafting up the hill from the tea factory in the valley.

This was Shiro's playground and her father's livelihood.

Shiro loved everything around her. The mountains that made her feel so tiny. Eucalyptus trees with their leaves that smelled like the oil her mother rubbed on her when she had a cold, wildflowers that clung to every nook and cranny, the dragonflies that hovered over her head, even the bumble bees buzzing around the lilies that lined the moss and mud path she was on. She raised her hands above her head and swung round. She was no ugly duckling. She was a ballerina, like in the storybook she was reading with her mother. She was a star and this was her stage. Every tea bush and butterfly her audience. The rush of the water in the nearby stream echoed the applause she heard in her head. She stretched out one foot and bowed. 'Thank you, thank you.'

The chatter of women's voices brought Shiro crashing back to reality. She wrinkled her nose and sniffed – sweat and *betel*.

'Coolies,' she groaned. 'Wish they'd go away. This is *my* place.'

The women moved through the tea bushes like a chain of multicoloured beads. Indian tea pluckers, coolie women, dressed in gaudy cotton saris with rough pieces of hessian tied around their waists like aprons. Most wore no blouse under their sari, showing a generous amount of dark brown flesh. Heavy ornamental faux-gold earrings dangled from stretched earlobes and coloured glass bangles jangled on agile wrists. Strong, weathered hands flitted like brown butterflies over the tops of the tea bushes, plucking the fresh bloom, two leaves and a bud. With practiced ease, they flung it over their heads. The leaves collected in the wicker basket on their backs, supported by a rope stretched over the cumbly – a rough blanket on their heads.

The single man in the group stood on the mud path by the tea bushes. '*Angé pore. Ingé pore*,' he shouted in the guttural Tamil dialect of the Indian estate labourers. He was dressed in an old flannel shirt and a faded brown pair of trousers. A towel, wrapped turban-like on his head, announced his status as *Kangani*. He stabbed his finger this way and that to places the women had failed to pick. They darted around on their calloused bare feet. Their fingers flew over the bushes, striving to pick the mandatory twenty pounds of fresh leaves that would assure them a full day's wage.

Shiro stood, hands on hips, watching the daily ritual of the harvesting of tea leaves, leaves that would soon be in the tea factory, ready to be processed into black tea. The babble of the coolie women and the occasional barked command of the man mingled with the bird calls in the eucalyptus shade trees and the distant hum of the machinery in the tea factory. These were the sounds of a work day in the tea plantation – the background of Shiro's life.

Leaving the path, she picked her way down the steep slope, careful not to dirty her pretty purple dress or get mud on her neat white socks and buckled black shoes. Thundershowers were common in the hill country and the damp ground was slippery from last night's rain. She stepped over the mossy patches, hanging on to the sturdy branches of the tea bushes so she wouldn't slip.

This was, strictly speaking, still school time. But it was different when you're being home-schooled by your mother. You can go to places like where Shiro was heading, to the place where a small waterfall interrupted a clear bubbling stream. It was a private spot; where a cluster of trees and a shield-like rock separated Shiro from her home. Her parents and older brothers knew about it, but they never went there. This was her special place – where she came to think, read and be alone. It was her place of magic, where she made plans and dreamed dreams.

She looked at the coolie women – wanting them to notice her.

'*Chinnamma, kavanam, vallukum*,' one of the coolie women called out, warning her of the slippery mud track. The woman smiled, exposing her chipped teeth, stained red with the betel leaf she was chewing. Another waved her hand at Shiro. Shiro wasn't sure whether it was in greeting or to shoo her away. She edged closer to the group. She should say hello to the second woman, whom she recognised as the mother of her friend, Lakshmi.

'Chinnamma, *veeté poungé*!!' Kangani scowled at her and pointed towards the Tea-maker's house. He wanted her to go back home. She read in his face the threat to tell her father if she spoke with the coolie women. The women around him chortled and continued with their plucking.

'Humph!' Shiro crossed her hands in front of her. She glared back at Kangani. Who did this man think he was? How dare he tell her, the Tea-maker's daughter, what to do?

She wiggled her head, imitating her mother. She knew what her mother would say. '*Aiyoo mahal*, you mustn't chat to those Indian coolie women. You will begin to talk Tamil like an Indian. You are a Jaffna Tamil girl; you must speak *chenthamil*, the pure Tamil that belongs to your people. That is your heritage. You have nothing in common with Indian coolies.'

As a Sri Lankan staff child, she accepted that she was not supposed to mix with the Indian coolie labourers. It was a no-no in the tea plantations. Lakshmi, of course, was an exception. She was a coolie girl, but Lakshmi was her special friend. Her mother and father allowed her that, although they never called her a friend. They said Lakshmi was her nanny.

There was no one else for her to play with, except the apothecary's children, Dawn and Elmo. They were burghers, descendants of the Dutch who invaded Sri Lanka a long time ago. But for some reason, her mother didn't like Shiro being with them. Shiro, who wanted reasons for everything, had asked why.

'You might pick up burgher ways,' her mother had replied. She wondered what that was. Probably something that didn't fit into how pure Jaffna Tamil girls behaved.

Right now, she had to get the better of this stupid man. Shiro glowered at Kangani. He nodded and raised his right hand to his turban, then pointed again to the house. She got the message: *I respect your father, but you cannot be here or talk to these women.* Maybe she would squeeze into the bushes and say hello to Lakshmi's mother. That would annoy him. But her dress would get dirty and her mother would know what she had done. It wasn't worth the lecture that would follow.

Shiro tossed back her mane of curly black hair. The purple stone pendent on the gold chain around her neck danced and sparkled in the sunshine. Ignoring Kangani, she settled down on the rock ledge overhanging the stream. Her feet hung over the edge, the tip of her shoes just above the water. Out of the corner of her eye, she saw Kangani smile, turn and mutter something to the women. The women guffawed and moved away down the hill.

She didn't need them. Here in this place, she could make her own world. Shiro opened the poetry book she had brought with her. Her Uncle George had sent it by post from Colombo. He wanted her to read what he called classics – learn to speak the Queen's English.

'*There Was a Little Girl* by Henry Wadsworth Longfellow,' she read out loud, and then giggled at the words that followed. 'There was a little girl; who had a little curl; right in the middle of her forehead. When she was good, she was very good indeed. But when she was bad she was horrid.'

Drawing out a strand of her hair, she twirled it around her finger. There. Now she had a curl in the middle of her forehead. She had the poet's permission to be horrid.

Shiro heard her mother's voice in the distance. 'Shiro, mahal, where are you? We have to finish study time before Daddy gets home.'

Shiro groaned. Tamil literature and history to learn, so she could grow up to be a good Tamil lady – just like her mother. She raised her sun-browned face to the sky, and reached her arms up. Flapping her hands, she pretended that she had wings and could soar up in the sky like the eagle circling above her. The eagle swooped down and round her. The swept-back crest on its majestic head looked like a back-combed hairstyle. Her father had told her that it was a Crested Hawk Eagle. The bird looked so wise, so old. How long did eagles live? Forever?

'He clasps the crag with crooked hands. Close to the sun in lonely lands. Ringed with the azure world, he stands.' Her father had read from his book of poems to her last night. She could die for poetry. She dropped the book and lay back on the warm rock ledge.

'Shiro, mahal,' her mother again.

Getting up from her spot by the rock, she dragged her feet back up the path towards home.

Yesterday, she had overheard her mother and father talking in the bedroom. 'I can't get through to Shiro,' her mother had said. 'She never listens to me. It's like she withdraws into a shell when I ask her anything.'

Shiro didn't listen because most of the time she couldn't understand what her mother wanted of her. Maybe it was because her mother had grown up in the north of Sri Lanka – in Jaffna, in the middle of what she called Tamil heritage and culture. And she wanted to train her only daughter to be just like her. But Shiro was a child of the mountains, born in the tea plantation. Her father told her there had been a full moon on the night she was born, and that the fireflies had lit up the trees and the cicada had sung a special song for her.

4

He said that, against the wishes of her mother and grandmother, he had taken her out into the garden the next morning and the eagle circling in the sky above the house had dipped down in a blessing. He told her she had smiled up at the bird.

She didn't want to be patient, or forbearing or anything else that her mother pointed out as womanly virtues. She didn't want to be like her mother. She wanted to be free. To travel to places where people didn't care whether you were Tamil or Sinhalese, British, Sri Lankan or Indian. She would make it happen – when she grew up.

She ran back to the house, her hair flying behind her in the wind.

The British superintendent's black car skid to a halt as she dashed across the road. Shiro stopped on the grass edge and waved.

A boy, a lot older than she was sat in the back seat with the superintendent, Mr Irvine. He was white, like Mr Irvine. The sun glinted on golden hair that looked a lot like the hair on her walking-talking doll.

Shiro hadn't seen him before. He looked back at her and raised his hand as if to wave back, only to have Mr Irvine pull it back down.

So you won't wave back? Shiro knew how to deal with that. She put her hands on her hips, bent forward, and stuck her tongue out at the receding car.

Shiro turned and skipped past the jasmine hedge and rose bushes that formed the garden fence of their house, then ran up the drive to the veranda.

'Irvine picked up the Ashley-Cooper boy from the station today.' She heard her father's voice in the sitting room. Her father was back already. She must be really late. Now her mother would be truly angry with her. 'He's Anthony, the white bastard who'll inherit Watakälé.'

Her mother's voice was, as always, soft and controlled. 'So he's James Ashley-Cooper's younger son?'

'Yes.' Her father's voice was gruff. He sounded annoyed – even angry. 'The other one, William I think his name is, spent time last year at Udatänná.' He barked a laugh. 'The next generation Ashley-Cooper Empire, probably more degenerate than their father.'

Shiro tiptoed into the house. She crept along the wall of the sitting room. Maybe she could get into her bedroom without them seeing her.

Her father's voice got louder. He waved his hands around over his head. That meant he was furious. 'And Thambiah, the chief clerk at Udatänná, says that older son was a stuck up fool. He was apparently going at the coolie women. Can you imagine? At just seventeen?'

'*Appa.*' Her mother put her fingers on her father's arm. 'Don't talk like that.' Her voice dropped to a whisper. She rolled her eyes towards Shiro. 'Not in front of Shiro.'

Her father spun around. His face changed. He chuckled and scooped Shiro up in his arms. 'Ah, princess, late again? And all muddy. Been talking to eagles and playing with butterflies? Never mind, let's go get you washed up for dinner.'

Shiro wriggled down from his arms. 'I saw the British bastard.'

'You what?' her father tried to look stern, but his lips twitched in a smile.

'Yes, the car just went by. I waved. He didn't wave back.'

The smile left his face and was replaced by a glare. 'Who the hell does he —'

Her mother grabbed Shiro's hand and dragged her towards the bathroom. 'Hurry up and wash before dinner, mahal.'

Scrubbing her hands and face in the bowl of warm water, she heard her mother grumble to her father. 'See what you've done? Nice vocabulary you're teaching your daughter.'

She wondered what a vocabulary was.

Chapter 2

Lakshmi squatted by the water surrounded by a pile of dirty clothes. Her shoulders ached from scrubbing the mud and dirt from her mother's old cotton sari and her father's thick trousers. Her hands were sore from the harsh rough soap she used daily.

She glanced up and saw Shiro Chinnamma in the distance. Chinnamma, wearing her favourite purple dress, skipped along the path to the Tea-maker's house. Her hair hung loose and bounced on her shoulders. The evening sun caught the tiny stone pendant at her neck and sent a spark of light. Even from a distance, Lakshmi could see that she was singing. Lakshmi stood up and waved to her friend but Shiro Chinnamma didn't look down into the valley.

Holding the wet clothes in her hand, Lakshmi continued to watch Shiro Chinnamma's figure. She remembered the first time she had gone to the Tea-maker's house. She had been about ten years old, or so her mother told her. Of course, like the other coolie children, she had no real way of knowing how old she was.

She had been so frightened that day.

'You are lucky that they want you. You must do anything *Periamma* tells you,' her mother had rasped at her. 'And keep your mouth shut. Don't talk back. They will hit you if you say anything.'

She hadn't wanted to go. Her father had twisted her ear. 'Idiot girl,' he had yelled at her. 'You think you can just stay at home like a lady and get me to feed you? Who do you think you are? Go! Work and earn your keep.' She learned later from Periamma that Tea-maker *Aiya* had given her father money.

But it had been so different from what she expected.

'Your job is to play and look after Shiro,' Periamma had explained. Little 3-year-old Shiro Chinnamma had smiled and held out her chubby arms. At that moment, Lakshmi fell in love with the little girl.

'We have arranged with your parents.' Periamma had continued. 'You will finish your washing and cooking in the line room in the morning and evening and spend the day being a nanny to Shiro.'

Lakshmi didn't understand what it meant to be a nanny. But she did what she was told and five years on she was still at the Tea-maker's house daily.

Lakshmi turned back to her washing. She was cold and wet and she hadn't eaten anything since the afternoon meal at the Tea-maker's house. But she had to get the washing done before it was too dark. She stepped to the edge of the stream, scraped dried mud off the edge of the sari in her hand, dipped in the water, and then dashed it on the rock to break up the dirt.

The water came from the clear waterfall. But here, downstream in the bottom of the valley, the water was cloudy and had a constant smell of rubbish and worse. It served as washroom, laundry, and rubbish dump for the line rooms where the coolies lived.

'*Kaluthai, kaluthai!*' Lakshmi looked up to see Meena, the coolie girl who lived with her family in the line room next to theirs, slap a stark-naked little boy who had been doing his job at the edge of the stream. The boy, whom Lakshmi recognised as Meena's little brother, ran howling up the mud path into the line room. Lakshmi sighed as she saw a brown smudge float down the stream. She couldn't wash the clothes in this dirty water. She would have to come back tomorrow. At least she had finished washing her mother's sari.

Lakshmi spread out the sari on the rocks to dry. She heard an insistent wail, '*Acca, Acca, pasikithu.*' Sighing, she picked up her 3-year-old sister, who had been playing in the mud behind her. The little girl grabbed the sleeve of Lakshmi's faded dress and wiped her nose on it.

Lakshmi perched her sister on her hip. She squatted down and gathered the rest of the half-washed clothes in her other arm. Her mother would yell at her for not finishing washing them. She might even hit her. Blaming Meena's little brother wouldn't make any difference. The unwashed clothes would have to be rinsed out later in the night under the single, shared tap at the back of their line rooms.

Lakshmi stopped to watch a car wind its way along the road on the other side of the stream. It was the *Periadorai*'s black car. There was another person in the car; he looked younger than Periadorai, must be about her age. As she watched, Periadorai reached over the boy and wound up the window, separating their world from hers.

Lakshmi's eyes met that of the boy as the car drove by. His eyes were the deep blue of the sky after a thunderstorm. He seemed to look right through her.

She watched as the car drew away up the hill towards the Tea-maker's house, and then turned toward her home in the line rooms.

Lakshmi stepped between scrawny chickens and listless goats, deftly avoiding the garbage and animal droppings that lay around in the line room's common compound. She headed for the single room that she, her mother, father and sister called home. They had one room in a row of five – the coolies' line rooms. The room was always damp and smelled of smoke, stale sweat and rancid curry. It was all so different from the large, sweet-smelling rooms in the Tea-maker's house where her friend Shiro Chinnamma lived.

Getting to the line room, Lakshmi dumped the half-washed clothes in a corner. She slipped her sister into a homemade cloth swing hanging from a metal hook on the rafter and gave her a piece of dried bread to chew on. Ignoring her continued whimpers and sniffs, she went out to the back veranda, which doubled as their kitchen. She needed to get started on the evening meal of rice and dried fish. First, she had to wash and clean the uncooked rice of stones. She lugged the heavy pan to the tap in the garden that the families in the line rooms shared. Squatting down by the tap, she rinsed the rice and picked out the stones and sundry weevils.

Her sister started wailing again. '*Vayapothu!*' Lakshmi yelled back. Her sister howled louder. Lakshmi ignored the screams.

Carrying the heavy pan of washed rice on her hip, she walked back to the veranda. She set the pan on the open fireplace and turned to the sticks she had collected last night. Lakshmi chose a couple and broke them into pieces. She groaned and cursed. They were damp from last night's rain. Picking up the newspaper she had brought from the Tea-maker's' house yesterday she shoved it into the fireplace. Thank God that was dry. She would have to use it to light the fire. Now to find the box of matches. Her mother hid the matches in the box with her clothes. That way her father could not find it when he wanted to light his *ganja*. Lakshmi rummaged through the tea crate that contained her mother's clothes and found the box of matches.

With the fire finally going, she squatted by it and stirred the pot of rice. Impatient, she blew on the fire. She had to finish the cooking before her father got back from his work in the factory. Yesterday, she had been late coming home from playing with Shiro Chinnamma. The rice had not been ready when her father wanted it. He had called her a lazy cow and had hit her.

Smoke swirled up from the damp wood and drifted into the line room. Her little sister coughed and screamed louder.

Lakshmi saw her mother in the distance, walking down the mud path with the other women, returning from her day's work as a tea plucker. Her mother was younger than Periamma. And yet with her greying hair and stooped walk, she looked so much older. Her mother never smiled, while Periamma sang and laughed all the time. As she looked at that lined face, Lakshmi saw herself in twenty years' time. She suppressed a shudder and quickly dashed a tear from her eye with the back of her hand.

Reaching the line room, Lakshmi's mother dropped her tea plucker's basket at the door and came through to the back veranda. 'I saw Shiro Chinnamma today. She tried to talk to me, but Kangani wouldn't let her. You tell her that she will have to behave. It is wrong for her to talk with us.'

'What did she do wrong?' Lakshmi stirred the rice. 'She likes to be friendly.'

She ducked to avoid the blow her mother directed at her head. 'What are you talking about, idiot! Staff and coolies can't be friends! You think that just because Periamma teaches you English and sews you dresses out of left over pieces of cloth, you're better than the rest of us? You think I don't notice that you are trying to speak Jaffna Tamil like they do? You're a coolie, you fool! An Indian labourer! You may be fairer than me, but that is nothing. You will never ever be anything other than a coolie! The staff and Periadorai are all alike. They will use you, and then throw you in the drain when they are done.' She hawked and spat into the back garden. 'Tea-maker Aiya doesn't care for you. You are a servant there. A servant, that's all. Remember that when you're playing big sister to that spoiled brat!'

Lakshmi's vision blurred. Hot tears filled her eyes. Leaping up from her squatting position at the open fire, she left the half-cooked meal, ran out of the room, and scrambled up the hill towards the Tea-maker's house. Behind her, she heard her little sister's familiar loud wail. Her mother yelled, 'Lakshmi, come back here at once, kaluthai!'

Lakshmi ducked into the tea bushes, hiding in them as she climbed up the hill. Her mother's foul curses and her sister's loud screams followed her.

Someday, Lakshmi told herself, somehow, she would have a better life. Periamma would teach her to read and write English, and to sing and sew. She would learn to live and speak like they did. She would get away from the ugly, dirty life in the line room.

She thought of Shiro Chinnamma's parting words yesterday evening. 'Lakshmi, there will be a day when you won't have to go back to the line room, when you and I live together in a little house that we will build in my own special place on the rock by the stream.'

Shiro Chinnamma was, as usual, making things up. Imagining and playing, she called it. But maybe … just maybe.

Lakshmi heard the hoarse, drunken laughter of the men returning from the tea factory. Today was payday, and that meant many of them, including her father, would be drunk on the cheap alcoholic drink, *arak*, sold at the little local shop. She cringed into the tea bushes and lay there till the raucous voices and crude language faded into the distance.

Clambering up the hill, she popped out of the tea bushes across from the Tea-maker's house. She ran around the back, through a little gate, and into their garden.

By the time she reached the back door of the Tea-maker's house, Lakshmi was smiling.

Chapter 3

The BOAC Lockheed Constellation bumped down onto the Katunayaké Airport runway. Its four turboprop engines roared in reverse thrust and the aircraft slowed.

'Ladies and gentlemen, welcome to Ceylon.' The captain's voice crackled over the speaker system. 'The local time is four pm. The temperature is ninety degrees Fahrenheit and the humidity is seventy four percent. The distance from Katunayaké International Airport to Colombo is 18 miles. It is a ninety minute drive.'

Anthony Ashley-Cooper stretched his lanky, 16-year-old frame in the seat. He rubbed the film of sleep from his eyes and rotated his stiff shoulders before taking a peep out the tiny window. So this was Ceylon.

A mirage-like haze rose from the ground. Brown-bodied natives with black hair and beady dark eyes, dressed in coloured skirt-like garments, scurried like so many gaudy insects towards the plane. *What a dump. What the hell am I doing here? Stupid question. Checking out my little part of the British Empire in the colonies, of course!*

The British cabin steward swung open the door. A damp and malodorous cloud invaded the cool, crisp air of the plane. Excited, hoarse shouts streamed into the cabin. Anthony gagged. *Is this what I'm going to have to breathe for the next few months? I think I'm going to be sick. Someone get me an oxygen bottle!*

Anthony unbuckled his seat belt, stood up, and walked to the exit. He stepped out of the aircraft and scrambled down the metal stairs. The handrail burned his palms. When he reached the ground, the heat of the tarmac sizzled through the soles of the hand-crafted leather shoes his mother had insisted he wear for the journey. The sunshine was blinding, a burning heat on his unprotected head. Sweat oozed from every pore of his body. He squinted and reached into his shoulder bag for his sunglasses.

The natives who had disembarked behind him rushed into the single-story building in front of the aircraft. That was the airport terminal? It was only a little bigger than the stables in the Ashley-Cooper manor. Anthony followed them.

Sweaty, bare-chested men trailed after him, chattering and pushing wooden trolleys laden with luggage from the aircraft. Anthony winced and stepped aside. He could smell the sweat streaming off them and see the gleaming whites of their teeth and eyes in the dark faces. One of them pointed to Anthony and said something in their native language. The others guffawed. How dare the idiots laugh at him?

It was only a fraction cooler inside the airport terminal. Ceiling fans circulated the fetid air. People formed what could pass as a queue in front of a table where officious-looking natives in white uniforms checked passports.

'Sir, this way, sir, special table for British, sir.' A man in a white uniform gestured towards a table with a printed sign 'Foreign Nationals ONLY'. There was no line of people at that table. Anthony held out his papers and passport to the man at the desk. The man leapt up and bowed from the waist. He accepted the papers in his right hand. His left arm bent and clasping his right elbow. 'Thank you, sir. Thank you. Welcome to Sri Lanka, sir.' He stamped the papers without reading them and handed them back to Anthony.

Sri Lanka, not Ceylon as his father and mother, and even the British cabin steward called it. Interesting.

Anthony passed the official desks and entered the arrival area of the airport terminal. The racket in the room stopped him in his tracks. Shrieks and squeals engulfed him. All around him people were shouting out what he assumed were welcomes and greetings in a language or languages he didn't recognise. *Can't these stupid natives talk without yelling?*

The letter from his Uncle Irvine had said Anthony would be met by someone from Oriental Produce. His grandfather, Sir Thomas Ashley-Cooper, had founded Oriental Produce in the early years of colonisation. Now, in 1957, it had grown into the largest and most prosperous tea company in Sri Lanka with branches in Africa. He and his elder brother, William, were heirs to the business. He had a family tradition to uphold. Anthony straightened and tilted his head back.

He scanned the crowd for a British face. Brown faces with shiny black eyes stared back at him. A few smiled. One man even said 'Good afternoon, sir.' Anthony ignored them all.

And then he saw a sign that read MR. ANTHONY ASHLEY-COOPER. It was fixed onto a pole and held above the heads of the milling throng. Anthony watched the sign stutter its way towards him. Finally, a short, portly native stood facing him. His white suit and shirt were crumpled and his dark round face shone with perspiration. A green tie, bearing the distinctive silver Oriental Produce logo of two leaves and a bud, hung in a crude half-knot around his thick neck. The man's lips split in a grimace of a smile as he lowered the sign. His black eyes looked up at Anthony with spaniel-like eagerness.

'Sir, I am Mr Emmanuel, the manager of the Colombo office of Oriental Produce, sir. Your uncle Mr Irvine, Superintendent of Watakälé Plantation, he asked me to meet you, sir.' He spoke in a loud, fluid, almost sing-song tone. 'He could not get away from the plantation, sir. A very busy time of the month for tea manufacture, sir.' His head nodded side to side like a pendulum. 'I am sorry I am late, sir. Hard to find parking and people won't give room, no, sir? Sir, I hope you had a good journey, sir?'

He wondered whether he should shake hands with a native. *Better err on polite.*

'Good afternoon.' Anthony held out his hand. Mr Emmanuel drew back. He placed the palms of his two hands close together against the chest in a prayer like gesture, bowed forward slightly, and said '*Ayubowan*, sir.' Puzzled, Anthony dropped his outstretched hand.

Mr Emmanuel continued. 'Sir, this is the customary greeting of the Sri Lankan people, sir. It means may you live long, sir. Don't worry, sir, you won't find the Indian coolie labourers using the greeting. It is only us Sri Lankans who use it.' His face split in a conspirator-like smile. 'But then, you will not be greeting any Indian coolies, no, sir?'

Chuckling as if he had said something amusing, Mr Emmanuel lifted Anthony's suitcases off one of the wooden luggage trolleys. '*Palayang yako!*' he snapped, shooing away a couple of men who had their hands on Anthony's bags. He tut-tutted and wiped fingerprints and dust off the bags. 'Can't trust these natives, sir. They will dirty your suitcases, no?'

Carrying the bags, he led the way out of the terminal building and across a wide strip of dry grass to a mud patch where a number of cars were parked. The humid, dusty air enveloped Anthony as he stepped out of the building. Rivulets of sweat moistened the collar of his white linen shirt, which now clung to his wet back. Damp patches of sweat were appearing under his arms.

The wind picked up and swirled the dust around them. Anthony's throat felt like sandpaper. He coughed into his handkerchief. Others around him hawked and spat great globules of spit on the ground.

Anthony recognised the Oriental Produce crest painted on the door of the dusty cream Ford Consul as Mr Emmanuel scuttled towards it. Mr Emmanuel placed Anthony's suitcase in the boot of the car with great care before scurrying over to hold the back door open for Anthony. 'Sir, it will be two hours to the hotel, sir.'

Anthony cursed inwardly as he squashed himself into the car's back seat. He had to listen to the ranting of this fawning old fool in his rundown motor vehicle for two hours!

Mr Emmanuel slid into the front seat, fired the car's motor, and pulled out of the airport carpark. Other cars started up around them, rumbling, rattling and trailing clouds of black smoke. They joined the line of traffic leaving the airport on a single-lane mud road, lined with tall coconut trees and other unrecognisable shrubs. A few people walked along the edge of the road, struggling with bags in various sizes.

After about fifteen minutes, Mr Emmanuel made a sharp left turn on to a larger, bitumen road with one lane of traffic in each direction. 'We are now on the main road to Colombo, sir. We can now travel faster, sir.' He proceeded to drive at exactly the same speed as he had before.

They wove their way between the motley sources of transport that blundered along the road to Colombo. Cars, buses and lorries shared the road with a variety of other modes of transport. They passed rickshaws pulled by barefooted and bare-chested men wearing the same skirt-like garment, this time tucked up to expose muscled brown legs and knees. Anthony looked on amazed at bicycles with two and three people together with what looked like all their household belongings hanging off the side. The traffic also shared the road with wooden carts, full to overflowing with fruit and vegetables, with scrawny bulls shackled at the front.

It seemed that the way to progress, if one were in a motor vehicle, was to blow the horn at an ear rending volume and drive to within a whisker of whatever other mode of transport one wanted to overtake. This evoked a loud and rude response from the other driver, be he the driver of a vehicle, a rickshaw puller, or the driver of the bull cart.

'Sir, sir, look sir, on the pavement – it is the *rambuttan* season. At other times it will be papaw or mango, sir.'

In between the piles of garbage on the broken rubble at the edge of the road lay mounds of reddish fruit with pink spikes on the surface, each fruit about the size of a golf ball. A little boy, wearing a blue t-shirt and nothing else, sat by one of the mounds sucking on a fruit. A man dressed in a coloured skirt-like garment and a threadbare shirt open to expose a caved-in chest, squatted by the boy. He smiled, showing red stained teeth.

Mr Emmanuel turned back to Anthony 'The Indians chew betel, sir. They combine the leaf and nut with lime. It stains their mouth red. You will see that everywhere on the tea plantation.'

Mr Emmanuel pointed to a group of well-proportioned swaying bodies, many walking with no footwear, some with colourful baskets of fruit and vegetables balanced on their heads. 'Sir, women wear cotton saris, sir. Six yards of material wrapped in one piece, sir.'

Ebony black eyes stared into the car with inquisitive interest. A couple of the younger women nodded and smiled and waved when they caught Anthony's eyes. He shrank back into the uncomfortable seat. 'People will all treat you very special, sir. You are white, no, sir – like a god. You will get used to it soon, sir.'

Anthony was thrown forward when Mr Emmanuel stomped his foot on the brake. 'What the –'

'Look sir, an elephant!' Mr Emmanuel pointed forward and spoke in a whisper. 'We mustn't excite it too much!' The car crawled past the mighty animal, once a king in his jungle domain, now reduced to carrying logs of wood with his legs shackled in chains.

Anthony gazed into the large brown eyes, fringed with long lashes. The animal gazed back at him. He wondered what memories of freedom this magnificent animal carried in its brain. The man riding the beast's back raised his hand in greeting to Anthony. He shouted a command and prodded the neck of the beast with a sharp stick. The elephant trumpeted and raised its trunk. Anthony's lips twitched. The largest animal in Sri Lanka salutes the visiting white god. He could get used to this.

The car bumped its way on towards Colombo. The roads grew even more crowded and polluted. Dust swirled around and into the car. Mr Emmanuel's voice droned on, lulling Anthony into a stupor. He heard less and less of what Mr Emmanuel said.

***

'Sir, sorry sir. We are at the hotel, sir,' Mr Emmanuel's voice broke into Anthony's drowsy state. He jerked awake to see an expanse of green lawn. Beyond it stretched the brilliant blue of the ocean with white-capped waves shimmering to the horizon. The setting sun was an orange orb in the pink and grey sky. Families and couples strolled along a mud path that seemed to serve as a promenade.

'Galle Face Green, sir,' Mr Emmanuel said. 'And that,' he said with an extravagant sweep of his arm, 'is the Indian Ocean.'

'Really?' muttered Anthony. 'I thought it was the North Atlantic.'

Mr Emmanuel smiled and bobbled his head.

They were parked in the driveway of a large sandstone two-storey building. Tall, white pillars reached up on either side of the large wooden-framed glass doors. Similarly impressive windows, also framed in wood, shone gold and pink in the evening sun. Native men in crisp white suits and white gloves stood at attention by the entrance.

Mr Emmanuel leapt out of the car. Bending at the waist, he held the door of the car open. Anthony unfolded himself from the back seat and walked up the worn, well-scrubbed marble steps of the hotel. Mr Emmanuel darted in front of him, carrying Anthony's luggage.

One of the uniformed men stepped forward and held the door open for them to enter. To Anthony's bemusement, a flash of resentment momentarily clouded the man's deep black eyes. Why would the doormen resent him? Mr Emmanuel had said he would be treated like a god.

He strolled after Mr Emmanuel into a large foyer with a high ceiling. The room was cool and carried the pungent smell of a hothouse full of blooms. Taking a deep breath he stood, looking around, hands in the pockets of his now crumpled linen trousers. Large wooden slatted ceiling fans circulated the air. Hand-crafted tapestries in bright reds, greens, blues and orange hung from white walls. They depicted outrigger canoes, half naked women balancing large urns on their heads, and a parade of elephants. Brass vases of multi-coloured flowers stood on round, ebony tables.

A slim, dark, young man emerged from behind the teak reception desk. He was dressed in a pale blue suit with an emblem embroidered on the breast pocket. He spoke to Mr Emmanuel in what Anthony took to be the native language. Mr Emmanuel nodded.

Putting the bags down, he turned to Anthony. 'The staff here all know your uncle, Mr Irvine, sir. They will look after you, sir. I will come for you tomorrow morning and put you on the train to Diyatalāwa. Good night, sir. Sleep well, sir.'

Mr Emmanuel pressed his hands together again in what must this time be a gesture of farewell. Anthony nodded, not wanting to extend his hand and definitely not ready to practice the Sri Lankan greeting in public. Mr Emmanuel then retreated backwards out of the hotel foyer, almost tripping over the welcome mat.

'Welcome to Galle Face Hotel, Mr Ashley-Cooper,' the young man addressed Anthony in flawless English. 'I'm Nimal, the maître d'hôtel of the Galle Face Hotel. We have booked you in the King's Suite. It overlooks the ocean. I am sure you will have a good night's sleep there.' His clipped, soft voice was a pleasant change after two hours of Mr Emmanuel's loud blather.

Nimal ushered Anthony towards the lift. A bellboy in a white uniform lifted his bags onto a small wooden trolley with intricate filigree handwork. He followed Anthony and Nimal out of the reception hall. They passed carved mahogany chaise longues, upholstered in thick woven material of the same bright and vibrant colours as the tapestries in the foyer. 'Sri Lankan handloom material,' said Nimal, following Anthony's gaze.

Anthony glanced at a large painting of a group of women carrying trays of flowers in their hands. His eyes widened when he realised that the women were topless.

Seeing Anthony's raised eyebrows, Nimal pointed to the picture. 'The Sigiriya Frescoes, Mr Ashley-Cooper. Sigiriya is an ancient rock castle used by King Kassyapa in the fourth century. There are paintings of hundreds of women like this on the walls of the rock. They were the Kings' princesses and consorts.'

Anthony looked at the tapestry and sniggered. 'He must have been quite a man to keep them all satisfied.' He ignored the look that flashed between Nimal and the bellboy.

In pointed silence, Nimal held the door of the lift open for Anthony to enter. The bellboy followed him with his bags. The wooden, box-like lift creaked up to the second floor and opened to reveal a carpeted corridor. Nimal stepped out and held the lift door open for Anthony. The wooden panelling, soft hidden lights and piped music gave Anthony a twinge of homesickness. *I could be in England*, he thought. On the other hand, if it were England, there wouldn't be paintings of fishing boats with half-naked men, and portraits of brooding, dark, mystic faces on the walls.

Nimal walked down the corridor and opened the door at the end. He stood aside and gestured Anthony to enter. The walls of the room were painted pale blue. Antique wooden armchairs and a writing table complemented the large, regency style four-poster bed in the centre of the room. Bowls of roses stood on either side of the bed and on the desk. The balcony door was open, and the lace curtain fluttered in the breeze to reveal tantalising glimpses of water. The fresh salt smell of the ocean wafted into the room, mingling with the perfume of the roses.

Nimal placed Anthony's bags on a stool. 'Your room, Mr Ashley-Cooper, I hope you like it.'

Anthony walked to a large, framed picture on the wall across from the bed. 'A tea plantation, sir,' Nimal explained. 'Similar to where you will be going tomorrow.'

***

Anthony lay on the soft linen sheets of his bed. He clasped his hands behind his head and stared up at the ceiling. Soon after Nimal had ushered him into his room, a waiter had brought up a dinner of rice, spiced roast chicken and mixed vegetables – all labelled in small script. Anthony had eyed the meal, poked around at the separate bits, sampled it and then enjoyed it more than he would be willing to admit. After dinner, he had a long soak in the old fashioned brass tub in the bathroom and now lay in bed trying to clear his head of the myriad images that filled his mind.

The sun sank slowly into the ocean. The light from the lamps on Galle Face Green filtered into the room, shrouding the picture of the tea plantation on the wall in an eerie yellow light. The swirls in the plaster ceiling took on the appearance of mountains and valleys, first of the rolling downs of his home in the Peak District of England and then of green hilled mysteries of yet unseen tea plantations.

Dinner parties at the Ashley-Cooper manor in Bakewell were never complete without stories about the tea plantations. He remembered the story of the itinerant Indian preacher. He heard his father's voice: 'The bugger came by every few months pontificating about the hellfire and brimstone that awaited me if I didn't repent of my sins. He bloody well knew I would set my dogs on him but he kept coming anyway.'

Even as a child, Anthony had felt vaguely uncomfortable at how much the guests at the dinner party in the manor enjoyed the idea of the old Sri Lankan man scuttling away with bulldogs chasing after him.

Other stories, mainly those concerning the coolie women and plantation hospitality, were explicit and bawdy. The dinner guests would snigger and chuckle, as Anthony's mother bundled him and his brother William out of the room. Recently, on one of these occasions, his father had grabbed William by his arm. He had raised his brandy snifter to his mother.

'Let him listen,' he had called out to her. 'He'll experience it himself soon enough.' William had enjoyed that, but Anthony had watched his mother's eyes burn with anger and then cloud in pain.

'The tea plantations charmed your father,' she had whispered in Anthony's ear the night before he left. 'Take care that the same doesn't happen to you.'

Sometime in the night, Anthony kicked the sheets off the bed. He realised why when he woke up. The doors to the balcony stood open, but the sea breeze did little to abate the cloying heat of the tropical morning. He picked up the sheet and wiped the sweat off his body. 'Like living in a bloody sauna,' he grumbled to himself.

A soft tap on the door heralded Nimal. 'Good morning, Mr Ashley-Cooper. I am sorry to wake you so early. Mr Emmanuel asked me to bring you breakfast. He will be here at eight-thirty to take you to the station.'

Anthony looked with grudging interest at the items on the plate that constituted his breakfast. 'Mr Emmanuel asked me to bring you bacon and eggs, sir, but I thought you may like to try the egg hoppers. It is a traditional Sri Lankan breakfast.'

'Leave it on the table.' Anthony looked at the tray of food, not particularly hungry. 'Please let me know when the car is here.' Nimal bowed and turned away.

Anthony stared at the two egg hoppers. They looked like pancakes with a crisp brown border, each with an egg fried sunny side up on a cushiony centre. On the rim of the plate were small bowls of colourful sauces. The blend of aromas was not like anything Anthony had experienced. And yet, it was enticing to his taste buds. Suddenly ravenous, Anthony sat down, and ignoring the knife and folk, devoured the food with his fingers – which, he reasoned, was probably the correct way to eat it.

Anthony showered and threw his overnight clothes into his bag. He rang for the bellhop and sauntered down to the foyer.

Mr Emmanuel arrived at eight-thirty, even more sycophantic than the day before. 'Sir, your uncle Mr Irvine called me this morning, sir. He will meet you at Diyatalāwa station.' Mr Emmanuel wiped Anthony's bags with his hanky before carrying them to the car with his customary delicacy.

Leaving the air-conditioned hotel, Anthony walked down the steps, opened the back door and got into the car. Mr Emmanuel came bustling after him to shut the door and then rushed over to the driver's side. 'Sir, I have booked a seat for you in the first class compartment of the train. I have also ordered chicken sandwiches for your lunch, sir.' Mr Emmanuel pulled away from the hotel.

Recovered from the half-asleep stupor of last evening, Anthony was more aware of the traffic and noise that surrounded them on the drive to the train station. Even in the business heart of the city, rickshaws and bull carts shared the road with bicycles in various states of disrepair and cars of indeterminate age belching foul brown fumes.

In contrast to the drive from the airport, however, there was a controlled purposefulness about the activity on the streets in Colombo. Men and women, many with bags tucked under their arms, strode along the pavement. The men were mostly dressed in white cotton business suits, the women in what he now recognised as saris. The women held up black umbrellas in a vain attempt to ward off the burning rays of the morning sun.

They wound their way through the traffic. Mr Emmanuel pointed to the Edwardian buildings lining the streets. 'Sir, we are driving through Colombo Fort. It used to be a British fortress in the nineteenth century, now all business and trade buildings, sir.'

Anthony turned to look at a group of men dressed in bright orange robe-like garments, their heads shaven and glistening in the sunshine. 'Buddhist monks, sir,' said Mr Emmanuel. 'Buddhism is the main religion in Sri Lanka. But in the tea plantation, the coolies are all Hindus. They are Indian labourers, no, sir? But sir knows that, of course.'

Half an hour later they drew into a parking spot in front of the railway station. The white arches bore the name 'Fort Railway Station' in English and what were presumably the two native languages of Sinhalese and Tamil.

A larger than life bronze statue of a bearded old man holding a large book stood in a fenced enclosure at the front of the station. Mr Emmanuel followed Anthony's gaze. 'Ah, you are wondering who that is, no, sir? He is a white man, sir. Colonel Henry Steele Olcott. He was important in taking Buddha's teaching to your country, sir. He wrote the Buddhist books here also.'

Anthony looked up at the stern countenance, now marred by pigeon droppings and adorned by two large cawing ravens. Railway lines, tea plantations, Christian missionaries and the Buddhist catechism. He was only beginning to understand the effect of the British Empire on the colonies. He turned to follow Mr Emmanuel into the railway station.

Mr Emmanuel ignored the offer of help from a number of scruffy urchins and carried Anthony's bags to the platform. The crowd of native men, women and children parted to allow the two of them passage. 'Sir, the British built the station in about 1910,' Mr Emmanuel said, his voice rising above the chatter that surrounded them. 'In those times the trains were used to transport tea and coffee from the hill country to Colombo, sir.' He flung his free hand to encompass the walls and arches, 'The sandstone blocks and the wrought iron arches were all made by local people, sir. Good work, no?'

Anthony looked around. The arches were imposing and the whorls in the metal delicate and beautiful, even under layers of grime and soot. The wooden doors were adorned with ornate brass handles and stained glass panels. It was an unabashed effort of his forefathers to replicate a British railway station in this squalid colonial outpost. And it was well done.

The announcement rang out, loud and strident, probably to make up for the hiss and wheeze of the big-wheeled steam locomotive at the head of the train and the clamour of the crowd struggling to board the carriages.

'The train on platform four is the day train to Badulla.'

It was repeated twice more. 'Sinhalese and Tamil, sir,' Mr Emmanuel explained. He ushered Anthony along the platform.

Native men walked up and down the platform hawking food, carrying their produce in cane baskets on their shoulders. Their calls of '*vadai, vadai kadalai, kadalai*' and '*thambili, thambili*' had a practiced, almost musical rhythm.

Mr Emmanuel stopped at a carriage with FIRST CLASS emblazoned in large, intricate gold lettering on the side. Anthony looked around. The carriage was empty and no one seemed eager to enter it.

'The natives all travel second class and the coolies in third, sir. No one will bother you, sir.' Opening the door, Mr Emmanuel scrambled into the carriage. He stored Anthony's suitcase in the overhead luggage shelf and wiped the seat with his handkerchief. 'You will be comfortable here, sir?'

'Thank you, Mr Emmanuel.' Anthony climbed in after him and sat back in the leather seat covered with white linen. The shrill whistle from the locomotive sent Mr Emmanuel scuttling off the train.

With another loud, drawn-out whistle and a bone rattling jerk, the train drew out of the station. A cloud of steam and smoke drifted from the locomotive, partially obscuring the platform. People were hanging out of the windows, waving and screaming goodbyes. Anthony looked back. He could just about make out Mr Emmanuel, waving in the air with both hands. Anthony raised his hand in goodbye – and good riddance. Flecks of dust and soot flew in the wind and into the compartment. Hooking his fingers in the brass knobs, Anthony dragged the glass window shutter down.

He wiped his face and hands with his linen handkerchief and then cursed when he saw that it was black with soot and dust. Oh well, he would be ready for a shower when he reached his uncle's bungalow. He thrust the handkerchief in his pocket and sat back with his eyes shut.

Tchaikovsky's piano concerto piped through the sound system, competing with the racket outside the compartment and the clickety-clack of the wheels on the rails. The carriage swayed as it gathered speed. The locomotive whistle was muffled and distant. Tired and jet lagged, Anthony dropped back into a stupor.

'Welcome aboard the *Uderata Maniké*, sir.'

Anthony's eyes jerked open. A young man in a white uniform stood in front of him. 'The name is meaning upcountry girl. I am the rail supervisor in charge of first class carriages. My name is John.'

The man poured some mysterious fizzy orange fluid from a bottle bearing the label 'orange barley' into a glass and offered it to Anthony.

Anthony groaned. Eight hours with another one of these idiotic natives, just as he had got rid of Mr Emmanuel.

'You must not mind him, young sir, he is only trying to look after you. This must be your first visit to Sri Lanka.'

Glass in hand, Anthony looked at the stout figure of the Sri Lanka man settling into the window seat in front of him. He wore a white shirt that reached down to the knees with what looked like a long, white skirt under it. The lower garment was held up by a leather belt. The hair on his balding head was well oiled and combed down, stretching down to his ample neck. He sported a walrus moustache, which wobbled as he leaned forward.

A native in first class?

'I am Don Mudiyansalage Premawansa Somaweera Hemachandra …'

Anthony's eyes widened at the cascade of syllables.

'But people call me Hemachandra Mudalali.'

Well I'm not people, thought Anthony, *and I'm damned if I'm going to make a fool of myself by trying to say your name.*

'I own a big fleet of lorries that take tea from the estates to Colombo. I employ ten drivers. I own the biggest shop in my town, where everyone comes to buy their food and clothes and things. That's why people call me Hemachandra Mudalali – it means Hemachandra, the town merchant.'

Hemachandra Mudalali did not stretch out his hand to shake Anthony's hand, neither did he put his palms together in greeting. Noticing Anthony's eyes on his clothes he smiled. 'Native dress. You can say sarong and shirt. How far are you going?'

Anthony appraised the man. The two of them were stuck with each other for the better part of the day; he might as well make the most of it. 'I'm travelling to a station called Diyatalāwa.'

'Why, that is where I am going too, sir! My shop is in Diyatalāwa. Are you staying with the Superintendent of Watakälé?' Hemachandra rubbed his palms together. 'Ah, that is why you are looking so familiar. Your brother visited last year, no? Stayed in Udatänná?'

Anthony nodded his response, then opened his carry bag and took out the book his mother had given him to read on the plane – Bunyan's *Pilgrim's Progress*. He'd ignore the old fool. Let him think it was colonial arrogance.

'So you also are going to take over and be the Superintendent in Watakälé one day, sir? Just like your brother will in Udatänná? You will be called the Periadorai – did you know that?'

It was probably another word for white god. 'Yes,' Anthony mumbled into the book.

'Then it is a good thing that we have this time together, no?' Hemachandra Mudalali continued, ignoring Anthony's aloofness. 'After all, my lorries are going to take your tea to Colombo to get sold.'

Anthony looked at him over the page of his book.

'Come, young sir. Let me tell you something about our country. It is very pretty, no? See, already we are leaving the city behind.'

Anthony sighed again. He put the book away in his bag.

As the train chugged out of Colombo, the grey smoke and soot-stained buildings fell away. Lush, green fields and a myriad of multi-coloured flowers Anthony did not recognise took their place. Hemachandra pointed out of the window. 'Paddy fields,' he said. 'The ground is dug by buffalo and the rice planted in steps. See, sir.' He pointed. Anthony gazed at the immense grey animals with graceful curved horns yoked in pairs at the ploughshares.

Hemachandra Mudalali pointed out rivers and mountains, villages of mud-walled cottages and coconut plantations. Listening to him, Anthony found himself drawn into the beauties and mysteries of the country.

When the train drew into a station called Māwanella, Hemachandra bought a young coconut from one of the itinerant vendors, who lopped its top off and stuck a straw into it. Hemachandra passed it to Anthony. 'Very refreshing drink, thambili. You will miss it when you leave Sri Lanka. But then you will come back, no? To take charge of Watakälé?'

Hemachandra pointed out a mountain he called Utuwankandé. 'The Robin Hood of Sri Lanka lived there. His name was Saradiel. Apparently, he enjoyed taking from the white man and giving the villagers the money.' He chortled, his moustache and stomach wobbling with mirth. 'Fortunately he was arrested and executed, so you are safe.'

At a station called Nawalapitiya, a muscular Garrett locomotive added power to the front of the train. Anthony soon understood why. The track became steep, climbing higher and higher. The two locomotives laboured in unison. The air became progressively cooler and clearer, even sweeter.

Anthony saw a station sign for Hatton flash past the window. A wide valley stretched before them, backed by a broad-shouldered mountain range. The lower regions of the mountain were swathed with brilliant green bushes. From its upper flanks, dark, ominous rock faces clawed upwards towards the sky. Distant waterfalls cascaded down the rocks. Hardy trees and bushes clung like mountain goats to the almost vertical slopes.

'The Great Western Range.' Hemachandra waved his hand out of the window. 'This is the area for high-country tea – the best kind. Not bitter but full of flavour.' He raised his hand to his mouth in a gesture to mimic holding a tea cup. 'They are saying it is like a good wine. Your plantations are high country too.'

The train passed a wide waterfall, which Hemachandra Mudalali identified as St Clair's Fall. Anthony leaned out the window to get a better look. The thunder of plunging water filled his ears. The water billowed out, fanned by a brisk breeze. Anthony felt the sting of icy cold drops on his face.

Soon the train laboured its way up the face of the Great Western Range. Anthony gazed back across the valley from which they had come. Range after range of mountains, like a petrified blue-green ocean, faded into a purple haze in the distance. This was a primitive, rugged and yet strongly seductive country. He began to understand why his father had grown to love it.

Hemachandra Mudalali pointed out a sharp-pointed triangle, jutting up out of the mountain range to the south. 'You would call it Adam's Peak,' he said, 'but we Sri Lankans call it Sri-Pāda. It's an important pilgrimage site for all the religions. You should climb it some time. Buddhists take the imprint at the summit of the mountain to be the hallowed footprint of the Buddha, hence the name Sri Pāda – holy footprint. To the Hindus, the footprint is that of God Shiva. Christians took it to be from St Thomas, who was thought to have brought Christianity to India and Sri Lanka. And to Muslims, it is an impression of Adam's foot, hence the name "Adam's Peak". Another name for the mountain by the Sinhalese is *Samanala Kanda*, meaning Butterfly Mountain. Flocks of butterflies wing their way to the mountain every year. They die when they get to the top – a sort of divine sacrifice.'

Cool mountain air now filled the carriage. Anthony closed his eyes and filled his lungs. Yes, it would be good to breathe this every day.

Hemachandra Mudalali chuckled. 'Nothing like this in England, no?' He pointed to the hills. 'It is nice here, young sir. No dirt and pollution like Colombo. You will be happy here -' He stopped and looked at Anthony. 'If you let yourself.'

The sun had dipped behind the towering green mountains when the train drew to a shuddering halt at Diyatalāwa Station. Dark-skinned men dressed in faded shirts and sarongs leapt like agile monkeys onto the train.

Hemachandra Mudalali pointed to the platform. 'Your uncle is waiting.' He raised his hand in a half salute. 'Young sir, we will meet again.'

Anthony had already seen his uncle, Phillip Irvine, standing on the platform, hands on his hips, feet splayed, a scowl of concentration on his tanned face. He was dressed in a white open-necked shirt, cream trousers and brown shoes. His brown hair was receding and there were more lines on his forehead than Anthony remembered from a year ago when they had met in England.

Mr Irvine's face creased into a smile when Anthony stepped down out of the carriage and onto the platform. 'Welcome to the tea plantations, son.' He shook Anthony's hand. 'You must be tired. Your Aunt and the girls are waiting for you at the bungalow.' He led Anthony out of the tiny station and into a mud yard where Anthony's bags were being packed into the boot of a black Wolseley.

Mr Irvine drove the car through the town of Diyatalāwa. The going was slow. They shared the narrow road with large lumbering lorries carrying crates of tea and small trucks and bull carts full of fresh vegetables. There were also dogs, cats, goats, cattle and even a sundry buffalo.

Leaving the town behind, the road climbed into the tea plantation. It was as if an emerald green carpet had been thrown over the undulating hills to welcome him. Mud roads curled through the hills like dusky brown ribbons. Anthony felt a frisson of excitement. So this was it. Tea – his father's legacy, soon to be his.

Anthony looked around, trying not to gawk. He wound down the window and sniffed.

'The aroma of fresh tea leaves,' explained his uncle. He pointed to the smooth-topped tea bushes that reached right up to the edge of the road. 'Don't look like individual plants, do they? Decades of pruning to keep then waist high and regular plucking of the bloom makes the tops grow together.' He pointed to one hill of a brighter green, which seemed to be alive with multi-coloured dots. 'Coolie women, Indian labour. They don't usually pluck so late. They're the backbone of the industry. Efficiency depends on them working fast. But quality depends on their ability to pick just the flush of two leaves and the bud.' He chuckled. 'We're always trying to improve both, of course.'

The car stopped at a boom gate. Bold black letters on a white wooden board read 'Watakälé Estate, Oriental Produce Tea Company'. A man ran from a small wooden hut at the side of the road and swung the gate up. He was dressed in a tattered black sweater and what Anthony now recognised as a sarong. He shuffled back into the ditch at the side and stood with his head bowed as the car swept by.

The road dipped and wound into a valley. They rounded a corner and a foul odour invaded Anthony's senses. 'What a stench.' He gagged and covered his mouth and nose with his hanky. A row of rooms, looking like filthy stables, came into view. Half-naked children played in the mud in front of them. Girls in loose, faded dresses squatted by the stream that separated the road from the buildings. They seemed to be washing clothes in the polluted water.

His uncle reached over Anthony to wind up the window. 'I'm sorry to have to subject you to this, son. These are what we call the line rooms. The indentured Indian labourers – coolies – live here. We have given each family a room. There are common toilets and taps. They are sturdily built rooms. Well ventilated. But the coolies have no sense of hygiene and the place is filthy. I'll explain this all to you later. I've applied to your father for money to re-route the main road so that it doesn't go past this area.'

One young girl with a baby perched on her hip, stood by the stream looking at the car. Her eyes met and held Anthony's. They bore an expression of patient forbearance, not unlike the look in the eyes of the elephant he had seen on the road from the airport.

The smell and sight of the line rooms fell away behind them as they drove up a hill. In a few minutes they passed a little cottage with trimmed jasmine and rose bushes lining the front garden.

'The Tea-maker's quarters,' explained his uncle. Just then a girl ran across the road. His uncle braked and swore under his breath. 'The Tea-maker's daughter,' he explained with a frown.

The girl stood by the road, smiling and waving to the car. The sun glinted on a purple stone pendant hanging round her neck and shimmered off her black hair. A single curl hung at the centre of her forehead.

'Please don't acknowledge her greeting, son,' his uncle said, with a restraining hand on his arm. 'We don't associate with the natives in public.'

Anthony turned to look back at the girl just as she stuck her tongue out to the receding car.

No patient forbearance there.

Chapter 4

Shiro shot up in bed. What had woken her? The old grandfather clock whirred and chimed the hour. Shiro counted, one - two - it was two o'clock in the morning. She slid down in bed and pulled the purple blanket over her head, wiping her tears with the edge of the blanket. Nicky, her little cat, was gone, his head crushed by a falling Jak fruit. Her mother had said he was dead. What happened when cats died? Did they go to cat heaven? What was dead, anyway?

Suddenly she was afraid. Flinging off her blanket, she ran barefoot across the hall to her parents' bedroom. She flung herself into their bed. Her father yelped as she landed on top of him.

'Promise me you won't die,' she cried, burrowing in between him and her mother.

Her father cradled her in his arms. 'Of course not, princess. I'll never leave you.'

She cuddled in between them. 'Can we have a cat funeral in the morning?'

***

Later that morning, Rajan and Lilly Rasiah stood with their daughter and Lakshmi around a little hole at the bottom of the vegetable garden. Tears streamed down Shiro's face. Lakshmi stood quietly, shuffling her feet, looking at Lilly Rasiah and then down the path leading away to her home.

'Earth to earth, ashes to ashes, dust to dust,' Lilly read from a tattered old prayer book. Rajan shovelled dirt into the shallow grave, covering the motionless little bundle that was Nicky, wrapped in his favourite blanket.

'I'll always love you, Nicky.' Shiro placed a twig from the rose bush on the fresh soil. 'I'm going to plant a rose bush over you and I'll pick a rose from it every day, wear it for you and tell everyone what a nice kitty you were.'

Rajan patted down the dirt, smoothing it over the grave. Lilly held her hand out to Shiro. 'Come, darling, we must finish class early so we can get ready for the tea party this afternoon.'

'Shiro Chinnamma, I am going home now,' Lakshmi said to Shiro. 'I have to cook and wash and do other work.'

'Mummy, I want Lakshmi to stay for the tea party,' Shiro swung around to face her mother. She stamped her foot.

Her parents exchanged glances. 'No darling, the superintendent's children are not allowed to play with coolies and Lakshmi has things to do in the line room,' Lilly replied.

'But Lakshmi will like playing with Janet and Sarah,' Shiro said, her eyes filling with tears again. 'Lakshmi is my best friend. I want Janet and Sarah to meet her. I want us all to play together.' Shiro crossed her arms across her chest, planted her feet firmly on the ground, and stared at her mother, ready to defy the world.

'Mahal, control yourself,' Lilly sighed. How was she to explain to precocious young Shiro that this afternoon tea party broke all conventions of tea plantation life? Shiro wasn't to know that British children weren't meant to talk to native Sri Lankan children, let alone Indian coolies. Poor little Janet and Sarah, the two daughters of superintendent Irvine, were stuck with only each other for company, just because they were white. *Appu*, who cooked for and supervised the superintendent's household, had said that the girls spent most days getting on each other's nerves and driving their mother and their English nanny to distraction.

Lilly didn't want to entertain them, but in the estate hierarchy it would have been unheard of for the Tea-maker to refuse a request from the superintendent, however unusual it was. And a request from the British superintendent that his family visit the native Tea-maker's house for afternoon tea was probably a first in the tea plantation's history.

Lilly squatted down so her eyes were level with Shiro. 'Lakshmi will not stay for tea. She will come and play with you tomorrow. Isn't that right, Lakshmi?'

Lakshmi nodded.

Shiro folded her arms and glared at first her mother and then Lakshmi. With a toss of her curly head and a disgruntled snort, she stormed off to a corner of the garden.

Lilly nodded to Lakshmi, who turned and darted down the dirt track that led to the line rooms.

Lilly looked at the path where her daughter had disappeared. *Someday, my darling, you will learn that you can't always get what you want from life*, she thought. *I pray it won't be too painful a lesson for you.*

Lilly Rasiah stood in the sitting room of the Tea-maker's house. She glanced at the clock. Three o'clock in the afternoon. They should be here soon. She looked out of the window. She was anxious but determined to not show it when her guests arrived. She repeated her husband's words to herself like a mantra: 'you can match it with the best.'

'Can I show Janet and Sarah the new dolls house Daddy made for me? Please? Please?' Shiro pranced around the sitting room, almost knocking over the tea table. She was dressed in her favourite purple dress. Lilly had brushed Shiro's hair and it hung loose to her shoulders, curling around her face. Tiny gold earrings peeked through the bouncing black tresses. Her favourite single stone amethyst pendent shimmered around her neck. She certainly was a cute little thing. She deserved much more than the tea plantation atmosphere and a coolie girl as a friend.

A plan began to form in her head, one that would give her precious, only daughter the education and refinement that Lilly herself had craved.

Lilly steadied the tea table. On it she had laid out the Wedgwood china tea set she had received as a wedding present from her grandfather. 'Yes, you can take them to the playroom. And please be careful, darling.' She steered Shiro away from the table. 'Why don't you stand on the veranda and let me know when the car draws up? Don't do anything to dirty your dress.'

Shiro skipped out to the veranda.

Lilly stepped back and surveyed the room. She had covered the chipped tea table with a hand embroidered white linen cloth. Roses from the garden nestled in the little crystal vase, and linen napkins with handmade lace edgings sat neatly folded on the rose-edged tea plates. The egg sandwiches and frosted cupcakes she had made that morning were both elegant and appetising.

She looked around at the worn lounge suite. Not for the first time, she noticed the frayed edges of the chintz covers and the scratches on the wooden armrests. She had covered the headrests of the lounge and chairs with chintz overlays and polished the wood as best she could. She would never think of complaining to her husband about something as trivial as new furniture. His salary barely met the school fees for their two sons and upkeep of his widowed mother and brothers.

This would be far inferior to what Mrs Irvine and the girls would be used to in the superintendent's bungalow. They would have to make the best of it.

Shiro's excited squeal preceded the rumble of the approaching car. Lilly glanced quickly into the old, ornate mirror that hung on the wall over the gramophone. She adjusted the fall of her light green cotton sari, slipped her feet into a pair of brown slippers, and went out to join Shiro on the veranda.

The black Wolseley, driven by a white uniformed Indian chauffeur, slowed and drew to a precise stop at the stone steps that led up to the front veranda. The chauffeur leapt out of the car and opened the back door. He stood holding the door with his head bowed.

Lilly watched a pair of cream leather high-heeled shoes emerge from the back seat.

Mrs Irvine glided rather than stepped out of the car. Her pale yellow silk dress clung to her slim body and fell in graceful pleats that reached just below her knees. Its Chantilly lace collar framed her pale oval face. A wide brimmed, cream hat with what looked like a peacock feather sat on brown hair drawn back in a tight chignon. Matching pale amber jewellery completed her ensemble.

'How very kind of you to invite us to tea.' Mrs Irvine removed her white linen gloves and extended slender manicured fingers with rose coloured nail polish to Lilly. The voice was soft, accented and genteel.

What a paragon of perfection. For a moment Lilly felt a clumsy oaf. Dismissing the thought, she stepped forward and took Mrs Irvine's hand. The white soft palm lay limp in her brown, work-worn one. 'It's good to have you and the children visit,' she said with what she hoped was a welcoming smile.

Out of the corner of her eye she noticed that for once, Shiro stood speechless, watching Sarah and Janet follow their mother out of the car. The girls were dressed in rose pink pinafore dresses and matching shoes with long lace fringed socks, their plaited hair tied back with pink ribbons. They both smiled at Lilly and Shiro and stood side by side, holding hands with each other.

'You must be Shiro.' Mrs Irvine looked down at the girl. 'Janet and Sarah have been looking forward to visiting with you today.' She drew Janet and Sarah forward, 'Haven't you dears?' She bent down with a little frown to pat down their hair and straighten their dresses. 'You girls will have to behave today with no Nanny to watch over you.'

She looked up at Lilly. 'I am sorry, but we ran out of room in the car for Nanny.'

'I don't have a Nanny,' Shiro broke in. 'But I have Lakshmi who –'

'Please come into the house,' Lilly cut in, steering Mrs Irvine and the girls towards the front door. She looked back to see Shiro stand staring at the car.

'Is that your brother?' Shiro asked Janet, pointing to the person getting out of the front seat of the car.

'No dear, that's their cousin,' Mrs Irvine's smile was strained. 'My husband's nephew, Anthony, is spending some time with us.' She turned to Lilly. 'Anthony's father, James Ashley-Cooper, owns the Oriental Produce Tea Company. Anthony and his brother William are heirs to the tea plantations. Anthony will one day be the superintendent here in Watakälé. My husband suggested that it would be useful for him to visit with a staff family.' The pretty dimpling on the cheek didn't hide the flush of embarrassment.

'Who's James Ashley-Cooper? And why would his son want to play with us?' Shiro slanted her head and stared up at the tall figure dressed in a crisp white, open neck shirt and slim fitted, blue linen trousers. He in return, glared at Shiro as if she were a piece of flotsam on a beach. Shiro's eyes narrowed. Lilly could sense that she was barely restraining the urge to stick her tongue out at him.

Lilly felt a prickle of anxiety. James Ashley-Cooper's son here – in their house. Was he checking out how they lived? She was glad she had sent Lakshmi back to the line rooms. It would have been terrible if he reported back to his father that the Tea-maker was consorting with the Indian labour.

'Please do come in.' She ushered the party into the drawing room. Mrs Irvine and the girls moved in. Lilly bundled her daughter towards the door of the playroom. 'Darling, why don't you take Janet and Sarah to the playroom? I will bring you some cake and orange juice in there.'

She turned to Anthony. 'You are most welcome to join us, Mr Ashley-Cooper. Please come in.'

'What a lovely tea set.' Mrs Irvine nodded permission to the girls to go with Shiro and sat down. 'And cupcakes. How delightful! Did you make them yourself?'

Where does she think they came from? Lilly nodded, forcing a polite smile.

Anthony stood just inside the front door and looked around the room. Taking a white linen handkerchief from the pocket of his shirt, he dusted a chair and sat down. Lilly suppressed a twinge of annoyance and held the plate of cakes out to him.

'Thank you.' His tone of bored condescension hung thick in the air.

Lounging back, Anthony bit into a cupcake. 'Why, these are almost as good as those from the kitchen in the manor,' he said. 'You – folk certainly know how to entertain.'

Mrs Irvine blushed. 'Anthony, would you please check on your cousins? And please take them some cake?' She held up a plate of cupcakes. 'Sarah and Janet will love the frosting and sugar flowers.'

With a shrug of his shoulder, Anthony took the plate and left the room.

'I apologise, Mrs Rasiah.' The flush of colour raced through her pale cheeks. 'Anthony and his brother don't understand the relationships here in the colony.'

'It's all right.' Lilly smiled at the other woman's obvious discomfort. 'These class distinctions – British superintendent, native staff and Indian coolie labour – they used to upset me when I married Mr Rasiah and first moved to the tea plantation. But they don't bother me anymore.'

***

Anthony followed the sound of chatter and giggles to the playroom. Lifting the purple cotton curtain, he stood leaning on the doorpost, the plate of cupcakes held in his long fingers.

Janet and Sarah sat on small stools, their dresses draped around their knees. They each held a doll in their hands. Shiro lay flat on the floor on her stomach, her dress riding up her thighs, her head and hands inside a wooden doll's house. Her voice came muffled from inside, 'Quick, Moses, come out of there! The superintendent's daughters are about to kidnap your sisters!'

'Your mother sent you some cake,' Anthony said, holding out the plate.

Shiro uncoiled herself from her inelegant position on the ground. She jumped up and pulled her skirt down over her thighs. 'Thank you, but why did you not knock?' She stood with her feet apart, her hands on her hips, her face tilted up. Her eyes locked with Anthony's.

'My apologies, I didn't know I needed to.' Anthony forced his voice to drip contempt, barely controlling his amusement at her rumpled clothes and tumbling locks.

Shiro continued staring at him. 'Can't you read?' Placing her right hand on her forehead, she pointed with her left to a sign on the door. Handwritten in purple ink, it read 'PRIVATE PROPERTY: KNOCK'.

No one had ever looked at Anthony with anything like the expression of amused scorn that he saw on Shiro's face. He looked at her, speechless. Who the hell did she think she was?

Shiro continued staring at him for a few seconds, then stepped closer to him. 'Oh, never mind. You brought food. We're famished.' She took the plate from his hand. 'Thank you. Do you want one?' She picked up a cupcake in fingers dusty from poking around in the doll's house and held it out to him – a peace offering. The brilliance of the smile that flashed across her face made Anthony step back.

'No thank you, Miss Rasiah, I don't eat with children.' Anthony realised with increasing irritation that his tone and words had no effect on this little black-eyed minx.

Shiro giggled. She was enjoying his discomfort. How dare she laugh at him?

'Okay then, starve if you want.' Shiro turned to the girls. 'Oh by the way, my name is Shiro, but you can call me princess.'

Princess? What an audacious brat. Anthony leaned on the doorpost and watched the girls eat. Janet and Sarah sat nibbling the cake, careful not to drop crumbs. Occasionally they glanced at Anthony with a shy smile. Shiro seemed to have forgotten his existence. Quickly stuffing a cake into her mouth, she dusted her hands on her skirt and went back to her play in the doll's house.

Anthony continued to watch her.

After a while Shiro stood up and looked at Janet and Sarah. 'Come on, let's go visit the grave.' Ignoring Anthony, Shiro took their hands. Together the girls ran out through the outer door and skipped down the garden.

How dare she ignore me like this? Anthony fumed. *Doesn't she realise that I could have her father dismissed from his job?* He followed the girls down a dirt path to the bottom of the garden, to a fresh mound of earth with a twig on it. He arrived just in time to hear Shiro say, 'He was a beautiful cat and I will never ever forget him. The roses on this bush will remind me of him for the rest of my life.'

'The poor thing.' Janet brushed a tear from her eye. She placed a daisy on the mound of earth. All three girls knelt quietly around the grave.

Anthony brushed past the girls and then turned to face them. His face twisted with scorn. 'For goodness' sake, all this rigmarole for a silly cat? Who cares?' He fixed his eyes on Shiro, 'Stupid. That's what you natives are – stupid!' He stamped on the little twig, snapping it in two.

Janet and Sarah stared up at him, their eyes wide in amazement. They jumped to their feet and scampered back into the playroom.

Shiro continued to kneel with her head bent. Two tears escaped from her tightly shut eyes and slid down her brown cheeks.

Anthony stood looking at her. He felt uncomfortable. After all, she was only an uneducated native child. He didn't need to bite her head off like that.

After a few seconds, she scrambled to her feet. She threw back her head and stared into Anthony's eyes. Her lips quivered, then formed into a pout. It was as if she carried the fire of her race in her dark gaze. It ignited a corresponding blaze in Anthony's belly that spread through his body.

A distant rumble of thunder was accompanied by a few heavy raindrops.

They clung like diamonds on Shiro's upturned face. A flash of lightning on the hill behind them made Anthony jump. Shiro didn't flinch. Her lips curved in a hint of disdain.

'Afraid of a little thunder storm?' She leant forward. 'Well, why don't you go home then, you – you – British bastard?'

Anthony's jaw dropped. 'I will have you know, Miss Rasiah, that we British are the only reason that your father has a job and you have bread and butter on the table.'

Shiro burst into laughter. 'And you should know that we never eat bread and butter. Maybe if you said rice and curry or *string hoppers* and *hodhi*. But you have no idea what those are, do you, *sir*?' With that, she turned and skipped back into the house.

Anthony watched Shiro's curls bounce on the collar of her purple dress. Arrogant native kid. Why did he let her get under his skin like that?

Shiro swung round as if she felt his eyes on her. She looked back at him and smiled. It made her look so angelic that Anthony stopped in his tracks. Then, as if changing her mind, she stuck her tongue out at him, twirled around and ran into the playroom.

Anthony stood in the back garden of the Tea-maker's house. *This is crazy*, he thought. *I shouldn't let her get to me. She's a child – a stupid, illiterate native child. She is nothing.*

Anyway, he would be going home soon. When he came back, he would be the superintendent of Watakälé Tea Plantation.

Chapter 5

Lakshmi opened her eyes to the chirping of parakeets in the mango tree outside Shiro's bedroom. The first rays of morning sunshine slanted through the curtains. It was Christmas Eve. And she was spending the holiday at the Tea-maker's house, getting the house ready for the festivities.

Shiro was huddled under the blanket, still asleep. Lakshmi rolled up the reed mat she slept on and placed it with the folded sheets in the corner of the room. She tiptoed out the back door to the servant's toilet at the bottom of the garden. The water gushed out of the tap. It was bitterly cold. She shivered and then smiled. Early morning ablutions at an indoor tap and a squatting toilet were pure luxury for a coolie girl. Other days she, like all the other coolies, would relieve herself in the tea bushes and wash in the stream.

Washed and dressed in her work clothes, Lakshmi picked up the bucket and mop and started scrubbing the floor in the sitting room. Raaken, the Indian coolie cook was busy in the kitchen making coffee, and Tea-maker Aiya and Periamma were talking in their bedroom. The daily sounds of the Tea-maker's house – echoes of heaven to Lakshmi.

***

All that day, Lakshmi swept and cleaned, washed and polished.

When Tea-maker Aiya returned from the tea factory at noon, the house sparkled clean and neat. Shiro and Lakshmi sat amid a pile of paper streamers and silver stars – decorations for the Christmas tree. Seeing the Tea-maker enter the house, Lakshmi got up and started clearing up the inevitable mess Shiro had created.

'I see all is calm with Shiro. I thought she would have been crazily excited with Victor and Edward due.' Tea-maker Aiya touched his wife on her cheek.

'Oh, we had our tantrum this morning when I would not let Lakshmi play with her. She is getting too stubborn and spoilt. She needs to learn proper manners. We have to send her away to school. I have the application forms to Bambalawatte Methodist Girls' School in Colombo. We can send it in after Christmas.'

A shadow crossed Tea-maker Aiya's face. 'I don't know why you want to send her to boarding school in Colombo. What can they teach her that you can't? It's not like she has to go to university or anything like the boys.'

Periamma lowered her voice. Lakshmi strained to listen. 'You can't protect her and keep her here all her life. It's unhealthy. She lives in a fantasy world of imaginary people and events. She needs better company. Do you realise she considers Lakshmi her closest friend? A coolie girl. You know that isn't right. She needs to meet children of her own social class, to behave like a lady.'

At that moment, Shiro looked up from scrunching another tinsel star. She scrambled to her feet and flew into her father's arms. 'Daddy, I've been working so hard!'

'So you have, my princess, so you have. Let's go get ready for Victor and Edward and Uncles George and Paul, shall we?' He turned to his wife. 'You tried to give her better friends with the Irvine girls. A lot of good that did. She's still sad that they don't reply to her letters.' He kissed Shiro on the cheek. 'Let her be. Don't try to make her into some parody of a British madam.'

Periamma rolled her eyes and followed father and daughter from the room.

Lakshmi cleared up the streamers and stars from the playroom floor, putting them in boxes. Her heart was heavy. Her mother had said just yesterday that Tea-maker Aiya only wanted her as a servant. Maybe she was right. They didn't want their precious daughter to get any closer to her – a coolie girl. They were sending Shiro Chinnamma away to separate them. Her mother said that she was cursed from birth. Maybe she was.

Lakshmi took a deep breath and blinked away her tears. She carried the decorations to the sitting room and placed them in the corner where the Christmas tree would be put up later that day, then went to the kitchen to join Raaken in the cooking.

***

Dusk descended like a soft blanket on the hills. Shiro and Lakshmi stood on the back porch of the house. Lakshmi rubbed her hands on her jumper. Periamma had knitted it for her from leftover bits of wool. It was big for her and a mix of colours and textures, but Lakshmi loved it because Periamma had made it just for her.

Soon the mountains lay shrouded, dark and quiet. The trees came to life, glowing with the twinkling of dozens upon dozens of fireflies. Cicadas began their night chorus. Shiro slipped her hand into Lakshmi's. Hand in hand, they stepped off the porch and stood in the garden. Darkness surrounded them like a gentle coat and dew drops settled on their hair and eyebrows.

Lights cut through the dark and could be seen meandering down the mountain across the valley. Excited, the girls ran to join Shiro's parents at the front of the house. The blue Ford Consul wound its way up the gravel road, its headlights cutting through the thick mist. Large moths, drawn to the light, danced in their brightness before being squashed on the fender.

The car stopped right by the steps. All four doors opened and the Rasiah family tumbled out. Tea-maker Aiya's brother, George, got out of the driver's side and shook his hand. Another brother, Paul, leapt out of the passenger-side front door. Shiro threw herself into his arms. Shiro's two brothers, Victor and Edward, emerged from the back doors. Victor hurried up the steps to his mother, while Edward tickled Shiro, who was still clinging to Paul. She laughed and released her grip. Edward promptly scooped her up and hugged her. Tea-maker Aiya helped his mother, a frail old lady of seventy years, out of the car.

Paul went around and opened the boot of the car. Lakshmi reached in and hauled a suitcase out. She felt a hand brush her neck. She shivered and turned to find Paul's face inches away from hers.

'Why, hello, Lakshmi,' he said, 'I hardly recognised you. You look all grown up and pretty. Not like a coolie at all.' The smirk on his face frightened her. She looked down and dragged the suitcase into the house.

Lakshmi jerked her head up at Shiro's shriek. Edward was chasing Shiro with a water pistol. Edward let fly a squirt of water, but he missed and hit Raaken on the backside. Raaken exclaimed and stepped back. The suitcase he was carrying into the house slipped out of his hands and bounced down the steps into the garden.

Periamma smiled and shook her head. 'Mahal,' she called out to Shiro, 'control yourself.'

***

The boxes and suitcases had been stored and the car parked under the mango tree. Everyone was seated around the dinner table. Lakshmi brought in the *pittu* and beef curry. She and Raaken would eat later in the kitchen.

'God bless our family, and bless this food to our bodies,' Tea-maker Aiya said. 'May we have many more Christmases together.'

'Amen,' the family chorused.

Lakshmi looked around the table at the crazy, joyous chaos that constituted the Rasiah family dinner. Victor, George and Tea-maker Aiya were discussing the exams Victor had taken a few weeks ago and his prospects for university placement. Edward gestured as he narrated how he and his friends regularly stole out of boarding school in the middle of the night for a snack. 'We go to the *kade* for a *thosai* feed,' he boasted. 'Nearly got caught once, when the headmaster had the same idea.'

While still talking, Edward tickled Shiro, making her squeal, choke and spray pittu all over the table. Everyone erupted in laughter. Periamma shook her head, and gestured to Edward to settle down. Turning to Shiro she said, 'Mahal, control yourself.'

Paul gobbled his food, ignoring all conversation. He looked up at Lakshmi when she placed his glass of water on the table. The look in his eyes made her shiver.

After dinner they all sat around the Christmas tree in the sitting room. The smell of fresh pine filled the air. The room glittered with coloured tinsel streamers and silver and gold balloons. Everyone 'oohed' and 'aahed' at the stars and baubles Shiro and Lakshmi had hung on the tree.

Lakshmi brought in mugs of Ovaltine for the family. After she had served them, she made one for herself in her tin cup.

The family sang carols late into the night. Shiro cuddled up on her Uncle Paul's lap, and Lakshmi sat on the floor by Periamma's seat. At one point they sang what Lakshmi knew to be Shiro's favourite song.

'Jesus loves the little children,
All the children of the world;
Red and yellow, black and white,
All are precious in His sight,
Jesus loves the little children of the world.'

Shiro had once told Lakshmi that she was a black child and the Irvine girls were white. Shiro had decided that as God's princess, she did not need a colour. The two of them had puzzled over what a red or yellow child would look like. Finally, Shiro decided that the boy Anthony who came last year was a red child since he seemed to go red easily. They never worked out what a yellow child was.

The grandfather clock whirred and chimed eleven times. Everyone was droopy-eyed and yawning. Tea-maker Aiya's mother was asleep and snoring on the sofa. Shiro had transferred herself from Paul's lap to her father's. She was more than half asleep, but keeping herself awake because she didn't want to miss a moment of the fun. Lakshmi was still at her spot by Periamma's seat. She leaned her head against its cool polished oak arm, longing for some sign of affection from Periamma, but there was none.

'I think that's enough for now,' Tea-maker Aiya announced. 'We have to leave early for church tomorrow.' Weary nods and grunts came from everyone else. Well, nearly everyone.

Paul threw up his arms. 'The night is still young. Let's sing something different. Anyone for a *baila*? Everyone ignored him and filed out of the room. Soft good nights and God-bless-you's were exchanged.

The room emptied. Tea-maker Aiya led a sleepy Shiro into her bedroom. Lakshmi walked around picking up the dirty mugs.

'You can clean them in the morning, Lakshmi.' Periamma smothered a yawn.

'They might attract cockroaches, Periamma,' Lakshmi replied, continuing to pile the mugs on the tray. 'It will only take me a few minutes to wash them.'

Periamma put her hand on Lakshmi's shoulder. 'You are so hardworking, dear girl. Good night.'

Lakshmi carried the tray of mugs out of the room. She passed Paul, asleep and snoring in the armchair. Lakshmi walked down the corridor and into the pantry. She set the tray by the side of the sink, opened the tap and started rinsing the mugs one by one. Lights were switched off across the house. The house was now completely dark except for the single bulb in the pantry.

'You are certainly grown up now, Lakshmi.' She heard a gruff voice behind her. Before she could turn around she felt arms reach out from behind her and pull her away from the sink. She could smell alcohol and stale beef curry on his breath.

Although she could not see him, she knew the man's voice. 'Paul Aiya, what are you doing?' she gasped. 'Let me go!'

'Why sleep on the ground in Shiro's room, Lakshmi?' She heard his heavy breathing and felt the roughness of his unshaven cheek against her own. 'Come sleep on my bed tonight.' She felt a sharp sting as his teeth closed on her earlobe.

'Let me go!' Lakshmi cried out and struggled. He grunted and held her tighter. His hand reached under her blouse and squeezed her breast. Lakshmi gasped in pain. His mouth was wet on the back of her neck. He groaned and pressed his body against hers. Holding her tight with one hand, he pulled her skirt up with the other. His hand was rough on her thighs. Squeezing, pinching and sliding upwards. 'Please please let me go,' she begged and wriggled. He growled and dragged her around to face him.

The door to the pantry flung open. 'Let go of the girl, you idiot!' Periamma's voice was low and angry, almost a hiss.

Paul released his grip. Lakshmi staggered and then sprang away from him. She pulled her skirt down and clutched her arms around her body. Shivering, she sank to her haunches by the door.

Periamma stood in the doorway of the pantry. Her hands were folded in front of her. 'You fool! Keep your philandering to the whorehouses in Colombo. In my house you *will* behave like a gentleman!'

Paul put his hands on his hips and laughed. 'Come on acca, she's only a coolie.' His laugh grew louder. 'Pretty and fairer than most I accept, but a coolie nevertheless.'

Periamma turned briefly to the sobbing Lakshmi, crouched by the door. 'Go to bed, Lakshmi.'

Lakshmi ran out of the room. She heard the sharp sound of an open palm strike a cheek. 'Your brother slaved and sacrificed to give you an education and this is what you end up as?' The anger was gone and in its place was sadness and tears. 'How dare you do this? She's only a few years older than our Shiro. How can I trust you with Shiro when she goes to Colombo? Wait till I tell *annai* about this.'

'No. no, please don't tell annai!' Lakshmi peeped back into the pantry. Paul was on his knees in front of Rasiah Periamma. 'Acca, acca, please. I'll never harm Shiro. She's my angel, my princess.'

Lakshmi turned and ran into Shiro's room, flung herself onto the mat and covered her head with her arms, cutting off the voices from the pantry. She squeezed her eyes shut, curled up like a ball and lay there, choking her sobs so as to not disturb Shiro.

Her eyes were still shut, her arms still over her head, when she felt another presence in the room. Had Paul returned, to finish what he had started? Trembling, she opened her eyes to see the shadowy figure of Periamma standing over her.

Periamma frowned. Her eyes in the dim moonlight filtering into the room were sad and seemed to have aged ten years.

'It's all right Lakshmi,' she whispered. 'Go to sleep, he won't come near you.'

She stood there for a few seconds, walked out and then did something Lakshmi had never seen her do before. She shut Shiro's bedroom door.

Lakshmi lay in the darkness, curled up tight. Her mind filled with fear, misery and memories of Paul's rough hands on her body. So this was the life of a coolie girl, was it? Clean up other people's dirty dishes and then be used by men for their pleasure? Maybe that was what her mother meant when she said no good would come of her?

No. She wouldn't live like that, she couldn't. Surely Periamma would look after her. Wouldn't she?

But what choice did a coolie girl have? Maybe she could be a servant in someone's house, but there was no safety there either. She thought of the girl who had gone to Colombo to be a cook. She had returned a year later, pregnant. She wouldn't talk about what happened. She lost the baby. A few months after that, she killed herself by drinking kerosene.

Lakshmi could hear Shiro's steady breathing and the occasional rattle and rustle of insects in the garden outside. The moon slipped behind a cloud, leaving the room almost pitch black. She wrapped her arms around her knees and rocked back and forth. Fresh tears trickled down her cheeks.

She *was* cursed.

She heard the grandfather clock in the corridor chime. Midnight – Christmas day.

Chapter 6

The shrill clamour of the wall-mounted telephone sliced though the stillness of the Tea-maker's house. Lilly sat up in bed and rubbed her eyes. It was still dark and the room was chill.

'Get up, Appa!' She shook Rajan.

Rajan groaned, turned over and pulled the blanket back over his head.

Lilly continued to shake him. 'Telephone, Appa. Take it, will you?'

'What time is it? It's freezing!' Rajan grumbled.

The telephone continued braying.

'Answer it, Appa,' Lilly patted her husband on the shoulder again.

Rajan groaned, sat up and lurched off the bed to his feet. Shivering and coughing he dragged the blanket and coverlet off the bed, wrapped them around him and stumbled across the room towards the light switch. He switched on the light and staggered into the corridor, swearing when he tripped on the rug.

The telephone continued its clamour. 'I'm coming, I'm coming!'

Lilly sat up in bed. She wrapped the remaining blanket tightly around her and squinted at the clock on the table by the bed. Five-thirty am? Who could be calling at this hour?

She heard Rajan shout into the telephone. 'I can't hear you. What did you say?' There was a pause. She could hear his grunts and heavy breathing. 'Race riots started in Colombo yesterday?' He sounded panicked and frightened. 'Trains being stopped and Tamils killed?' There was another pause. Rajan continued, his words now slow, laboured and ragged. 'Are you okay?'

Colombo? Race riots? Her two boys were in the city! Lilly flung off the blanket and leapt out of bed. Grabbing her housecoat off the bed end, she threw it over her nightclothes and ran down the corridor to the sitting room. Raaken, wrapped in a threadbare blanket, was already there. Shiro and Lakshmi came dashing in just after her.

Rajan put the receiver back on the phone cradle and turned to face the gathered group. 'That was George,' he said. 'The Sinhalese are rioting against the Tamils in Colombo. It's bad, very bad. The boys, mother and George are okay – for now. But Paul didn't come home last night after dinner with friends.'

Rajan started panting, as if he had just run a race. His face was pale, his lips drawn down in a grimace. 'They're trying to trace him through his Sinhalese friends. But his friends say they don't know.' He paused and sighed. 'Or maybe they won't tell.'

Lilly's body burnt hot and then cold. The stark horror in Rajan's eyes made her burst into tears. Rajan's arms went around her. Such public demonstration of affection was not correct in front of the servants and children, but today she needed it and she knew Rajan wanted it too.

'George wanted to get to us before we left for the railway station,' he said, holding her close and rocking back and forth. 'Thank God they were able to. George said they are -' He dropped his voice so the others could not hear. 'They are raping and murdering people on the trains.'

Lilly's head spun with even greater fear. She and Shiro had planned to take the early morning Uderata Maniké train down to Colombo. Shiro was scheduled to start as a student at the Bambalawatte Girls' boarding school next week. The phone call had saved their lives – and more. Little Shiro and herself, at the mercy of rioters. Her mind recoiled at the thought.

Lilly saw the fear and vulnerability on her husband's face. She felt faint but she knew that her husband needed her to be brave. Their two boys were still down there. Breaking convention, she cradled his head in her hands. 'Don't worry Rajan. The children will be all right. God is good. He has protected us this far. Trust him.'

'George said he's trying to get everybody out of Colombo and come here,' Rajan whispered in her ear. 'He has some Sinhala friends who might help them.'

The look of anguish in his eyes sent a chill through her body. She could tell he knew more than he was willing to say to her. Lilly broke out of his embrace, ran to the study and flung herself on her knees.

The study was a special family room for the Rasiahs. The furniture in the study belonged to Rajan's parents. It had been moved to Watakälé when his father died fifteen years ago. A small, round, mahogany table stood in the middle of the study with the family bible on it. The roll-top desk that Rajan worked at stood on one side of it. On the other was the equally old but comfortable rocking chair where Lilly sat to knit. A small, wooden cross hung on the wall above the family bible. Lilly flung herself on her knees before the cross. 'Oh dear God …' She hesitated. Words would not come. She burst out in tears again. Laying her head on her arms, she continued kneeling, her body wracked with sobs.

She heard Shiro's voice – soft and hesitant. 'Lakshmi, maybe it's my fault?' Lilly looked up. Shiro was seated on the trunk packed with her things for school. Lakshmi stood by her, holding her hand. Lilly looked at the tear stained faces. Shiro sobbed. 'Maybe I brought this on by praying that I don't have to go to school?'

Lakshmi sat down on the trunk and put her arm around her friend's shoulders. 'Don't cry, Chinnamma,' she said. 'I am here with you.'

'Did you hear what Daddy said about Uncle Paul? I love Uncle Paul.'

Shiro couldn't see the cloud that crossed Lakshmi's face when she mentioned Paul but Lilly did. Neither of them had spoken again about what happened last Christmas.

Now he was, in all probability, dead.

Lilly got off her knees. She bent and kissed Shiro. 'We won't be going to Colombo today.'

***

Lilly spent the day praying. Tea-maker Aiya went to work as usual, but didn't get much done.

As evening fell, Shiro and Lakshmi stood at the front of the house, watching the winding road across the valley, waiting, longing for the car which would bring the rest of the Rasiah family out from the savagery that had fallen on the rest of the country. Day slipped into night. The temperature plummeted. The wind whipped around the girls, making them shiver. Nobody called them into the house.

Lilly prayed and prayed and prayed.

Rajan sat in his favourite armchair with an open newspaper, listening to the radio.

And then they saw it – the headlights of a vehicle snaking down the mountain. Everyone rushed out to the front veranda.

The minivan drew up at the front door. The Rasiah clan stumbled out of the vehicle, their faces drawn. Lilly hugged Victor and Edward. 'Thank God, thank God,' she kept repeating between gasped sobs. Rajan held his weeping mother in his arms, talking to his brother George over her shoulder.

The stories tumbled out of them. Rape, stabbing, people in boiling tar, dismembered bodies lying on the road, burning tyres around bodies, houses burning with people still in them. Above it all, the sound of screaming and the shouts of the mobs. The things they'd seen in Colombo and on the drive up to the tea plantation poured from their lips. The usually impeccable George Rasiah sobbed as he described the scenes to his older brother. The boys clung to Lilly.

Lilly looked over her sons' shoulders at the two men standing by the car. They looked tired and yet they were both smiling. One, dressed in a white shirt and belted sarong, was by the driver's door. The other man wore a white shirt, dark tie and slacks. The clothes of both men were crumpled.

Shiro walked over to the man in slacks and took his right hand in hers. 'Thank you for saving my brothers,' she said, looking up at him and the driver. 'I prayed to Jesus to send a guardian angel to look after them. He sent both of you.'

The man squatted down so his eyes were level with Shiro's. 'God heard your prayers, darling,' he said. 'We were protected by a whole army of angels.'

This conversation made the adults aware of the two men. 'Annai, this is Mr Ranasinghe,' George said to Rajan. 'He and his driver are both Sinhalese. They risked their lives to get us here.'

Lilly moved away from her sons. 'Oh, Mr Ranasinghe,' she mumbled, tears sliding down her cheeks again, 'how can I – how can we …'

Mr Ranasinghe waved a hand in the air. 'It's the least we could do. I think it's sickening, what my people are doing. Disgusting doesn't begin to describe it.'

Lakshmi hurried into the house to help prepare a hot meal for everyone.

***

No one sent Shiro to her bedroom that night. She sat on her father's lap and listened to her family, and their guest Mr Ranasinghe, discuss the turmoil in the capital. This was the first she'd heard of the long-standing rivalry between the Tamil and Sinhalese people of Sri Lanka. She hadn't known that Sinhalese were Buddhists and Tamils were Hindus.

For once, overawed by what was being said, she kept silent, storing up words to ask her mother about later: looting, rape, murder. The exact meanings puzzled her, but the hushed and broken voices told her that they were bad things to happen to anyone.

'It's all the bloody Britishers' fault,' her father groused. 'The divide and rule policy over the last fifty years. Putting Tamils in administration and giving the Sinhalese land to farm.'

'Yes,' Mr Ranasinghe nodded. 'Pretty much guaranteed the dissent after the 1948 independence. The Sinhalese majority were never going to be happy that way.'

The white man's empire again, thought Shiro. *No wonder Daddy hates the British*.

'It was only a matter of time after Prime Minister Solomon Bandaranaike declared Sinhala the official language in 1956. We could all sense the racial tensions between Tamils and Sinhalese at work,' George said.

The only ministers Shiro knew were nice, old gentlemen who talked about Jesus at church. *Why did they go around changing languages and upsetting people?*

'It's a good thing our school's trilingual and made us study Sinhalese, Tamil and English. The rioters were in the buses picking out people who couldn't read the Sinhalese newspapers.' Victor's voice was rough with emotion. 'Won't help us get into university, however.'

Mr Ranasinghe sighed. 'A recipe for disaster. Trying to make sure that more Sinhalese get into university than Tamil kids.'

Exhausted by the fears she had faced that day and the conflicts she had learned of that night, Shiro drifted off to sleep, still cradled on her father's lap. The last thing she heard was her grandmother's cry, 'Sinhalese bulls have killed my son!'

That is so rude, Shiro thought as she dropped off to sleep. *A couple of those bulls just saved your life.*

Chapter 7

Picking up the slate and the piece of chalk, Lakshmi copied the words Periamma had written on the piece of paper. The chalk screeched on the slate. Lakshmi struggled to form the words. It was hard work writing English. The letters were different from the Tamil alphabet she had learned in the few years she had gone to the estate school.

It was almost seven years since Shiro had gone to boarding school in Colombo. Lakshmi had settled into a routine. She went to tea fields to pluck in the morning then finished the work in the line room and spent the evening with Periamma. She was supposed to help out in the house but with Shiro gone to school and the boys in Colombo there was little to do. So the evenings were times when Periamma taught her English. Lakshmi lived for the evenings and for the twice-a-year holidays when Shiro came home.

Shiro wrote long letters to her. They were about the boarding school in Colombo. Lakshmi still couldn't read all the words in these letters. Lakshmi numbered the envelopes and saved them in a box under Shiro's bed. Then begged Periamma to read the letters to her over and over again till she knew them by heart. Periamma didn't mind reading Shiro's letters. She said it brought Shiro closer to them both. Lakshmi repeated the letters to herself when she felt alone in the line room.

Putting the chalk down, she pulled out the box of letters and picked up letter number three. She traced the scribbled handwriting of her friend. This was an early letter.

Periamma walked in. 'You're travelling memory-lane again are you, Lakshmi?' She laughed at Lakshmi's expression. 'It means you are thinking back to what is in that letter.'

Lakshmi nodded. That was a nice word, memory-lane.

She held out the letter. 'Periamma, do you have the time?' She said in English, happy to see a smile of acknowledgement.

Periamma took the letter from her and picked up the slate full of Lakshmi's poorly formed words in her other hand. 'You are getting good in your English writing. Soon you will be able to write letters back to Shiro.' Smoothing down the purple cover on Shiro's bed, she sat down.

> Miss Grace Rowling told us today that the British missionaries built the Methodist boarding school in Bambalawatte in 1910. In her words, it was to be a little seaside oasis of England in the busy, hot and humid capital of Sri Lanka. Miss Grace is our school principal – she also looks after the God side of what we study, like reading the Bible and praying. Miss Grace is old.

Periamma stopped and smiled. Lakshmi knew why! She continued reading.

> Not as old as Mummy and definitely not as ancient as Achchi. Miss Grace is white like the Periadorai's daughter, Janet. She is a little like the angel we put on top of the Christmas tree. She wears starched print cotton dresses that reach to below her knees, the neckline of the dress high with a pure white lace collar. Her golden hair is curly and shiny.

> Now about the school. I am going to tell you about it so you can imagine what I am doing every day – all the time.

> A high brick wall, six feet tall, separates the school from the seaside railway line and the sea. You will love the sea, Lakshmi. Remind me to tell you about it when I come home at Christmas. The wall is topped by barbed wire and broken glass. I asked Miss Grace if it was to keep the girls from escaping. She thought it was very funny. She said no, it was to keep, in her words, undesirable elements from the compound. I told her that I would like to see an undesirable element, which made her laugh even more. She has a laugh like little bells ringing. The buildings …

Lakshmi's thoughts drifted as Periamma continued to read about the rooms and the verandas, the study and music areas and the tennis and netball courts. She listened again as Shiro described a typical morning at the school.

> The rattle and hoot of the train carrying early morning

workers from the villages down south into their work in Colombo shakes our second floor dormitory. We have a big fat ayah – a sort of servant called Soma who wakes us up at five forty-five in the morning. She stomps around opening all the windows, letting drops of salty sea spray and wind into the room. Then to make sure we are up she clangs a huge big brass bell!

We have prayer time every morning. I like prayer time. Miss Grace reads the Bible. Lakshmi, you MUST learn to read the Bible. At least get Mummy to read it to you. It's full of really interesting stories. The other day she read to us about this guy who had to never cut his hair…

Shiro's letters were full of happy, fun things. But when she'd visited last December, she had a different story to tell. She told Lakshmi that there were girls who bullied her because she was an estate girl. She said she hated the boarding, but loved going to classes. Lakshmi had to swear on the eagle to keep their secret. She was never to tell Periamma that Shiro was not happy.

Periamma finished reading the letter. Lakshmi reached into the box and handed her another one. It was a new one, written just a month ago.

She laughed. 'You want to hear about Shiro's new friend? It is good that she is making friends in Colombo.' She stopped and glanced at Lakshmi. 'Don't worry. You will always be important to our Shiro.'

Important. No one cared for her. Maybe it would be different with Shiro? Maybe they would stay friends? Soul-mate was the word Shiro had used last December. Periamma continued to read.

There's a new girl in the boarding this term. She actually came in about halfway through. Poor thing was so lost. Miss Grace asked if I would help her settle. Lalitha Pragasam is a Hindu. She's a little older than the others in our class. She grew up in a rubber plantation, so we sort of fit together. Her mother is an Indian like Lakshmi, but her father owned a small shop in a village down south near a place called Kalutara. He is dead and her mother married again. Lalitha says that's why she is in the boarding. Lakshmi, you will like Lalitha. I'd like to bring her home one holiday. We could have the best times ever – the three of us.'

Shiro wanted Lakshmi to write to her. What was there to write about? That she had started working as a tea plucker? Walking barefoot between the tea bushes, trying to pluck more leaves than the others? She could describe life in the line room – the smells, the dirt. Maybe she would write of how Periamma has taught her to clean her nails every evening. How she now had her own toothbrush in the toilet in the garden.

Periamma folded the letter and put it back in the box. 'You miss her, don't you Lakshmi? I do too, but it's good for her to be in Colombo. She is learning to behave like a lady. Making friends of her own class. She is happy there.'

Lakshmi nodded. She understood. Shiro needed friends of her own class, not like her, a coolie. 'Yes, she is happy.'

'And,' Periamma continued, 'I have a surprise for you. Shiro is coming home next week for the Christmas holiday.'

Lakshmi leapt to her feet, beaming. 'Periamma, that is very good.'

A rumble of thunder drowned out her words. A flash of lightning lit up the room. Periamma switched on the light. 'You should go home now, Lakshmi. It's getting dark and –' they both jumped at another closer crash.

Lakshmi slipped the slate and chalk under the bed. She ran down the corridor to the back door.

'Take a sack to cover your head, Lakshmi,' Periamma called after her.

'No Periamma, I am used to the rain.' Lakshmi shut the back door and ran down the path leading to the line rooms. She would love to stay forever at the Tea-maker's house. But her mother wanted her at home to help in the night. And she had to go out in the morning with the coolie women plucking tea leaves. It was a hard job. She was tired by afternoon when they carried the leaves to the weighing shed. Worse still, she didn't get to keep the money she was paid. Her father took almost all of it. He bought ganja and arak with it. She owed it to him for tolerating her, he said. He threatened to beat her and worse if she refused.

Lakshmi did whatever her father and mother told her to do. That way they didn't stop her from going to the Tea-maker's house.

Lakshmi slowed down as she came close to the line rooms. Meena was in the front veranda of the adjoining line room, sweeping with a broom made of dried coconut fronds. 'Oh, you are wearing a nice frock,' she called out. 'Ribbons on your hair also. Soon you will be wearing socks and shoes, no?' Meena grinned, her betel stained red lips parting to expose chipped teeth.

Lakshmi looked down at her dress. In her hurry to get home, she had forgotten to change back into her own clothes! She wouldn't dare tell Meena that Periamma had already given her a pair of socks and shoes.

Her mother came out of the line room. 'My, my, you look like a bride today. So now they are buying you clothes also? What do they expect in return? Are you sleeping with Tea-maker Aiya? Or maybe he is hiring you out to the Periadorai?' She guffawed in laughter. Meena joined in.

The insult stopped Lakshmi in her tracks. 'Amma, Tea-maker Aiya and Periamma are good people. They are kind to me because I am Shiro Chinnamma's friend. They would never harm me.'

Her mother swung on her with a scowl. 'A friend? You think you are a friend to Tea-maker Aiya's daughter?' She laughed, then hawked and spat at Lakshmi's feet. 'You're more stupid than I thought if you believe that. People always want something from us coolies, you fool. If it's not your body, it will be your sweat and work. Don't think you are any different. Just because –'

Lakshmi stared at her mother 'Just because what, amma?'

Her mother spat in the dirt, then turned and shuffled back into the line room. 'Go and get the food ready before Appa gets home.'

Lakshmi slipped into a corner of the line room. She removed and folded her dress and wrapped herself in her threadbare skirt and blouse. Sighing, she went out to the back veranda and started the fire for the rice and lentil meal. She cooked the food and set it aside. She picked up Shiro's old blanket and the cloth that served as her sheet. Wrapping them around her, she found a dry spot in the corner of the room, curled up and fell into a fitful sleep.

Lakshmi heard the clatter of the tin plate as her father gobbled the food she had made. He hawked and spat before coming back into the room. Lakshmi smelt the arak on his breath as he leant over her. His hand crept under the blanket. He ran his hand down her body. She squeezed her eyes shut and prayed that he would think she was asleep.

A little later she heard her father and mother arguing. Her father growled at her mother: '*Nandri illatha kaluthai.*' She heard the sound of a heavy slap and a gasp of pain from her mother. Lakshmi screwed her eyes tight. She heard a scuffle and groans and grunts from her father. Lakshmi turned to the wall and tried to shut out the moaning sounds coming from her mother.

Dear God, she didn't want to end up like this.

Chapter 8

Heads bent, the coolie women vied to fill their baskets. Their work-worn, brown hands flew over the dense tea bushes, picking their fresh green shoots. Soon the siren from the factory would signal the end of the morning shift. They would form a line at the weighing shed and have tea leaves weighed and entered in the ledger. That would determine their daily wage.

At twenty-three years of age, Lakshmi had the wiry figure brought on by the active life of a tea plucker. She was however, fairer, prettier and healthier than the other young coolie women. She had good teeth and skin thanks to Periamma's training and the food, toiletries and medicines she gave her. She also bathed regularly at the Tea-maker's house and didn't chew betel. Her hands were soft with the sesame oil Periamma got her to rub on them every day.

Lakshmi smiled. Today Shiro was coming home for the holidays, She was now sixteen and very pretty. In her last letter she had promised to bring Lakshmi some things she called makeup. Her fingers flying over the tea bush, Lakshmi smiled to herself, as if she would have any need of all that stuff that Shiro used to colour her nails and lips.

'Over there,' Kangani shouted, pointing to a couple of tea bushes by the mud road that the coolie women had missed as they swept the hill.

Lakshmi lowered her head and moved to where Kangani pointed. She continued plucking.

'Aiyoo, Lakshmi can't pluck fast like us, no,' one of the other women, Sunderi, called out with a hoarse laugh. 'She thinks she's a lady because Tea-maker Aiya looks after her. Look at her hands! She must keep them soft for her other jobs in the Tea-maker's house.' A cackle of laughter rolled through the women.

'She won't chew betel also, no? Must keep her teeth white. What use she must have for her mouth when she is there?' Meena called out. She hawked and spat a red spray of spittle into the roadside ditch. The laughter grew louder.

'Shut up! Get to work.' Kangani yelled. Continuing the chatter, the multi-coloured chain of women swept through the tea bushes, their bags now almost full of fragrant green tea leaves.

Lakshmi looked up at the rumble of a motorcycle on the mud road.

'What are you looking at?' Kangani hollered, poking a figure in Lakshmi's direction. 'You want Periadorai to think that I am letting you relax? Go on, work!'

It was a new Periadorai. One they hadn't seen before. The coolie women glanced at each other and giggled. 'Go on plucking! Work, work,' Kangani shouted.

The Periadorai parked his motorcycle and walked over to the tea pluckers.

Kangani pushed his way through the tea bushes to the edge of the road. Removing his towelling turban he held it in both hands and stood in the drain by the road, his head bent and eyes lowered, looking at the ground. 'Periadorai – Aiya …' he stammered.

The Periadorai stood at the edge of the road a few feet away from where Lakshmi was plucking. She continued working, keeping her head and eyes down. She could see his brown leather shoes and white socks. He was so close that she could smell him. It was a sharp sweet smell, nothing like the stale smell of sweat, curry and arak that reeked from the coolie men.

Maybe white people smelled like lime pickle?

He reached his hand out to the tea bush she was working at and picked a shoot. Lakshmi had a glimpse of his hand, white skin with long fingers. Clean pink nails and finger tips, tiny flecks of gold on the back of the hand. It was the hand of a statue, even a god.

The other coolie women stopped plucking and stared at the Periadorai. Lakshmi continued working.

After a few moments, he turned to Kangani. 'I am Anthony Ashley-Cooper. I am taking over from Mr Irvine. Do you speak English?' His voice was soft, like music. His words were slow and clear. Lakshmi understood every word.

Kangani shook his head.

Lakshmi raised her eyes to the Periadorai. 'I speak a little, Aiya, sir,' she said in English.

'Shut up!' Kangani barked at her.

The Periadorai looked straight at her. His eyes were deep blue, like a clear morning sky after the rain. Lakshmi looked down at the tea bush. The other women fell silent.

'What is your name, girl?' he asked.

Lakshmi kept her eyes down. 'Lakshmi, Aiya,' she murmured.

'Luksiimi.' A wave of soft giggles from the women acknowledged the mispronunciation of her name. 'Can you please ask the ladies if they are happy?'

She turned and translated his words to Tamil.

Kangani turned to the coolie women. 'Nod your heads, everyone,' he commanded in Tamil. They all responded.

'Good, good. Now please ask them if they are paid enough.'

Again Lakshmi translated it to Kangani.

He repeated his order. The women nodded again in unison.

'I am glad. Thank you, Luksiimi.' Ashley-Cooper Periadorai smiled at her. His teeth were white. They sparkled like jewels. Lakshmi didn't smile back. She looked down and continued plucking.

The Periadorai raised his hand in salute to Kangani. Swinging onto the motorcycle, he roared off up the road.

The coolie women broke into excited chatter. Kangani clapped his hands. 'Enough, enough.' He yelled, 'Go on, work harder. You have wasted time.'

'Lakshmi won't have to work much longer. She will get a summons from the Periadorai's house. She is fair, no? White men like girls like that!' one of the older women called out.

'Then she can use her soft hands, no? And her mouth also.' Meena hooted with laughter.

Lakshmi lowered her head and plucked faster. Her face burned with shame.

The strident hoot of the siren signalled the end of the morning plucking. It was a welcome respite. Lakshmi bowed her head and ran towards the weighing shed.

Mocking laughter followed her.

***

Shiro was due home anytime now. She would travel as usual in Hemachandra Mudalali's lorry. Hemachandra Mudalali had one driver he trusted completely. This man was the one he sent when Shiro or her brothers hitched a ride from the station.

Lakshmi bent over the ironing board, eager to get her work done before Shiro arrived.

Periamma and Tea-maker Aiya sat at the dining table with their mugs of hot tea. Periamma leant forward towards Tea-maker Aiya. 'That Anthony Ashley-Cooper who replaced Mr Irvine looks like a nice young man. I met him when I was returning from the staff wives meeting at the Wrights.' I was so surprised when he stopped his motorcycle, and said good morning.'

She lowered her voice, and Lakshmi listened carefully to get the words that followed. 'You know how Mr and Mrs Irvine always ignored us on the road? Anthony didn't seem to mind that someone may see him talking to a staff wife. We had a little chat about when we last met – he was only sixteen. He said that since then, he's done a university degree in political science and international diplomacy, or something like that. He said he understands the situation in the tea estates much better now.'

A shadow crossed Tea-maker Aiya's face. He frowned at his wife. 'Don't tell me you got taken in by his behaviour? You should know better than that, Lilly. He just wants to wheedle some information from you that he can use against the staff.'

Periamma shook her head. 'No, Appa. I think he was being nice. He said he had done research on colonial rule and independence. He even knew about the race riots. He asked if we had been affected by them. He sort of hinted that he wants to improve things for the coolies and native staff.'

Tea-maker Aiya's frown settled into a scowl. 'A white Raj, an Ashley-Cooper, do things for the coolies? Help the native employees? Bah! If he thinks that, he is more naïve than I thought he was. Someone at that all white Nuwara-Eliya club of theirs will put him right soon enough.'

'And,' she continued with a smile, 'He remembered Shiro. Wanted to know what she's doing.'

Tea-maker Aiya stood up. The chair rocked back, almost toppling over. Lakshmi jumped forward and righted it.

'Enough!' he raised his voice and waved his hands over his head. 'Lilly, you are not to talk with that man. Not about the staff. Not about the boys. And never, never about our daughter.'

Periamma stared at him for a couple of seconds. She shook her head. 'Don't be like that. Why can't he be different?'

He leant across the table making it even harder for Lakshmi to hear what they were saying. 'Be careful, Lilly,' he muttered. 'He and his brother William have been here only for three months. Already that William has a terrible reputation in Udatänná. No coolie girl is safe around him they say. There are stories of the way he entertains his friends from the club – bad stories.'

He glanced at Lakshmi and lowered his voice even more. 'You remember what father said about James Ashley-Cooper, when he was superintendent and father was Tea-maker? And the trouble that it caused for father? William is supposed to be just like his father James, or worse.'

'Aiyoo!' Periamma gasped and shivered. 'That is so bad.'

'You know what mother said about James Ashley-Cooper. How he used to entertain?'

Periamma nodded. 'She said that he even had one coolie woman live with him like … like a slave, even that she got pregnant by him. And there were others.'

Tea-maker Aiya snorted. 'More to that story.' He glanced at Lakshmi. 'You don't know half of it. Better you don't.'

Lakshmi continued ironing, pretending she heard nothing.

'Anthony has an honest face and clear eyes, Appa,' Periamma persisted. Lakshmi smiled to herself. Periamma always wanted to believe the best of everyone. 'I'm sure he's not like his brother. Anyway, we would have heard if anything had happened here.'

Tea-maker Aiya shrugged and dropped back into his chair. He glanced at Lakshmi. 'Maybe, maybe not.' They continued drinking their tea.

'Anyway, Appa.' Periamma's voice was low, sad. 'I wish there wasn't such a big gap between the British superintendents and us. How old are the Ashley-Cooper brothers? They must be only about twenty-three or twenty-four, just a little older than our boys. It must be depressing for Anthony in that big bungalow on the hill, with just Appu and the dog for company.'

'Don't you worry about him! He'll find people to talk to when he wants. Even to entertain him.' Tea-maker Aiya's lips turned down in a sneer.

'Don't talk like that, Appa.'

Lakshmi picked Tea-maker Aiya's shirt from the clothes pile in the basket and smoothed it on the ironing board. 'He spoke to us when we were plucking today,' she said, frightened of what their response would be.

Tea-maker Aiya's head shot up. He swung round in the chair to face her. 'He did what?'

'This morning. He didn't know Tamil. I told Kangani what he wanted.'

Tea-maker Aiya thumped his mug on the table. 'You translated for him? You idiot girl.' He shoved a pointing finger across the table at Periamma. 'Now see what you've done. Everyone knows that coolies don't learn English in the estate school. That Ashley-Cooper fellow is going to wonder where she learned it.'

He shook his head. His voice dropped. It was as if he had forgotten that Lakshmi was there, listening. 'You know what can happen to a coolie girl who knows English.' He slanted his head towards Lakshmi. 'Especially one who looks like her.'

Lakshmi knew what they were thinking. A coolie girl who was clean and could speak English, could understand and talk with the Periadorai, who was fairer than most Indian women. She had heard stories of what happened.

Why? Lakshmi wondered. Why did it have to be like this in the tea plantations?

The familiar rumble of Hemachandra Mudalali's lorry sounded outside the front door and Periamma and Tea-maker Aiya quickly got to their feet.

Chapter 9

The minister's manse and the little sandstone church were perched on a hill. Unfurled in front was the township of Nuwara-Eliya, the hill country capital of Sri Lanka. It was the main centre for trade, education and entertainment for the populace of the tea plantations that spread around it.

For the white British superintendents, this latter need of entertainment was provided by the all-white, members' only club – the Royal Hotel.

Anthony leaned back on the worn leather lounge. He shut his eyes and swirled the tea in the mug. He sniffed, opened his eyes and studied the deep amber colour, then sipped. He did this as a habit with every cup he drank, ever since Mr Rasiah, the Tea-maker, had showed him how to taste and classify the teas manufactured in Watakälé. The fragrance, the bouquet, the mellow warm stimulation to his taste buds; this would be a brew of broken orange pekoe tea leaf.

Bob punched Anthony on the shoulder. 'You should recognise it. You brought that tea along last time you came over.'

'Sorry Bob. Sheer habit.' Anthony said. He set the mug down and stretched. 'I'm bloody glad you took up the position here, old friend. And that you found your true love in Grace Rowling.'

Reverend Robert Kirkland, recently appointed British pastor of the Reformed Church Nuwara-Eliya, and new husband to the missionary principal of Bambalawatte Girls' School, gazed down at his long-term friend. 'Finding out that extending the Ashley-Cooper Empire in the tea plantations is not all your father said it would be, Anthony? Why not come visit us on a Sunday? Grace will be here on Wednesday. A couple of other superintendents attend the morning service. In addition, the Rasiah family from your place attends church regularly. Mrs Rasiah and the other ladies are planning a special welcome lunch for Grace after the church service.'

Anthony shook his head. 'I'm mighty glad you'll have Grace with you Bob. But no thanks, church is not my thing. You're right though. I need to get away from the plantation occasionally. Clear my head so I can think.'

'Your brother William seems to be getting around, making a reputation for himself too. Although, I must say I don't like the way in which he's doing it.'

Anthony stood up and moved to the window.

Anthony turned to Bob. 'What's William been up to this time?'

'Booked a room in the Royal with a couple of his chums; smuggled in a couple of coolie girls. One of them needed medical attention in the morning.' Robert walked over to stand by Anthony. 'I've visited his estate in Udatänná. They're all terrified of him, Anthony, the coolies and the native staff, men and women.'

Anthony shrugged. He looked away, across the town. 'That's how father wanted us to work, Bob. You've been at the manor when he's berated us about it. Make sure they know their place, he said the night before we left England. Instill fear in them. Make them think they would be sacked if they didn't toe the line. Tell them that they would not get a recommendation letter. Make them understand that they would never be able to work on a tea plantation again – the only job they know.' He sighed. 'And William drank it all in.'

'You know that's wrong, Anthony. You believe that all men are equal. You wanted to make a difference here. Surely you haven't forgotten that?'

Anthony shrugged again.

'What do you plan to do about it?'

Anthony laughed – even to his own ears, it was a cheerless sound. 'You could always get a rise out of me, Bob. Actually, I'm working on a savings plan for the coolies and a retirement fund for staff. I have a report written. I've talked to Mr Rasiah the Tea-maker about it. He doesn't really trust me, but he was willing to listen. He even advised me on some changes. I need to put it to the coolies and staff and then send it to father. I'll make suggestions on the living conditions and health care later.'

'A savings plan. You think that'll work? Will your father accept it?'

'I honestly don't know, Bob. But I have to try. It's all so wrong how we treat them.'

Bob jumped off the chair and punched Anthony in the shoulder. 'My friend, the moral crusader. You'll find a way. Trust your instincts.'

***

'This report is absolutely idiotic, Anthony. Father will be furious.' William sneered. 'The coolies have no idea about planning for the future. They live in the moment. All they want is their arak and their next meal.' He chuckled. 'And sex, of course!' He ripped the four sheets of closely typed paper in half. Ignoring his brother's muttered expletive, he crushed the fragments into a ball and aimed it at the brown cocker spaniel sitting under the mahogany office desk.

The dog yelped as the paper ball hit him on the nose. He jumped up and scampered over to Anthony. Anthony reached down and fondled the dog's smooth head. 'Shush Pegasus.'

William chuckled. 'You named that floppy eared mongrel after your horse in Bakewell? How pathetic can you get, little brother?'

They sat across from each other in the superintendent's bungalow at Watakälé. Angry blue eyes locked and held. William rocked back in the mahogany office chair. He crossed his legs and flicked the dust off his hand-crafted leather shoe.

He pointed to the crushed up paper ball that had been Anthony's typed report. 'Father wants results, man.' Leaning towards Anthony he banged his clenched fist on the arm of the chair. 'He wants the award for silver tip tea at the London auctions. You're not going to get that by doing good deeds for your slave labour.'

Anthony turned away from his brother's mocking eyes. Getting up, he walked over to the window and looked out on the manicured hedges and the rose bushes that bordered the lawn of his bungalow. Two coolies were trimming the hedges and another was watering the garden, working hard to keep things perfect for the British superintendent. Anthony took a deep, shuddering breath, fighting to keep his voice under control. 'The Indians are indentured labour, William – not slaves. They deserve to be cared for in their old age! That's why I created that pension and savings plan. It's simple – we give them a raise, but require them to invest it for the future, for when they can't work. They won't be worse off in terms of their take home pay. Mr Rasiah and I have discussed it. We told some of the labourers last week.'

'Sure you did. Is that why they almost went on strike?' William's voice dripped contempt. 'Come on, man. The Indians – they're savages. That's all. You can call them labourers, workers, whatever you will, but they will remain ignorant brutes, more animal than human.'

Anthony swung around to face his brother. 'And how did they become like that, William? Ever since the plantations were set up, we, the British Raj, have kept them dependent on us for their daily bread. They have no proper schooling, no health care, and no rights. Just look at the state of the line rooms! It's bloody wicked! It's – cold-hearted cruelty!'

The dog slunk away from William and Anthony and whimpered in a corner of the room.

William unfolded his lanky frame from the chair and stood facing his brother. His open-necked, white linen shirt clung to his tense muscled frame. Hands rested on the hips of his soft wool tailored pants. The morning sun slanted through the wide windows, accentuating his tan and glinting off his golden hair. His eyes were chips of cold blue flint.

'Get off your high horse and face the situation, little brother!' he snapped. 'We were sent here to make the best of these plantations, before the stupid natives nationalise them. Our father and grandfather worked hard to build up these estates. We have to get everything we can out of them, before the locals take it over and wreck it all! And if that means making both natives and coolies work harder – so be it! We owe it to our father!'

The flush extended to his neck where an angry pulse beat was visible. 'You are an Ashley-Cooper, little brother. You are an Englishman. This measly little third world country is a colonial cog in the empire our family has built. You better remember that when you try to play saviour to the slaves.' He thrust his face close to Anthony. 'It's that bloody do-gooder pastor friend of yours in Nuwara-Eliya isn't it? – The Reverend Robert Kirkland and his English rose of a wife. Don't think I haven't heard what they say about me!'

For a moment, the brothers stood glaring at each other. Anthony clenched his hands by his side. He wanted to smash his fist in his brother's face, but he couldn't. Not in full view of the coolies and the house staff.

With an angry snort, William walked over to the liquor cabinet. He picked up a half bottle of scotch malt whisky and poured himself a drink. 'Black Bowmore. Good quality whisky! Well, it's nice to see that you enjoy the money your dear natives and coolie friends make for you.' Raising the glass, he downed his drink straight.

Anthony closed his eyes. He battled the waves of anger that engulfed him. 'So how do *you* plan to manage Udatännä?'

William stood at the cabinet, checking out the bottles of liquor. 'All staff bonuses will be tied to productivity and London auction prices. Coolies will be expected to meet minimal quotas of tea plucked and hours worked or risk losing their jobs,' he examined an unopened bottle of Amaretto almond liqueur.

Anthony snatched the bottle from William's hands and banged it down on the table. 'That's immoral. How the hell can you get away with that?'

'With the blessings of father, that's how, little brother. I've talked to him.

Called him just yesterday. I updated him on your activities also.' William grinned back at Anthony and picked up a bottle of Bailey's. 'Stop being so bloody naïve. The coolies have no power, no organised labour union, nothing. And the natives have to do what we say – they know that their survival depends on us. They have to keep in our good books.'

Anthony heard a soft cough to his right. Appu stood next to the mahogany table with a tray in his hands, bearing a fine china tea set and a tray of homemade ginger biscuits. He was dressed in a white long-sleeved shirt buttoned to the top and tucked into his white sarong. A leather belt with shining buckle circled his waist. Not a grey hair was out of place on his head or in his handlebar moustache.

Appu had told Anthony that he had joined the staff in the Watakälé superintendent's bungalow as a houseboy when he was fifteen years old. That was thirty years ago. He had risen through the ranks and now ran the household staff. Anthony had grown to trust him.

Appu's hands trembled as he placed the tray on the mahogany desk. He stepped back and stood waiting. His face expressionless as he looked at Anthony. 'Will Udatänná superintendent Aiya be staying for lunch, sir?'

'You heard what I just said, didn't you Appu?' William's lips curled in amusement as he leaned in close. 'You look like you'd like to poison me, not feed me.' He laughed in Appu's face. 'Don't worry, I'm leaving. I have things to do in Udatänná.' Appu didn't flinch as a spray of saliva hit him. 'Very important things.' Williams laugh grew louder and he continued to stare into Appu's eyes. 'Ever the expressionless minion, eh Appu? You are well trained.'

William swung round on his heels, strode out of the room and down the steps to the drive. He mounted his motorcycle, kicked it to life and roared down the road in a cloud of dust.

For a moment, Anthony and Appu stood next to each other on the veranda watching William's receding form.

'Can he do it, sir?' Appu looked at Anthony.

'Yes, Appu. In Udatänná he can do anything and he will start after Easter.'

Anthony walked back into the office and flopped into the seat that William had just vacated. He was tired, drained. Leaning forward, he put his head in his hands. 'I want to help the staff and labourers, Appu, but I don't know if they'll understand. I don't know what else I can do.'

Appu was quiet for a while. 'The staff party, sir. Will he come?'

'Oh yes, Appu, we've already put up the money for it. Father insists that we both attend. It's supposed to be a sign of our generosity to the natives. Pretend to be nice guys while we're bleeding them dry. What a load of hypocritical bullshit.'

Anthony rubbed his face with his hands. Their father – James Ashley-Cooper – it came back to him, didn't it? No one opposed the Ashley-Cooper name and got away with it. Their mother had tried to resist and had been exiled back to England, a discarded wife. Now his two sons were doing his bidding, and William loved every minute of it.

Anthony glanced at the dog. Pegasus looked up at him, the crumpled report in his mouth. He had tried to do some good and it ended up as a scrunched up paper ball with dog drool on it.

No. He could not – would not give up.

Anthony looked up into Appu's compassionate eyes. Appu smiled. 'You are a good man, sir. God will bless you.'

A chill wind blew across the lawn and into the house. Both men shivered.

Chapter 10

A cold, wet mist snaked its way through the valley. Clammy tendrils sneaked through the closed windows into the dining room of the Tea-maker's house. Periamma pulled her sweater tight around her. She shivered and looked at Tea-maker Aiya across the table.

His mood matched the weather that Easter morning – dark and foul.

Lakshmi carried the food into the dining room from the kitchen. Raaken had taken the weekend off to visit his family in the next estate and she was helping out in the house. Shiro and her brothers were in Colombo that Easter. So it was just Tea-maker Aiya and Periamma who sat at the traditional Easter breakfast of boiled eggs and pancakes. In an attempt to be festive, Periamma had coloured the eggs with food dye. But Tea-maker Aiya was in no mood to notice.

'It was probably the chief clerk who decided to have the party on Easter Sunday,' he said. 'He's a Hindu. What does he care about this day? That idiot, Wright, would have gone along with it. He would take any chance to get drunk.'

Periamma sat silent, picking at a pancake. She had explained to Lakshmi that organising the staff party was traditionally seen as women's work, and there being no female staff, the wives did the organising for the day. Periamma was by far the best cook and the most organised. Over the last few days, Lakshmi had helped her and the other women make pretty coloured eggs and cakes. Periamma had instructed the other women on how to make little triangular pastries with minced meat and potato filling and small cupcakes with frosty icing of different colours. Patties, she called the pastries. In the beginning the other wives had done all the things wrong, but they had learned and now almost everything was ready for the staff party later that day.

'I have half a mind to not go. You can go with the ladies, if you want.' Tea-maker Aiya grumbled. 'This isn't a time for partying, what with the coolies all set to go on strike and all.' He sliced an egg in half – probably imagining it to be the chief-clerk Supramanium's throat – poked one half into his mouth and chewed.

Rasiah Periamma poured him a fresh cup of tea. 'You know we have to go, Appa. The Tea-maker and his wife have always attended the party.'

'I know, I know,' He groused, his mouth still half-full of egg. Pausing to swallow he continued in the same angry tone. 'And not only is Anthony Ashley-Cooper coming, his brother's going to be there too! We'll have both high-and-mighty Ashley-Coopers there at once!'

'Why do the superintendents come for these parties?' Periamma's brow creased in worry. 'I can understand with the Irvines. It was some entertainment for Mrs Irvine and the girls. But two single men?'

'Tradition, Lilly, tradition. They pay for it, they attend it. It's pretence of good will while they squeeze the place dry. This time we get the Ashley-Cooper look-alikes – Anthony and William.' Scowling he poked at a pancake.

Lakshmi picked up the empty plates.

Tea-maker Aiya glanced at the clock. 'Before we leave for church, I have to visit the factory and check how the withering of the tea leaves is progressing.' The chair scraped on the bare floor as he stood up, wiping his mouth with a napkin. 'Just be careful with Anthony and William today – they're two peas from the same Ashley-Cooper pod.' He strode out of the house.

Periamma watched as her husband walked down the path to the factory. She sighed and turned to look at Lakshmi. 'Yes, yes,' she said. 'We have been married for twenty-five years, but there are still times when he treats me like a young girl.'

'Periamma, it is beautiful. The way you both care for each other and the children.' Unable to control her emotions, Lakshmi turned and ran into the kitchen.

***

The Tea-maker's house was abuzz with the frying of spicy snacks and the last minute baking of cakes and biscuits. Periamma and Tea-maker Aiya had returned from Easter church service. Lakshmi had come immediately after she finished the morning shift of tea plucking and was busy cooking for the party.

Lakshmi bent down over the wood-fired oven to take out another batch of biscuits. Periamma watched her fan the biscuits on the serving tray. 'You must learn to cook the Sri Lankan Tamil way, Lakshmi. Making cakes is good, but you must learn rice and curries also. Then we can get you employment in a house. That is the only way you will get away from being a tea plucker.'

Last evening Lakshmi had heard them talking. 'She does not belong in the line rooms,' Periamma had said to Tea-maker Aiya. 'She is pretty and fair complexioned. Maybe we could arrange a marriage for her with a lower level staff member? There is that nice young Indian man, Sundaram, the junior book-keeper.'

Lakshmi winced as she remembered Tea-maker Aiya's reply. 'Don't be silly, Lilly. What staff member in his right mind would marry a coolie girl? That would be the end of his promotion chances in the plantations.'

***

The staff members were putting up the last of the streamers and balloons and people had begun to trickle in for the party.

Lakshmi stood behind Periamma looking around the clubhouse.

Tea-maker Aiya came in, carrying a book. 'Look at all this rubbish,' he grumbled. 'And these women. Who taught them to dress, for goodness' sake? What do they think they are, *Vesak* lanterns? Or at a *Thovil* ceremony.'

Periamma shushed him as the assistant Tea-maker's wife, Mrs Wright, approached. She was dressed in a maroon and green silk sari with a shiny green jacket under it. The sari was decorated with sequins, which shone and sparkled as she moved. The jacket rode high on her body, revealing a generous bulge of brown flesh. The hair piled up on her head was adorned with a bunch of red plastic orchids. To top it all, she had plucked her eyebrows and coloured her eyelids dark blue. Mr Wright, carrying six bottles of arak, followed her across the room. His eyes were glazed and he staggered as he walked.

Tea-maker Aiya rolled his eyes. 'I am glad you look normal.' He shoved a finger in the direction of the Wrights. 'Look at that man. Drunk already!'

Periamma looked down at her blue cotton sari, then across to her husband, the only staff member who had not bothered to change out of his casual factory clothes. 'Yes, we are different, aren't we?'

'This is all very nice, no?' Mrs Wright teetered up to them, her round, fleshy face beaming. 'You like my makeup? My daughter Roshni has just finished the beautician course in Nuwara-Eliya, no? She helped the other ladies also. Shall I ask her to do your face also?' She peered into Periamma's face.

'Thank you Mrs Wright, that is so kind, but I am afraid we don't have time for that. I have to make sure the food is served.' She turned to Tea-maker Aiya, 'Will you help me please?' Periamma grabbed his arm and moved him away.

'She can stick her daughter's makeup where the monkey stuck the nuts,' Tea-maker Aiya mumbled under his breath as he followed her.

Lakshmi went into the kitchen at the back of the clubhouse and opened the trays of food. After laying out the food as Rasiah Periamma had asked her to, she slipped out and stood by the kitchen door. No one took any notice of her. After all, she was just a coolie helper.

The party was in full swing and the baila music blaring over the speakers when the two Ashley-Cooper Periadorais drove up to the clubhouse. The uniformed chauffer held the door of the black Wolseley open as the two men got out of the car. Someone turned the volume of the music down and a hush descended across the room.

Mr Wright was swaying from side to side and hiccupping. Mrs Wright hustled him into the kitchen. Lakshmi caught Periamma's eye and shut the kitchen door.

Lakshmi recognised Watakälé Periadorai as the one who had spoken to her in the field. The other one looked a lot like him. He was a little taller and broader. Watakälé Periadorai was smiling. The other man had a scowl on his face.

He must be Udatänná Periadorai.

The task of welcoming the Periadorais had fallen to Periamma. Naturally! Tucking the fall of her sari around her waist, she walked over to the door of the clubhouse. Everyone else in the room was silent and her words carried to Lakshmi.

'Welcome to the staff party. It is a pleasure to see you both,' she said to the men.

Watakälé Periadorai bowed at his waist slightly and held out his hand. 'The pleasure is all ours, Mrs Rasiah.' He turned to the other man, 'You have not met my brother, have you? William is the superintendent of Udatänná. William, Mrs Rasiah is the wife of the Tea-maker in Watakälé.'

William, Udatänná Periadorai, ignored his brother's words. He looked around the room, keeping both hands firmly in the pockets of his pair of trousers.

Periamma spoke directly to Udatänná Periadorai. 'I am glad you could join us, Mr Ashley-Cooper. It is good of you to come all the way from Udatänná. Would you like to sit down?'

Udatänná Periadorai raised his eyebrows and stared back at her. The blue eyes were cruel and cold.

Lakshmi shivered. It hurt her to see Periamma being treated like that. She could see from Watakälé Periadorai's face that he didn't like it, either.

Udatänná Periadorai shrugged his shoulders and sat down. Watakälé Periadorai settled in another chair.

Periamma looked around. The staff members and their wives seemed to have either gone into the kitchen or were in a huddle by the drinks trolley.

Tea-maker Aiya was nowhere to be seen.

Elmo, the 18-year-old son of the apothecary, was standing by the record player. 'Come, Elmo.' Periamma beckoned to the young man. 'I am sure the superintendents would be interested to hear about how you play rugby for Kandy schools.'

Having settled that, Periamma nodded to Lakshmi. Lakshmi went into the kitchen. The women were crowded together, talking. '*Aney*, they are both very handsome, no?' Mrs Wright giggled. 'I must introduce Roshni later. Could be useful in job hunting, no? A reference from the superintendent is a big thing.'

'And so young,' another woman commented. 'Wonder how they will *manage?*'

This comment reduced them all to giggles. A couple of women looked at Lakshmi and nudged each other.

'They will find a way I am sure. Like their father did.' one sniggered.

Lakshmi shuffled from foot to foot, then spoke to Mrs Wright. 'I think Periamma wants some food taken out.'

Mrs Wright picked up a tray of cakes and spicy snacks and shoved it in Lakshmi's hands. 'You take it out.'

'But –'

'Don't argue with me, you idiot. Do as you're told.' Mrs Wright shoved Lakshmi out through the kitchen door into the clubhouse.

It was wrong for a coolie girl to serve the Periadorai food. But what was she to do? She looked at her long maroon cotton skirt and white satin blouse with sequined lace at the collar. Periamma had sewn it for her. The new pair of slippers on her feet was Shiro's Uncle George's Christmas gift to Lakshmi.

At least she was dressed all right today.

Taking a deep breath, she walked tray in hand, across the room towards where the Periadorais were seated. Periamma looked up as Lakshmi approached. Her brow knit in a frown. Lakshmi saw the look of worry, almost fear in her eyes. She turned to the Periadorais. 'Would you like to try some of our Tamil snacks? They are called *palaharams*. These are *vadai*, a spicy fried snack of pulses. Those yellow ones are semolina and honey. Or maybe some love cake?' She pointed out the various sweets on the tray that Lakshmi was holding.

Udatänná Periadorai kept his hand on the sweet tray and stared at Lakshmi. Lakshmi met his eyes and quickly looked away. Periamma flinched. Lakshmi stared down at the tray, shivering with fear.

'Is this pretty lass your daughter, Mrs Rasiah?' Udatänná Periadorai drawled.

'No, Mr Ashley-Cooper, my daughter is studying in Colombo,' Rasiah Periamma's voice was soft, controlled.

Lakshmi stood rooted to the spot, not knowing what to do. The tray wobbled in her hands.

Watakälé Periadorai reached out and took a piece of cake. He smiled at Lakshmi. 'Thank you.' His voice was gentle, even kind, and completely different from his brother.

'I thought all staff children studied in Nuwara-Eliya or Kandy?' Udatänná Periadorai released his hold on the tray long enough to take a piece of cake. Lakshmi promptly backed away, placed the tray on a table and rushed back toward the kitchen.

'No, our daughter is in Colombo,' she heard Periamma reply. 'She is studying at a Methodist missionary girls' school. She should be finished and back home next year.'

Lakshmi glanced back. 'A missionary school?' Udatänná Periadorai's lip curled in a sneer. 'I thought all you natives were heathens?'

Stepping behind a pillar, Lakshmi peeked out to watch and listen to them talk.

'No, Mr Ashley-Cooper, we are Christians,' Periamma continued. Others wouldn't notice, but Lakshmi heard the hurt in her words. 'All three of our children have attended missionary schools in Colombo. My elder two boys are in university there.'

'Wonders will never cease.' Udatänná Periadorai waved his hand, dismissing her and her comments as irrelevant. He scanned the room, his eyes narrowed, cruel and calculating.

Mr Wright moved towards Udatänná Periadorai with a tray of drinks. 'Sir, what will you drink, sir?'

'Straight whisky, man,' answered Udatänná Periadorai with a yawn. 'Anything to liven up this place.'

'Sir, you have not met my wife and daughter, have you, sir?' Mr Wright continued, motioning them forward. Mrs Wright minced across the room. She held her daughter Roshni by the hand. Roshni was dressed in a low cut red blouse and a skirt that barely covered her shapely bottom. She wriggled and smiled at Udatänná Periadorai.

He pointedly stared at her breasts and then dropped his eyes to her waist and lower.

Periamma got up and moved over to the group in charge of the music. 'Let's get the music going.'

***

The staff members relaxed as the night wore on. People danced the baila. Others got drunk. Mr Wright vomited in the tea bushes. The women gathered and gossiped. Periamma hovered, making sure the food and drinks were served and cleared up. Lakshmi washed dishes and cleaned the kitchen.

A couple of hours passed.

Udatänná Periadorai stood talking with Mr Wright and Roshni. He had a number of empty whisky glasses next to him. His hand rested on Roshni's waist.

Lakshmi walked around the room with a tray, collecting empty plates and glasses. Udatänná Periadorai stared at her as she picked up the empty glasses on the table next to him. He bent down and whispered to Roshni.

Roshni looked at Lakshmi and giggled.

Watakälé Periadorai was chatting with some of the younger staff members about the relative merits of the Sri Lankan and Indian cricket teams. He moved over to Udatänná Periadorai. 'I'm sorry to break up the party.' His eyes fixed on his brother. 'But we should be going.' He turned to Mr Wright and Roshni. 'My brother has a long ride back to Udatänná.'

Udatänná Periadorai scowled. He stared at his brother, but said nothing. He turned away without a further word to anyone and sauntered to the front door.

He jumped in the back seat of the car, then yelled out, 'Come on, Anthony, I've had my gutful of hobnobbing with your minions.'

Watakälé Periadorai ignored him. He went round the room, shaking hands and thanking the staff. He smiled as he did so, but his eyes were dark and angry.

Periamma walked with Watakälé Periadorai to the front door. Lakshmi slipped out of the back door of the kitchen. She stood behind the tall canna plants. She wanted to be there to help Periamma if needed.

Watakälé Periadorai shook hands with Periamma. 'Mrs Rasiah, thank you very much for a lovely evening.' His voice dropped. Lakshmi leaned forward to hear his words. 'I must apologise for my brother –'

'No,' Periamma spoke clear and loud. 'The staff party can be overwhelming for someone unused to boisterous Sri Lankan entertainment. Thank you both for attending the event.'

Watakälé Periadorai shook her hand again. 'Thank you.'

'Let's go, little brother,' Udatänná Periadorai hollered from the back seat of the car. 'I need some fresh air.'

Watakälé Periadorai slipped into the front seat by the driver. The car rumbled down the drive, away from the clubhouse.

Lakshmi stepped out of the shadow just in time to hear Periamma mutter

'Rajan is right. William is an arrogant bastard.' She looked at Lakshmi. Her eyes were tired, sad. 'Lakshmi, where is Tea-maker Aiya?' Together they walked back into the clubhouse.

Tea-maker Aiya came out of a side storeroom, carrying a book. He scratched his head and yawned. 'Have they gone?'

Periamma shook her head. 'Appa, that was rude.'

Tea-maker Aiya chortled. 'I don't think anyone even noticed.'

The Periadorais' departure signalled an end to the party. People started packing up. Mrs Wright grabbed Periamma's arm. 'He is a very nice man, no? The superintendent of Udatänná – Mr William? He has told Roshni that if she wants a good job to contact him. You should talk to him about your children also.' Giggling, she lurched away on her high-heeled slippers.

'I can imagine what job he will have for Roshni to do,' Tea-maker Aiya said under his breath.

By the time Lakshmi and the Rasiahs finished packing up it was past ten o'clock at night. They drove to the Tea-maker's house. 'It's very lonely on the road at this time, Lakshmi,' Periamma said as the three of them unfolded themselves from the old Morris Minor. 'You should sleep here tonight.'

'No, Periamma,' Lakshmi said with a chuckle. She ran into the storeroom and changed into her old clothes. 'We all go about at this time. It is safe. I will run all the way to the line room. I won't take the short cut. I'll go by the main road past the weighing shed.' With that she dashed out the back door, shutting it behind her.

'Be careful,' Rasiah Periamma called after her.

Lakshmi meandered along the road, forgetting her promise to run back to the line room. What was there to run back to? She wished she had accepted the offer and stayed overnight in the Tea-maker's house. Lakshmi looked up. The moon was a silver ball hanging in the velvet black sky. Fluffy grey clouds moved across its shining face. Fireflies glittered and glimmered in the trees. An owl hooted in a tree.

She thought of Shiro. She missed her so much. Soon Shiro would finish school and get married. She had heard Tea-maker Aiya and Periamma talking about appropriate boys and arranged marriages. Lakshmi giggled. Somehow Shiro agreeing to an arranged marriage was difficult to imagine.

Lakshmi heard the motorcycle just as she walked past the weighing shed. It must be Periadorai. As was proper, she moved to the side of the road and stepped into the small ditch. She turned her face away, waiting for him to ride pass.

The motorcycle screeched to a stop. Glancing up, Lakshmi saw him get off.

'Well, well, well, if it isn't our little cake server.' The words were heavy, slurred. He was drunk. She turned to run away.

White hands reached for her. She saw his face, sparkling teeth grinning like a mad dog, gold hair glistening in the moonlight. Sharp blue eyes filled with lust. She smelt alcohol.

***

She was on the floor of the weighing shed. How had she got there? She screamed and struggled.

He slapped her. Her head snapped back, smashed on the cement floor.

'Shut up and enjoy it, you bitch,' he snarled. 'This is all you're good for anyway.' He ripped her blouse off in one movement, laughing as she tried to cover her breasts with her hands.

And the pain, oh dear God, the pain. Would it never end?

She lay on the floor sobbing.

The clouds passed and she saw his face in the moonlight filtering into the weighing shed – Periadorai.

He stood over her, fastening his clothes. Reaching into his trouser pocket, he threw a wad of fifty rupee notes on her as she laid sobbing and bleeding on the floor of the weighing shed. He reached down and held her face in his hands as she tried to crawl away. His nails cut into her skin. 'You could make more money this way than as a tea plucker.'

The motorcycle roared away. She heard his laughter echoing into the night. A sound she would never forget.

Lakshmi sat up. She screamed and doubled up in pain.

Where could she go? What could she do?

If the other coolies found out, she would be subject to more agony and humiliation. Everyone in the line rooms would laugh at her. Her father would beat her. He would accuse her of going to Periadorai and offering herself to him. Worse still, now that Periadorai had used her once, he would expect her to be available for him whenever he wanted her. That was the way of the tea plantation.

Periamma – she would help her.

Gathering her clothes around her, she staggered to her feet. Pain shot through her lower body. She looked down at the blood trickling down her thigh. Sobbing and limping she scrambled up through the tea bushes to the Tea-maker's house.

The kitchen light was still on. Lakshmi looked through the window. Tea-maker Aiya and Periamma were sitting at the dining table. Lakshmi tried to open the back door. It was locked. She banged on it. 'Periamma, Periamma,' she yelled. She heard footsteps. Tea-maker Aiya pulled open the latches that had been set for the night. Lakshmi stood there, looking at them, alternately sobbing and screaming. She knew she looked frightening. Her blouse was muddied and dirty and ripped across the front. She held the torn scraps together in her shaking hands. The scratches down her arms were bleeding stripes. There were red streaks of blood on her skirt. Her lips and face throbbed with pain, swollen and bleeding. She could hardly see from her right eye.

'Lakshmi!' Periamma gasped. She grabbed her hand and pulled her into the house. Tea-maker Aiya slammed the door shut behind her.

'Who did this to you?' Periamma whispered. Tears streamed down her face as she looked at Lakshmi. Tea-maker Aiya stood with clenched fists, breathing hard.

Lakshmi shivered, she couldn't stop her body shuddering. Her teeth chattered. She couldn't walk. She opened and shut her mouth. Then between sobs she shrieked. 'Periadorai, Periadorai.'

Periamma held Lakshmi's arms and helped her to a seat. Lakshmi tried to sit and then shot off the seat. '*Nohuthu, nohuthu,*' she moaned. She collapsed on the floor, whimpering and writhing. The pain spiralled though the core of her. It was in her body but also in her mind.

Periamma sat on the floor by Lakshmi and took her hand. Lakshmi lay where she had dropped, curled into a ball, her body trembling, tears trickling down her cheeks.

'Periamma, why did he do it? I thought I would die.'

Periamma didn't answer. She squatted by Lakshmi, stroking her head. Taking the hanky she had tucked at her waist, she wiped Lakshmi's face. Then, standing up, she went to the bathroom and turned on the hot water heater.

Lakshmi heard Periamma sob.

Tea-maker Aiya came over to her with a mug of tea. It was one of the family mugs, not the old tin one she usually used. He knelt by Lakshmi and offered it to her. Lakshmi struggled up. She reached out trembling hands to the mug, clutched at it and took a sip. She clasped the mug to her body, rocking herself back and forth. For a while, they remained in silence, Lakshmi sipping hot, sweet tea, Tea-maker Aiya and Periamma standing by her.

'Come,' Periamma took Lakshmi's hand and helped her stand up. She led her to the bathroom. Lakshmi took off her torn clothes. Periamma looked at the bruises and teeth marks on her breasts and the blood on her thighs. 'Aiyoo, how could this have happened?'

Lakshmi shook her head. There were no words.

Leaving Lakshmi in the bathroom, Periamma walked out.

Lakshmi bathed slowly. She scrubbed her skin with the soap. The scratches and bruises stung as she rubbed them, but she continued, trying to take away the shame, the pain. She washed away the blood on her thighs, but she continued to bleed.

She heard them talking just outside the bathroom door. She strained to listen

'It is such a brutal rape, Appa. Dear God, how could any man do this to a helpless girl?' Periamma's voice was ragged and interrupted by deep gasping sobs.

'It's the way of the estates Lilly, plantation hospitality for the white Raj, the nightcap to the staff party.'

'Can we do anything?'

'Officially, no,' Tea-maker Aiya said. 'It's the word of a coolie against that of the British superintendent. But I intend to confront Anthony with it tomorrow morning.'

'Be careful Appa.' Periamma's voice caught on a sob. 'Don't get into trouble with Anthony Ashley-Cooper. You remember what happened when your father questioned his father's actions.'

Tea-maker Aiya sighed. 'I know, I know. Like I can ever forget. Let's think about it tomorrow. For now, let's just help Lakshmi.'

Lakshmi came out of the bathroom, dressed in a nightdress Rasiah Periamma had given her. There was already a fresh trace of blood on it.

Rasiah Periamma glanced at the blood stain. 'You'll have to go to the apothecary tomorrow,' She helped Lakshmi lay out a mat in their bedroom.

'Periamma,' Lakshmi clung to her hand, 'please don't get into trouble because of me.'

Periamma squatted beside Lakshmi as she lay curled up on the mat. 'Lakshmi, when you were just a little girl you came as a nanny for Shiro. You were frightened then and I told you I would look after you. You trusted me then. We will help you now also. Now go to sleep.'

Sleep? Lakshmi lay on the mat, hearing Periadorai's laughter.

The house was dark. She could hear Tea-maker Aiya snore. Lakshmi lay curled on the mat. The pain between her legs now a dull ache.

What would become of her?

Chapter 11

Anthony tossed and turned in bed. A vague feeling of unease, almost fear tingled through his consciousness, keeping him awake.

He lay in bed, mulling over the evening.

The Easter staff party had not been a total disaster. William's behaviour was reprehensible as usual, but the staff seemed happy enough. Chatting with Mrs Rasiah had been interesting. She was so proud of her children and her sons' achievements. And young Shiro, he wondered what she looked like now. He dosed off, remembering the riotous curly hair, the defiant glow in her black eyes.

Anthony sat up in bed and looked at the clock. It was midnight. Surely William must have got home by now? He rolled out of bed and padded barefoot through the dark house. In the office, he picked up the telephone and dialled William's number.

The phone rang for a few anxious seconds. 'Yeah?' William snapped. Anthony breathed out a long, relieved sigh. 'Oh, good you're home,' he said. 'I was worried about you riding back tonight. You were so drunk.'

William hooted with laughter. 'Sorry, little brother, you won't get rid of me that easily.' Anthony heard a sound of swallowing.

'Are you still drinking?'

William ignored the question. 'I had a very interesting ride home, little brother,' he said, 'a very interesting ride indeed. You never told me how much fun there is to be had in Watakälé.'

William's words sent a chill down Anthony's spine. 'William, what happened?'

'You'll find out soon enough, little brother. Go to sleep. Good night.' With another sharp bark of a laugh, William dropped the handset.

William, what have you done now?

Anthony woke to the jarring ring of the phone. He glanced at the clock – six in the morning. The morning after the staff party – who'd be awake at this time? He turned in the bed, shivered and pulled up the doona, waiting for Appu to pick up the phone.

'Still sleeping.' Appu said into the phone. Anthony rolled over and listened to the conversation. All he could hear was Appu's repeated '*aiyoo, aiyoo,*' every exclamation more shocked and distressed than the other.

It sounded serious.

Scrambling out of bed, Anthony started dressing. There was an insistent tap at the door. 'Come in, Appu,' he called out. 'What is it? Has something happened in the factory?'

The door opened with a crash. Appu stood holding on to the doorpost with both hands. His eyes were wide open and tears streamed down his creased cheeks. The look in his eyes shocked Anthony to the core of his soul.

'Come on man, tell me! If it's so bad, I need to do something fast.' Anthony reached for his shirt.

'Nothing you can do, sir,' Appu babbled. 'Mr Rasiah, Tea-maker Aiya, sir. He is angry, sir.'

'What about, man? Stop shivering like a leaf in autumn, and tell me. What is he angry about?'

Appu looked down at his feet. His Adam's apple jiggled as he swallowed. 'The coolie girl who was serving at the party, sir; she – she was hurt last night. Somebody did – did a bad thing.'

'A bad thing? What are you saying man? Was she raped?'

Appu nodded.

'But who the hell would do that in Watakälé? One of the staff, maybe? Most of them were drunk.'

Appu stared at the ground. He was shivering. 'She said – said it was you, sir,' he stammered.

'Me?' Anthony exclaimed in horror. 'I came straight home and went to bed! You know that. I hope you told him?'

Appu nodded again.

'Damn it!' Anthony slammed his closed fist into the wardrobe door. 'It was William! That's what he was laughing about last night! He raped the coolie girl!'

Anthony dropped down on the edge of the bed and rubbed his eyes.

What a mess. The bloody idiot, why couldn't he keep his whoring away from Watakälé? 'Where is Mr Rasiah, Appu?'

'At the apothecary's, sir. The girl needed treatment, sir.' Appu was now sobbing. His shoulders stooped. His words came out in drawn out gasps.

Anthony reached out, and ignoring all proprieties of behaviour, placed a hand on Appu's shoulder.

'I'll go immediately.'

'No sir, not to the apothecary's, sir,' Appu shook his head. 'Tea-maker Aiya said she is too frightened of seeing you. He said to meet him in the factory.' Appu shuddered and gasped, wiping his tears with the tea towel he was carrying. 'I'll serve breakfast, sir,' he said in a strangled voice. Pulling his body erect with obvious effort, he looked at Anthony.

'No, just coffee. Thank you, Appu. And please ring Mr Rasiah and tell him that I'm on my way to the factory.' Anthony spoke over his shoulder as he went into the bathroom. He splashed water onto his face. Rape on Watakälé, God only knew what that would do to his credibility with the staff and coolies.

When Anthony came out of the bedroom, freshly brewed coffee was on the table. Appu stood by the door. His face was washed. He was back to his groomed and dignified best. But his eyes were pools of sorrow mixed with anger.

Anthony downed his coffee and strode to his motorcycle. He knew Appu would testify that he had come home after the party and been in bed all night. But William, he would never be held accountable for this. The rape of a coolie girl by the British superintendent would never be reported to the police. Even if it was, it would never be followed up. That's how things worked in the tea plantation under the British Raj.

This was plantation entertainment – colonial style.

***

'No, Mr Ashley-Cooper, nothing you can do can make amends for your brother's disgusting behaviour. You can't buy off pain and shame.'

Mr Rasiah stood with his arms folded over his chest. Anthony wilted before the raw anger and blatant disgust in his eyes.

'It's what your family do well – rape.' Mr Rasiah stepped back and leaned on the tea tasting bench. His lips twisted and black eyes flashed fire. He raised his voice. 'My father worked for your father. Did you know that?'

Anthony shook his head.

'He, your father – James Ashley-Cooper – kept an Indian coolie girl, a 15-year-

78

old in the house. She got pregnant. He set her up in a house in Diyatalāwa.'

Anthony felt faint. He grasped the corner of the office table. 'My father? A child? Here in the tea plantations?'

'Yes, Mr Ashley-Cooper. The girl was in the bungalow when he brought your mother there as his bride.'

Anthony stifled a gasp. Memories flooded his mind – his mother's refusal to speak of those early years. His father's sarcasm. His mother's words to him when he asked her about the plantation: 'There are people who know what happened …'

'But surely someone would know if he had a child by a –'

Mr Rasiah laughed. Lips curled in a sneer he leant towards Anthony. 'Notice a half-breed coolie? For goodness' sake, look around you, Mr Ashley-Cooper; you'll see them everywhere. Olive skinned coolie men and women, boys and girls. Brown, grey and blue eyed. You probably have more than one sibling around here. But don't take it personally. Your father was not the only British superintendent spreading his sperm in the tea bushes.'

Anthony stood dumbfounded. 'Dear God, how could they?'

Mr Rasiah's voice lost the painful edge. 'It wasn't all rape. Some coolie girls consider it a notch in their belt to bed the white Periadorai.' Mr Rasiah stood silent and then sighed. 'You aren't like that, are you? I would have heard if anything happened.'

Anthony met his gaze. 'Mr Rasiah, please let me help the girl. I want to make a difference.'

'You can't help her, Mr Ashley-Cooper. As to making a difference, you already have. Follow through on the coolies' savings plan and staff provident fund.'

'That I will do.'

'As for the girl,' Mr Rasiah continued. 'We'll take care of her. Your involvement would make it look like you were the one responsible, an admission of guilt.'

Anthony flushed at the implication and looked down. 'I see. What do you think I should do?'

'Don't get involved in this incident. Look after Watakälé. Show that you care for the labourers and staff. Get down to the tea fields with the coolies and get into the factory during manufacture, Mr Ashley-Cooper. Let the coolies know you are interested in the tea plantation – in the plucking, the manufacture – but also in them as people. And you will truly learn what is happening. The coolies will feel you care and they in turn will work better for you. Let them see you as a man, not the white lord of the British Empire.'

They looked at each other across the large old wooden desk of the Tea-maker's office. The tall, young British man dressed in Savile Row woollen trousers, linen shirt and hand-crafted leather shoes; his sun bleached golden hair drooping over his tanned angular face. The dark skinned native Tamil Tea-maker, dressed in khaki trousers and a flannel shirt, his feet in worn leather sandals.

Finally, Mr Rasiah smiled. 'Mr Ashley-Cooper, you are so unlike your father and brother. I'll do something for you, Mr Ashley-Cooper. Watakälé will have the best price on the London tea auctions within six months. It'll take some doing but it can be done.'

Anthony's heart raced. Top the London tea auctions. That would be something to excite his father. 'Can we aim for gold tip?'

Mr Rasiah shook his head. 'No, wrong altitude, but we could try for silver tip.'

'Let's do it.' Anthony held out his hand to Mr Rasiah. They shook hands and parted. Anthony looked back at Mr Rasiah as he climbed onto his motorcycle.

Friendship with the native staffers, wage increases for the coolies. This was definitely not what his father wanted.

But maybe it would go some small way towards paying back the hurt and pain his family had heaped on these people.

Chapter 12

July 1966 Watakälé

The roar of the approaching motorcycle and the crunch of tyres on gravel sent a shudder through Lakshmi's body. She knew now that it was not Watakälé Periadorai who had hurt her, yet the site of his face with the piercing blue eyes, so like his brother's, sent shafts of fear and pain through her. It was as if she were back on the floor screaming for mercy and getting none. She moved away from the gravel path, deeper into the bushes. Her trembling fingers struggled to pick the two leaves and a bud. She slowed, then stopped picking.

Meena and the other women giggled and pointed.

From the corner of her eye she saw Periadorai get off the motorcycle and walk towards Kangani. Kangani scuttled to the edge and stood in the ditch, his towel turban in his hand.

Periadorai stared at her. She felt beads of sweat gather on her brow and slide down her face. Her eyes blurred. The other women nudged each other and giggled. Surely they could not know?

'How is the picking today?' Periadorai addressed Kangani in English, then repeated his question in slow halting Tamil.

'Sir, sir, yes, yes, good sir, good sir,' Kangani's head bobbed.

Periadorai stood watching them work for a few moments, then flung his leg over the motorcycle and rode off towards the factory.

The silence was broken by guffaws of laughter. 'Maybe he is checking us out?'

'No, he was staring at Lakshmi!'

'Ah, she has soft hands no? And fair skin also!'

'Soft other things must be also.'

Lakshmi continued plucking. Soon the women moved on to talking about other things. Lakshmi listened to the talk around her.

'He won't get away with it!'

'My husband said that they will fight.'

'We will all do a stop work.'

'Bad enough Periadorai, Tea-maker Aiya is also in it, no!'

'Shut up,' Kangani supervisor shouted. He tilted his head towards Lakshmi. 'Somebody might tell what we are talking.'

Lakshmi knew what they meant. They thought that she and Watakälé Periadorai –

No, it was too frightening to even think about. Not caring that her basket was only half full she pulled it off her head. 'Kangani Aiya, I'm sick. I will go early to the weighing shed.'

Laughter followed her as she ran down the muddy path to the shed.

Later, on her way back to the line room she stopped to watch Kangani and other labourers, including her father, talk at the kade. In the past, these meetings would include plain tea and a shared betel chew, laughter and crude jokes, sometimes also a smoke of ganja. But recently the talk was serious, even angry. There was a new man there, a man from outside the tea plantation. A man they called Union Aiya.

That night, huddled in the corner of the line room, she heard her father Raman shouting outside in the veranda of the line room. 'The white pig and Tea-maker Aiya will all be sorry soon. We won't wait for Union Aiya to do it – we will see to it ourselves. I have had enough.' A few other coolies joined him, shouting, clapping. She crept to the door and listened.

What she heard made her heart burn with fear.

***

The first rays of light crept through the old piece of cloth that hung across the door of the line room. Lakshmi rubbed the sleep from her eyes. Soon she and her mother would need to leave the line room and trudge to the weighing shed for the attendance muster before starting another days tea plucking.

She had to hurry. Lakshmi stepped over her sleeping sister and crept out of the room. If her mother got up before she returned, she would assume that Lakshmi had gone into the bushes to relieve herself. She pulled her skirt and blouse tightly around her and scrambled up the hill towards the Tea-maker's house.

Lakshmi's stomach churned. Stopping she bent over and retched. She washed her mouth in water from a little stream and hurried on. She must have an upset stomach. She was vomiting a lot these days.

Shivering in the cold, she scrambled up the path leading to the Tea-maker's house. Her bare feet slipped on the moss and wet mud. Cursing, she clung to the tea bushes. She stopped to vomit again and then hurried on.

There was not a moment to spare.

The house lay shrouded in darkness. She ran to the back of the house and tapped on the window of the store room where Raaken slept. She heard the hiss and rattle of his snores. "Raaken, Raaken,' she called.

Raaken stopped snoring and groaned. The mat rustled as he got up. He opened the window. 'Lakshmi? What are you doing here at this time of the morning?'

'Big problem, Raakan! Come, come.' The anxiety in her voice had the effect she hoped for. Opening the window completely, Raaken climbed through to join her in the garden.

'Why, Lakshmi? What has happened?'

'Some of the coolies have done a *soonyam*, a death charm, and placed it under the mango tree,' Lakshmi's voice cracked as she stumbled out the words.

Raaken's eyes widened. 'Aiyoo, don't even talk about such horrible things. Something bad will happen to you.'

Lakshmi trembled and grasped Raaken's arm. 'I heard my father talking about it. He is the leader of the group. It's right in the path Tea-maker Aiya takes to the factory. It's a death charm. He will step on it and die.' She shook Raaken. 'We have to do something.'

Raaken pulled the old blanket around his shoulders. He drew his brows together in puzzlement. 'Who would want to kill Tea-maker Aiya?' he scratched his head. 'Everyone knows he's the only staff person who looks after us.'

'It's something about him keeping part of our pay and giving it to us when we are old. They say it is Periadorai's idea and Tea-maker Aiya is supporting him. They say we will get less money and that the estate will take the rest. There is a new man who talks to Appa and his friends. They call him Union Aiya.' She shook Raaken again. 'I am frightened. One way or the other they want to kill Tea-maker Aiya and Periadorai.'

Raaken frowned. 'Be quiet, Lakshmi! We don't want to wake them.'

Lakshmi continued to tug on his arm. 'Quick, hurry. Let's find it first.'

Raaken pulled his arm from her grasp. 'All right. We'll go check under the mango tree and see if anything has actually been put there. Why frighten them for nothing?'

They walked round the house to the mango tree. Neither spoke. The wind picked up and whistled up from the valley. The early morning mist swirled around them. Carefully they examined the mud around the mango tree, their eyes straining in the dim pre-dawn light.

Lakshmi grabbed Raaken again. Her fingers clawed on his arm. 'There!' Her voice was a frightened mumble. 'What is that?'

Lakshmi and Raaken stared in horror at a spot where the soil had been freshly dug up and covered over. On the surface lay a triangle of three twigs. The sign of a death charm – a soonyam.

'What did they put in there?' Lakshmi stuttered. She put her hand on the mango tree and then drew back as if stung.

'Probably some of Tea-maker Aiya's hair, a nail and charms bought from the old *swami* in Diyatalāwa,' Raaken responded in a hushed voice. 'You go home before your parents get up. We don't want your father to suspect anything. I'll look after this.'

'Thank you, Raakan, thank you,' Lakshmi ran from the Tea-maker's house and scrambled back down the path to the line rooms. She got to the line room just as her mother was getting off the mat.

'Why are you crying? Are you not well?' her mother snapped.

'Just a little stomach ache,' Lakshmi mumbled in reply, reaching for her clothes.

Together they dressed in their work sari and hessian apron and cumbly, the blanket they wore over their heads. Picking up their baskets, mother and daughter made their way to the weighing station for muster before another day of tea plucking.

But Lakshmi could not work. She was scared and worried. She was also vomiting over and over.

'Go back to the line room, Lakshmi,' Kangani yelled. 'You are useless here today.'

Grateful to be let off, Lakshmi left the tea field.

She heard her mother's voice. 'That silly girl must have eaten something at the Tea-maker's house.'

The loud guffaw from Meena's mother chilled Lakshmi's heart. 'Maybe there is something else in her belly that is making her vomit!'

***

Lakshmi veered away from the line room and ran to the Tea-maker's house. She looked through the kitchen window.

She watched as Raaken mixed the rice flour to make the pittu for breakfast. Carefully he set the bamboo tube on the pot of boiling water and filled it with the soft while balls of rice flour. He didn't always get this right, but today the texture looked perfect.

Periamma came into the kitchen.

'Raaken, you are up early today. And already made the pittu.' She stood at the door to the kitchen, dressed for the morning. *She looks so happy*, thought Lakshmi. *How will Raaken tell her that Tea-maker Aiya will die today? She will be so upset.* Lakshmi was glad she was there.

Lakshmi slipped in through the back door into the kitchen. Periamma turned to her. 'Lakshmi! What are you –'

They heard Tea-maker Aiya clear his throat as he brushed his teeth in the bathroom.

'Periamma –' Raaken cut in quickly. He shivered and swallowed. Lakshmi watched him. Soonyams were dangerous and powerful. To even talk about it was to invoke its power.

Maybe she should go forward and tell Periamma herself.

'Periamma –' Raaken repeated.

'What is it, Raaken, what is happening? First thing in the morning, what are you looking so frightened about? And why is Lakshmi here at this time of the morning?' She moved into the kitchen and stared at Raaken.

Raaken cleared his throat. He dropped his eyes and mumbled 'I need to talk with Tea-maker Aiya.' Sweat slithered down his trembling body.

Periamma stood in the kitchen staring from one to the other. 'Why can't you tell me?'

Raaken held on to the edge of the table and shook his head. The table shook with the shudders running through his body.

Periamma stared at him for a few more moments. 'Oh, all right,' she sighed. 'Appa,' she called out. 'Can you stop and come here? Raaken has something he says he wants to tell you right now.'

Tea-maker Aiya walked into the kitchen. He was in his sarong and t-shirt with an old frayed jumper over it. Traces of shaving cream clung to his cheek.

He stared at Raaken and then gestured at him with the shaving razor. 'Stop shaking, man. What the hell's the matter?'

Raaken's words tumbled out. 'Aiya, I don't know who did it, Aiya. Everyone knows you are a good man, no? No one should ever want to hurt you. But they have done a bad thing, Aiya. A very bad thing.'

'Raaken,' Tea-maker Aiya said as he shoved his finger in Raaken's chest. 'Slow down! Stop blathering! Who has done what bad thing?'

'The coolies, Aiya! They have done a – a soonyam – a curse!' Raaken stopped and gulped. The table he was leaning on fell over with a crash. 'They have put it in the path, under the mango tree. You will step on it on your way to work this morning,' he rushed on, 'and then … you will die, no, Aiya. We must contact the devil dancers, the sorcerers. We must get them to come and cancel the curse, Aiya.'

Lakshmi watched round-eyed. Maybe the soonyam was working on Raaken already?

She expected Tea-maker Aiya to shake in fear. Much to her surprise, he started laughing. Not a gentle polite laugh as he usually had, but a loud, happy laugh that echoed around the kitchen.

'Is that all it is?' Tea-maker Aiya said, wiping his eyes. 'I know the troublemakers who did this. They don't understand Periadorai's proposal for a savings plan. The idiots will cut off their noses to spite their faces.' He gestured a scissor movement to his nose and chuckled again. 'Come, Raaken, let's go find this soonyam.'

He looked at Lakshmi standing in the corner of the kitchen. 'Ah, you're the one who brought the bad news.' He laughed again, 'Come on, both of you.' He strode out of the kitchen into the garden.

Still shivering, Raaken led the way out of the kitchen and round the house to the place where he and Lakshmi had seen the disturbed soil. Tea-maker Aiya and Periamma followed, both of them smiling. Lakshmi and Raaken exchanged looks. It was a madness spell, they were now sure of it. Why else would they be so happy at a time like this? Standing at a distance, Raaken pointed, and then looked away. 'There, Aiya – that is the soonyam spot.'

Tea-maker Aiya hooted with laughter again. He went to the spot where the soonyam was. First he stamped his foot on the spot. Then he jumped up and down on it. 'Raaken, Lakshmi,' he called out as he leapt up and down. 'My God is more powerful than all the devils and soonyams in this world and out of it! I am protected by the God who made the world and the stars! This curse can have no effect on me!' Still laughing, he stepped away.

'Aiyooo' Raaken squealed. His eyes rolled up. He sagged and dropped to the ground in a faint.

Lakshmi felt her head spin. She turned and vomited at the gnarled old roots of the mango tree, right over the spot where the soonyam lay.

***

Raaken lay twitching on the ground. 'Aiya, Aiya, you will die – die – die.'

Tea-maker Aiya looked at Lakshmi and Periamma squatting by Raaken. 'I can't be hanging around with this idiot. I'm meeting Ashley-Cooper at ten to announce the plans to the coolies.' He walked away into the house.

Lakshmi and Periamma sat by Raaken till he sat up. 'Go to the kitchen and get some tea,' Periamma instructed. Raaken got to his feet and staggered to the kitchen.

Lakshmi followed Periamma, knowing where she would go – to the study, to kneel by the cross. Lakshmi watched and listened. 'Dear God,' Periamma prayed between sobs, 'look after him. I need him, the children need him.' Lakshmi turned and crept away to join Raaken in the kitchen.

They sat cross-legged on the kitchen floor, strong, sweet tea in their tin mugs. Raaken bent to thump his head on the floor, then leapt up and walked round and round the kitchen. 'They will beat him, throw him off the top floor of the factory and stab him. I know they have knives, maybe even guns. They will shoot him and Periadorai, they will chop up the bodies and throw them in the river.'

Lakshmi drained her cup of tea, and then leapt up to follow him round the kitchen. She clung to his shirt. 'Shut up, you idiot. Don't worry Periamma.'

Periamma's voice stopped them. 'What is happening here?'

Lakshmi ran to her. 'Periamma, can I go to the factory and see what is happening, please?' Periamma looked at her, then at Raaken and nodded. 'I'm worried too. But I don't want you to go alone. Take Raaken. Both of you go.'

'Aiyoo, amma,' Raaken cowered back behind Lakshmi. His sarong was damp. He had wet himself in fear.

Lakshmi didn't want to waste time. She held up her sari and ran down the road to the factory. Raaken followed her. 'Run, Raaken, run,' she yelled out to him.

They slowed as they approached the factory. It was quiet. There was no noise of machinery. No rumbling of the rollers and dryers. No whining of the blowers in the withering troughs. And above all, no chatter of workers.

Then they heard it – a faint sound from the back of the factory.

Raaken stared at Lakshmi. Suddenly he stood straight. He seemed to grow taller. 'Let's go,' he said. 'If I can't save Tea-maker Aiya, I will die with him.' Hitching up his sarong, he ran round the factory. Lakshmi followed. She stopped once to vomit in the drain.

A group of sixty to seventy factory workers were gathered on the back lawn. Some of them shook their fists at Tea-maker Aiya and Periadorai. Others at the back hooted and yelled obscenities. Bellows of 'traitor, lies and robber' mingled with screams of 'kill him'.

Tea-maker Aiya and Periadorai stood on the raised end of the factory lawn. Periadorai looked nervous. But Tea-maker Aiya was calm and relaxed. He looked at the howling mob. The men's eyes were glazed and there was a smell of stale arak around. One man at the front hawked and spat at Tea-maker Aiya's feet. Lakshmi recognised him as the union man at the kade. Lakshmi felt the bile rise in her throat, again. Raaken worked his way through the crowd until he stood close to Tea-maker Aiya. Lakshmi crept along behind him.

Tea-maker Aiya cleared his throat and faced the crowd of men. 'Periadorai is concerned that you all have no money to live on when you are old and can no longer work in the factory.'

There were loud jeers from the crowd.

Periadorai said something to Tea-maker Aiya in English.

'Periadorai, has a plan for you. He will increase your pay, but you must put ten per cent in a savings account for when you can no longer work,' Tea-maker Aiya translated.

'You're lying!' one of the coolies yelled.

'Periadorai wants to cut our pay and keep the money,' shouted another.

'We will not work till you stop this plan,' another screamed out.

A couple of the men picked up logs of firewood. Raaken looked around desperately. Everyone was shouting and moving towards Tea-maker Aiya and Periadorai.

Periadorai stepped back, but Tea-maker Aiya stood with his arms folded, facing the crowd.

'Have I ever cheated you?' His voice was clear and calm, echoing around the lawn. 'When have I ever done anything wrong to any of you? Have any of you ever been turned away from my house without tea and a meal?' He stared around at the coolies.

Then he stepped down and walked right up to one man. He stabbed his finger at Murugan. 'Who helped your women when they were pregnant?'

The crowd parted as Tea-maker Aiya walked through. He stopped at another man, Santhanum. 'Who gave medicines to your children?' He stepped back and spoke louder. 'Who gave you extra rice rations? Who wrote your appeal letters for you? Now tell me – why do you want to attack me? Come forward anyone who has a complaint against me. Come.' He stood with his arms extended outwards.

'Don't listen to him,' the union man yelled. 'He is a puppet and the white man is pulling the strings.'

Lakshmi looked around. Suddenly, nobody was paying attention to union man.

The crowd became quiet. A few cleared their throats. Others fidgeted. They put down the logs of wood they were holding. They broke into groups. The rumble of talk replaced the yells and hoots.

Suddenly, one labourer pushed forward and stood facing Tea-maker Aiya. Tea-maker Aiya didn't flinch. He looked the man directly in the eyes. The labourer turned and faced the crowd. 'Tea-maker Aiya is right. He has never done anything to harm us. Why hurt him? Let a few of us talk to him and find out about this plan.'

Lakshmi looked on – shocked – it was her father, Ramen, the very man who had placed the soonyam for Tea-maker Aiya. Here he was supporting him!

A chattering erupted among the men. After a couple of minutes, the crowd broke up. A few of the coolies, led by Lakshmi's father, went into the Tea-maker's office. Others picked up the large bags of fresh tea leaves the women had collected and carried them into the factory. The chug and roar of the dryers and rollers filled the morning. The factory was getting back into production.

Lakshmi and Raaken looked around, wide-eyed. Tea-maker Aiya was right. His God was definitely more powerful than all the devils of the soonyam.

Lakshmi turned and ran back to tell Periamma what had happened. She ran back to the house, stopping to vomit in the drain.

Chapter 13

August 1966 Watakälé

Tea-maker Aiya and Periamma sat on either side of the dining table. It was their usual morning ritual before he went off to the factory. They didn't see Lakshmi stand by the door.

'I am worried about Lakshmi, Appa,' Periamma sipped on her tea.

'Worried?' he mumbled, his eyes fixed on the newspaper.

'Yes, she has been throwing up a lot and isn't eating. And yesterday when she was doing some work I noticed that her waist is thickening.'

'So?' he looked up from the paper. 'She must have eaten something at the kade. Don't know why she needs to when you feed her so well, Lilly. And she's a growing girl.'

'No Appa, it's not that. I'm worried. It's five months since … since.'

Tea-maker Aiya dropped the paper on the table. He leaned toward Periamma. 'You can't mean?'

Silently, Periamma nodded.

Suddenly Lakshmi knew. The vomiting – the nausea – four months without the monthly flow. A shiver ran through her body. She clung on to the door post. Slowly she slid to the floor.

'No! Dear God, No! No!'

***

Lakshmi lay curled on the floor in Shiro's bedroom clutching Shiro's purple blanket. She rocked her body back and forth. Deep sobs rent her body. Dropping the blanket, she clawed at her stomach. A baby? Her child? A half British bastard.

She laid her face on the tear soaked blanket. *My friend, my only friend, how will you understand? You are so innocent, how can I tell you? Will you hate me? Will you think I went to him? And Periamma and Tea-maker Aiya, will they even want me near you? You are so pure. I am soiled, dirty … useless.*

'That idiot William, he must be made to pay for what he has done,' Tea-maker Aiya shouted. 'At the least, we should tell his father James. I will write to the Oriental Produce offices in London today.'

'Appa,' Periamma pleaded, 'Please, Appa, don't do anything rash.'

Lakshmi's heart ached at the sob in Periamma's voice. 'Please remember what happened to your father when he tried to question what happened.'

Lakshmi crawled to the door of the bedroom. Tea-maker Aiya and Periamma stood in the middle of the sitting room.

Raaken watched from the kitchen door.

'Yes, yes.' Tea-maker Aiya yelled. 'So we let them get away with it – again. There is no justice in the plantations.'

'Appa,' Periamma clung to his arm. Tears streaked her face. 'Never mind them. We must help Lakshmi. What are we going to do?'

'Damn the British bastards.' Tea-maker Aiya glanced at Lakshmi crouched by the bedroom door. 'Come, Lilly,' he drew Periamma into the study.

Raaken came into the bedroom with a cup of sweet milky tea. He held it to her. His weathered face was set in deep lines of worry. 'Drink this,' he said. His eyes were filled with tears. He squatted by her side. 'Lakshmi, they are good people, they will do something to help you.'

Lakshmi sobbed. She felt Raaken's rough, calloused hand rub her head. Kindness she had never received from her parents.

They both listened as the study door opened. Tea-maker Aiya went to the phone. 'Reverend Robert Kirkland, it's Rajan Rasiah,' he paused. 'I need your advice …' Periamma stepped close to him and said something in an undertone. Tea-maker Aiya cupped the receiver in his hand and spoke in a soft murmur.

Lakshmi and Raaken looked at each other. *Podeher Aiya* – the church minister Shiro called Bobsy, was a white man. He was probably a good friend of the Periadorais. What could he do to help Lakshmi? Why would he want to? No white man cared about a coolie girl.

Tea-maker Aiya put the receiver down. He turned to whisper something to Periamma. 'I have to go to the factory. I'll talk to Hemachandra Mudalali from there. You tell Lakshmi.' He turned and walked out of the house. The front door slammed shut.

Lakshmi remained crouched by the door to Shiro's bedroom.

Periamma came in and squatted on the ground beside Lakshmi. Raaken scrambled to his feet and hurried off to the kitchen.

'Lakshmi, you remember how when you came as a nanny to Shiro Chinnamma I told you that we would help you when you were older?'

'Yes, Periamma,' she whispered. She felt in a trance. It was like she was outside her body, hearing words spoken to someone else.

Periamma's eyes brimmed full of tears. She put out her hand and stroked Lakshmi's hair away from her face. Her hands were shivering. Periamma bowed her head. She didn't look at Lakshmi.

Lakshmi sobbed. She clung to Periamma's arm. Her heart was breaking. And Shiro Chinnamma was not here to share the pain with her.

'Lakshmi, I wanted to train you to cook and sew. To knit and arrange flowers. Get a job for you in a house in Colombo. But with what has happened to you. I am sorry. There is so little that we can do.'

A shaft of icy fear cut through her heart. She couldn't breathe. 'Periamma, what will happen to me?'

'You can't stay here Lakshmi,' Periamma whispered through her tears.

'Periamma,' Lakshmi's wail brought Raaken scurrying back to the room.

'No, Lakshmi. People will say things. You see, Tea-maker Aiya is the only man in the house, people will think —'

'Aiyoo, Periamma,' Lakshmi screamed. She clutched Periamma's sari. She needed to hold on to the only person who cared for her. The only place she felt safe, wanted — sometimes even loved.

Periamma took Lakshmi by her shoulders and moved her away. Lakshmi let go the sari. This was the end. She stared at Periamma. Lakshmi would never forget the look in her face. It was the face of *Parvati*. The face of a goddess who suffered all things, endured all things for her man. She knew that to Periamma, her family would always come first. She, Lakshmi, would take second place.

Lakshmi placed her hand on her stomach. 'Periamma,' she mumbled through her tears, 'other girls say there are ways to get it out.'

'No,' Lakshmi cringed at the anger in Periamma's voice. 'We cannot kill a baby.' Her fingers tightened on Lakshmi's shoulders. 'We have talked to the church minister in Nuwara-Eliya. They have a place for girls like you.'

'Periamma,' Lakshmi clutched her stomach. She felt a twitch — it was alive.

'You will be looked after at the Salvation Army home till you have the baby.'

'And then what?'

Periamma held Lakshmi's hand tight. Lakshmi's own pain mingled with that of the older woman's as Periamma continued. 'The baby will be taken away.

It will be put up for adoption. And you -'

'Will I come back?'

'No, not with Periadorai here and his brother at Udatänná. It is too dangerous for Tea-maker Aiya. We will talk to your parents.'

It pierced her — a knife to her soul, more painful than her father's beatings. Worse even than the horror of that night in the weighing shed. They were sending her away. Periamma had promised to look after her and now it was finished. They were discarding her when she needed them most.

'Tea-maker Aiya will talk to Hemachandra Mudalali in Diyatalāwa.' Periamma continued. 'Hamine his wife told me they need someone to help in the house. You will go there after the baby is born. They are a good Sinhalese couple. People here will be told that we got you a job as a servant in a house.'

Lakshmi picked up the purple blanket, held it to her lips. 'Shiro Chinnamma?'

'Shiro is too young to understand all that has happened to you, Lakshmi. She is very innocent. We have to spare her.'

'But,' Lakshmi stammered. 'Won't she be upset when she comes for the holiday and I am not here?'

Periamma stood up. Her next words were a death sentence to Lakshmi's hopes and dreams. 'Lakshmi, we will help you with the baby and later find you work at Hemachandra Mudalali's house. But you must promise me that you will not contact Shiro or tell her where you are. We will tell her that you got married and moved away.' Periamma sighed. 'Lakshmi, it is best you never see Shiro Chinnamma ever again.'

Lakshmi stared open mouthed at Periamma. Never see her friend again? *How could that be?*

Her mother was right. They were discarding her like a piece of shit. All the love and devotion she had felt for Periamma collected in her chest and congealed into a hard lump of hate.

Chapter 14

December 1966 Watakälé

The train puffed into Diyatalāwa station. Hurling herself off the train, Shiro threw herself into Victor's arms and then hugged Edward with equal vigour. 'It's good to be home.'

'Hey, princess. I thought you loved school?' Edward hugged her and set her down on the platform. Victor jumped on the carriage and pulled her bags off.

Love school? Please! But they all thought she was happy in Colombo – all except Lakshmi, of course. Lakshmi knew the truth.

With a wheeze and a loud hoot the train pulled away from Diyatalāwa station.

Shiro looked around. 'Where's Lakshmi? Mummy said she was sick.' Was it her imagination or did a shadow flit across Victor's eyes? 'I told mum in my last letter. I so want to see her. Surely she can't still be sick? I asked mum to send her to the station.'

'She's sick, Shiro. And stop being a drama queen.' Victor snapped.

Shiro stared at her oldest brother. Victor never scolded her. A gentle reprimand tempered by a hug was the worst that ever passed between them. 'But Lakshmi hasn't replied to my letters for about six months. She couldn't have been sick all that time. What kind of illness could that be?'

Victor and Edward exchanged glances. This had to be bad. They were keeping something from her. The three of them never had secrets.

'What's happening?' She looked from one to the other.

Edward threw an arm over Shiro's shoulder. 'Come on, Shiro. String hoppers and chicken curry awaits you at home. Let's find Hemachandra's lorry.'

Hemachandra Mudalali was one of their father's good friends. Whenever they arrived on the train from Colombo, they rode his lorry from Diyatalāwa to Watakälé. Edward and Shiro squeezed into the front of the lorry with the driver, while Victor hopped in the back among the sacks of rice and bags of produce. Shiro liked Hemachandra Mudalali. He was fond of her too. Often they stopped at his store or house for tea before driving home with the lorry driver. Today she found a box of Black Magic chocolates on the passenger seat with a note 'from Hemachandra Uncle to Shiro baby'.

Edward ripped it open and shoved a mint cream in his mouth. 'Here.' He held the open box to Shiro. 'Stop being a glum puss and stuff your face with some cherry chocolate.'

'No.' Shiro pushed the box aside and turned to look at Victor through the back window of the driver's cab. 'What happened to Lakshmi? Why are you not telling me about her? She will be better when she sees me.'

She rummaged in her bag and pulled out a box. She opened it to show a bracelet and chain of blue semi-precious stones set in silver. 'You know how Lakshmi loves brightly coloured jewellery. All she has ever had are those stupid glass bangles her mother discards. I saved my pocket money all year to buy her these as a Christmas present. Don't tell her though, okay? She'll love them, I know she will.' Shiro shut the box and clasped it to her bosom, as if the jewellery were Lakshmi herself. 'If this doesn't make her feel better, nothing will.' She prattled on about Colombo. Her brothers remained silent.

Forty-five minutes later, they were home. Jumping out of the lorry, Shiro dashed inside and flew into her father's arms. Her mother hugged her with a dignity Shiro now knew came from an upbringing where people didn't act intimate in public. 'Mum, I got an "A" report. That should make you happy. And guess what? I passed Tamil literature. I can now put all that behind me and concentrate just on the science subjects.' Shiro looked closely at her mother. 'Mum, you look so tired. Isn't Lakshmi here to help you with the Christmas cooking?'

'Come, darling,' her mother took her hand and hustled her into her bedroom. 'I made you a new purple and white quilt. You can take it to school next term. Now you must wash and get ready for dinner.'

Shiro followed her mother. Why was everyone dodging her questions? What was going on?

Soon they were sitting at dinner table. Usually Lakshmi would serve them. Today Raaken brought in the food. Shiro looked around at her brothers and parents. Everyone seemed to be avoiding eye contact with her. Even Raaken shuffled out without greeting her. Then Edward caught her eye and winked. Victor frowned at Edward and looked down at his plate. They all picked at their food.

There was silence around the table. The family were never this silent at the beginning of the Christmas break.

'Tell us about school, darling,' her mother smiled across the table.

'Mum, you know all there is to know. I write it all to you weekly,' Shiro looked around the table. 'What's with you all? How come everyone's so quiet?'

No one replied. Shiro reached for a string hopper. 'Mum, where's Lakshmi?'

Everyone froze. Shiro looked around, puzzled. Her mother's eyes filled with tears. Victor and Edward looked at each other. Her father stared at his string hoppers as if he'd never seen one before. Raaken stood with one hand on the door post.

Long moments passed by. Shiro stared from one to the other. 'I will talk with you about it later, darling,' her mother waved her hand, dismissing the topic.

A memory flashed into Shiro's mind – memory of a cat, its skull crushed by a falling Jak fruit. Her mother had said exactly the same words in exactly the same tone.

She wanted to throw up the string hopper she had just swallowed. Something had happened to Lakshmi. Maybe she was not just sick. 'Is she dead?' she whispered.

'Of course not, darling.' Her mother frowned. 'Why would you think that? She's just – well, not in a fit state to come play with you these holidays.'

'Then she's dying!' Shiro's voice rose in pitch. 'She'd never keep away from me unless she was dying! I must go see her at once.' Shiro sprang up, tilting the plate, spilling the string hoppers on the tablecloth. The chair rocked and crashed to the floor.

'For goodness' sake, tell her the truth. She's sixteen, she can handle it.' Victor's voice was sharp with anxiety.

There was silence around the table as the family looked at each other.

Raaken rushed in and wiped the spilt string hoppers. He pulled up Shiro's chair.

'Handle what?' Shiro said.

Her mother reached over and took Shiro's hand. 'Darling, Lakshmi isn't actually sick,' she said. 'She can't come to be with you because she's pregnant.'

Everyone watched Shiro. No one spoke. The grandfather clock in the sitting room droned out seven chimes.

How could she be pregnant? Pregnant meant sex. Sex meant marriage. She realised what must have happened. 'What do you know? Lakshmi beat me to it! So what's the big secret there? She got married and is pregnant.' She laughed and looked around the table. 'Relax, okay? I've learned about how people get pregnant.' Shiro sat down and reached for another string hopper. 'Who did she marry, Mum? Can I go visit her tomorrow? When's the baby coming? Guess it must have been a real rush thing? We promised to be at each other's weddings. But then she's so much older, I guess she couldn't wait!' She mixed in the chicken curry and took a mouthful. 'I can't wait to see her.'

Silence descended around the table again. Shiro stopped eating and looked around the table. Her mother had her head bent. Her eyes were shut tight. Tears trickled down her cheek. Her father leant his elbows on the dining table, his hands tented as if in prayer. Victor stared at the floor. Edward rocked back, staring at the ceiling, his fingers interlaced on his stomach. Shiro looked from face to face. The air around the table was oppressive, frightening.

Her father scraped his chair back and stood up. 'I'm going back to the factory to check the withering,' he said. 'Victor, you said Shiro can handle it. You tell her.' He turned and walked out.

Victor took a deep breath. He got up, took Shiro's hand and walked with her out into the garden. A cold breeze blew from the valley, working chilly fingers into their clothes. Victor drew her down on the little wooden bench under the mango tree. She moved close to her brother and pulled her purple jumper around her.

Victor put his arm around her. 'You see, Shiro, Lakshmi is pregnant, but she's not married. The father will never marry her. He doesn't want anything to do with Lakshmi or the baby.'

'Who?'

'I don't know who the father is. Mum and Dad are trying to help her. She has gone away to have her baby. Dad will get a job for her after the baby is born. That's the best we can hope for.'

This could not be happening. They had shared their most intimate secrets, planned to spend their lives together. Lakshmi had promised to be at her wedding. Their children were going to play together among the tea bushes, maybe even marry each other. Lakshmi and she were to grow old together as best friends.

'The baby?' she stammered.

'Will go to an orphanage. Probably be adopted out.'

The pain and sorrow that Lakshmi must feel weighed down on Shiro's heart. She should have known. Deep sobs tore through her. She should have insisted that she come home when Lakshmi stopped writing. She could have done something. Found the man. She, Shiro, could have made him marry Lakshmi.

She leapt up and spun round to face Victor. 'But Victor, what if we could find the father? What if we told him what a wonderful girl Lakshmi is? What if he saw the baby? Surely he'll want them both back in his life!'

Victor sighed. He took Shiro's hands in his. 'No, Shiro. I told you. He doesn't want to know anything about it. He never wants to see Lakshmi ever again. I don't even know who he is.'

Shiro glanced up. Her mother stood at the back door, watching.

Shiro closed her eyes. She let her tears burn their way down her cheeks. This was her life, her family watching over her, always. Making sure she did the right thing, spoke to the right people and acted in the right way. Protecting her, keeping her innocent. Sending her to the right school so she could be ready to wed the man they choose to be a suitable mate for her.

No more.

She shook Victor's hands off. 'Some bastard raped her, right?' she shouted.

Victor jumped up and grasped her shoulders. 'What do you know about rape? And I thought school taught you not to swear!'

Shiro squirmed away from him. She felt hysteria bubble up in her. She gestured to her body. 'Victor, look at me! I'm an adult! I have breasts! I get periods!'

Victor's jaw dropped to the ground.

'I know about sex and babies! Boys and men stare at me! They want to kiss me, make love to me. I know they do!' She laughed. 'Even on the train today.'

'Aiyoo, mahal. Where did you learn all this?' Her mother stood beside Victor. Her face pale, her eyes wide. Hands covered her mouth.

Shiro spun around to face her mother. 'Not from those prudish teachers at that boarding school you sent me to. Where you think I am incredibly accepted and happy. The girls had a book. It had drawings of penises and vaginas and what happens with them. Some girls have boyfriends. They have sex with them and then talk about it. They boast about what they do. And rape – that's what happened to the girls during the riots, remember? You said you saw it, Victor!'

Edward came out to join Victor and her mother. 'Shiro, darling,' Victor started.

'No!' Shiro broke away from the circle of her family and fled to her room. She hurled herself onto her bed, buried her face in her pillow and howled.

She stayed in bed, breathing heavily, her face buried in her pillow. She had no more tears to shed. Her mother and brothers stood talking outside her room. 'Now what can we do? We can't let her see Lakshmi, she won't understand.' Her mother spoke in a hushed whisper.

Victor responded, his voice tinged with concern. 'She's not as ignorant about these things as we thought, Mum. Let's just get through Christmas. She's young; she'll outgrow her attachment to Lakshmi. She talks about her new friend, Lalitha. She'll be okay.'

Shiro felt incredibly lonely. Outgrow her attachment – is that what they call it – her love for her best friend? Her soul-mate and she was supposed to outgrow it over Christmas. Replace Lakshmi with Lalitha. She loved Lalitha, but it was different. Nothing would be the same again.

Her mother came in and sat on the corner of her bed. She caressed Shiro's back, as if to absorb some of the pain.

'I want to see her!'

'You can't see her, darling. She's not here; we've arranged a job for her. It's best you don't see her again. I'm sorry. I'm very, very sorry.'

'No you're not. None of you are.' Shiro mumbled into her pillow. 'None of you understand, do you? You wanted me to stop seeing her because she's a coolie and you want me to make friends with high-class Tamil people and move up in society. You think that the private school and Colombo will do that. You don't know anything. The girls are snobs. I don't fit in there. And now I don't fit here either. Lakshmi was my best friend. And now she's gone. You sent her away! I have no one.' she sobbed.

Her mother continued stroking Shiro's back. 'Darling, please try to understand. Lakshmi got pregnant. If we acknowledge it, people will think Daddy or one of the boys is responsible. I know how you loved her and she loved you too. But this is not just about you, darling. It's about family honour.' She got up and left the room.

Shiro stayed in bed, hugging the pillow. Deep shudders rent her body. She thought of Lakshmi's Christmas present – the blue bracelet and chain.

Lakshmi, her dearest friend, pregnant — a bastard baby — what will become of it? *Who is the father? What will become of you, Lakshmi?*

No. She would find Lakshmi. She knew who would help her.

Chapter 15

December 1966 Watakälé

A lazy mist drifted across the valley, now hiding, now revealing the mountaintops, caressing the bright green flush of tea leaves reaching up to be picked.

The hill was across the valley from the Tea-maker's house. It was the highest point in the plantation. The single gnarled and windswept tree on the top commanded an all-round view of Watakälé Tea Plantation.

The chill wind ruffled the golden hair of the young man standing at the summit. He leant on his motorcycle, enjoying the sun on his head. The sharpness of the wind stung his neck and brought tears to his eyes. He fixed his binoculars on a crested hawk eagle circling overhead, then lowered them to survey the tea plantation and the progress of the tea pluckers.

Anthony Ashley-Cooper was the happiest he had been for the last few years. Last week his father had told him that the last batch of tea from Watakälé had received the prestigious 'Silver Tip award' at the London tea auctions. This was the ultimate accolade for flavour, colour and quality in tea production – a winning combination largely due to the expertise and hard work of the Tea-maker, Mr Rasiah.

When Anthony received the news, he had gone down to the factory and congratulated Mr Rasiah. Ever since the Tea-maker supported him in the savings plan fiasco, Anthony held him in high esteem. Of course, as the superintendent, it would be unseemly for him to voice that admiration to a native staff member.

Anthony recalled the conversation on the day after the staff party incident with William. Mr Rasiah was probably the only member of the native staff who didn't address the superintendent as 'sir' and had the nerve to advise him how he should run the plantation. Anthony had heeded his words and had taken to early morning walks through the plantation. He had come to enjoy the songs of birds at dawn and the pink and violet hues that lit the hills as the sun dispersed the misty haze from the mountain tops.

During these walks Anthony would observe the women doing the tea plucking. He watched as they trooped, chattering, to the shed for muster, where the tea leaves they plucked were weighed and recorded by the Indian Kangani. Later in the morning he rode up a hill and looked around using his binoculars, watching the transport of tea to the factory and the men working in the field – pruning, fertilising, and conducting the daily jobs of a successful tea plantation. Sometimes he rode down and talked to them.

After lunch, he went down to the tea factory and walked with Mr Rasiah through the process of tea making. He had learned from the older man's wisdom on withering times and roller settings, drying temperatures and grading. Finally, standing with the Tea-maker, he would go through the process of tasting and classifying the black tea produced that day.

He liked this hill. It gave him a good vantage point. Anthony picked a group of tea pluckers just finishing the morning shift and watched them laugh and chatter as the Kangani marshalled them up the hill to the weighing shed. Some of the women were young, just teenagers. His thoughts went to his brother, William, and the horrible incident after the staff party.

He hoped the girl was all right.

'You are such a prude, little brother,' William had taunted him last week at the Royal Hotel at Nuwara-Eliya. William, Anthony and some other superintendents from adjoining estates had been at the bar. Much to Anthony's disgust, the conversation had drifted to discussing how sexy some of the young coolie women were. William had described a recent encounter with a coolie girl in Udatänná. The crude, obscene language turned Anthony's stomach. 'You've no idea what you're missing, little brother,' William had said, his disparaging tone belying the fact that he was only sixteen months older than Anthony. Revolted, Anthony had walked away. Drunken, mocking laughter had followed him out of the club.

Anthony watched the tea pluckers as they moved up the hill towards a stream and a waterfall. His gaze was captured momentarily by a girl in a purple dress seated by the stream on a ledge of rock, engrossed in a book. As he watched, she flopped over on her back and folded her hands behind her head. The blouse of her dress hugged the curves of her shapely body. The gesture sent Anthony back in time to when he was sixteen.

A thrill of excitement spiked through his body. Could it be her? He continued to watch through his binoculars. She jumped up and scrambled up the hill towards the Tea-maker's quarters, her skirt riding up above her knees. It brought back memories of a little girl lying face down on a nursery floor. A scornful young voice rang in Anthony's head: 'Well, why don't you go home then, you British bastard?'

You certainly have grown up to be a beauty, Shiro Rasiah.

***

Back in the Tea-maker's house, the Tea-maker and his wife waited for Shiro.

'She's a dreamer!' Lilly grumbled. 'She lives in her fantasy world. Not in the least interested in cooking or sewing. You heard her this morning. What can we say for the marriage proposals? That she recites Shakespeare beautifully? That she can come up with some cock and bull imaginary story at the drop of a hat? You must stop encouraging her to try for the university entrance exam. She will get spoiled even more in university.'

Rajan had returned from the factory for lunch. They stood watching Shiro wind her way up the hill. She was late for lunch, but in the laid-back life of the tea plantation, twenty minutes meant nothing.

'What about the Chelliah boy?' Lilly grizzled on. 'He's from a good family. He wants to get married soon. And he likes Shiro a lot.'

'Lilly, Shiro is seventeen. She has just learned that she has lost Lakshmi, her best friend. She is heartbroken. Let her grow up.'

'I left school at sixteen. We married soon after.'

'And you make me a wonderful wife, Lilly. Shiro is different. Surely you can see that. Let her spread her wings and sit the university entrance exam. If she gets in, let her go to university.'

'Aiyoo. That will be the end. What if she meets some Batticaloa boy or something in university?'

'She will meet Batticaloa boys and Indian boys, she will also meet Muslim and Hindu boys, Lilly,' Rajan said. 'We'll just have to trust her to make wise choices.'

Lilly swatted her forehead with her palm. 'Make wise choices! Since when has your daughter made wise choices? You will let her do what she wants, as usual. Someday you will be sorry.'

Rajan nodded. 'Yes, she has never had to choose. And you know what? It's our fault, yours and mine. We need to stop protecting her and let her have her space and freedom.'

Shiro ran the last few yards.

'Sorry I'm late. I was reading and watching the eagle. Isn't he gorgeous? I kept thinking that somewhere out there Lakshmi is also watching the eagle.' She threw her arms up. 'I could see you watching me. You were talking about me, weren't you? I'm safe anywhere in Watakälé. Everyone knows the Tea-maker's daughter.'

'We know you're safe here, sweetheart.' Rajan laughed and hugged Shiro.

Chapter 16

December 1966 Watakälé

Shiro made her way to her special place, her book hugged to her chest. The rays of the morning sun slipped through the mist and teased the tea bushes with flickers of light. White butterflies flitted around her, a swarm on their way to Adam's Peak. *Lakshmi, I miss you so. This is all no fun without you, my friend.*

She looked up at the sky. It was her eagle again. He'd been flying around over this area every day for the two weeks that she had been at home. She watched as he swooped and settled on a high branch. She wished she could fly away with him – be free.

Shiro loved this place – and yet she longed to have a new and different life far away from the tea plantations. Maybe she could travel to some distant country like Africa or Australia. Maybe she could be a missionary doctor or maybe even a flying doctor in Australia.

The tea bushes reached to her waist. She remembered a time when she had to stand on tiptoe to see over them. That was a time when Lakshmi had been with her.

Reaching her place, she spread her purple blanket and flung herself down on her stomach. She opened up her book. Soon she was lost in reading *A Midsummer Night's Dream.*

'Lovers and madmen have such seething brains,
Such shaping fantasies, that apprehend
More than cool reason ever comprehends.
The lunatic, the lover and the poet
Are of imagination all compact.'

The image of the lovers' behaviour made her laugh. So that's what the stupid girls at school meant when they said they were madly in love. She would take her time. Study and hopefully university – then love and sex!

'Princess Shiro, I presume.' The voice was distinctly British.

Shiro swung her eyes up from her book. Brown leather shoes led up to a neatly creased pair of brown wool trousers. Tilting her head further revealed a brown leather belt then a white shirt open at the neck and tucked into the trousers.

She leapt to her feet, her hands on her cheeks, ready to scream.

'Please don't be frightened, Miss Rasiah.' The words were soft spoken, soothing.

Shiro looked up at the tall Englishmen. He stood with his hands up in a mock gesture of surrender. The sun behind him turned his blonde hair into a golden halo. His cobalt blue eyes creased at the corners. A smile dimpled his cheek and lit up his angular face. 'Please, I didn't mean to frighten you. I've been watching you for two weeks. I had to walk down and say hello.'

Shiro continued to stare at him. Who was this picture book perfect white man? 'Watching me?' She stammered, stepping back from him, tensed, ready to run. She must not get familiar with strange men, especially not white ones. She should leave. But the look in his deep blue eyes kept her rooted to the spot. Somewhere in the hidden recesses of her memory the angular face and blue eyes were familiar. Who? When?

Shiro screwed up her face, searching for the lost memory.

'I've watched you through my binoculars on my daily rounds of the tea plantation. You seemed to be having a great time with your books. What are you reading?'

Shiro ignored his question. 'I'm sorry. I have to go home. My parents won't want me to talk to you.'

His smile widened. 'You don't recognise me, do you, princess? I'm Anthony Ashley-Cooper. We met when you were eight years old. I wasn't very pleasant. May I proffer a belated apology for my boorish behaviour?'

Shiro gasped. The British bastard who stamped on the rose bush she planted over her cat's grave! She put her hand to her mouth, remembering how she had insulted him that day. She pushed her knuckles into her mouth. Her body shook with suppressed laughter.

Anthony laughed with her. 'Remember? The day your cat died. Did you get another cat?'

'Oh, I remember you.' Shiro dropped her hand, collecting herself as memories of the day flooded back. Puckering her lips she made a vain attempt to look stern. 'You didn't want to play with a native child, remember?' Surely, this was not the churlish spoiled brat who had come with the Irvine girls for tea all those years ago? The grown up Anthony was actually quite cute. Keeping serious was impossible. Amusement tweaked at the corners of her lips.

'I apologise for my crass manner. What are you staring at? Have I a smudge on my face?'

'No. It's just that you've changed. You aren't -'

'Obnoxious? Pompous? Pig headed? I can think of a string of adjectives to describe what I was. It's called growing up.' He looked down at her. 'And you? What are you up to, princess? Finished school yet?'

'No, I'm still in school. And please, not princess!'

'In case you've forgotten, you asked me to call you princess.'

'That was a long time ago. Like you said, before we grew up.' She stood up straight. 'I believe it is proper that you call me Miss Rasiah, Mr Ashley-Cooper.' She picked up her blanket and turned away. 'Anyway, we shouldn't be talking like this.'

'Why?' his voice called her back.

Shiro stopped and hugged her blanket and book to her chest.

'Because you are the white superintendent and I am the Tea-maker's daughter.'

Anthony stepped closer to her. He smelt of lemon and something else. Shiro couldn't recognise it, but it was nice. Shiro swung round and looked into his eyes, expecting anger, exasperation. To her surprise his eyes twinkled with laughter.

'Come on, Miss Rasiah – relax. You don't honestly believe those archaic rules, do you? The girl I remember would have stuck her tongue out at anyone who dared tell her what to do.'

Shiro chuckled. He was right. She shook her head, sending her hair tumbling around her face, blowing in the breeze. 'I was incorrigible, wasn't I? Now I realise that nothing's quite that simple in the tea plantation.' She shrugged turning to the path leading up to the house. 'Some things you can't fight.'

'We were children, Miss Rasiah. It's been eight years. Could we start again? Be friends?'

Shiro stopped. She turned. Their eyes locked. His eyes dared her.

When could Shiro ever refuse a challenge?

Chapter 17

December 1966 Watakälé

Anthony stood, looking up the path. He felt an overwhelming impulse to run after her, to beg her to stay and talk to him. He put his head in his hands and massaged his temple. *She is a child*, he told himself, *a native child. I am the British plantation owner. It is wrong – forbidden.* He should take a leaf out of her book.

***

The light blue cotton blouse, demurely buttoned up to her neck, and blue pleated skirt looked like it could have been part of the uniform of a school girl.

'You came.' Shiro's words were a cross between a statement and a question.

Her black hair lay unbound on her shoulders, curling around her dark, young face. Anthony wanted to reach out and tangle his hands in it. Did it feel as thick and heavy as it looked?

'Are you glad to see me?' Anthony had agonised over what to do all last night. The look on her face told him that he had been right to keep the appointment.

'Only if you will read with me.' She leaned forward and smiled, holding the book she was carrying behind her back. The movement stretched the thin material of her blouse.

'What are you reading today?' Reaching for the book brought her closer to him. The smell of freshly crushed rose petals flooded his senses.

Shiro placed the palm of her right hand between them. Her fingers touched his chest. Surely she would feel his erratic heartbeat?

'Move away. I hate being manhandled. Here, have the book.' She thrust the book at him and stepped back.

Manhandled, what an interesting way to put it. Anthony let her go and accepted the book, bursting into laughter at the title. '*Romeo and Juliet*! You want me to read Shakespeare with you?'

'Why *sir*, do you think us natives not literate enough for it? What did you expect? Nursery rhymes?' Shiro mocked. 'Let me quote for you.'

She stood straight with hands behind her back, face turned up to the sun. Like a little girl reciting poetry in school, thought Anthony, or an angel about to sing.

'My only love sprung from my only hate!

Too early seen unknown and known too late!

Prodigious birth of love it is to me,

That I must love a loathed enemy.'

Anthony clapped. 'Well done, Miss Rasiah.'

'Here, sit down.' She shook out the purple blanket, dropping down and patting the spot beside her. 'You can be Juliet and I'll be Romeo. And stop trying to be all official. You can call me Shiro now. Only friends read Shakespeare together.'

Anthony lowered himself on the edge of the blanket.

Shiro groaned and slid across the blanket towards him. 'Why are you sitting so far away? Are you scared of me or something? You can't see the book from so far.'

'Here, let me start. I am Romeo.' Shiro cleared her throat and feigned a serious and deep voice.

'If I profane with my unworthiest hand

This holy shrine, the gentle fine is this:

My lips, two blushing pilgrims, ready stand

To smooth that rough touch with a tender kiss.'

'Come on,' Shiro prompted him. 'Read your part as Juliet.' Leaning over, she pointed to the words. The touch of her skin on his arm made Anthony catch his breath.

'Why are you Romeo?' he mumbled. 'Shouldn't that be my part?'

'Because I always play the male lead in the school plays, silly. I'm the toughest and the most masculine in the class.'

'Tough and masculine somehow would never cross my mind when I think of you.' Anthony muffled a laugh. *She's treating me like one of her class friends*, he mused. *I'd better play along.*

'And, you are sweet and fair and golden-haired, like Juliet would have been.'

This time Anthony laughed out loud. 'I've been called many things Shiro, but never sweet and Juliet-like. But have it your way.' They bent over the book, their faces close together.

'Good pilgrim, you do wrong your hand too much,

Which mannerly devotion shows in this;

For saints have hands that pilgrims' hands do touch,
And palm to palm is holy palmers' kiss.'

'Oh dear, you're such a bad actor. Here, let me show you.' Sliding even closer to him on the blanket, she looked into his eyes.

'For saints have hands that pilgrims' hands do touch,
And palm to palm is holy palmers' kiss.'

Anthony remained silent, surprised at the sudden longing to take her in his arms. Was he falling in love with her? This feisty and lovely young woman was a far cry from the naughty little eight year old he remembered.

But there was no passion in the black eyes that locked with his. Just innocent trust.

This was dangerous ground. 'I don't think we should continue reading this section.'

'Why not? Don't you like *Romeo and Juliet*?' She pouted, making it even harder for Anthony.

'No, I love it, sweetheart. It's just that I think Juliet kisses Romeo at this point.'

'No. She does not.' Turning away she scanned through the page. 'I know this story, I even acted it. I was Romeo and I was not instructed to kiss Juliet.' Shutting the book, she looked up at Anthony. Black eyes narrowed. Long lashes dropped, curtain-like, over obsidian pupils. 'You're teasing me, aren't you? And by the way, I am not your sweetheart.'

'Are you someone else's sweetheart?'

'Really, Mr Ashley-Cooper, what an inappropriate question. But for your information, I have no time for sweethearts.' She giggled. 'Not that I don't know what it's all about. I have a year more in school.'

Shiro dropped back on her elbows, looking over the mountains. Her eyes filmed with tears. 'After that, I have a major problem.'

'A problem?'

'Yes, as to my future. My mother wants me to get married, but I want to go to university. Then I'd like to get away from here. To some exciting and wonderful place – Africa or Australia, maybe. Preferably as a doctor.'

'You will have to get yourself an African or Australian sweetheart then.'

'Oh dear, I'll never be allowed to do that!' The dismay in her voice would have been amusing if it wasn't so obviously real. 'My parents will arrange a marriage for me with a good little Tamil boy. But all the ones I meet are so boring. All they're interested in is making money and buying a house. Not exciting things like books and poetry.'

Anthony leaned towards her, looking into her eyes – deep pools of worry. 'Don't do it, Shiro.'

'Do what?'

'Don't agree to an arranged marriage. Follow your heart.'

Her eyes cleared and sparkled with mischief. 'Mr Ashley-Cooper, do you realise what you're doing? You're encouraging me to rebel against my parents! You'll be in such trouble if I tell my father!' Her expression changed as she looked at Anthony through half closed eyes. 'But then, we can't tell anyone we met and talked, can we? It's our secret.'

The seductive allure in her was as old as the hills around them and as unaffectedly natural.

Shiro glanced at the watch at her wrist and scrambled to her feet. 'My goodness, I have to run. I promised Mummy I'd help with the cake and the palaharams.' She picked up the blanket and book. 'Are you coming to church on Christmas day? Ten-thirty in the morning in the Reform Church in Nuwara-Eliya? Bobsy the minister's great fun.'

Anthony grimaced. 'I'm not exactly a church person.'

But she was gone, scrambling up the path to the Tea-maker's quarters.

Bobsy the minister? *Well I never …*

Chapter 18

Grace's hand nestled in Bob's. Their heads bowed and eyes closed in prayer.

The romance that had bloomed at Bambalawatte Methodist School, fired by late night hot chocolate between school principal and assistant minister, was consummated in their loving marriage partnership. Today Grace's face glowed with the special bloom that comes to a woman who has just learnt that she is pregnant by the love of her life.

'Thank you, Father, for this wonderful season of Christmas when we celebrate the baby in the manger, the gift of your son. Bless this food to our bodies.'

Stuffed roast chicken lent a festive note to the curried fish and vegetable rice lunch. Handmade bonbons lay by the plates. It was a simple meal. Anthony felt a knot of envy in his chest. They had so little in their church manse, yet they were so content – so in love.

Bob opened his eyes. 'Why the distant look of distress, Anthony? Missing the festivities in the manor? Afraid we can't compete with that, old chap.'

'Gracious no. You know how I always hated the extravagance. It's the plantation, I just don't seem to be able to fit into my role as superintendent.'

Grace reached over to fill his glass with freshly squeezed pineapple juice. 'You're lonely, Anthony. Appu and a dog aren't enough company for you. Do you have any friends on the estate?'

'Friends? Only a girl I met a few weeks ago, the Tea-maker's daughter, Shiro.'

'I see.' Bob chuckled. 'That explains the impish glances she directed at you from the choir stalls. And I thought you were in church because I invited you.'

Grace's eyes continued the appraisal of his face. Anthony reddened under her questioning gaze.

'I watched Shiro grow up in the boarding school, Anthony,' she said. 'She's different from the run of the mill kids we saw there. She's deep and intelligent.

She was bullied.' She glanced at Bob. 'We tried to protect her.'

Bob nodded. 'She's an intense kid, charming, witty and brilliant, capable of deep affection. Shiro fought a group of girls who teased her best friend, Lalitha. And I mean a real rough and tumble eye gouging battle.'

Shiro in a fight. Yes, he could believe her capable of it. A smile tugged the corners of his mouth.

'She's not a child, Anthony.' Grace's soft words were tinged with concern.

Bob's eyes met Grace's. Frowning, he reached over the dining table and grasped Anthony's forearm. 'Be careful, Anthony. You don't need any complications in the plantation. I counselled young Shiro when I was assistant minister in Colombo. She's impulsive, but capable of deep emotions.' His eyes clouded with concern. 'She's also a very attractive young girl.'

'Why would there be complications in the plantation? Shiro's a naive little girl. She treats me as a friend and confidante.' Anthony chuckled. 'Come on Bob. Or Bobsy, as Shiro calls you. Be direct with me. What you truly mean is don't get involved with a native.'

'Anthony, it won't work, man. It can't. I know your father. He'll never tolerate your alliance with a Sri Lankan.'

Anthony's eyes flashed with deep blue fire. 'Alliance. What an interesting turn of phrase. Shiro and I just talk, chum. She's lonely too. Apparently, she lost her best friend recently.'

Anthony frowned as he intercepted another glance between Bob and Grace.

'Damn it, Bob, what the hell am I supposed to do? Maybe you'd rather I go in for some plantation hospitality like William and his cronies do? Like our father did?'

'You are a British planter, Anthony. You cannot have a relationship with a native Sri Lankan or Indian.'

'I don't believe I'm hearing this in this house – from you! Whatever happened to your catch cry of all men one before God? We sang about it, remember? "In Christ there is no East or West – one great fellowship of love throughout the whole wide earth". How do you advise me to live that out?'

Anthony dropped his gaze at the compassion in Bob's eyes.

'Be a friend to Shiro Rasiah and her family and to the rest of your staff.'

'A friend? That's a joke! How am I supposed to do that? The coolies turned down my savings plan.'

'We heard about the near riot,' Grace reached over to serve Bob a slice of roast chicken.

'But your plan for the staff provident fund was taken to the London board by your father.'

Anthony stopped with his fork halfway to his mouth. He looked from Bob to Grace, his eyes slitted. 'How do you know that?'

'William,' Bob responded with a dry chuckle. 'He was here last week. Furious at what he sees as your father pandering to your preposterous plans to wreck the plantations. His words, not mine. He wanted me to talk you out of doing something that would destroy all his good work. Rein you in was what he said.'

Grace looked at Anthony, her grey eyes clouded with worry. 'He also accused us of spreading rumours about him.'

'Damn him. He had no right to talk to you that way.'

Grace continued her appraisal of Anthony. 'Maybe you should put back your plans. Take it slow?'

Anthony choked, coughed, then chewed and swallowed. He took a gulp of water. 'I can't just let it go, Grace. My family raped and pillaged the plantations. William is of the same ilk. I have to do something to atone. Whatever the consequences, I have to act.' He swung to face Bob. 'Surely you can understand that?'

Bob tucked into his rice and chicken. He didn't look at Anthony. 'Stop punishing yourself.'

'What?'

'You're punishing yourself for what your father and your brother have done. And for all of us – the British.'

Bob put down his fork and knife. He leaned across the table.

'Anthony, you can't bear the sins of your people. Only one person can do that.'

Chapter 19

January 1967 Watakälé

'I was really sad when you didn't come here after Christmas,' Shiro grumbled. 'I thought you were annoyed that I giggled when Daddy introduced us. Maybe you didn't want to see me ever again.' She imitated her father's deep drawl, 'Mr Ashley-Cooper, I believe you have not met my daughter, Shiromi.' She rolled her eyes. 'He doesn't remember that we met when you came to visit with the Irvines!'

She sat curled on her blanket, bits of coloured wrapping paper spread around her. Her eyes were half closed, intent, as she flipped through the slim leather bound book of Lord Byron's poems.

Anthony sat with his back to the rock, his hands clasped around his knees. 'I was not mad at you and you were not heartbroken.'

'How do you know?'

'I watched you every day through the binoculars. You had heaps of fun with your brothers. Scrambling up the mango tree and riding your brother's bicycle hands-free across the factory lawn does not indicate deep distress.'

'You spied on me!' She fisted her fingers and punched Anthony on his arm. 'That's awful of you. Anyway, they're just brothers. They're gone back to Colombo now. It's you I want to be with. You're my special friend – the only one on the estate now.' She stopped and bit her lip.

'I'm sorry,' Anthony caught her hand and straightened out her fingers. 'I also happen to know that you were at the bungalow speaking with Appu. What are you up to, princess?' He held tight to her hand when she tried to pull it away.

Shiro watched as he skimmed his thumb over her palm. 'How did you know? I asked Appu not to tell you. He promised.'

Anthony held on to her hand as she tried to pull away. 'I hung him up by his thumbs in the bungalow dungeon and burned the soles of his feet with my cigarette as we British do when we want information.' He reached out with his other hand and touched the tip of her nose. 'Out with it. What are you up to?'

Shiro pouted and held his hand in both of hers. 'Would you believe me if I said I wanted to know what you eat for dinner?'

Anthony smiled and tweaked her nose. 'Watch it, Pinocchio. Your nose is growing longer.'

'Okay, the truth. My parents sent away my best friend. They did it because they don't want me to have an Indian coolie best friend. They want me to have high class Tamil *Vellalar* friends, as fitting for a young girl ready to enter society and the marriage market.' Shiro stopped and shuddered. 'I was asking Appu to tell me where she is. He knows everything there is to know about the coolies in Watakälé. So there.'

'Did you find out?'

'Are you kidding? He would die rather than go against my parents' orders. But I got one concession.'

'Meaning ...'

'I send one letter a month to him and he will send it to her.'

'You could ask her where she is.'

Shiro groaned. 'You don't know your Appu very well, do you? He will censor her letters before he sends them to me. And my letters in the boarding school are checked by the teachers anyway. No matter. I'll deal with that later.' Shiro drew her hands away from Anthony. 'Let me look at your present. Hmm, what shall I read – Here we are.'

She sat up, crossed her legs and looked down at the book. Anthony clenched his hands by his side. He should have taken Bob's advice – stayed away. This was too risky. He had tried to keep away. But he had been drawn to this place – to her.

He heard her voice as if from a distance. 'Ye friends of my heart, Ere from you I depart, This hope to my breast is most near, If again we shall meet, In this rural retreat, May we meet, as we part, with a tear.'

She looked up. 'Why are you staring at me?'

Anthony reached forward and touched her hair. A thick curl wound itself round his finger. 'Don't let them do it to you, Shiro.' He withdrew his hand.

She looked back at the book. She flicked the pages. 'Do what?'

'Don't agree to an arranged marriage. Don't allow them to make you a possession – a chattel to any man. Study hard and get into university. Go to medical school.'

Shiro shut the book. She frowned. 'I'd love that. You think I should do it,

115

don't you? But could I?'

She trusted him. This much he could do for her. Give her a future. 'Course you can, sweetheart.'

Her eyes darkened, flickered with uncertainty. Damn, he wanted to see her eyes burn with love for him. *What are you thinking, Anthony? She's not for you.*

Anthony struggled to keep his voice calm. 'Sweetheart, you told me that you get high marks when you try. Try harder this year. Once you get into medical school, they won't stand in your way.'

Shiro rested her elbows on her knees and cupped her face in her hands. 'Hmm. I believe I may be able to.' Suddenly her eyes lit up and her lips curved. She glanced at his face and let her eyes rove down his body.

She's up to something. She knows the effect she's having on me. The little imp!

'But,' Shiro mused. 'It will be hard. I have no encouragement from anybody.' She drew her lips into a moue. Damn, he should leave – right now.

'Surely, your brothers and uncle –'

Shiro rolled her eyes. 'Oh, please! They all think I should get married, or at least engaged, before even considering university.' She lay on her back and looked up at the sky.

'They think I'll fall in love with someone totally inappropriate in university. Like a Sinhalese, or Muslim. Or even worse –' She chuckled and sat up. Her eyes flickered back to his, sending his pulse racing. She lowered her voice to a soft, breathless whisper, clasped her hands together and leant forward. 'Someone like you.'

She looked serious, except for a tiny twinkle deep in the wide black eyes.

She was Juliet in *Romeo and Juliet*; Beatrice in *Much Ado about Nothing*; Ophelia in *Hamlet*. The little minx! It was an ice cold shower on his passion.

He took her hand. 'To be, or not to be, that is the question: whether 'tis nobler in the mind to suffer the slings and arrows of outrageous fortune; or to take arms against a sea of troubles.' He laughed at her look of outrage. 'Maybe you should forget medicine and get on the stage, princess?'

She shook her head. 'It's not that. You are such a bad actor. And your words are so out of context.' The curls danced in the sunshine.

Stop it, girl. Anthony drew his hand away.

'I'm serious, Anthony.' She grabbed back his hand. 'No one in my family believes that I want to study. But I plan to stay in Colombo all year and study. I need help.'

'Help? Tutoring?'

'Not in my subjects, silly. Help as in encouragement.' She was quiet for a few moments. He could almost hear the cogs in her brain click.

Her eyes widened. 'I've got it. You can do that for me.'

'And how do you see that happening?' She played with his fingers, sending streams of fire streaking up his arm and into his chest. He clenched his teeth, willing his fingers to stay limp as she played with them.

'Anthony, don't look so terrified! I'm asking you to write me an occasional letter.' She chuckled again. 'Not drive down to Colombo or study zoology and botany or do whatever other scary thought crossed your mind just now!'

An occasional letter – that was safe. She wouldn't be back here till next December. That gave him plenty of time to get his head and heart under control. 'I guess that wouldn't do any harm.'

'No harm at all, just lots of help.' Shiro uncurled herself and got on her knees. She slapped her hand to her forehead and leaned back. It was theatrical to a point of exaggerated absurdity. 'Oh, I forget. We aren't allowed to get letters from boys.' The dangerous twinkle was back. 'No matter. We'll pretend you're a girl. You can be Juliet … Mary. No, Ann. That's it. You're my friend Ann, daughter of the superintendent.'

'Shiro.'

She leapt to her feet. 'Mummy will be looking for me. I've got packing to do. I'll write soon. Ann, care of Anthony Ashley-Cooper. Has a nice sound. Bye.'

She jumped up and scampered up the path to the house. Stopping halfway, she turned and blew him a kiss.

Anthony stood open-mouthed as she disappeared up the path.

Chapter 20

Lakshmi leant over the sink in the kitchen of Hemachandra Mudalali's house, rinsing the used lunch plates and stacking them on the draining board. After sweeping the kitchen floor and wiping the tabletops, she served the leftover rice and curry into a tin plate and sat on a small stool in a corner of the room.

It was now four months since she started work as a servant at the Hemachandra Mudalali residence. She had come to Hemachandra Mudalali's directly here from the Salvation Army home for unmarried girls, a week after she had given birth to Daniel. Reaching into her jacket she pulled out the black and white picture of her son that the matron of the Salvation Army home had given her. Tears coursed down her cheeks. 'Aiyoo, my child, my child.'

Hemachandra Mudalali's wife Hamine stood at the kitchen door. 'What are you crying about? Are you sick?' She glanced at the picture in Lakshmi's hands and shook her head. 'The child will be well looked after. It is a good thing that Tea-maker Aiya had connections with the Salvation Army.'

Lakshmi leapt to her feet. The tin plate on her lap slipped off, sending the rice and pieces of fish sliding across the cement floor of the kitchen. 'Why are you talking of Tea-maker Aiya and Periamma as if they did some good thing?' tears tore out of her. 'They wanted to get rid of me. They used me as a servant and then when I was in trouble threw me away. They dropped me off five months pregnant like a bag of dirt at the Salvation Army hostel. I begged them to let me stay in the estate. I said I would work for them without any pay. But no, they wanted me out of their life.'

Hamine shook her head. Her hand was firm on Lakshmi's shoulder. 'They are good people, Lakshmi. We have known them a long time. We gave you this job because Mrs Rasiah asked us to. You could not stay on the estate after what happened.'

Lakshmi slid the photograph back into her blouse. 'No! They just wanted an excuse to get rid of me. They didn't want their daughter to be friends with me. I know. I heard them. They even sent her to Colombo to study to separate us. And after I got pregnant, they refused to tell her what had happened to me, even where I was.'

Hamine shook her head. 'Lakshmi, listen to me. Shiro is a bright young girl. Mudalali and I have seen her grow up. She needed to study in Colombo. It was not about you.' Her eyes narrowed. 'How do you know that they didn't tell her where you were?'

Lakshmi looked at the floor, scuffing the coir mat with her bare toes. 'Shiro Chinnamma sends letters to Appu and he brings them to me. I give him letters to post to her. He made me promise that I will not tell her where I am.' Frightened, she stared at Hamine. 'Please don't tell Tea-maker Aiya or Periamma. I don't want to get Shiro Chinnamma into trouble.'

'I guess a letter once in a while doesn't matter. But you must never tell her that you are here. If she comes here, we must tell Tea-maker Aiya.'

To never see Shiro Chinnamma again would break her heart, but what options were there? 'I will never tell her.'

'Lakshmi, I know you are sad about your son, but we like having you here.' Hamine smiled. 'In fact, you being able to read and write English is like having a secretary at home for Mudalali. And you read the English papers and tell the news to us also. Before you came, the Sunday paper would lie unopened all week on the table in the sitting room.' She stopped and chortled. 'Mudalali wanted to impress people that came to visit. I felt bad to tell him that an unopened English newspaper folded and creased as it had been in the shop with the original rubber band around it is hardly evidence of our interest in world news.' She reached out and touched Lakshmi's hand.

'Lakshmi, you were the one who refused to see Mrs Rasiah when she came. She was very upset. Who do you think sends you the money and clothes through Appu every month?'

Hamine walked to the door, then turned and looked at Lakshmi. 'Well, tomorrow is Sunday. You will feel better when you have visited your son. Go and visit, but don't get too attached to the child. You know he'll be adopted out soon.'

Lakshmi stood at the kitchen sink. Hemachandra Mudalali and his wife Hamine, were kind to her. They had no children and the work wasn't hard. Lakshmi's lips twisted in a grimace. She earned more here than a tea plucker and only did as much cooking and cleaning as in the line room for her family, probably even less, in much more comfort. She looked at the wood burning fireplace and the sink with the tap and compared it with the years she had spent cooking in the back veranda of the line room and standing in line for a pot of clean water from the common tap. No, her life was better here.

Yet, there was a time when she had hoped for better things. A home of her own, a husband who loved her. But it was an unreasonable dream for now.

Periamma, Lakshmi clasped the edge of the sink as the face once so beloved swam into her consciousness. Just a few old clothes and rupees sent through Appu. It was the way of the plantations, after all. The coolies used as unpaid servants, abused, raped and then thrown into the drain. Her parents had been right – once a coolie, always a coolie. She was on her own. She thought of Shiro Chinnamma's monthly letters. Shiro Chinnamma was still a dreamer, getting ready for her university entrance examination but still the same girl that she was when they had sat together by the stream. Shiro Chinnamma begged Lakshmi to tell her where she was. But telling her would bring her there and that would make Hemachandra Mudalali and Hamine angry. No, that wasn't worth the risk. Not yet.

The little room next to the kitchen was her room. In it was a little bed and a trunk with all her belongings. Lakshmi sat on the bed and unlocked the trunk. Pulling out Shiro's last letter she started reading:

> 'You remember Watakälé superintendent Aiya? We are friends now! Can you believe it? A white superintendent and a brown native girl! We meet in our place. No one knows, well, no one but you. And there's more. I write to him monthly too, except I have to address it to 'Ann Ashley-Cooper'. I ask him to do things like kiss the eagle! Ha, ha. I think I'm a little in love with him. But of course, that is crazy! Sri Lankans and white people can't be together, ever!'

Shiro Chinnamma's letters were all like this, full of bits of news and exclamation marks. Lakshmi skimmed down to the end of the letter. Tears filled her eyes as she read:

> 'When I get married, I will adopt Daniel. Then you can live with me and we can both be mothers to him.'

There was no doubt that Shiro meant it. But Lakshmi couldn't wait so long. Daniel may be adopted out any day. The lady who organised the adoptions had said that she had never seen such a fair Eurasian baby. She had also commented on his blue eyes.

Hemachandra Mudalali paid her monthly salary direct into a savings account in the post office, but that was not enough. It would cost a lot to get a small house and get her son Daniel back from the orphanage. And it had to be done quickly, before someone adopted him.

Appu, when he visited her last month, had given her an address of a woman here in Diyatalāwa. He had said that this woman, Malar, may be able to help her. He didn't tell her how or why. Tomorrow was Sunday, her day off. She would go see this woman, then visit her son in Nuwara-Eliya.

'Lakshmi, it looks like rain,' Hamine yelled from the upstairs bedroom window. 'Take the clothes in.'

'Yes, Hamine,' Lakshmi picked up the laundry basket and ran out to the backyard. Heavy drops of cold rain fell on her face and neck. Lakshmi shivered.

**

It was seven in the morning and Hemachandra Mudalali and Hamine were still asleep. The morning breakfast of kiribath and seenisambol was ready and on the dining table. Hamine would take care of lunch. Lakshmi shut and locked the back door of the house. She drew her multi-coloured woollen jumper tight around her. The ever-present morning mist of the tea plantations surrounded her with fingers of damp and cold. Thin rays of sunlight struggled through. She raised her face to their caress.

Leaving the garden, she secured the wooden cross bar across the garden gate. Last week the milk delivery man had left the gate ajar and two of the egg laying hens had wandered out into the street. Hamine had insisted that Lakshmi and Hemachandra Mudalali walk the streets looking for them. They were never found. The hens probably ended up as chicken curry by that evening.

Lakshmi pulled the crushed piece of paper out of the pocket of her blouse and looked at the address. Number 32, Gemunu Street. That was a small road off the main highway, towards the army training camp. She walked quickly. That area of town would be crowded today. Sunday morning was pola time, the market day, when all the locals brought their vegetables and fruit for sale and the traders had pavement displays of clothes, jewellery and all sorts of incense and other treasures. The population of Diyatalāwa increased about tenfold on pola days, transforming the sleepy country town into a busy market town that could rival Nuwara-Eliya.

Lakshmi pushed past women carrying baskets of vegetables and bull carts laden with coconuts, thambili and multi-coloured boxes woven from the coconut palm leaf. She stopped at a display of baby clothes. No, she shouldn't waste her money. Apparently people donated clothes and money to the Nuwara-Eliya orphanage. The children there, including her son Daniel, were always well dressed and clean.

The shouts of vendors describing their wares and the loud chatter of people bargaining with them for the best price rose in volume as she pushed through the crowd. The smell of ripe Jak fruit tickled her nose. Hamine loved ripe Jak. She must remember to buy some on her way back.

A group of uniformed soldiers approached her. Her movement to the edge of the road into the drain was automatic. Cursing, she stepped back. These were soldiers from the army encampment in Diyatalāwa, not British Periadorai or estate employees. There was no need to behave like a plantation coolie. The men laughed. One pointed at her and said something that sounded like '*vesi*'. The laughter grew louder. Lakshmi scurried down Gemunu Street. Surely she must have heard wrong? Why would they think she was a *vesi*, a prostitute?

Number 32 was painted in small letters on a fence made of six foot high roofing sheets. It clashed with the other houses in the street, which had front fences of rows of canna plants and jasmine bushes. There was a wide gate also of the same material. Lakshmi walked up to it, half expecting it to be padlocked. The gate was shut but not padlocked. It swung open with a loud squeak. Shutting the gate behind her, Lakshmi hesitated, shifting from foot to foot. What was she doing here? And who was this Malar? How could she help her make money? Well, no use standing here.

Number 32 was an old fashioned brick single story house set in a garden with rose bushes, daisies and other colourful flowers Lakshmi didn't recognise. A wide gravel path led to the front veranda. Two cane chairs and a small table stood there. Lakshmi took a deep breath and walked up the path to the front of the house.

The front door swung open. A middle aged man in the brown uniform of the Sri Lankan army stepped out from the front door of the house. He held his army cap under his arm and was buttoning his coat. He was followed by a woman dressed in a pale green cotton sari. Lakshmi stepped behind a tree. The woman looked about the age of Periamma, maybe a little younger. Her black hair was slicked back in a bun and her lips a red slash in her dark face. Lakshmi watched while she fluttered the eyelashes of her *kohled* eyes at the man, who shook hands with her and handed her an envelope. The woman smiled and slipped it into her sari blouse. The man turned and strode down the path and out of the gate.

The woman had half turned towards the front door when she saw Lakshmi. She bent towards her. 'Who are you and what are you doing here?' she snapped in Tamil.

Lakshmi recognised the rough, guttural accent. This was an Indian Tamil woman like herself. What should she say? But Appu had sent her, and he was a good man. At least she should talk with this woman.

'What do you want?' the woman repeated.

Lakshmi stepped out from behind the canna plants and took a couple of steps toward the woman. 'Are you Malar – Amma?' she stammered. 'Appu Aiya from Watakälé sent me to see you, Amma.'

'Hm, Watakälé Periadorai Appu sent you, heh?' The woman gestured to Lakshmi to come closer. Lakshmi climbed the two steps to the polished cement of the veranda, slipped her sandals off and stood barefooted. The woman looked Lakshmi up and down like examining a cow or goat on sale at the market. 'Yes, I am Malar. Come in and tell me what you want.'

Lakshmi followed Malar through the front door and into the sitting room, then stopped dumbfounded, gaping at the rich furnishings. A red velvet covered sofa and two matching chairs, all with thick, carved wooden arms, stood around a brown and red carpet. The two windows had what looked like thick red velvet curtains tied back with black cord. Along the walls were three and four shelved glass fronted cabinets with plates, bowls, dishes and statues in glass and white porcelain. Hamine had a few of these types of things. That was how Lakshmi knew what they were. Hamine cleaned and dusted them all herself, telling Lakshmi repeatedly how expensive and precious they were because they were all imported from England. She used words like Royal Doulton and Wedgewood, which were apparently written on the bottom of the pieces. To Lakshmi they had looked no different to the regular plates and dishes they used in the kitchen.

This woman, Malar, had cupboards full of them. Malar walked through a back door and down a red carpeted corridor. Lakshmi followed. There were two closed doors on either side of the corridor and Lakshmi could hear voices and laughter from behind one door.

The kitchen at the end of the corridor was completely different from the sitting room. It was a simple room. A wooden table with four rattan chairs stood in the middle. On one side was a wood-fired stove, the sink, a cupboard of plates and other bits and pieces. On the other side was a large chest of drawers. Malar pointed to a chair and sat opposite Lakshmi. A book that looked like a factory ledger lay on the table between them. Opening it Malar looked across it at Lakshmi. 'So you want a job? I can do with more girls like you. Tell me your name. How old are you?'

'My name is Lakshmi, Amma. I am about twenty-three years old,' Lakshmi stammered.

'You must call me Malar.' She scribbled something on the book. 'Have you had any children?'

'I had a baby four months ago Amm – Malar,' she whispered.

'You have given him away?'

Why did Malar want all these details? 'He is in the Salvation Army orphanage in Nuwara-Eliya.'

'Who is the father?'

Lakshmi couldn't take it any longer. 'Am – Malar, please help me. My child, Daniel, I must take him out of the orphanage. Make a home for him. Please, please help me. I will work for you.' Her voice broke on a sob, 'I have the Sundays free. I will do anything. Please.'

Malar stood up and walked around the table. Her hand was gentle on Lakshmi's head. Lakshmi's sobs subsided. 'This Daniel. Your son,' Malar's voice was soft. 'He is the child of a Periadorai? A white man?'

Lakshmi nodded. Her body trembled with remembered pain and horror. 'And this man, the father, did you go to him willingly or did he force you?'

'He forced me.' The memory was still a shaft through her soul.

'You are working somewhere already?'

'Yes,' Lakshmi whispered, 'At Hemachandra Mudalali's place.'

'But you want a lot of money fast, right?'

'Yes,' Lakshmi raised her head and looked into Malar's eyes. A tear formed in the corner of Malar's eyes and slipped down her cheek. 'Lakshmi, I too had a child by a British Periadorai. But he didn't throw me away. He bought this house for me. Got the furniture and all the things you saw. He paid for me to bring up the boy.'

Lakshmi followed Malar's eyes to a colour picture on top of the refrigerator. It was of a young man about Lakshmi's age, maybe a little older. He was dressed in a blue suit and stood in front of a red brick building. Lakshmi could see that he was fair, a little like Daniel.

'That is my son, Jega. He is studying in England. He will come back soon as Dr Jega Jayaseelen. His father in England is paying. He will be a doctor. A specialist, he tells me, whatever that is.'

A sob rent Lakshmi's body. 'You are lucky.'

'Lucky?' Malar's lips twisted. 'Taken from the line rooms at fifteen and kept as a slave by the British Periadorai. Then when he went to England and brought his wife back. I was thrown out by her. She hit me. Called me a prostitute. She was a white pissasu – a devil. I was pregnant with my son.'

'But at least your son's father looked after you?'

Malar nodded. 'So that is why Watakälé Periadorai's Appu sent you to me. He knows what happened.'

Lakshmi watched as Malar wiped her face on the end of her sari and sat down at the table, picking up her pen again.

'Lakshmi, do you know what type of work the girls do here in my house?'

Just then a short, dark and chubby woman dressed in a red blouse and long black skirt came down the corridor into the kitchen. 'Malar, the army man gave me an extra two hundred rupees.' She giggled.

Malar glanced at Lakshmi and then addressed the other woman. 'You can keep it. And here's the rest of your payment for today.' She handed a few folded notes to her. Lakshmi recognised them as hundred rupee notes. The woman counted it and laughed. 'Nice. I can go shopping at the pola markets.' She left by the back kitchen door. The laughter hung in the air between Malar and Lakshmi.

Lakshmi remembered the army men she had passed on the road, their mocking laughter and the word they had used – *vesi*. The truth dawned on her. This was a whorehouse. It provided women to the army camp. Yes, she wanted money, but to sell her body? To go through that pain and shame over and over again? No. She couldn't do it. She pushed back her chair and stood up. 'Malar, I am sorry. I can't, I shouldn't have come.' Even as she spoke she realised that she had said the last few words in English.

'You speak English?' Malar gasped.

Lakshmi nodded, her hands grasping the edge of the table.

'Lakshmi, sit down. You want to make money? I can do that for you. Let me help you.' Her eyes met Lakshmi's. 'You don't have many choices, girl. You are young and pretty.' Her eyes roved over Lakshmis body. 'You look after your hands and your nails.' She looked at Lakshmi's mouth. 'You don't chew betel and have good teeth.'

What am I doing? Lakshmi pulled the chair back and sat down. The world slowed down around her. She was about to agree to be a prostitute. What would Periamma say if she knew? Why think of her? She didn't care about her. Anger boiled up in her heart and spilled over.

'I'll do it.'

Malar nodded. She bent and wrote in the ledger then turned the book around to Lakshmi. 'Sign here. I will set up appointments for you on Sunday, your day off. It is the busiest day of the week. On a good day, you can get through five or even six appointments. I will pay you two hundred rupees for one session. Like you saw, whatever else you make is yours. The men who come to you will pay you well if you are good.'

Lakshmi picked up the pen and signed her name in English. Lakshmi Ramen. It was an act of defiance and a renunciation of all that the Rasiahs stood for. To use the manners Periamma had taught her and the English she had learnt to earn money as a vesi.

Malar smiled. 'That's better. Now I will give you a medicine you have to take. This will keep you from getting pregnant. If something still happens, we will see to it.'

There was a sharp knock on the front door. Malar glanced at the clock on the wall over the drawers. 'Goodness, it's ten o'clock. Sumi was supposed to be here.' She bit her lip. 'Lakshmi, when did you have your periods?'

'I just finished. Why?'

'Would you like to start work today? This is an important client and the girl he asked for hasn't come. I think he will like you.'

Lakshmi glanced down at her white cotton blouse and threadbare skirt. 'I am not ready ...'

Malar interrupted her with a hoarse chuckle. 'Don't worry, girl. Clothes are the last thing on their minds when they come here.' Grasping Lakshmi by her hand, she dragged her to the nearest bedroom door, opened the door and pushed her in. 'There's a nightdress on the bed. Take all your clothes off and put it on. Pull your hair down. And from today, when you are working, you will be called Devi.'

Lakshmi stood by the bed. She picked up the lace nightdress. It felt like she was out of her body, watching herself take her clothes off and put on the lace attire, changing from Lakshmi with the dream of a better life into Devi the prostitute. She pulled her hair free of the tight knot and let it cascade down her back. She sat on the edge of the bed and waited.

Daniel, my child, this is for you.

She heard a male voice, speaking in accented British English. 'A new girl, you say? Better than Sumi? Well, I'll expect a bang for my bucks. Let's see what she has to offer.'

The door opened and Lakshmi stared into the white skinned face. The expression of arrogant lust in his eyes made her shudder. Bile rose in her throat. Her breathe caught in her chest.

His hands reached for her. Lakshmi muffled a scream as his lips came down on hers.

Chapter 21

December 1967 Colombo

'Memories, pressed between the pages of my mind, Memories, sweetened through the ages just like wine, Quiet thoughts come floating down, And settle softly to the ground, Like golden autumn leaves around my feet.'

Shiro hummed her song, the one Lakshmi had sung with her when they were children. *Lakshmi my dear, dear friend. You sounded so sad in your letter. I wish I knew where you are. I feel you thinking of me.*

Images of Lakshmi from two years ago were imprinted in her memory. Lakshmi dressed in her simple, long skirt and white blouse hugging goodbye at the station. Lakshmi waving as the train drew away. Now it was all gone. And no one would tell her where to find Lakshmi. Her letters spoke of her baby. But Shiro, who knew Lakshmi well, sensed the hopelessness, and under it, anger.

There were new friends in Colombo. There was Lalitha and others. But there was no one who could enter that special corner of her heart where Lakshmi lived. Not even Anthony.

'I'm so proud of you.' Her uncle George looked at Shiro sideways as he wound his Ford Consul through the cars and other sundry vehicles crowding the entrance to Fort Railway Station. 'When you next come to Colombo, you'll be starting medical school.'

Shiro leaned over and kissed her uncle on his cheek as he pulled into the parking lot. 'You spoil me, uncle. The way you were running around telling everyone. Honestly, I thought you were going to put posters in the streets.' She waved her hands above her head. 'My niece is going to be a doctor!'

They got out of the car. Uncle George opened the boot of the car. 'Bag, sir?' A sarong-clad, bare-chested porter, smelling of sweat, appeared as if from nowhere and placed her trunk on a trolley. 'Badulla train, no, sir?' together they negotiated the motley group of people bustling and shoving their way onto the station platform.

Shiro hopped on board the carriage and found a seat. She pulled the window up and leaned out. Uncle George stood on the platform just below. 'Have a good trip,' he called out. 'Send me your booklist for medical faculty and I'll buy them all for you.'

'Oh Uncle, you've bought me all those lovely clothes already. I'll ask Daddy to call you when I get home.'

The diesel locomotive's horn echoed through Fort station. The Udarata Menike pulled away from the platform among the usual shouted goodbyes in English, Tamil and Sinhalese. Leaning out, Shiro waved to her uncle until the train drew away and around a bend.

With a contented sigh, Shiro flopped into the linen-covered, leather first class seat Uncle George had booked for her. She opened her bag and pulled out the university entrance examination certificate. Three distinctions and a credit had guaranteed entry to the Colombo Medical Faculty. School teachers and fellow students had been amazed. Bratty little Shiro, drama queen and dreamer, top of the class and one of the best results in all the Colombo schools. Now, one of only two from her school accepted to the Colombo medical school. The other, her best buddy and study partner, Lalitha.

How Shiro longed to share these experiences with Lakshmi, the one person who would understand her dreams. No. Not the only person. There was now Anthony – or Ann. The letters had kept her focussed on her study, kept her mind away from what she knew her family were planning for her.

In the last letter under the nom de plume of Ann, he had promised to be at their place. She needed advice on how to deal with her parents. Anthony would help.

She pulled out her mother's last letter to her.

'Darling Shiro,' her mother had written.

> 'Daddy and I are so proud of your achievements. Victor explained to Daddy that the grades you have achieved are hard to reach. We are honestly happy for you.'

Then followed the rider:

> 'However, we would like you to consider if this is what you want to do. Five years in medical school and then two years internship is a long hard road for a girl like you.'

A girl like her indeed! The train rocked and rattled through the dusty, dirty

Colombo suburbs. Shiro sat back and imagined the conversation that would have preceded the letter.

Victor would have said something like, 'She loves her study and she's smart. We shouldn't stand in her way.'

Daddy would have responded with, 'True, but can she stand the pressures of university life on her own in Colombo?'

Mother would have pounced on that. 'Why does she need to go to university? She's already well educated. There are such nice boys available. That Chelliah boy has just finished university. I hear he's looking for a bride.'

Sure, Mum, Shiro thought. *Marry a nice Tamil boy and settle down. That's what well brought up Tamil girls do, isn't it?* The boys studied and went to university, the girls went to a good school and married a suitable boy. If the girls were lucky, their parents sent them to finishing school to learn the finer points of cooking, entertaining and flower arrangement. Medical school? For a girl? Heavens, that's not part of the Jaffna Tamil script.

No. I have a place in university and no one, not even you, my beloved mother, is going to stand in my way. I will go to medical school and be a doctor. Marriage, arranged or otherwise, can wait.

The familiar scenery sped past. The deep, rushing, muddy waters of the mighty Mahaweli River was filled with cattle and even a couple of elephants having their daily bath. The bright green, terraced rice fields stretched into the distance beyond the river, the endless undulating sea of paddy stalks interrupted by collections of shanty dwellings. Little children in colourful cotton dresses and shirts stood on the verandas of the little homes by the railroad track, calling out and waving to the passengers on the train.

Shiro reached out and threw a handful of wrapped lollies to one group of children. She looked back as they swooped on them.

Shiro's heart throbbed to the beat of the diesel locomotive as the Uderata Maniké wound its way through the Nawalapitiya Ranges. She could see the shiny silver-blue shape of the locomotive as the rail track weaved around the mountains.

The sound of the locomotive's diesel engine changed to a deep rumble as the train muscled its ascent into the tea country. Shiro breathed in the clean mountain air. The train entered tea country. The smell of partially processed tea drifted into the carriage, making Shiro's heart long to be back in Watakälé, back in her special place by the stream.

Rolling hills in shades of green and lavender reached as far as the eye could see. Gossamer fingers of mist clung to the top of the hills, loath to let go of their hold on the tea bushes, even in the afternoon sun. Standing in stark contrast to the green of the tea bushes were three and four storey silver-white tea factories, each announcing their name in bold, black letters on the roof. Shiro read off the names as the train rumbled past – St Clair, St James and St Coombs. All these saints. The original British owners must have been very superstitious!

The superintendents' tudor-style houses or bungalows were perched on the hills. The manicured lawns and neatly trimmed rose bushes were hidden from the eyes of native, coolie and commoner by tall cyprus and eucalyptus trees planted by the British when they first developed the plantations. As a child, she and her brothers had played a game they called 'spot the bungalow'. Whoever saw one first got a chocolate. Shiro laughed at the memory. She was usually mighty sick of chocolate by the time they got to Watakälé. She knew now it had been their way to keep her entertained on the eight hour steam train ride. At least the onset of diesel had cut the travel time by almost half.

Shiro pulled out her book, Jane Austen's *Pride and Prejudice*. She imagined a scene from the book in each of the bungalows as they whooshed by the window.

She thought of the tea parties the new school principal hosted for the senior girls in the boarding school, teaching the girls how to entertain 'the British way'. Apparently it was an important skill for an accomplished young lady. Did British planters in the bungalows actually take their evening tea around lace-covered tables, laden with a silver tea service? With dainty cupcakes and cucumber sandwiches on crystal plates? She would have to ask Anthony about that. If he did, she would like to entertain for him one day. Show the budding British Raj what natives could do.

The Uva valley signalled to Shiro that the train was approaching Diyatalāwa. The hills, now shadowed in the evening sunshine, stretched out to eternity. When she was a child, Victor had called this God's playground. She had believed him, as she always did, and looked for angels frolicking on the hills.

With the loud wheeze of air brakes, the train sidled up to the platform at Diyatalāwa. Shiro hung out the window and looked around. Her brothers were not on the platform. Victor was working that day and Edward was still in Colombo. She waved to Raaken, the man servant from Watakälé, who was there to help her with her trunk. As usual, they would travel home in Hemachandra Mudalali's tea lorry.

Raaken boarded the train, grabbed Shiro's suitcase and hauled it onto the platform. Shiro picked up her handbag and followed.

The train drew out of the station with a long, drawn-out hoot. Shiro glanced at her watch. There were ten minutes before the lorry was due. Time enough for some discreet snooping.

'Raaken, do you know where Lakshmi –' A sharp voice cut across the chatter on the platform. Shiro turned to the source, but not before she caught the look of fear on Raaken's face.

'Where the hell are those coolies? And where is my car? I told that bloody Tea-maker to make sure it was here to meet the train!' The British-accented voice dripped with conceited authority.

The tall Englishman towered over the cowering form of Mr Velu, the Diyatalāwa stationmaster. The man was strikingly handsome, with a muscular and athletic body, his hair blonde and thick, curling at his neck. The lean, angular features of his face were relieved by a generously sculptured mouth.

Shiro gasped. Anthony? No, of course not! This must be the older brother from Udatänná. He looked like Anthony, blue eyed and blonde, but taller and broader. The petulant expression on his face was that of a spoiled child. His eyes shifted to catch hers for a fraction of second before returning their icy stare to the hapless Mr Velu.

Shiro recoiled. Anthony's brother, if that is who the man was, had the eyes of a devil.

'Sir, I am very sorry sir, there has been no telephone message from Udatänná, sir,' Mr Velu stammered. Shiro looked away, sickened by Mr Velu's grovelling. A year away and she'd forgotten the power dynamics and cultural divides of tea plantation life.

The Englishmen raised his hand and waved Mr Velu away. The sun glinted on the slim gold watch on his wrist. 'Well go on, don't just stand here, call them and get them to send the car immediately. I can't spend my day here in this godforsaken rat hole of a station.'

Mr Velu scurried away with a deferential, 'Yes sir, at once, sir.'

The Englishman placed his foot on his suitcase and packed his pipe. The shoes were of hand-crafted leather like those Anthony wore. The handkerchief used to flick dust off his suitcase pure white linen.

Conceited eyes swept over at the station peons bustling around on the platform. *These are my minions*, his posture said. *I am lord of my domain*. Then, as if sensing Shiro's eyes on him, the eyes pivoted to stare at her. They were the same deep blue as Anthony's but hard as flint and as menacing as a crouching tiger awaiting its prey. The look sent a chill down her spine.

Shiro shuddered and turned away, just as Hemachandra Mudalali's lorry rumbled into the station parking lot.

'Shiro missy, I am sorry to be late. How are you?' The driver jumped out, 'Hemachandra Mudalali sent you sweets.' He handed her the obligatory box of Black Magic chocolates. Seeing the Englishman, he lowered his voice. 'Come, missy. Let's go.' The driver bundled Shiro into the front seat of the lorry. Raaken heaved her suitcase and bag in and then leapt in the back with it. The driver loosed the handbrake and lurched out of the railway station parking lot.

'Shiro missy, did you see that English man?' the driver asked as they bounced their way along the rough road which ran through Diyatalāwa town and on to Watakälé Tea Plantation. 'He is the superintendent at Udatännā. Not a good man at all. He did not talk with you, did he? I will get into trouble with Mudalali if he talked to you.'

'Come on, driver! What could happen in broad daylight on a station platform?'

Shiro stumbled over the words remembering the lechery in the man's face in those moments they had gazed at each other. It was as if he had stripped her naked just with his eyes.

She hoped to never see him again.

***

Watakälé

'What is wrong with you?' Her mother nagged Shiro. 'I hardly know you now. Why can't you talk to me about what is going on in your head?'

Three days into her holiday and nothing had changed at home. She was dying to go to her place by the river. However, her mother had set her mind on teaching her all the womanly tasks. This meant that Shiro was expected to help in the cooking and cleaning. The fact that she would be a medical student next year was ignored by her mother and even by her beloved father.

Mother had been hassling her that morning about her traditional role as a woman and a daughter. Worse still, she wanted Shiro to agree to an arranged marriage. Shiro was sick of it.

'What is wrong with me,' she erupted, 'is that I cannot, and will not be what you want me to be! I'm sick and tired of being the perfect daughter! I love cooking and craft and I will do it for me! For me, do you understand? Not for a man you choose. I don't want to marry a suitable boy and be a housewife and mother like you! I want to be a doctor! I want to make a difference in the world! Is that so wrong?' Shiro's face was red. Her hands were clenched by her side.

Tears streamed down her face.

Mother remained calm. As usual, she turned to the men in the house to resolve conflict. 'Appa,' she said to her husband, 'can you see what I mean? Can you explain to her that we only want what is best for her? Boys don't want a highly qualified, independent woman.'

Before her father could reply, Shiro's brother Victor intervened. 'Mum, boys today are different. They admire brains. Shiro has that, as well as beauty and charm.' Seeing the shocked look on his mother's face, he continued. 'Of course, they still expect her to be a good housewife but you've taught her all that.'

Her mother rounded on him. 'But this boy, Yogan Chelliah. They will be in Nuwara-Eliya for Christmas. They want to meet with us. You have met him in Colombo. He's a nice boy and a friend of Edward's also.'

A good housewife? Arranged marriage? A nice boy? Ha! Shiro tossed her head in mockery and disgust. Spinning on her heels, she stormed out of the house. As she left, she heard her father mumble, 'I'm going to the factory. Call me if you need anything.'

That's right, Shiro thought, as she wound her way down the familiar path to her place by the stream. Leave the issue unresolved and run away to your precious workplace. Any wonder I don't want a traditional arranged marriage?

Shiro hoped Anthony would come. She needed to see him.

***

'Tears, princess?' Anthony squatted by her side. He drew her hands away from her face.

Shiro swallowed a sob, and then remained silent. Her lips quivered. Anthony held her hands, stroking her fingers. The touch on her lip was feather light but it comforted her. The anger and frustration drained out of her.

He pulled a white linen handkerchief out of his pocket and wiped the tears from her face. 'Talk to me, Shiro. You should be happy, thrilled even. You came top of your class, won every award. Your father couldn't stop talking about it. You've been accepted to medical school. It's everything you wanted. Whatever's happened?'

She stared up at him. Her lips quivered. 'I don't want to get married.'

Anthony lips twitched. 'I don't recollect asking you, sweetheart.'

The words had the desired effect. 'Not funny.' Her lips lifted a smile.

'That's my girl.' He sat down beside her. 'What's up?' He placed his right hand behind her.

Shiro rested her head on his shoulder. She breathed in the familiar sharp lemon smell of his body. It had been a year since they had sat here last but it felt like yesterday. This was what she needed – Anthony, her friend, her confidante, her rock. The one person in the world she could say anything to.

'My mother.' She snuggled into his shoulder. 'She wants me to meet this guy. His name's Yogan Chelliah. She wants me to agree to an arranged marriage. Get engaged, even have the marriage registered before I go to medical school.' Her body shuddered as she gulped back another sob.

Anthony's arm tensed and then slipped from behind her to around her shoulder. Gentle fingers moved in slow circles over her arm. 'When and how does this arranged marriage thing happen?'

'The families meet tomorrow for lunch at the Nuwara-Eliya River View Hotel. His family is already there.' The feel of his fingers on her skin was amazing. It sent little ripples of happiness shooting to her brain.

'Can you say no?'

'To marrying him? I can, but only after I meet him."

Anthony was silent. His hand slipped down her arm and rested round her waist.

He turned his head towards her and spoke into her hair. 'Meet this Yogan,' he said. 'Then come here in the evening and tell me about it. We'll decide what to do about it together.'

Tears forgotten, Shiro threw her arms around him and hugged him. 'You are the best ever. I couldn't live without you. Thank you.'

Chapter 22

The beige Savile Row wool suit and white linen shirt were more suited to a business meeting in the City of London than a drive to the hill capital of Nuwara-Eliya. Anthony was taking no chances. He planned to impress. He rummaged through his drawer of ties. 'Something with purple,' he mumbled. Appu placed Anthony's brown leather shoes polished and ready at the foot of the bed and then stepped back. 'Sir, the car is at the front. Are you sure you don't want the chauffeur, sir?'

'I'll be fine.' Slipping on his coat, Anthony jumped in the Wolseley and drove out. He noticed that the Tea-maker's car was not in the garden. They must have left early.

The swirling wind and rain made for heavy going. It took Anthony an hour to negotiate the winding roads to Nuwara-Eliya. He ripped into the car park of the River View Hotel in a shower of gravel and parked some distance from the Rasiah's old Morris Minor. Slipping his jacket on, he picked up his briefcase and sauntered to the hotel. He tried to look casual, like he had decided to stop there for lunch on an impulse.

He pretended not to notice the minor kerfuffle as the staff at the front desk saw him climb the steps. A man in a black suit with the badge 'Anton Perera – Manager' emerged from the side room and approached Anthony. 'Sir, welcome to River View Hotel, sir. It is good for you to come here, sir.' His voice and demeanour were both delighted and surprised. Few British came to River View Hotel. It was obviously a coup to have the heir apparent of Oriental Produce visit.

'Mr Perera, you have a family from Watakälé dining here, the Rasiahs.'

'Yes, sir. They are with a family from Colombo who are holidaying here.'

'Well, give me a table close to them. But,' his eyes bored into the managers, 'I don't want them to know I am here.'

The manager's eyes glazed like a deer in the spotlight of the hunter. 'Yes, sir, at once sir.' He recovered and gestured to the dining room. 'There are lot of families here today, sir. But we got a really nice table by the window in the dining room, sir.' He bowed as he ushered Anthony towards a table for two by the window.

The chatter in English and Tamil indicated that the meal was well under way. Anthony adjusted his seat so he had a clear view of Shiro. He was close enough to hear the conversation at the Rasiahs' table.

'Yogan is very musical, Shiro,' said a large lady in a red silk sari on Shiro's left. 'And he has a lot of opportunities for travel also in his job. He will go up in the company fast. You will be well looked after.' She had a flabby paw with a multitude of rings clasped on Shiro's arm.

Dismissing her, Anthony concentrated on the young man sitting on Shiro's right. Yogan Chelliah was dressed in a white cotton shirt and dark blue pair of trousers. *Damn the man.* Yogan was younger than Anthony and very good looking.

Yogan's eyes lit up and crinkled at the edges as he gazed at Shiro.

Shiro fluttered her eyelids at him. *The little witch, she's playing with this man.* Even as Anthony watched, she lowered her eyelids, opened her mouth and licked her lower lip.

Yogan's expression went into an overdrive of adoration.

Anthony nibbled on his smoked salmon and salad, all the while watching Shiro across the room. Suddenly, Shiro's back stiffened. She swung around in her seat and looked across the room. Her eyes widened as they met his. Anthony put his folk down and raised a finger to his lips. A smile crept across her face. She turned back and looked up at Yogan, fluttered her lashes and touched his sleeve with her fingertips.

The young man looked like he would faint with pleasure.

The brat. He's already in love with her. A shaft of jealousy pierced Anthony's heart. His every impulse was to stride across the room and drag her away from the man and her family. His fingers tightened on the arms of the mahogany chair.

Shiro flashed a look at Anthony. Her eyes shone bright with mischief. *She's enjoying this. She has no idea what it's doing to me.*

There was a buzz of conversation around the Rasiahs' table and seats were pushed back. The lunch plates were cleared by the waiters. Mrs Rasiah walked over to Shiro and spoke to her. Shiro shrugged and stood up. With a side glance at Anthony she followed her mother and Yogan out of the dining room.

'Sir, more coffee, sir? Would you like to see the dessert menu, sir?' Anthony ignored the waiters pleading tone. He waited till Mrs Rasiah came back to the dining room.

'Coffee in the lounge please, waiter.' Anthony dropped a five hundred rupee note on the table and strolled out of the dining room. He avoided looking at the Rasiahs.

A log fire glowed in an ornate old brick fireplace of the lounge. This, along with two hidden wall sconces, provided the only light in the room. Deep two and three-seater velvet upholstered sofas and single armchairs with carved arms were placed in groups around the room. Large tapestries in muted oranges and reds covered the walls. The firelight threw flickering shadows on the burnt orange carpets and clotted cream walls. It was small and intimate.

Shiro and Yogan sat at either end of a three-seater sofa. Anthony walked in front of them and sat on a sofa with his back to them.

Pulling out a book from his briefcase, Anthony snapped his fingers at the uniformed waiter standing at the door. He pointed to the ceiling lights. He cleared his throat and put on his best colonial accent. 'Switch these lights on, man. This place is like a bloody mausoleum. How the hell am I supposed to get any work done in this darkness?'

The waiter leapt to obey and the lounge was flooded with bright yellow light.

Anthony ignored the giggle from the sofa behind him.

Yogan Chelliah spoke with an almost delicate intonation, a cultured Sri Lankan voice with a missionary school accent. 'Shiro, what do you want to do now that you have finished school?'

Tell him you want to be a flying doctor in the Australian outback, Anthony prompted silently.

Shiro's voice was louder than necessary for someone sitting across her on the sofa. 'I'm going to medical school and will specialise in something. Paediatrics, obstetrics –something crazily exciting.'

The tone of the response was anxious. 'But that will take a lot of years.'

'Perfectly true, Yogan. What did you expect? Did your parents tell you I was ready for marriage immediately?'

That's my girl – go for the jugular. Anthony punched his closed fist on the open book on his lap.

'No, no,' Yogan said. 'I thought maybe next year? When you are finished the first year exams?'

Shiro spoke slowly. Her voice dripped condescension. 'Yogan, I haven't even said I want to marry you. But talking about marriage, why do you want to marry me?'

Oh no, Anthony groaned. *He's going to tell her how wonderful she is. That he loves her and will give her the world.*

'Well, Shiro, our parents have known each other for a long time. You will be safe with me. We can have a good life together.'

Anthony barely contained a laugh, but Shiro didn't. She laughed loud and long. 'But Yogan, surely marriage is more than safety and a good life? What about love and romance?'

Yogan coughed. 'That will come later, Shiro,' he stammered. 'Like for your parents and mine. You are young –...'

Shiro's voice was rose in pitch. 'No. Don't hold my hand.'

Anthony clenched his fists, amazed at the intensity of emotion that ripped through him. He wanted to yank her away from this man. Tell her that he was the only one who had the right to touch her. Instead, he stood and picked up his briefcase. He walked halfway to the door, then stopped and looked back at Yogan and Shiro.

'Well, Miss Rasiah, fancy meeting you here. I thought I recognised your family in the dining room.' He walked over to the couple on the sofa. Yogan stood up as he approached. Anthony gazed down at Yogan, pleased to note that he was a good four inches taller than the Sri Lankan. 'And this would be one of your brothers?'

'No, Mr Ashley-Cooper.' Shiro's face was a picture of innocent virtue. 'This is a family friend, Yogan Chelliah.' She turned to Yogan. 'Mr Ashley-Cooper is the superintendent in Watakälé.'

Anthony smiled down at Yogan. 'I see. You must all be very proud that Miss Rasiah is going to medical school?'

'Y-yes,' Yogan stammered.

'And yourself, Mr - eh - Mr Chelliah, do you work around here?'

'I'm an accountant in Colombo.' Yogan Chelliah visibly withered under the cold, blue gaze.

Anthony put on his best British colonial persona. 'Ah, accountants. Boring but necessary.' He flicked back his cuff to glance at his gold Omega watch. 'Well, I have to go. Running a tea plantation doesn't allow for lazy afternoons by the fire, I'm afraid. It was good to see you again, Miss Rasiah.' He turned on his heel and walked out. He heard Shiro giggle.

He didn't look back.

Chapter 23

December 1967 Watakälé

'No, I will not marry Yogan Chelliah. In fact I will not marry anyone till I finish medical school.' Shiro stood with her head thrown back, eyes flashing defiance at her mother.

'Aiyoo, by then you will be too old to find a man,' her mother wailed.

Shiro felt a deep resentment build up in her soul. 'So? Why is marriage the be all and end all of everything? I'll stay unmarried, travel, be a missionary doctor. Mum, you are so pathetic.'

She ran out of the house.

Behind her, Victor spoke to her mother. 'Let her be, Mum. She's a complex little thing. You can't force her. Someday she'll meet a man who will understand her.'

Shiro part ran, part slid down the damp path. She stood panting by the stream, shivering. It was cold and she hadn't stopped to pick up her coat. She flung her head back and scanned the familiar landscape, searching for the peace she had always been able to find in this place.

The eagle was there, roosting on a nest high on the tallest eucalyptus tree. Shiro leant back against the rock to wait for Anthony and then slid down to sit crosslegged on the rock ledge.

She thought what marriage to Yogan would be like. He had touched her when they were on the sofa. His touch had been gentle … but awful. She had hated it. She imagined his hands on her body. It made her want to throw up. She giggled, that would be a bad beginning to the honeymoon.

Thoughts of Anthony's long, slender fingers crossed her mind. His fingers on her shoulder, his hand on her hair. How wonderful it felt when he touched her. But then he was special, her best friend.

Shiro frowned at the growl of the motorbike and the screech of the brakes on the rough gravel. *That's careless. Anthony always parked his bike some distance away and walked to the stream.* They had decided that it was safer that way. It wouldn't draw attention to their meetings.

Shiro looked up as she heard footsteps. 'Anthony …?'

'Waiting for my brother are you, sweetheart?' The voice was a vicious parody of Anthony's.

Shiro leapt to her feet. 'Who are you?' Anxiety and fear raised the pitch of her voice. Even as she spoke, she knew who he was. This was Anthony's brother, William, the awful man she had seen on the platform of Diyatalāwa station.

The laugh was arrogant and dismissive. 'I could ask the same of you, my sexy little kitten. But no, I'll tell you what I think you are.' He gestured at the stream. 'You're the mermaid of the waterfall, sent to seduce hapless sex-starved men like me.'

William reached out a suntanned hand to touch her cheek. Shiro shrank back against the rock wall behind her and turned her face away.

'Stop it,' she gasped.

William moved closer and slid his fingers down her cheek. 'So you had an appointment with my little brother Anthony, did you? Maybe I could stand in for him today?' She stared back at him. His blue eyes were cesspools of dark desire. Her heart raced. She needed to get away.

William sneered. His eyes slid from her face to her breasts. Shiro gulped and grasped the top of her blouse.

He stepped closer, blocking her path. A strong smell of alcohol emanated from him. She glanced around. The tea fields were empty. There was no one to hear her if she screamed.

Suddenly, a wave of anger replaced her fear. Her father's voice echoed in her ear. 'Bastard whites think they can have any native woman.' Well, she was not just any native woman. She was Shiro Rasiah. She was no pawn and definitely not a white man's plaything.

William's right hand slid down from her cheek to her shoulder and her arm. His fingers cut into her flesh. His other hand reached for her. His fingers played with the amethyst pendant of her chain nestled on her neck, then moved lower to rest on her breasts.

Damn him and all his kind to hell. Shiro drew her hand back. She lashed forward with all her strength. Her hand slashed across Williams face. Her fingernails gauged his cheek.

He pulled back. She saw the red stripes on his face where her nails had drawn blood.

'Get your filthy hands off me,' she screamed.

'You little she-devil,' William growled. His hands held her arms tightly.

Shiro struggled. 'Don't you dare touch me you damned white bastard!' she spat.

'Fighting words, my lovely.' He pulled her to him. 'I'll show you that I'm a far better lover than my little brother.' William lowered his mouth to Shiro's.

'Take your hands off her, you idiot!' Anthony was on the path just above them, his body tense and eyes blazing. With two strides, he bridged the gap between them. He gripped William's shirt and yanked William away from Shiro. William staggered and fell, sprawling in the mud. Anthony stood between William and Shiro, hands clenched into fists by his sides, breathing in sharp gasps. Shiro stepped back against the rock.

William sprang up. 'How dare –' He stopped, looked from Anthony to Shiro, and laughed. 'Come on, little brother,' he scoffed, smoothing his rumpled shirt. 'I was just keeping your bit of fluff warm for you.' He leered at Shiro again. His face reminded her of the demon masks the local sorcerers used for witchcraft.

'What the hell are you doing here in Watakälé, William?' Anthony hissed through clenched teeth. 'Go. Get out of here before I do something we both regret.' He looked at William's scratched and bleeding face. 'Get your face seen to. It looks like you've been trying to rape someone in broad daylight. That would be disgusting, even for you.'

William hooted with laughter. 'Relax, Anthony, she's all yours. Unlike you, I don't find the natives tempting. The coolie girls are much more sexy and willing.' He looked past Anthony at Shiro. He raised a hand in a mock salute. 'But my compliments. This one's truly a delectable piece of flesh. What fire, what spirit! Let me know when you tire of playing with her.' He turned and walked away. They heard his laughter as he revved his motorbike and sped away.

Eyes on fire, Anthony turned to face Shiro. His breath was ragged, his knuckles white in clenched fists. The look in his eyes made her shiver. 'Are you okay, Shiro?' Anthony ran a finger over the bruise on her arm where William had seized her.

There was no thrill in his touch. Shiro shrunk further back against the rock. 'Don't touch me.'

'You're shivering, sweetheart.' He stripped off his light sweater and wrapped it over her shoulders.

Tears stung Shiro's eyelids and trickled down her cheeks. 'He called me your bit of fluff and said you were playing with a native. Is that what you're doing, Anthony?'

Anthony winced and shut his eyes. 'The idiot.' Then he sighed. 'Shiro, my princess, please sit down. We need to talk.'

Shiro gulped and shook her head. She stood with her back pasted to the rock. 'No. It's gone.'

'What's gone, Shiro?' Anthony reached forward and touched her arm. His touch calmed her but it was not enough. She turned her head away from him.

'The magic – this place. He's spoiled it all. See?' She flung her hand to the sky. 'Even eagle isn't here anymore.'

Anthony slid his hands down her arms. He picked up her hands and brought them to his face. He kissed her fingertips one by one. 'I'm here, sweetheart.'

'For how long, Anthony?' She dragged her hands away. 'Till you're bored with being a best friend to me? Get tired of playing with the natives? Till you get me into your bed? The Englishman and the Sri Lankan native girl. This is all just a game for you, isn't it Anthony?' Tears flowed down her cheeks, unchecked.

'Princess, no.'

Ripping off his sweater, she flung it at his feet.

'Just go back home, you … you British bastard!'

Chapter 24

December 1967 Watakälé

Shiro kept her hands anchored in the pockets of her purple skirt as she strode along the gravel path. The wind swirled around her, blowing her hair around her face. Diamonds of water glistened in the curls.

Anthony rode his bike by her side, keeping pace with her. The mist rose from the valley, reached damp fingers between them. 'Talk to me, Shiro. Please.'

She shook her head. 'Why?'

'Because I care.'

She twisted round to face him. Fury and pain warred in the depths of her eyes. 'Care?' She tossed her head and laughed. It was a sound of sorrow and anger that sent spears of anguish through Anthony. 'How could you care? You are white – British. You pretended to be my friend. But of course we can't be friends, can we?' Her voice rose in pitch, took on a twinge of hysteria. 'Just like Janet and Sarah couldn't be friends to me. The wonderful white Raj, rulers of the empire, the lords of the plantation and us – the stupid, untouchable natives! The conquerors and the conquered.'

'Shiro, sweetheart, please.'

'No. Every time I think of you, I feel a deep burning pain here.' She pushed her clenched fist to her chest over her heart. 'Leave me alone.'

'No Shiro. Please. It isn't like that for us. We need –'

A spear of lightning rent the lowering sky. Thunder drowned his words and a curtain of icy rain dropped from the clouds. Shiro spun round and dashed off the road into the weighing shed. Anthony left his motorbike in the rain and followed her. They stood panting, looking at each other in the half-light of the musty room. A flash of lightning illuminated Shiro's face. She flinched, closed her eyes and bit her trembling lower lip.

Anthony moved closer to her. He whispered her name. 'Shiro.'

Her voice caught in a sob. 'I wish I had never met you. I would have gone to medical school, married some stupid Tamil boy of my mother's choosing. But you've spoiled it all. Now I don't know who I am.'

Anthony was lost. He groaned and drew her into his arms. Stabs of longing lanced through his body.

How could loving this glorious girl be wrong?

He caught her chin and turned her face up to his. She gazed at him, her eyes wide with wonder, longing and a dawning awareness.

'Shiro, sweetheart, the feeling you have here,' he placed his hand over her heart, thrilling at her sharp intake of breath, 'what you feel for me is not hate, Shiro.'

Shiro's lips trembled. 'I've never felt this way. I don't like it.'

'Let me show you what it is, my love,' Anthony whispered, a breath away from her mouth.

Her lips were soft and yielded to his. When his tongue touched her mouth, she parted her lips for him. He thrilled to the taste of her, the soft sweetness of her tongue on his. The drum beat of the rain on the tin roof of the weighing shed echoed the mad rhythm of his heart.

Shiro's arms reached around his neck. She clung to him. Opening the top button of his shirt, she let her hand drift over his chest, exploring the contours of his body. Little whining sounds came from her throat.

Anthony groaned. With a little mew, she curved her body against him. His kisses deepened, demanding a response, drawing her essence, her soul into his keeping.

Surely this was love. Not the mild everyday affection punctuated by angry outbursts that seemed to keep his parents together, but a love that coloured life with an almost unbearable intensity – part wonder, part fear and pain.

'I love you, Shiro. I love you more than life itself. I want you with me forever.' He covered her face with kisses.

She nuzzled closer to him, her cheek warm on his bare chest. 'Love, Anthony? How is that possible? There can't be a forever for us.' She raised her face. 'Can there?'

The words brought Anthony crashing back down to reality. Her black eyes were clouded with desire and her lips swollen with his kisses. Her hair tangled on her shoulders. He caressed her face, feeling the warmth, the soft pliant acceptance of his touch. Then he kissed her again, storing up the feel and taste of her.

He did not want to let her go, not now, not ever. She was everything to him.

He held her tight, stroking her back. 'Shiro, I need to go now, darling. I have to see to some things – important things. Come to our place tomorrow evening sweetheart. We will be together, Shiro. I love you.'

Her eyes glowed with joy and trust. Reaching up, she kissed him on the cheek. 'I love you too, Anthony.'

He watched her leave the weighing shed and walk towards the Tea-maker's house. He would never let her out of his life. They would find a way to be together.

This had to be his destiny.

Chapter 25

Anthony rode up the path to the bungalow. He needed Shiro. He had been crazy to not acknowledge it earlier. He would call Bob, tell him about her. Get his advice. He would do whatever he had to do. He could not, would not, let her out of his life.

The sight of the Oriental Produce crested white Rolls Royce parked outside the bungalow sent a ripple of anxiety through Anthony. It meant a stopover by the visiting agent from London or a member of the family. No local used that car.

A visit without warning signified an emergency of some sort.

Anthony jumped off the motorcycle. He ran up the steps to the veranda and froze.

His father sat at the carved metal table. A plate of sandwiches and a tray with scones, cream and jam lay before him. Appu stood by his father's side, his eyes fixed on the floor.

James Ashley-Cooper stirred milk into his cup of tea and then looked up at Anthony.

Anthony stood on the top step. He was soaking wet, his shirt still unbuttoned. He pulled his shirt together and shook the water from his hair.

'Been working in the field, Anthony? Isn't it a little late in the day to be supervising the plucking? Or were you otherwise occupied?'

Anger replaced anxiety at the sarcasm in his father's voice. 'Father, I didn't know you were coming over. When did you get in?'

'I landed this morning.'

'Is something the matter?'

James Ashley-Cooper remained seated. Grey eyes locked with blue. As always, Anthony's gaze dropped first.

'Go get yourself changed before you catch pneumonia. I'll wait for you in the study.'

'Father?'

'Go!'

Anthony capitulated, as always. He walked towards his bedroom. Appu's mouth and throat worked soundlessly as Anthony walked past. He turned to follow Anthony into the house.

'Appu, I will see you in the study now.' James Ashley-Cooper's tone brooked no argument.

Appu looked at Anthony.

Anthony nodded. 'Do as he says, Appu.'

***

James Ashley-Cooper sat in the leather padded mahogany armchair at the office table. He had changed from his travel clothes. The crisp blue wool suit and silk shirt he now had on were unwrinkled. The overhead light glinted on his polished black leather shoes and shimmered off the whisky and ice in his hand.

His father was dressed for confrontation. Anthony recognised it and accepted the challenge. He stood across the table from his father, dressed in woollen trousers and a polo neck white wool jumper, his hair damp.

His father gestured to the drinks trolley. 'Fix yourself a drink, Anthony. You'll need a stiff one.'

'Thank you. No.' *What the hell was this about?*

His father gestured to the chair opposite. 'Sit,' he ordered.

'Father, whatever is the matter?' Anthony lowered himself into the chair opposite his father.

'Anthony, I am not one to beat about the bush. You, more than anyone else know that.' His father leaned forward and tented his hands on the edge of the desk. His lips compressed. His eyes glinted grey flint. 'I am here because of reports of your behaviour on the plantation.'

'My behaviour? What the hell are you talking about? I had the best tea prices for you at the auctions. The visiting agent himself told me that he has never had such glowing reports from the staff in Watakälé –'

His father's imperious voice cut him short. 'Your personal behaviour.'

Anthony leapt to his feet. 'My personal –'

His father rocked back. 'Yes. You raped a coolie girl and now you are sleeping with the Tea-maker's daughter. Less than three years in the superintendent's job. That is unacceptable and you know it.'

Anthony gasped. His breath caught in his throat. He stared at his father.

'Father, I don't know where you get your information. You are wrong. William raped a coolie girl last Easter. I had nothing to do with it. You can ask Appu –'

'Appu,' his father responded with a dismissive wave of his hand, 'is loyal to a fault to the superintendent he is working for. I know that all too well.'

'Ask the Tea-maker Mr Rasiah and his wife, then. They were there at the staff party.'

'This is your estate, Anthony. The girl told the apothecary that the superintendent raped her. And as for the Tea-maker, you are sleeping with his daughter. I don't know what arrangement you have with him, but of course he would lie for you.'

Anthony felt the walls close in. He gritted his teeth. He didn't care what his father said about him. He would not draw Shiro into this. 'Shiro Rasiah and I are friends. She is a child, Father. Just seventeen. I am not sure where you got your information from but I am not, as you so delicately put it, sleeping with her.'

His father got to his feet. They stared at each other across the table.

'So, this Shiro Rasiah is a child. So was the coolie you raped. So you have a penchant for young native women. You wouldn't be the first.'

The bitterness of years spilled out of Anthony's soul. He smashed his hand on the desk. The glass of whisky toppled and rolled off to shatter on the ground. 'It's William, isn't it? My God, Father, you know he's lying. I caught him trying to force his attention on Shiro and stopped him. I should have known he would run to you.'

'He called me, true. However, I checked with the apothecary. I also called the assistant Tea-maker, Mr Wright. He didn't know the details but reported gossip from the coolies that there was a girl who was raped by you and was helped by the Rasiahs. Sent away, he said. I hope she isn't pregnant by you.'

Anthony reeled back. He hadn't even thought of the possibility of a pregnancy!

He looked into his father's eyes. 'Damn it, Father, surely you know that I wouldn't act this way. It's William –'

His father's grey eyes hooded over. 'Your mother is distraught. She insisted I come over and prevent *you* making the biggest mistake of your life.'

'Mother sent you?' He remembered her words – *the plantations charmed your father; take care that it doesn't happen to you.*

His father dropped back into the chair. He shut his eyes. Seconds passed. His father shuddered and re-opened them. Anthony gazed into grey pools of deep sorrow.

'Your mother and I discussed it. We both feel it would be better for you to get out of here before it's too late. We want you to take over the British arm of the company. Leave William to run the plantation for whatever years are left. You are not suited to this life.'

It was as if he had been dealt a physical blow. Anthony staggered back. 'You're sacking me from my post as superintendent of Watakälé?'

A band of fear and anger constricted his heart. He couldn't breathe. He glanced at Appu standing by the door. Appu turned and hurried away but not before Anthony saw the tears streaming down his face.

Anthony stared at his father. 'You can't do that. I have made progress here. The silver tip tea at the London auctions, the staff provident fund for retirement, fresh water to the line rooms. The health care plan for the coolies ...'

'Anthony, I accept that the silver tip was a coup. But all the other things you are doing cost good money. We can't afford to do this. Not now, when the stupid natives are set to nationalise the plantations. We don't have the time for such frivolities.'

'Father, you're a millionaire, a billionaire more likely. You made it on the backs of these people. The least you can do is put some back before –'

'Before we are thrown out by the stupid Sri Lankan government,' his father interjected. 'You are a naïve idiot, Anthony. We're here to make money, not spend it on grandiose feel-good schemes. William understands that.'

Anthony collapsed into the chair. 'It's not about rape and sexual liaisons at all. Is it, father? It's an excuse to get me out. To give William a free hand in Watakälé to do what he's done in Udatänná. Rape the entire bloody plantation but keep the Ashley-Cooper coffers filled with blood gold.'

'You are wrong, Anthony. Your mother is concerned about you. I am too. You may not believe it now, but we only want the best for you. Look at you! You're acting like a raving lunatic. Your mother was right. You don't have the temperament for this job.'

Anthony got to his feet and walked to the window. He stared out into the dusk. His estate, his people, his soul mate; he felt it all slipping through his fingers. He was helpless against his father's will.

Had he truly thought he could do it? Bitterness laced through him. He turned to face his father.

'And what does Mother think? That I'll end up like you? With an Indian sex slave in the house? Ashley-Cooper bastards roaming the plantations?'

His father leapt to his feet and strode round the table. Anthony flinched but didn't move.

His father grasped Anthony's shirt and stared into his eyes. His words were slow and calculated. 'What I did is none of your business, Anthony. Yes, there are things I did that I now regret. And I will do whatever I need to stop *you* making the same stupid mistakes. And since *you* brought up the past – I meet my responsibilities.'

Anthony ripped himself out of his father's grasp. 'I will not leave Watakälé.'

His father placed a pad with the Ashley-Cooper crest and a monogrammed pen on the table. He drew up the chair. 'Sit. Write to the Tea-maker's daughter. Tell her you will not see her again. I will inform the staff that you are leaving.'

Anthony looked at the paper

It was over. He had lost.

'No. I will tell her and the staff personally.'

For three years, here on the plantation, Anthony had believed that he could make a difference. Do something meaningful. Now it was finished. Not just finished, in his brother's care all would undone. Anger, bitterness, disappointment spiralled through him, but nothing compared with the pain that tore his heart apart. He was losing Shiro. His love – his life.

His father placed a firm hand on his shoulder. 'Pull yourself together, son. You're an Ashley-Cooper. You will make a life for yourself away from this place.'

Anthony looked up at his father. James Ashley-Cooper's eyes shadowed with memories. 'You are *my son*. I need to protect you.'

'An Ashley-Cooper?' Anthony laughed. 'Forgive me for not feeling too proud of my heritage right now.'

James Ashley-Cooper withdrew his hand from Anthony's shoulder. He turned away. 'Someday you'll understand. I'm driving over to Udatänná. I need to talk to William. You have three days to finish up here. I have tickets booked for us back to London.'

James Ashley-Cooper walked out of the house and climbed into the car.

Anthony stood watching. Three days to say goodbye. A day for every year he had spent on Watakälé.

Chapter 26

December 1967 Watakälé

Shiro flew down the path and threw herself into his arms. Anthony held her. Bitterness and fear clouded the glory of her in his arms.

'Anthony,' Shiro twisted her arms around his neck and slid them into his hair.

He moved his lips over her face, her neck. She was so radiant, so happy. He brought his lips back to hers. His kiss was a desperate communication of despair.

Shiro kissed him back. He held her close, his lips on her forehead. The tears he couldn't control slid down his cheeks.

He felt her body tense and grow still in his arms.

'Anthony, what's wrong? You're different. What has happened?'

She was the one precious thing in his life and he was about to break her heart. He was helpless to do anything about it. 'I love you so much, Shiro. Please my darling, my love. Always remember that you are the most special and important thing that has ever happened to me. Nothing will change how I feel about you. You will always be a part of me – always. You will be in my heart. No, you are my heart.'

Shiro drew away from him. Her eyes clouded dark with fear and foreboding. 'But –'

He pulled her back into his arms. What he was about to say would destroy her happiness. He could not look into her eyes when he told her. 'We can't marry. Princess, it would never work between us.' Every word felt like a bullet to his heart. How must it feel to her?

She stiffened and pulled away. 'You said you loved me!'

His soul turned to ice. How could he explain it to her?

'Shiro, I love you so much. But we can't be together, sweetheart. You remember how you asked me what it was like to be a superintendent.' She stood staring at him, still as a statue. 'Well, I've got to maintain – certain expectations.'

Shiro nodded. 'Like not marrying a native.' She closed her eyes and stepped back.

'It's not just about me!' Anthony reached out and turned her face up, his eyes pleading. 'No one would respect you, either. We'd both be laughed at. And our children. They'll be half caste mongrels.'

'You think I care about any of this? All this time and this is all you know of me?' Tears clung to her lashes. 'It's your father, isn't it? Appu told my dad this morning that your father was here.'

'Shiro, my love.' He reached out to touch her but she drew further away. His hand fell to his side. 'You don't understand, sweetheart. If it were just about here – the plantation – I wouldn't care either. But there's my family, too. I'm only here as long as my father's happy with me. Sweetheart, you grew up here. You know that. If I married a native, he'd sack me and disinherit me. He warned me. We'd be penniless!'

'Your father! The rich and famous owner of tea plantations in Sri Lanka and Africa. You're frightened of him, aren't you? That's all our love means to you.' She bowed her head. He could tell she was biting her lips to keep from crying.

'But what about your life? Your career?' He stopped, shocked by the look of despair on her face. 'You're about to go to medical school and be a doctor. You said you wanted to go to Africa or Australia. You can help hundreds of needy people – thousands of them. I cannot – I will not – take that away from you.'

'Anthony, of course I want to go to medical school. But I want to be with you. You know that Anthony. Please. You can't do this.'

She stood before him shivering. Her eyes were pools of misery. 'Please, let me be with you.'

He had to tell her the truth. She deserved to hear it from him. He took her hands. Her fingers curled and clung to his. 'My father has heard about us. He has removed me from my position as superintendent of Watakälé. I have to leave for London in three days.'

Shiro's eyes grew wide with horror. 'He sacked you? Because of us being friends? What kind of a man is he?'

He raised her fingers to his lips. 'No, Shiro. It's an excuse. He doesn't approve of what I'm doing in the plantation.'

'But my father said that you were the first superintendent to care about the staff and the coolies. How can that be wrong?'

The rage in his heart spilled over. He squeezed her hands. 'It's wrong in the British overlord's books, Shiro. I know I should be angry about it all. But all I care about now is you.'

Her body grew stiff and her hands were cold in his. She was drifting away from him and he could do nothing.

'It's finished, isn't it?' She pulled her hands out of his grasp and turned away. Her voice was barely a whisper. Anthony strained to hear her words. 'You, your father, your brother – you're all the same, aren't you? You use us natives and coolies then spit us out when you're done.'

He stepped close, held her shaking shoulders. 'No, Shiro. You know I'd never intentionally do anything to hurt you. I love you.' He felt the shuddering sobs rend her body.

She quietened. 'Where is your father?'

'He's at Udatänná. He'll be back in three days, in time to drive to Colombo.'

She turned to face him. Her eyes were coal black orbs of pain and determination. 'Anthony, this morning my parents asked me for a decision on the Chelliah marriage proposal. I asked for time, till tomorrow.' She laughed. It was a mirthless, hollow sound. 'I believed I would have news. We would have something to tell them. Stupid, stupid me.'

'Shiro. What have I done to you?'

'I'll tell you what you have done to me, Anthony. You've made me grow up. Change from a naïve, trusting child into a woman. I guess I should thank you for that.' She stared at him. 'Now I have one last favour to ask. Give me this and I promise I will never ever ask anything of you again.'

'What do you want of me?'

'I will accept the marriage proposal, go to medical school, do all these things, but I want you to make love to me.'

Anthony reeled back, stunned. 'You want me to make love to you?'

Shiro nodded. 'Yes.' She moved close to him. He could smell her. Reaching out, she placed her hand on his chest, over his heart. She opened two buttons of his shirt. 'You say you love me. And you are going away.' Her eyes bored into his. 'I want you to be the first. Let's not talk of marriage or forever. I want to be with you. Once, just once. After that, I'll accept the marriage proposal. Get on with my life.'

He pulled her close, dropped his face into her hair.

'Anthony,' she whispered into his chest, 'Make love to me.'

What would it matter? He would hold her, make her his. They would both have a memory to last a lifetime.

He took a deep, ragged breath. She stiffened in his arms. This would be the hardest thing he would ever do in his life.

'Go home, sweetheart,' he said. 'Go back to your life. This time of our friendship – our love – it's a dream, Shiro. A fantasy.' A shudder went through her body. He pulled her closer. 'I can't do it, princess. You will regret it later. And you will hate me for doing it. Please, please forgive me, forget me and move on with your life.'

She clung to him. Her fingers bit into his shoulders. 'Forgive you? Forget?' she rasped. 'I asked you for one thing, one small act of love from you to make life worth living. You won't give me even that. I can't go on like this. I won't.'

He enfolded her in his arms and held her. There was nothing left to say.

She pulled away and walked to the edge of the path, then turned to stare at him. Anthony recoiled at the expression in her eyes.

'You will be sorry, Anthony.' She turned and scrambled up the hill.

Anthony looked up. The eagle rose from his nest and circled above him.

Chapter 27

The wind whistled around the Tea-maker's house and rattled the window. It was five-thirty, far too early in the morning for anyone else to be up.

Shiro sat up in bed.

Are you awake, Anthony? Are you thinking of me? Well, soon you will know what your betrayal has done to me.

Shiro pushed back her purple blanket. She had no further use for it. She glanced at the corner of her room where the mat on which Lakshmi used to sleep still stood, rolled up and gathering dust. *My friend, you would have understood the pain in my heart.*

Never mind. It's over.

She had to hurry. Raaken would be up by six to fix breakfast. By then it would be too late for them to do anything. She would be gone.

Shiro tiptoed past her parents' room. Stopping for a moment, she looked through the open door. Her mother lay on her side. Her breathing regular. Her father was on his back, snoring.

'I am so sorry' she whispered.

She stood staring at her parents' sleeping forms. *I am truly sad to do this to you but I can't go on. The whole thing is too much.*

In the dark she stubbed her toe on the edge of the stove, causing a slight clattering sound. The cat sleeping in the ash under the stove mewed.

'Shush.' She bent to pat its head.

The pesticide bottle was on a waist-high shelf in the corner of the kitchen, alongside mops and cleaning fluids. She picked it up. The lid was screwed on tightly. She managed to get it open and raised the bottle to her mouth.

She felt the sting of the fluid on her lips. She swallowed. The first drops burnt her throat.

The cat meowed.

The kitchen light flashed on.

Raaken shrieked.

He dashed the bottle out of her hands. 'Aiyoo Chinnamma,' he screamed.

The bottle flew across the kitchen and shattered against the wall. Pesticide dripped down the wall and onto the floor.

The cat squealed and shot out into the garden.

Raaken, who had never touched Shiro in her life, held her in a tight grip as she struggled to get free. 'Periamma! Aiya!' he yelled.

Lights came on all over the house. Her parents came running into the kitchen.

Shiro howled. She had no words. Just demon cries from the hell her soul inhabited.

Raaken let go of her. Shiro sank to the floor. The pieces of glass from the broken bottle pierced her bare legs. The pesticide soaked her purple nightdress.

As in a dream, she heard her mother sob, 'Mahal, mahal.'

With the help of Raaken, her parents coaxed and dragged her to bed.

She had no energy to fight them. She had failed. The family would rally around her again. They would protect her as they always did. She would have to live – and face life – without him. She lay curled in bed. The tears refused to come.

Her mother came in with a foul tasting mixture. 'Drink this, darling.'

The drink made Shiro violently ill. She retched into the bowl her mother held.

'Mahal, Shiro, why? Why did you do it?' her mother sobbed.

Shiro lay shivering in bed. *Let me die*, she wanted to shout to them all. *Can't you see that I can't live without him?*

The rain eased and the sun struggled through the curtains of her bedroom window. The apothecary came and sat beside her. She obediently put her tongue out and moved her eyes and head as instructed.

She had known the apothecary since she was a little girl. He stroked her hair. 'Shiromi,' he said. 'Do you want to talk about anything?'

She shook her head. What was there to say?

She heard the mumbled conversation outside her door. 'Depression. Colombo – immediately.'

Soon after, she heard a car drive up. Victor came running into the room and sat on her bed. He took her hands in his. 'Shiro darling, talk to me.'

Talk, talk, they all wanted her to talk. How stupid. She had nothing to say.

Shiro realised she hadn't spoken a word since waking up.

The thunder and rain echoed the turmoil in Anthony's heart as he rode down to the tea factory that morning. He had been awake all night listening to the rain on the roof and thinking of the dark future he faced without her.

He longed to turn into the Tea-maker's house, to take Shiro in his arms and tell her he was wrong to send her away, that together they could face the world. Nothing mattered more than their love.

No, he could not. He would not do that to her.

He would go back to England. She would go to medical school, be a doctor. Be free to travel the world and fulfil her dreams. She was young. She would meet someone else. Learn to love again. He tortured himself with the thought.

Today he would tell Mr Rasiah that he was leaving, that all their plans for the betterment of staff and coolies were finished, crushed by the word of the mighty British Raj, his father, James Ashley-Cooper.

Anthony saw the apothecary's motorcycle and Victor's car parked in the drive of the Tea-maker's house. A chill of fear raced through his body and centred in his heart. He heard her voice in his ear: 'I can't go on like this –' He rode faster down to the factory, struggling to keep the motorcycle upright on the road slippery with mud after the rain.

Anthony pulled into the factory driveway. Through the office window, he saw Mr Rasiah pacing up and down. Anthony leapt off his motorcycle and walked into the office.

The usually impeccable Mr Rasiah was dishevelled. He looked like he had not washed his face or combed his hair. Even the buttons on his shirt were on wrong.

'Mr Rasiah, is something the matter?' Anthony asked. His heart cried out, *please tell me she's all right.*

Mr Rasiah wheeled round to face him. 'Mr Ashley-Cooper, I need to leave immediately for Colombo. I don't know when I'll be back.'

'What's the matter, Mr Rasiah?' Anthony took a deep breath. 'Can I help at all?'

The Tea-maker's face and shoulders sagged. 'Mr Ashley-Cooper, you're a good man. I wouldn't normally share this with anyone outside the family, but I trust you. It's my daughter, Shiromi. She tried to kill herself.'

Anthony's chest constricted. Mr Rasiah was looking down and didn't notice the fear and horror on Anthony's face.

'She tried to drink pesticide. The cook, Raaken, stopped her just in time. But the apothecary says she's depressed and needs specialist treatment in Colombo.'

Anthony turned away from him and looked out at the clearing sky. He breathed deeply, trying to focus on the moment, not on the memory of her face and her tears.

'Do you know what caused it?'

'No, she won't talk to us. She hasn't said a thing since it happened early this morning. That's why we need to get her to Colombo as soon as possible.'

Anthony stayed silent. *I caused it*, he wanted to scream back. *She loved me. I tried to do what is right and I nearly killed her in the process. So, Mr Rasiah, what do you think of your trustworthy, good-man superintendent now, eh?*

Anthony turned. 'You can have the leave, of course. Take as long as you need.' Reaching in his pocket, he took out his cheque book. He wrote out a cheque for fifty thousand rupees, tore it out and handed it to Mr Rasiah. 'Consider this an early bonus payment for your work this year. Psychiatric treatment is expensive. Please get her the very best.'

The Tea-maker looked at the cheque and then raised his face to Anthony. The gratitude in the eyes of the usually proud man wrung at Anthony's heart.

He held the cheque in both hands. 'This is an answer to prayer, sir. Thank you.'

'God go with you, Mr Rasiah.'

Anthony watched Mr Rasiah jog up the path to the Tea-maker's house.

It was the first time in their acquaintance that the Tea-maker had addressed Anthony as sir.

Chapter 28

Two years later ... March 1969 Nuwara-Eliya

Lakshmi stood before the matron of the Salvation Army children's home. Tears streaming down her cheeks, her body trembling with horror at what matron had just said.

'Aiyoo, amma. How can you just give him away like that? I am his mother. You know that I am saving money. I was going to get a proper job in Diyatalāwa and get a house. Aiyoo, my baby!'

The matron clasped Lakshmi's shoulders. 'Lakshmi, you signed the papers for adoption a week after you gave birth to Daniel. What happened to you is too common a story. But we could see even then how hard it was for you. Most girls don't even want to see the baby. You loved him. That is why we let you come to see him. But you would never have been able to care for him.'

Lakshmi dropped to the floor and cradled her face in her hands. 'Amma, I am earning. I am saving money. I work on my off day also.' She sat curled on the floor. The horror of rape, the shafting pain of rejection by the Rasiah's, these were nothing to the searing devastation of the loss of her child. What reason was there for her to live?

Matron squatted by her. 'Lakshmi, you are thinking of yourself, not of your son. What sort of life can you give him? A small shack in Diyatalāwa? Scraps of food you bring home from the Hemachandra house? And how will you continue working with a child in the house?' She stroked Lakshmi's head. 'Your son will be well looked after. The person who adopted him will give Daniel a good home and the very best education.'

'No,' Lakshmi wailed. 'Aiyoo. Tell me where he is. I will go and get him back.'

The rhythmic pressure of the matron's hand on her hair did nothing to calm the storm of agony in Lakshmi's soul. Yet even as she struggled, she knew the inevitability of what had happened. And she realised that it was best for her

160

son. He was only two years old. He would forget. She never would. She had taught him to call her amma. Matron hadn't been happy about that. Now he would have someone else as his mother. Her beautiful boy, conceived in pain and sorrow. His skin and hair all gleaming gold, his eyes the blue of a clear sky. Her tears were for her as much as for Daniel.

A thought flashed through her mind. Surely matron would not have given Daniel to that man? His … she couldn't even think the word. Daniel's father?

'Amma,' Lakshmi grabbed matron's hands. 'Amma, you didn't give Daniel to that man, Udatännä Periadorai – William Ashley-Cooper?'

Matron smiled. It was a tired smile, one that conveyed the emotions of having experienced great sadness. 'Lakshmi, the Rasiahs tell me that Udatännä Periadorai doesn't even know that there was a child from that day. No, we didn't give Daniel to him.'

'Then who, amma?'

'No. We can't tell you that, Lakshmi. It was part of the contract that you signed. The only way we will reveal your relationship to him is if Daniel himself comes to us. That will be when he is grown up.'

'I will never see him again?'

Matron got to her feet and drew Lakshmi up to stand with her. She led her to a bench. 'Lakshmi,' matron drew her down on the bench and put her arm around her, 'go back to the Hemachandra house. They are good people.' She looked into Lakshmi's eyes. 'Give up the other thing you do.'

Lakshmi drew back from matron's embrace. How could this be? How did she know? 'Amma,' she stammered. 'I don't know what you mean.'

'You work as Devi. I found out from another girl who saw you here with Daniel. She too, used to work with Malar. Got too old and no one wanted her. So she works here now. But she visits Malar in Diyatalāwa. She told me you work as Devi.' Matron looked Lakshmi up and down. 'That you are popular because you are clean and pretty and also because you speak English.'

Lakshmi stared away from matron. There was a spider's web on the ceiling. A fly flew into the web. She watched as the spider approached the fly. She couldn't tear her eyes away.

Matron turned her face back. 'Lakshmi, Hemachandra Mudalali and Hamine are good people but they will not like it if they know about Devi.'

Lakshmi nodded. 'They will throw me out.'

Matron nodded. 'Stay with them. I know them. They will look after you.'

'And my son, Daniel?'

'You will never see Daniel again.'

She was back on the floor of Shiro's bedroom. It was Rasiah Periamma who was speaking. 'You will never see Shiro …'

Lakshmi howled. 'Never see … Never see …' she screamed in English.

A couple of other Salvation Army women, dressed in the traditional dark blue sari and white high neck blouse with the red and gold 'S', came rushing down the corridor. Together with matron they bundled Lakshmi into the office. One of them pushed a glass of water and a white tablet into her hand. 'Here, swallow this,' she instructed.

Lakshmi obeyed. What else was there to do? She would go back to Hemachandra Mudalali's. Do her daily work.

Lakshmi walked to the bus stop. This would be the last time she would come this way.

No more Devi. Devi was dead.

It felt like she was dead too.

What purpose was there for living?

Chapter 29

Melinda Kirkland's tiny white fingers clutched 2-year-old Daniel's olive brown ones. Together they tottered across the lawn of the manse. Daniel let go of the little hand nestled in his and continued his unsteady gait towards his adopted father. Melinda wobbled and plonked her nappy clad bottom on the wet grass of the lawn. Her tiny rosebud lips turned down and her brown eyes filled with tears. Grace Kirkland laughed and scooped up her daughter. She walked to the veranda and handed Melinda to the nanny.

'That was most unchivalrous behaviour, my son. I need to teach you how to treat a woman.' Anthony put the tea cup down on the wrought iron table and picked up Daniel. The little boy nestled into his lap.

Bob Kirkland cradled a mug of hot milky tea in the palms of his hands. His eyes met and held Anthony's.

Grace walked over to join them. 'I'll take Daniel,' She eased him off Anthony's lap. 'You boys can catch up. Take your time.'

The men watched Grace till she entered the manse.

'So,' Bob's expression conveyed a mix of compassion and impatient curiosity. 'You're away for two years. We hardly hear from you except for an occasional card. Now you turn up with an adopted son. What's the story? And as Grace said, take your time.'

Anthony took a deep breath. 'Okay, the beginning. Two years ago I obeyed my father's orders. Two years, he said, when I went back. Two years with the company in London. I sat in the plush leather chair of the Mayfair offices of Oriental Produce reading the reports from the plantations, seeing the increasing profit margins, knowing that the blood and tears of the coolies and natives were filling the Ashley-Cooper coffers.' He shook his head. 'Every page reminded me of what I had done. I betrayed them. I said I would help. Then I ran away to do my father's behest. I'm a Judas.'

Bob put his mug down on the table. He reached out and curled his fingers on Anthony's arm. This was how they had been when they shared their dreams as boys, sitting together by the river Wye in Bakewell. Bob tightened his grip, conveying unspoken love and friendship. Their friendship had lasted from childhood though university and adult life.

Anthony shut his eyes and then blinked to hold back the tears. He hadn't cried once since he left Watakälé. But here with Bob and Grace, he felt the wall he had built around his heart crumble. He looked over the lush green tea bushes and swallowed the tears.

'Every morning I would wake up in my Knightsbridge flat and feel the lifeblood seep out of my heart. I would go through the motions of living, go home to the manor for weekends. Father and mother would be overly caring, protective. Dad would come fishing and riding with me. But it all felt unnatural, forced. Finally, I confronted them both. I think they too realised that I had hit rock bottom. Life in England was not for me. The truth – I insisted on the truth. I told them of the rumours I had heard on Watakälé, the innuendos of impropriety. I believed, stupidly, that I was strong enough for anything they would tell me.'

Bob's fingers tightened on Anthony's arm. 'Your father came to see me after he ordered you home. He knew the coolie girl was pregnant. I don't know who told him, maybe Appu. He was upset, I would say even terrified. I explained clearly to your father that it was William not you who did it. I telephoned the doctor here who diagnosed and looked after Lakshmi's pregnancy. He spoke to your father. He confirmed that Lakshmi had identified Udatänná Periadorai as the man who raped her. Your father was visibly relieved. Your father loves you very much, Anthony.'

'Why didn't you tell me about the pregnancy when I came to say goodbye to you?'

Bob shook his head. 'I couldn't, Anthony. The Tea-maker Mr Rasiah and his wife, Lilly, asked me to keep it confidential. They couldn't be seen to be helping her. It would have seemed like he or one of his sons were responsible. I arranged for the Salvation Army home to take her in. After the baby was born, Mr Rasiah arranged employment for her. Even I don't know where she is now.'

Anthony dropped his head and splayed his fingers over his eyes. 'Father went to the Salvation Army home after he talked to you. He saw the coolie girl, Lakshmi. She was doing some sewing. She had looked up and their eyes had met briefly. That was when he knew.'

Bob kept his fingers on Anthony's arm. 'Knew?'

Anthony's voice dropped to a tortured whisper. Bob leaned forward.

'He said he knew by her eyes. He had seen her as a baby. Her father, Raman, brought her to him. The coolie demanded money to claim the child as his. Father gave it to him. I have seen Lakshmi but I didn't pick the Ashley-Cooper slate grey eyes.'

Bob was silent. Moments passed. 'Anthony, I know.' His voice gentled. 'It's common knowledge in Watakälé. Ramen offered his wife to your father. It was after your mother left for England. It's a ruse the coolies use to get money from the superintendent.'

'What else do you know, Bob? That my father came to the plantation as a young man and kept a coolie girl in the house? How he got her pregnant and then married Mum – his English rose. How he paid for the education of the Indian woman's son – even his postgraduate medical training? I'm sorry, Bob, but I consider that behaviour totally reprehensible. Unforgivable.'

Bob smiled. 'You're forgiven by God and therefore you too, can forgive Anthony.'

'He made mother's life miserable.' A shudder ripped through Anthony's body.

Bob placed his other hand on Anthony's head. It calmed him. 'So there's more?'

'Once the cupboard was open, the skeletons were jostling each other to leap out. I insisted that father tell me why he was so relieved that it was William and not me who impregnated Lakshmi.'

'And he said it was because William was not his son.'

Anthony didn't try to control his tears. 'You knew that too?'

'I work in the church, Anthony. People tell me things. Apparently your father was furious when your mother threw his Indian mistress out of the house. He ignored your mother – acting as if she wasn't there. Set up the woman in a house in Diyataläwa and went to her whenever he wanted to. There was Roger Hands, a trainee planter; a creeper. He was just eighteen. He was lonely and so was your mother. It's a sad story. She got pregnant. Your father banished her to England. Where –'

Anthony finished his sentence. 'Where she had William.'

'It doesn't make the rape okay but at least Daniel is not the child of incest.'

'Suddenly it all made sense, Bob. The way he treated William, encouraging him to be ruthless, selfish and greedy. Laughing at William's affairs with the local girls. He started giving William whisky when he was just fourteen. I resented the attention he gave William. It's only now that I understand what he did and why.'

'Did your mother never object?'

Anthony's laugh was bitter. 'Oh, she tried. I remember her begging him to discipline William, to teach him some boundaries. Father's reply was that he would mould William to be an Ashley-Cooper. He always laughed when he said it.'

'What was the tipping point, Anthony? What made you decide to make the break? Leave England and adopt your nephew, Daniel?'

'Bob, when I left two years ago, you encouraged me and tried to help me see that something positive could come out of anything. And that God cared about my situation.'

'Yes, I remember how angry you were. '

Anthony gazed over the tea bushes. His eyes cleared. He looked back at Bob. 'I sat across from father and mother in the morning room of the manor. Dad outlined his plans for the future of Oriental Produce. I thought of your words. Maybe, just maybe, God is with me in planning my future.' Anthony stopped.

'And what would that future be, Anthony?'

'Oriental Produce is pulling out of the tea plantations in Sri Lanka.' Anthony got up and paced up and down the lawn.

'I had heard rumours about it. How does that affect you?'

Anthony stopped pacing and looked down at Bob. 'I saw in my father's eyes the spark of business brilliance that made the Ashley-Cooper Empire what it is today. And listening to him, I too, felt the stirring of excitement.'

'Hey, don't keep me in suspense!'

Anthony smiled. 'We are diversifying. Going into wine production.'

Bob gasped. 'Surely not replanting tea bushes here?'

Anthony's smile widened. 'This is where it gets interesting. Not in Sri Lanka. The company's looking at vineyards in South Australia.'

'Wow. And where do you come into it?'

Anthony's voice took on a hint of irony. 'Me? For the first time in my life, my father asked me, not ordered me! He *suggested* that I may be interested in taking over the project in South Australia.'

Bob pushed out of his chair. He stood in front of Anthony and placed both hands on his shoulders. 'Tea producer to wine maker?'

'The term is Vigneron, Bob. The company is close to finalising a deal in the Barossa Valley area of South Australia. The estate has a couple of olive groves thrown in for good measure.'

'Wouldn't you need time to learn the art of being a winemaker or whatever it's called?'

'Remember Damian McNaughton?'

Bob nodded, 'The guy with the brains for big business.'

'Yes. His family owns a large wine export company in South Australia. I will train under him while Oriental Produce sets up our vineyards.'

'So you agreed to go to Australia?'

'Yes. But this time, I laid down conditions.'

'What conditions?'

Anthony pointed to the veranda of the manse where Grace and the nanny were playing with Daniel and Melinda. 'That he agrees to my adopting the boy and finding his mother, my sister, and taking them with me to Australia. The words stuck in his aristocratic throat, but he agreed. Now all I have to do is find Lakshmi.'

'How do you plan to do that?'

'I'll start with William. Father wanted me to check up on him anyway.'

Bob nodded. 'Good idea, that. I've heard that his wife isn't very happy ...'

Anthony grimaced. 'Poor Janet. She had such good memories of growing up in Watakale with her sister and parents.' He stopped and smiled. 'I first met Shiro when I visited her father, my uncle Irvine.' Bob watched as Anthony remained silent for a few moments. 'Janet as good as proposed marriage to me before we first took over the plantations. Then married William when he went back on leave. I'll check on her and see what William knows about Lakshmi. I have to find her and reunite her with her son.'

'We should have named the boy Moses, not Daniel,' Bob mumbled. He tightened his hold on Anthony's shoulder. 'You are still at it aren't you, Anthony? Trying to make up for what you feel your family have done to the coolies?'

'I have to, Bob.'

'I said this to you five years ago, Anthony, and I'll repeat it to you now. You can't give your life to make up for the sins of your father or your family.' Bob continued to hold Anthony's eyes. 'And Shiromi, does she come into this grand plan of yours?'

Anthony ripped his eyes off Bob and turned away. His voice faltered. 'Is she okay?'

'She is more than okay. She's top of her class in the second year at medical school. Her mother is apparently thrilled that she was crowned year queen! You did right, Anthony.'

Anthony shut his eyes.

'Then why does it hurt so much?'

Chapter 30

The Psychiatric clinic was not a place Shiro wanted to be. She refused to go. And Lalitha threatened.

'I'll call your mother,' she said when Shiro refused. 'Or I might tell Dr Jayaseelen.'

'No,' Shiro wailed. 'Don't you dare tell Jegs I'm seeing a psychiatrist. He'll think I'm a nutcase.'

Lalitha giggled. 'I think the lecturers think you're pretty nutty anyway.'

'Nutty?'

'Yes. I was at the staff room to pick up my essay and I heard Dr Jega talking with Professor Dias and Professor Fonseka.'

'And?'

'Professor Dias said you are a brooding brilliance of bleak moods and enticing conversations and can swing from darkness to sunshine in the blink of an eye.'

Shiro smiled. 'I like that. It's poetic. Didn't think Dias had it in him. What did Jegs say to that?'

'You won't like this. He said that it was as if you were acting a part, using your brains and rapier sharp wit without getting close to anyone. He was smiling as he said it. I think …' Lalitha stopped and stared at Shiro.

For a moment Shiro was back by her stream. Golden hair and blue eyes she would never forget. The feel of her hand in his. His voice. *Maybe you should forget medicine and get on the stage, Princess?*

Shiro shook her head. *No, forget Anthony. Move on. Make the most of today.*

'Tell. What do you think?'

'Not just me. It's like everyone thinks Dr Jega Jayaseelen has a soft spot for you.'

Shiro laughed. 'So what's wrong with that?'

Lalitha gasped. 'Stop it, Shiro. I covered for you during the holidays on the estate when you used to swan off to talk to that Anthony Periadorai fellow and look where it got you. I am not getting involved in that stuff again.'

'Don't talk about Anthony.' Shiro snapped. 'This is different.'

'How is it different? Dr Jega Jayaseelen may have a traditional Tamil name but look at him. His light skin and brown hair, not to mention those gorgeous grey eyes, brand him as a mongrel of mixed birth, a Eurasian.'

'He's got a MRCP and PhD from Queens University College Medical School. And he's tipped to be the youngest professor at the Faculty of Medicine Colombo, that's what's different. My parents will think that he's a good catch for a Tea-maker's daughter.'

Lalitha shook her head. 'This time I'm not keeping your secrets. Your family will never forgive me. I promised your brother Edward to watch out for you.'

As usual, Shiro ignored what she didn't wish to hear. 'In some ways, Jegs reminds me of Anthony.'

'Now you're dreaming!'

'Truly,' Shiro continued. 'When the sun shines on his hair and when he smiles, he does look a little like Anthony.'

'Shiro, stop it.' Lalitha pulled her hand. 'It's time for your appointment.'

***

'You have high distinctions in anatomy and physiology and a credit in biochemistry, Shiromi. First in your year batch of over a hundred students at the first exam is excellent.' Professor Mangala Jayasekara consultant psychiatrist glanced at her notes. 'You were also chosen year queen at the Law-Medical dance. And yet you're not happy, are you?'

Shiro sat looking straight ahead. Lalitha held her hand.

'Madam,' a shudder went through her body. 'I love my medical study, and it was fun to be chosen queen. My mother and brothers support me. And yet –' Her voice dropped to a whisper. 'I can't forget him.'

'Shiromi, your mother and brothers don't know the real story behind why you went into depression, do they? Your mother thinks it's because she wanted you to agree to an arranged marriage.'

Shiro shook her head. 'They have some idea. There was a letter.'

Professor Jayasekara glanced back at her notes. 'A letter?'

Shiro felt Lalitha's hand tighten on hers. 'Yes. Anthony's brother wrote to

169

my mother. Apparently Anthony gave daddy a bonus of fifty thousand rupees just when I tried to kill myself.' She took a deep, ragged breath, 'Anthony's brother, William, said in the letter that it wasn't a bonus. He said it was payment for Anthony sleeping with me.' She stopped.

'And?'

Shiro shrugged. 'Mum threw a tantrum. Made me kneel and swear on the Bible I hadn't slept with him. My brother Edward had to practically tie her down to the chair to restrain her. She said we couldn't tell Dad. What with his brother, William, being superintendent of Watakälé and Dad's boss and all. I think she was frightened that Dad would do something drastic.' Shiro laughed. The touch of hysteria in her voice was obvious to her own ears.

Professor Jayasekara touched her shoulder. 'Shiro, calm down.'

A tear escaped and slid down Shiro's cheek. 'I offered to have a virginity test done.' She laughed again. 'You know, madam, I begged Anthony to make love to me the day he sent me away. He refused. Now everyone thinks we did it anyway. Damn him. Damn him and his family to hell.'

Professor Jayasekara paused and scribbled on her notepad, then looked at Shiro. 'Shiro, you are angry. That is a good sign. It means you are getting better.'

Shiro nodded. 'Better? Doesn't feel like it. I feel like he is here.' She pushed her clenched fist into her chest. 'I can't stop thinking of him. I feel like there's a connection to him. I don't know where he is, what he is doing.' Her voice dropped. 'I keep imagining how it might have been if we were together. That makes me even angrier.'

'Shiromi, you loved him. A bond like that doesn't die completely, my dear. It will change from the searing pain you first felt, through the anger, to a gentle memory. It will take time but I promise you, it will happen.'

Shiro held her eyes. 'Is it wrong to want revenge?'

The smile on Professor Jayasekara's face was world weary. It spoke of years of sitting in the clinic listening to stories of broken hearts and broken lives.

'Revenge is a poisoned goblet to drink from, Shiromi. You have a bright future. Think of where you are now as a chrysalis – you will grow wings, break out and have a wonderful life.'

Doctor Jayasekara rested her hand on Shiro's shoulder. She left it there till Shiro smiled back at her. 'Now get out there and enjoy being a medical student. Go talk to your friends. Do something exciting and interesting. I'll see you next month.'

Shiro and Lalitha walked out of the psychiatry clinic. They passed the next patient coming in. He was a middle-aged man.

'I am god.' He gestured to the girls. 'Listen and obey!'

They were both giggling as they stepped into the sunshine.

***

There was a small statue of the Buddha, barely twelve inches high, at the base of the old Bo tree. Around it people laid offerings of flowers and incense. The flowers and garlands of jasmine were somewhat wilted at noon, but the pungent smell of sandalwood from the joss sticks hung in the tropical afternoon air.

A group of young men and women stood chatting and laughing in the shade of the twisted branches of the Bo tree. The supposed holiness of the surroundings didn't daunt them in the slightest. They were medical students and this was their daily ritual between ward rounds and lectures. It was here they came for a coke, cigarette, beer or even a cuddle with a colleague or an off-duty nurse.

Shiro and Lalitha ambled over to join them.

'Look at them,' Shiro whispered. 'What hope do we have of doing anything exciting and interesting with this mob? Most would get a high distinction if we had a subject on how to be boring!'

Lalitha giggled as one of the boys held out a paper cone of fried peanuts. 'Like some nuts, Shiro?'

Shiro rolled her eyes, smiled and shook her head. Lalitha could read Shiro's thoughts – 'nuts from the biggest nut of the bunch'.

Suddenly the chatter around the Bo tree muted. Shiro looked up to see Dr Jega Jayaseelen cross the road from the hospital. He was dressed in a pair of grey trousers and white shirt. The white coat with stethoscope in its pocket indicated that he had come from a hospital ward.

He looked at the assembled medical students. His grey eyes narrowed and his smile encompassed the group. 'So, this is where you hang out for some R and R.' He laughed at their bemused expressions. 'Sorry, that's Rest and Recreation. In London it was the pub at the corner. I guess that isn't available here in Colombo.'

He glanced at Shiro and Lalitha, his look of faux-surprise so obvious as to be comic. 'Oh, Miss Pregasam and Miss Rasiah. You said you wanted some help with the brachial plexus. I have some time now if you would like to come to the anatomy museum?'

Shiro remembered that she had stumbled when naming two of the branches of the brachial plexus in last week's upper limb tutorial. She didn't remember having asked for help. However, assistance from a lecturer was not something to be scoffed at. 'Why, thank you, Dr Jayaseelen.' Shiro half turned towards the assembled group of students. 'How nice of you to remember that we asked for help.'

She swung back and grabbed Lalitha by the hand. They followed Dr Jega Jayaseelen across the road and into the main building of the Colombo Faculty of Medicine.

The British had built the lecture rooms and administrative offices in colonial times. It was a tiny replica of an English university. The Anatomy laboratories and the museum with preserved body parts were used for tutorials and private study.

Shiro glanced back at the gathered group. Nandan, the boy who had offered her the peanuts, raised his hand, four fingers folded in and thumb extended in a 'go for it' sign. Shiro smiled back. She had a feeling that from now on Dr Jega Jayaseelen would be known in her year group as 'Brachial Plexus'.

As they entered the building, Lalitha clutched Shiro's arm. 'Shiro, I nearly forgot, I promised to help organise some stuff for the table tennis tournament tomorrow.' She looked up at Dr Jega. 'Sir, can you please explain to Shiro? I'll ask her about it later.'

Shiro swung on Lalitha. 'What tournament? You don't play...'

But Lalitha was already gone.

'Shiromi, do you mind very much being alone with me?'

Dr Jega's voice was Sri Lankan with a crisp British accent. It reminded her of another time, another place, a voice completely British.

Shiro looked into grey eyes. The sun streamed through the window, lighting up his brown hair with a golden halo. He looked so like Anthony. *You're dreaming, girl*, she scolded herself.

'I don't mind at all, Dr Jayaseelen. It's so kind of you to offer.'

He continued to smile down at her. 'And you and I both know that you don't need any assistance in naming and tracing the nerves that make up the brachial plexus.'

She met grey eyes that reminded her of blue. *Damn, damn, damn. Oh, what the hell.* 'I don't mind being alone with you –' she paused and let her smile flit up to her eyes, 'Jega.'

Chapter 31

The setting sun slanted through the shade trees, turning the tea fields into a tapestry of green, gold and grey. The mist clambered up the mountains, snuffing out the colours and replacing them with a blanket of black.

This was a last ditch attempt to locate Lakshmi. If William didn't know, he would have to ask Mr Rasiah, the Tea-maker. He was not keen to face the Tea-maker. Too afraid of how much he knew of his part in Shiro's suicide attempt.

'You're a bloody coward, Anthony,' he mumbled to himself.

It was dark when the car wound its way into Watakälé. The Tea-maker's house and garden looked unkempt. Mrs Rasiah's roses and jasmine plants were overgrown with weeds. She must be in Colombo with Shiro, and Mr Rasiah alone there. Anthony's heart constricted when a turn in the road showed him the stream with the ledge of rock.

The chauffeur, Sunil, drove up the steep, winding road to the bungalow. The lights were all on and the house on the hill shone like a beacon. Anthony saw Appu in the dining room, laying out the bone china plates for dinner. He noticed three other Indian coolies in white uniforms outlined in the sitting room light. Two were sweeping the room. The third was about to draw the thick damask curtains. William and Janet certainly kept a large staff, he mused, comparing it with his simple life there just two years ago with Appu and the dog.

The car drew up and stopped at the house.

The coolie at the window drawing the curtains noticed the car in the driveway. He stopped and peered through the glass. Then turned and scurried towards the study. Soon William and Janet came out and stepped out onto the veranda.

This is it, thought Anthony, *no turning back now*.

The car was parked in the penumbra of the lights on the veranda. Anthony slid the sleeping Daniel off his lap and opened the door of the car. 'Sunil,' he said to the chauffeur, 'Please watch the child for a few minutes.' He eased himself out of the back seat and took two steps forward so the couple standing on the veranda could see him.

'Anthony!' Janet gasped. She flew down the veranda and threw herself into his arms, surprising him with her tight embrace. With the same suddenness, she sprang back and shot a quick glance towards her husband on the veranda.

'Where have you been? I tried to find you. Your parents thought you were with Bob Kirkland, but –' She shot a glance at William. 'I didn't want to call them.'

Keeping his arm around his sister-in-law, Anthony moved her up the steps and away from the car. William remained on the veranda, his hands in his pockets. His eyes were cold and hooded, secretive even.

Anthony was shocked at how his brother had changed. He had lost weight and his face had the reddish blotches of an alcoholic. There were dark shadows under the blue eyes that locked with his.

'What brings you here, little brother?' William's tone was belligerent.

'You knew I was coming, didn't you, William.' It was a statement rather than a question. 'And that I was bringing the boy?' Anthony glanced back at the car where Sunil was lifting Daniel out of the back seat.

'A baby! Anthony?' Janet looked from Anthony to William, confused.

William came down the steps. He brushed Janet aside.

'Yes, Anthony, your dear friend the Reverend Robert Kirkland called a couple of hours ago. Informed me to expect a visit from you and your half-breed son.'

Anthony looked past him to Janet. He gestured to the child. 'This is my adopted son Daniel.'

'He's gorgeous. May I hold him?' Janet held her arms out. Daniel laughed and went to her.

Janet walked into the house, ignoring the tension between the two brothers. 'Come on, don't stand out here in the damp. Let's get this cutie into the house.' Daniel snuggled half asleep in her arms, his arms wrapped around her neck.

William shot a vitriolic glance at Anthony and followed.

'Appu,' William called out towards the kitchen. 'Your favourite Periadorai has returned.'

Appu stepped out from the kitchen. The tired eyes lit up and a smile creased the dark, weathered face setting the moustache wobbling. 'Aiya,' he exclaimed. His eyes then swept to the boy in Janet's arms and the look turned to one of horrified trepidation.

William was obviously enjoying the situation. 'Stop gawking and get us a meal, Appu. Our prodigal son and his bastard must be hungry.'

Appu took Daniel from Janet. 'I will take him to the kitchen and give him some food, madam. The driver and the other staff can help me.'

Anthony saw Janet open her mouth to protest. William flashed her a look. She stopped and handed over the boy to Appu. Then moved to stand beside William.

Appu took Daniel in his arms and went back into the kitchen.

Janet stared at William. 'Why didn't you tell me they were coming?'

'And spoil your surprise, darling?' drawled William. 'I wanted to watch your face when you saw your ex-boyfriend and his half-breed savage.' He laughed and turned towards the bar to pour a glass of whisky.

Anthony and Janet stood facing each other. 'I'm sorry things turned out this way between you and William, Janet,' Anthony said.

Janet turned away, but not before Anthony saw the tears in her eyes.

Appu appeared at the dining room door. 'Dinner is served, sir.' He stood at the door till Janet and William passed. Then he approached Anthony. 'Sunil and I will bathe and feed the child and put him to bed, sir. You don't have to worry.' Looking into Anthony's eyes, he lapsed back to talking in Tamil. '*Kavanam*, Aiya. Be careful, sir.'

Appu dished out the roast beef, boiled vegetables and baked potato with an expressionless face. Janet and Anthony chatted about their parents and the manor house. William was silent.

Appu served a delicious pineapple tart for dessert. Janet pushed back her chair. 'I think I'll go check on the baby.' She looked from one to the other of the brothers. She waited for a grunted permission from William before rising from the table and almost running out of the room. Anthony waited until her footsteps faded down the corridor before getting up.

'Stop,' William snapped. 'Sit down.'

Anthony paused, half up from his chair. William snapped, 'Sit down, I said.'

Anthony lowered himself back down.

'Why the hell did you come back with that half-breed creature?'

Anthony curled his hands on the arms of the chair. 'That half-breed creature, as you call him, is your son, William, and you know it. The girl you raped. She had your son.'

William clapped his hands and laughed. 'What a surprise! A coolie girl pregnant by a Periadorai. So, I had sex with her. She probably had sex with ten others before and after that.'

'Come on, William. She was a virgin when you took her. Even you would have recognised that. And you saw the boy. He's an Ashley-Cooper. Did you look at his eyes? It's Mother all over again.'

William picked up the glass. He gulped the whisky neat and coughed. 'Blue eyes and brown hair. Stop fantasising, little brother. She could have been impregnated by any of our gang.'

'No. He's your son. Father knows and accepts it.'

'More fool he.' William turned to refill his glass.

Anthony took the glass from William's hand. 'I need to find the boy's mother.' He leaned forward, not wanting Janet to hear. 'Where is she, William? Where is Lakshmi?'

William grabbed the glass back from Anthony. He sniggered and raised the glass. 'Don't be stupid, little brother. Do you think I kept track of every girl I screwed?' He guffawed. 'I didn't look at her face when I shagged her in the weighing shed and I have no idea what her name is. The bitch is probably just one of the prostitutes who roam the streets of Diyatalāwa. Why don't you go check them out? There's a great whorehouse there. I can give you the address. The Madame is pretty sexy herself.'

Anthony shut his eyes and prayed for patience.

'And you can wipe that self-righteous look off your face. Who are you to stand judgement over me?' William continued. 'What about your little fling with the Rasiah girl?'

Anthony felt the hairs on his neck stand up. 'What are you talking about?'

William leered at him. 'You thought I didn't know?' He pulled out a letter from his pocket and threw it across the table to Anthony. 'Read it. Father sent it to me when you left Watakälé. Or should I say were sacked. He wanted me to follow it up. I held on to it for a day like today.'

Anthony looked at the plain brown envelope. He drew out the piece of paper. The letter was in Mr Rasiah's clear long hand, the type he used for official correspondence.

'Dear Mr James Ashley-Cooper

Dear Sir

I want to thank you personally for the bonus of Rupees fifty thousand that your son, Anthony, so kindly passed on to me last week. It was very generous of you. It was very timely since we had to take our daughter to Colombo for urgent medical treatment and this sum will enable us to get the best doctors to see her.'

Damn, damn, damn! Anthony thought. Why did Mr Rasiah have so much integrity?

William was still leering at him.

Appu came in and picked up the dishes. Anthony could feel his worried eyes on him.

'There was no debit on the company account for that amount, was there, little brother? I checked. It came out of your personal account.' William tossed back his drink and coughed. 'That wasn't all you paid the Rasiahs, was it?'

William leant forward again and poked his finger at Anthony. 'There is the credit to Mr Rasiah's provident fund with the proviso that it be used for their children's education. The girl's the only one still in university, you might as well have stamped her name on it. You thought I wouldn't notice?' William laughed. 'What did you pay the Rasiahs for, Anthony? The services of their sexy daughter? The one you met by the stream? Were you paying for an abortion in Colombo? Or maybe you've got a bastard yourself, that you're supporting somewhere?'

Anthony lost it. All the years of pent up frustration and anger against his brother were in that one punch.

William roared with pain. He clutched his face and staggered back, crashing into the drinks trolley. The clatter of breaking bottles and William's screamed curses brought Appu and the other coolies running into the room. Janet followed after them.

'Damn you to hell, William,' Anthony panted, standing over a prostrate William. 'You are what Father made you, aren't you? Mother tried to change Father's attitude, and it killed her spirit. You're doing the same to Janet. You bastard! I will find Lakshmi. I will find the mother of your son! I will give her and Daniel a better life. I swear it!'

Janet dropped to the floor by William with a linen napkin in her hand. She looked up from where she was kneeling, holding the cloth to William's fast swelling cheek.

'Did you say his son?' she gasped and looked at William's rapidly swelling face. 'I thought you couldn't father a child.'

'Shut up, woman' William shoved her hand away.

'Yes, Janet,' Anthony said. 'William raped a coolie girl. Daniel is her son. I want to find the girl. I'm going to take the two of them to Australia to start a new life.'

William struggled to his feet. 'You'll never find her,' he muttered angrily. 'The bitch is gone. And you,' he pointed a finger at Janet, 'shut up and go to bed.'

Janet stood between the brothers. She looked from William to Anthony. 'Anthony, let it go. Please. Let's talk about this in the morning.'

William held on to his jaw. He jabbed a finger at Anthony. 'I'll get even with you. Both you and your precious Mr Rasiah.'

Anthony turned and walked down the corridor to the guest room. He could hear William swearing and Janet's voice, soft and weary. 'Come to bed. You need to sleep it off. It'll be all right in the morning.'

Daniel was already in bed, fast asleep. Anthony kissed him on his curly head. *Tomorrow, we'll find your mother*, he promised him silently. Sighing, he shut the door and opened his overnight bag. Just then, he heard a soft, insistent tap on the door.

'Anthony! It's me. Please, let me in!' It was Janet's voice in an urgent whisper.

Anthony opened the door a fraction to let her in and closed it after her. 'What the hell are you doing? You heard what he said. He's still convinced you and I were lovers in England. If he finds you here he'll kill us both!'

'I don't care, Anthony,' she said. Her face was drawn, her eyes dull. 'He's always drinking.' Her voice cracked on a sob. 'He even drinks with the native staff, especially the assistant Tea-maker, Wright. He spends nights away. Appu says he goes to Diyatalāwa. I think –' She took a deep breath. 'I think he has a mistress somewhere.' She sobbed into his shoulder.

Anthony held her. This was a girl whom he had grown up with, the closest he would come to a sister. He felt a wave of tenderness for her. 'Why do you stay with him? Why don't you go back to England?'

'I can't. It'd be too shameful for both families. I could bear it, just, if I had a child. But he stopped making love to me after we came here. He called me frigid. Said the coolie girls are fun.' She choked on her sobs. 'He said all I ever did was lie back and think of England. He said he couldn't father a child anyway. And now you say –' Her voice trailed into silence.

Anthony racked his mind for something to comfort her.

Daniel stirred and whimpered. Janet drew back from Anthony's arms. 'I'm so glad you came. It makes me feel better to have seen you. I hope you find Daniel's mother. Take care of yourself and keep in touch.' She kissed him on the cheek and slipped out of the room.

Anthony pushed the door shut. Dragging the heavy armchair across the room he lodged it under the door handle. Then pulled off his shirt and trousers and laid them on a clothes hanger by the bed. Setting his alarm for six, he lowered himself into the bed by his son.

Exhausted, his body cried out for sleep. But he tossed and turned.

Images kept jostling each other in his mind, images of a cowering coolie girl, a lonely wife, a leering drunkard and a laughing, black-haired girl who read Shakespeare by a stream amidst the tea bushes.

Will the pain ever get better?

***

Anthony opened his eyes. Something had woken him.

The clock on the wall told him it was five-thirty. He sat up in bed, instinctively looking at his son. Daniel had rolled over in the night and was lying cuddled against him. Anthony looked at the door, which was still securely shut.

He looked around the room. What had woken him? His eyes were drawn by a patch of white just in front of the door. It was a sheet of paper. Listening intently, he heard the soft footsteps of someone walking barefoot down the corridor. Whoever was padding down the hall had just slipped a paper under the door.

Anthony moved Daniel aside and slipped off the bed. He picked up the paper. There were two words printed on the paper: 'Hemachandra Mudalali'.

Anthony nodded. So that was where Lakshmi was. The only person who could have known this was Appu. He obviously did not want to be identified as the source of the information.

Anthony pulled on his shirt and trousers. He opened the door, shutting and turning the key in the lock. He padded barefoot through the length of the Bungalow and tapped on the door of the servants' quarters.

Appu opened the door. 'Please tell Sunil that I would like to leave at six-thirty,' Anthony said. 'I have to make a stop at Diyatalāwa on my way back to Nuwara-Eliya.'

'Yes, sir. That is good,' Appu said. 'I will pack some food for you and the child.'

Anthony nodded and turned to leave.

'Sir …' he heard Appu say.

Anthony turned back to him again.

'Aiya, Shiro Chinnamma is well. She is happy.'

They stood looking at each other for a moment – the Englishman and the coolie. Then Anthony placed his hand on Appu's shoulder. 'Thank you, Appu. I will not come here again. Please look after Janet for me.'

'Aiya,' the old man looked at Anthony with tear filled eyes. 'I will ask God to look after you.'

Anthony felt Appu's gaze follow him back down the corridor back to the bedroom and his son.

Janet came out when she heard the car draw up. She had a soft blanket in her hand. 'Please keep Daniel warm,' she said. Anthony touched her cheek as she reached into the car to kiss Daniel. 'Take care, Janet,' Anthony said. 'I will never come back here. Appu is a good man. He'll help you.'

Anthony did not look back as the car wound its way down the steep drive.

Sunil looked in the rear view mirror. 'We will be in Diyatalāwa by seven o'clock, sir.'

Chapter 32

Thick fog surrounded them in Diyatalāwa. They could hardly see a few feet in front of the car. The town was just waking. A few men, their heads swathed in towels to keep out the cold and rain, strolled along the road's narrow, uneven pavements. Children squatted around a tap on the roadside, brushing their teeth. They looked up and waved as the car passed. Daniel, wide-awake and with his nose pressed on the window, waved back.

Anthony signalled to Sunil to stop the car. He wound down the window. 'Hemachandra Mudalali *veedu*?' he asked a man who was just opening his shop. Yawning, the man pointed down the road to a two-storey building.

Sunil nodded. The car continued to travel up the road and soon drew up at the front door of the house.

Anthony got out of the car. 'Sunil, please watch the child.'

Sunil got into the back seat with Daniel. Daniel, wrapped in Janet's blanket and munching on a fruit bun from Appu's kitchen, stared around.

Anthony stood at the front door. The house was shuttered and dark. Seven in the morning was obviously too early for Hemachandra Mudalali.

There was no knocker or buzzer. Anthony tapped and then hammered on the door. The only acknowledgement was the strident barking of what sounded like a large dog from the house next door.

After a minute, Anthony pounded on the door again, even harder. 'Hello' he called. 'Mudalali, are you at home?'

A light came on in an upstairs room. A loud male voice called out 'Lakshmi, go see who is coming at this time.' Anthony's heart skipped a beat. Had he heard the name Lakshmi?

Soft footsteps approached the front door and the corner of the curtain was pulled back. Anthony stepped back into the light from the street lamp, so that

181

whoever was peeking through the glass pane of the window had a clear view of his face.

A bloodcurdling scream came from the house. 'It is him. He has come!' A female voice shrieked in Sinhalese. This was followed by the sound of running feet. Footsteps clumped down the stairs and towards the front door.

The door flung open. Hemachandra Mudalali stood there, his ample chest bare except for a red towel thrown over his shoulder. His left hand held his batik sarong up to his knees, exposing fat and hairy legs. He leaned forward and squinted into Anthony's face.

Anthony drew back as Hemachandra Mudalali's malodorous morning breath washed over him.

'Who is this?' Hemachandra Mudalali continued to stare into Anthony's face. Then his tone rose in pitch and volume. 'Aney, it is you, no, sir? Over two years since we saw you no?' He turned to shout into the house. 'Anthony Periadorai is here, Hamine.'

Hemachandra Mudalali reached out his arms and Anthony felt himself engulfed in the sweaty bosom. Over Hemachandra Mudalali's shoulder, Anthony saw Mrs Hemachandra in her housecoat, bustling around drawing the curtains open and arranging the furniture.

Hemachandra Mudalali relinquished his hold on Anthony. Anthony took a deep breath.

'Long time, no? We are missing you on Watakälé. Business is not good there, sir. You are visiting? Or you are coming back to work in the district? That would be good, no? Come in, son, come in.' Hemachandra Mudalali stepped back, gesturing for Anthony to enter.

Anthony held up his hand, palm out, to Hemachandra Mudalali, then turned and signalled to Sunil. Sunil lifted Daniel out of the car. Daniel clutched the blanket in his left hand. The thumb of his right hand was firmly secured in his mouth. Sunil handed Daniel to Anthony and went back to the car.

There was silence as Daniel and Anthony entered. Hemachandra Mudalali looked from the child to Anthony and back to the child. Daniel drooped on Anthony's shoulder, sucking his thumb, his head tilted to one side. His big, cobalt-blue eyes stared back at Hemachandra Mudalali.

'Sir.' Hemachandra Mudalali hesitated. 'Sir, is this –'

'Yes, this is Daniel. Lakshmi's son by my brother, William. I have adopted him. I want to find his mother. Is she here, Mudalali?'

There was silence in the room. Hemachandra Mudalali looked at his wife and back at Daniel. Mrs Hemachandra stood behind a sofa, her fingers clasped tight on the back of the seat. Anthony held Daniel closer to him. This was not going to be easy.

Daniel raised his head and looked at Hemachandra Mudalali and his wife. 'Girl.' He pointed at Mrs Hemachandra. His chubby little forefinger moved to Hemachandra Mudalali. 'Fat man.'

Anthony clasped his hand on Daniel's mouth. This was definitely not helping his cause. 'Daniel,' he whispered in his ear. 'Go back to sleep, son.' He turned to apologise.

Hemachandra Mudalali slapped his ample stomach and hooted with laughter. His moustache wobbled.

His wife let go of the back of the sofa and pointed to her husband. 'I am telling him he is eating too much,' she chuckled. 'Those days he is having bread for breakfast, no? Now since Lakshmi is here, we are having *kiribath* and *roti* for breakfast and fried rice for lunch and dinner also.'

There it was again, the mention of Lakshmi. So Appu was right. This was where she was. Anthony encompassed them both in his next words. 'So Daniel's mother, Lakshmi, is here?'

Mrs Hemachandra's hands tightened on the sofa back again.

Hemachandra Mudalali wiped his eyes on the corner of the towel hanging over his shoulder. 'Sir, why are you wanting to know?' He glanced back at his wife.

There were undercurrents that Anthony couldn't comprehend. What was Lakshmi's status in this house?

Anthony moved closer to Hemachandra Mudalali. He looked down directly into his eyes. 'Mr Hemachandra, I have adopted the boy. Daniel is the first born of the next generation. I will not let him be brought up as an orphan.'

A look of relief crossed Hemachandra Mudalali's face. 'Ah, I understand. You will be wanting to take him to England, no? So you want to tell Lakshmi?'

'No.' Anthony was beginning to get impatient. He took a deep breath and continued. 'I will not subject my son to the racist claptrap of British colonial arrogance. I am taking him to a place where he can be his best.'

Hemachandra Mudalali was now smiling. 'I see. You have come to say goodbye.'

'No,' Anthony repeated. 'I have come to find Daniel's mother and ask her to come with me.'

Mrs Hemachandra raised her hands to her mouth. 'Take her with you? What are you saying?'

'What I am saying is that I want Lakshmi to come with me to Australia.'

'Australia. That is like very far away, no?' Mrs Hemachandra gasped.

A look of anger flashed across Hemachandra Mudalali's face. He gestured his wife to be silent. 'So you are no different from your brother? He rapes her and you want to take her with you to Australia as your keep. A servant for easy sex. Just like your father.'

Anthony stood dumbfounded.

'I thought you were not like them.' Hemachandra Mudalali's face twisted in a sneer. 'What will you do when you are finished? When she is too old for you? Sell her as a slave?'

'Damn you for comparing me with my brother.' The fury in Anthony's voice silenced Hemachandra Mudalali. 'Or with my father, for that matter. I want her to care for Daniel. I am not looking for a lover for myself.' There was no way he was going to explain his relationship to Lakshmi to this idiot.

'But,' stammered Hemachandra Mudalali, 'how will they allow?'

Daniel was now asleep and drooling on Anthony's shoulder. Anthony silenced Hemachandra Mudalali with his other hand. 'It's all arranged. I have a visa to take a local woman as a nanny for the child. If she agrees, Lakshmi will be part of Daniel's life. When he is old enough, we will tell him the truth.'

Hemachandra Mudalali eyes bulged and his jaw dropped. 'You will do that? You will tell him she is the mother? A coolie? You are not ashamed?'

'The shame is what we the British have done to the plantations.' Anthony fixed his eyes on Hemachandra Mudalali. 'Is Lakshmi here?' he raised his voice. 'I must speak to her.'

'Yes, she is here.' Hemachandra Mudalali's voice was wary. 'But she is frightened of you. You heard her scream.'

'She thinks I'm William. Of course she's frightened. Let me talk to her. I have her son. Surely that makes a difference?'

Hemachandra Mudalali stood there, gazing at the floor, hands clasped behind his back, shifting his weight from foot to foot. Anthony stared at him, surprised at his hesitation. *He doesn't want to let her go. How preposterous. She's a servant here, and probably works for practically nothing out of gratitude. Damn the man.*

Anthony sat down and crossed his legs. He settled Daniel on his lap. Daniel opened his eyes, wriggled off Anthony's lap and flopped on the floor. Anthony held onto Daniel's hand. 'Mudalali, I am not leaving here until I speak with Lakshmi.'

Hemachandra Mudalali shook his head. Turning, he walked towards the back of the house. Anthony got up and went with him. Behind him, Mrs Hemachandra took Daniel by the hand and followed them.

A slim woman stood in the kitchen, holding on to the sink. She had her back to the door. She wore a threadbare blouse and skirt. Her shoulders were bent forward, as if to protect herself from further pain. She did not turn around or raise her eyes as they entered.

'Hello, Lakshmi,' Anthony said, pausing at every word. 'Can you understand me?'

Anthony leaned forward to hear her faint response. 'I know English.'

'Good. Lakshmi, I am Anthony Ashley-Cooper. I'm not William. I think you know that now. You must remember me from the days when I was the superintendent at Watakälé. Please don't be afraid of me.'

She remained frozen to the spot, turned away from them, her every muscle tense. She reminded Anthony of an animal, cornered, hurt, ready to flee or maybe to bite back.

'Lakshmi.' Anthony kept his voice soft and low, 'I've brought someone I think you'd like to meet. Your son, Lakshmi. Now my son also – Daniel.'

'My son? But how? He was adopted. Matron said I would never see him again.' Lakshmi swung round to face them. Even after years of hard manual labour, the clean lines of her face were evident. She must have been beautiful. Her eyes, a murky dark grey, widened with fear and surprise. Anthony flinched. The resemblance to his father was right there.

Anthony stepped aside so Lakshmi could see Mrs Hemachandra and Daniel. Mrs Hemachandra carried Daniel in and set him down to stand in front of Lakshmi.

Daniel looked up at his mother, his blue eyes wide. He tilted his head to a side and smiled. 'Amma, Amma,' he repeated.

'My son –' Lakshmi stammered. She covered her mouth with her hands. Tears filled her eyes and streaked down her cheeks. She sank down on her knees. 'You are here. My son. My son.'

Daniel held out his arms. He toddled towards her. 'Amma.'

Lakshmi drew him to herself and held him tight, tears flowed down her cheeks.

Hemachandra Mudalali, his wife and Anthony watched Lakshmi as she knelt there, her arms wrapped around her son, rocking him back and forth. Her tears fell unchecked on his curly brown hair. Daniel mumbled and rested his head on her chest.

This is right, Anthony thought, *there's a bond between them. Just for once, maybe I've done the right thing.*

'Let's go back to the sitting room,' he said to Hemachandra Mudalali. 'I think they deserve some time together.'

***

Hemachandra Mudalali and Anthony sat across from each other, cups of tea before them. Mrs Hemachandra hovered at the door to the kitchen.

'She is a good worker and a very good cook,' Hemachandra Mudalali said. 'Mrs Rasiah taught her English and even some mathematics. She is quite good at it, actually. I think Lakshmi and the Tea-maker's daughter, Shiro, used to read English books and study together.'

Anthony flinched at the memory. Shiro, talking of her friend, her soul-mate.

'Yes, she even helps with reading letters and helping me with accounts. Almost like having a secretary in the house.' Hemachandra Mudalali continued.

'How much do you want for her?' Anthony's voice grated. *You criticised me when you thought I wanted a sex slave, but you're using her too. Paying her a servant's wage and surreptitiously using her to help in your business. You mean for me to haggle a price for her, like some commodity you pack in the back of that lorry of yours, you capitalist son of a bitch.*

Hemachandra Mudalali sat back, his face shocked. 'No, I don't mean ...'

Mrs Hemachandra marched up behind her husband, her brow furrowed, her face pinched in anger. She leaned over Hemachandra Mudalali and mumbled into his ear. Anthony smiled at the fierce tone in her voice. For all his bluster, Hemachandra Mudalali was definitely not the boss in this partnership. Hemachandra Mudalali shifted in his seat. His wife poked him in the shoulder. Still scowling, she whirled around and stormed out of the room towards the kitchen.

Hemachandra Mudalali looked at the ceiling and sighed. 'No, you don't have to pay for her. She deserves a chance at a better life.'

Anthony nodded.

Mrs Hemachandra came in and spoke to Hemachandra Mudalali. Anthony strained to listen. All he heard was Lakshmi, Daniel and Sinhalese words for boy, father, mother.

'My wife says Lakshmi wants to come and talk with you,' Hemachandra Mudalali said.

Anthony got to his feet. 'Yes, I'd like that.'

Lakshmi was already at the kitchen door. She held Daniel in her arms. Daniel gurgled at Anthony. 'Dada,' he said, pointing to Anthony.

'Mr Ashley-Cooper, Aiya.' Lakshmi spoke in English, enunciating every word. 'When my Daniel was born, I held him in my arms for two days. Then they took him away to the orphanage. I visited him, watched him grow. Knowing I would lose him. The day – '

Tears filled her eyes and she hugged Daniel. 'I thought I would die the day they told me he was adopted. I was so frightened. I thought what if someone used him as a servant? Or worse?' Her lower lip trembled.

She took a deep breath and looked at Daniel. The love in her eyes lit up her face and the room. 'But now I know that you are his father. You are a good man, sir. I know that. You will look after him. You have given me back my life, sir. Whatever happens now, I am happy.' She placed Daniel in Anthony's arms.

She then knelt in front of Anthony. She placed her hands palm down just in front of his feet and bowed down. Her forehead touched the tip of his shoes.

Anthony stepped back and looked at her. He felt sick. *This is what we, the mighty British Empire, have done to the people in the plantation.*

He cleared his throat and put Daniel down. She didn't move. 'Lakshmi,' he mumbled, 'please get up. I have something more I want to say to you.'

Lakshmi stood up, wiping her eyes. The ghost of a smile wafted across her face as she looked at Daniel, who was climbing up Anthony's legs.

'Lakshmi,' Anthony said, 'You know I have adopted Daniel as my son. I am his father now. He will grow up as an Ashley-Cooper. Inherit his rightful name and place in the world.'

Lakshmi's eyes opened wide. 'Sir –' She gasped, then nodded her comprehension.

'I came to find you because the boy needs a woman to care for him.' Anthony stopped and watched hope and fear wage war on Lakshmi's face. 'Lakshmi, Daniel needs his mother.' He searched for words. 'I'm going to Australia. Do you know where that is?'

Lakshmi nodded. 'I have seen a world map.'

'Good. I plan to start a new life with Daniel. I want you to come with us.'

Lakshmi's hands flew to her mouth. She looked from Anthony to Daniel, then at Hemachandra Mudalali and Hamine. She closed her eyes and took a deep, ragged breath.

'Aiya.' She stared at Anthony. Her gaze was unwavering, defiant and determined. 'I want to be with my son. I will do anything you need for that.'

Anthony looked into her eyes. *She's letting me know that she's willing to be my mistress. This woman will truly do anything to be with her son.*

Holding her gaze, he shook his head. 'Lakshmi, I want you to look after

187

Daniel. I am not looking for a mistress or a lover. Do you understand that?'

'But what is there for you? Why are you doing this if not for –'

Anthony was fast losing patience. First Hemachandra Mudalali and now Lakshmi! *What makes them all think that the only thing that British men wanted from native women was sex?* Even as he thought it – he knew the answer. *Rule Britannia!*

He glanced at Hemachandra Mudalali and his wife. 'Can I have a few minutes alone with Lakshmi?'

'Of course.' Hemachandra Mudalali pointed towards a small side room that looked like a storage area. Mrs Hemachandra peeled Daniel off Anthony. 'I'll give him something to drink. You talk.' She marched off towards the kitchen, gesturing Hemachandra Mudalali to follow.

Anthony took Lakshmi's arm and drew her into the room. He tightened his grip when she flinched and pulled away. Shutting the door, he took Lakshmi by the shoulders and forced her to sit down on a low stool. He squatted in front of her and spoke in an undertone. He wouldn't put it beyond Hemachandra Mudalali to have his ear at the keyhole.

'Lakshmi, I want you to listen carefully. What I am going to tell you is going to sound like an unbelievable story. I don't expect you to take it all in right now. But I want you to trust me. I will explain it all later. Can you understand me?'

Lakshmi nodded.

'Will you trust me?'

'You are a good man,' Lakshmi whispered.

'Lakshmi, did you ever feel different from the other coolie girls?'

Lakshmi nodded. 'Yes, I thought that I was not dark like the others. Also my eyes are not like a coolie.'

Anthony nodded. 'That's because your real father is not a coolie. Your real father is a white man, Lakshmi.' Anthony took a deep breath. 'Your father is James Ashley-Cooper.'

'But, that is your name?'

'Yes, Lakshmi. My father is James Ashley-Cooper.'

Lakshmi shrank back from him. Then stared at him with a dawning understanding. 'That means that –'

'That means, Lakshmi, that I am your brother. But –' he continued quickly, seeing the understanding turn to fear in her eyes, 'William has a different father. He is *not* your brother.'

Anthony smiled at the confusion on Lakshmi's face. 'I know, Lakshmi. It took me some time to work it all out too.'

Lakshmi's eyes misted. 'Shiro Chinnamma said it would happen.'

Anthony flinched. 'Shiro?'

'Yes, that last Christmas we were together, she waved her pretend wand and made a wish. She wished that one day a handsome man would rescue me and take me to a faraway country.'

Anthony tried to sound casual. 'Do you hear from Shiro?'

'Oh, yes,' Lakshmi said. 'She writes once every month.' She stopped and smiled. 'You don't have to pretend with me. I know that you were friends.'

'Friends. She said that?'

'Yes, she wrote that you and she used to meet and talk after I went – was sent away. We never had secrets.'

'Does she still write? How is she now?'

'I haven't had a letter for a month or so. She has friends in medical school. In her last letter she wrote about a Professor Jega.' Lakshmi smiled. 'I think he is in love with her.'

A shaft of agony pierced through him. Shiro was moving on. It was what he wanted for her, after all. He too, had to move on. He realised that Lakshmi was speaking to him.

'Aiya, can I write to her? About Daniel and you?'

'No, Lakshmi.' Shiro must not know. She must not be hurt again. 'Let's leave it till we are in Australia.'

Chapter 33

Only the ticking of the old grandfather clock interrupted the silence. Dusk turned to darkness and no one switched on the lights in the Tea-maker's house. Raaken came in and left mugs of strong, sweet, milky tea next to father and son. He looked from one to the other and slunk out of the room.

Victor got up and paced across the room to stand by his father. 'You can't go on living like this, Dad.' He put his mug of tea down on the side table. 'Mum would want to know what is happening.'

Rajan leant forward. 'No, son. No one in Colombo is to know what is happening here, especially not your mother.'

'But you and Mum have always shared everything. Like when Shiro tried to kill herself. You went through that together. Nothing could be worse than that. Why not tell Mum how worried you are? Damn it Dad, this is serious!'

'Tell her what, son? That the superintendent William Ashley-Cooper has cooked up evidence to frame me for theft? How do I explain to her that my assistant Tea-maker, Wright, is in cahoots with him and is fiddling the books for him? She'll think I'm imagining it. And if she believes me, she'll blame herself.' Rajan Rasiah's voice was tired and resigned.

Victor switched on a light. The glare from the naked overhead lamp made them both flinch. He pulled a stool to sit close, facing his father. 'For heaven's sake dad, why should she blame herself? She hardly knows the new superintendent William Ashley-Cooper. She went to Colombo with Shiro before he started here.'

Rajan Rasiah sighed. 'Victor, there are some things we kept from you boys.' He sat forward, his hands clasped between his knees. 'Son, William Ashley-Cooper's the one who raped Lakshmi. He found out that your mother and I helped Lakshmi with the pregnancy and that we sent the boy to the Salvation

Army orphanage. William Ashley-Cooper is a vicious and vindictive man. I am the evidence of his actions. He wants me out. I am pretty sure he is working with the assistant Tea-maker Wright. I don't know what hold William has over Wright, but I might as well resign before he forces my hand.'

Victor leapt up. The stool toppled over. The crash brought Raaken running into the room. 'Dad, the plantation is your life. You can't give up so easily. I'll write to James Ashley-Cooper myself. William is a bastard.'

The look of calm acceptance in his father's eyes chilled Victor's blood. It was not like his father to not fight for his rights. 'Calm down, son. It won't do any good. You think I haven't thought about it? Why do you think I have kept duplicate ledgers at home?' He gestured to the top drawer of the cabinet. 'But no amount of evidence will make a difference. It will be his word against mine. No one will take the side of the native against the British. Can't you see, son? James Ashley-Cooper doesn't care about any of us. None of the white bastards do. They just want to rip everything from the plantations before nationalisation. That's why he sent Anthony Ashley-Cooper back to England.'

'But Dad –'

'No. It's finished.' Rajan stood up. 'I've made up my mind, son. I've written the resignation letter. I'll hand it to William tomorrow morning. Then I'll drive down to Colombo and tell Mum about it all in person. I've had enough of this life.'

Victor saw the tears in his father's eyes. He reached for the telephone. 'Dad, please, let me call Mum.'

Rajan shook his head. 'Goodnight, son.' He stood for a moment resting his hand on his son's shoulder. Victor watched as his father walked into his dark and silent bedroom. He seemed a lot older than his fifty-two years.

Victor switched off the lights. He sat alone, looking out of the sitting room window at the mango tree. As children, Edward and he had built a treehouse there. Later, with Shiro, the bench under the mango tree became the place where confidences were shared and problems solved. He remembered the story of the soonyam and Raaken's swoon.

It was dark outside. Fireflies lit up the trees like some out-of-season, ethereal Christmas decoration. With a sigh, Victor realised there would be no more Christmases in Watakälé. He would continue to work as a scientist in the Tea Research Institute at Talawakalé on the other side of the mountains. Soon he would go to England to complete his PhD. Edward would marry Lalitha after his degree in accounting. Shiro would continue her medical studies in Colombo.

A large moth flew crazily into the glass window and dropped down, its wings broken. He thought of Shiro, her enthusiasm and brightness dimmed by the depression she had suffered. Their mother said it was due to the stress of her not wanting an arranged marriage. But she was improving. He was sure she would, in her inimitable way, bounce back.

He realised that this would be the last night he would sleep in his room.

***

The string hoppers were leathery and the hodhi lacked salt. Victor and Rajan sat at breakfast. Raaken stood by the dining table. His eyes were red and his face drawn and despondent.

'Aiya, eat, Aiya,' Raaken urged.

Turning away, Rajan Rasiah picked up the phone. Maybe he should call his wife. Lilly would know what to do. He held the receiver to his forehead. Then replaced it in the cradle. No. He would handle this on his own.

'Aiya, Aiya,' Raaken kept repeating between sobs. Raaken had just learned from Victor that his master was leaving Watakälé.

Victor helped his father pack his bag. Raaken sobbed as he loaded it into the boot of the Morris Minor. The furniture and all the other household goods would be sent later.

Victor stood with his hand on the front door of the car. 'Dad, please let me come with you when you speak to William Ashley-Cooper.'

'No, son. He'll think I don't have the gumption to stand up to him. You go back to the office.' He put his hand in his trouser pocket and touched the resignation letter. He was no longer bitter and angry. Instead, he felt a deep sense of calmness and peace.

'I'm going directly to Colombo from the factory. I don't know when I'll be back.'

'Aiyaaaa,' Raaken howled.

Rajan drove down to the factory. He did not look back at the house. He recalled events and one by one, severed the chains that bound him to the house and the plantation. Memories of the day he brought his young, beautiful and nervous bride there. The day he heard of his father's death and knew he had to care for his mother and brothers. He shuddered as he remembered the day that Shiro tried to kill herself.

It was all done and finished. Today he would start a new chapter.

Wright, the assistant Tea-maker, was seated in the factory office when Rajan walked in. 'Mr Ashley-Cooper said he would like to talk to you,' he said, a smirk on his pockmarked face.

192

Rajan looked at the man he had trained. He remembered what an ignorant buffoon Wright had been when he was first hired five years ago. Rajan had spent hours teaching him the basics of tea manufacture and tea tasting. Now this man had ganged up with William Ashley-Cooper to discredit him. Rajan stared clear-eyed at Wright. Wright looked away and walked out of the office. Rajan sat at the Tea-maker's table for the last time.

The roar of the motorcycle and a cloud of dust heralded William Ashley-Cooper's arrival. Rajan remained seated as William strode into the office.

'Well, Mr Rasiah?'

Rajan sat back with his hands folded on the table. He stared into William's vicious blue eyes. He would not give this bully the pleasure of seeing him cringe.

William leant over the table. 'I can destroy you, Mr Rasiah,' he spluttered. 'I have evidence of fraud in your ledgers. I also have people who will support me.'

Rajan stood up and looked at William. 'We both know that Wright cooked the books, Mr Ashley-Cooper. I don't know exactly what you promised him. I suppose it is a promotion to head Tea-maker and a substantial pay rise.'

Reaching into his pocket he drew out the resignation letter. 'Here is my letter of resignation, effective today.'

William looked taken aback. He gaped at Rajan. 'You're giving up?'

'No, I am not giving up. As I say in the letter, I am resigning. There is no place for me here. You and your minions can ruin this place.' Rajan held out the letter. His hand was steady, his expression proud and distant.

William clenched his hands. His face contorted with fury. 'Why you filthy little insubordinate –' His mouth worked soundlessly for a few moments. Then he snatched the letter from Rajan's hand. 'I accept your resignation,' he snarled, 'with immediate effect. Get out!'

Rajan Rasiah nodded once. He turned and began walking out of the office.

'By the way, Mr Do-gooder Tea-maker. Do you want to know what brought on your daughter's depression?' William yelled out after him.

Rajan stopped, but did not turn around.

'That got to you, didn't it?' William laughed. 'She was having an affair with my brother, Anthony. He broke it off with her. That's why she got so ill.'

Rajan stood frozen to the spot for a moment. With an effort of will, he continued walking to the car.

He got in and started up the engine, drunken, demented laughter followed him. It sounded like a hyena dragged out of the darkest caverns of hell.

***

Rajan drove down the road away from Watakälé, his mind awhirl. William was lying. Anthony wouldn't have had an affair with Shiro. He was too honest, wasn't he? And where would she have the chance to meet him?

She was always near the house. Wasn't she?

But as the winding road unfolded before him, seemingly disconnected events began to fit together. He remembered Shiro's long absences, her high spirits when she came back home. He remembered Anthony's questions about Shiro and her health, the cheque towards her treatment in Colombo, the extra bonus in his provident fund account. Unconsciously, Rajan's foot pressed heavier on the accelerator. The speedometer steadily crept up. He didn't care.

Anthony –the best superintendent he'd worked for. A man who treated the staff with dignity. He never played around with coolies. Well, he didn't need to, did he? He had a much fairer prize. Rajan's heart contracted at the thought. His beloved daughter in the arms of – no! It was too horrible to think about.

Then he remembered Lilly's words on the telephone from Colombo a couple of weeks ago. *Watch out for William*, she had said. *He will do anything to make trouble.* Did she know something? Was he the only one in the dark?

He wrenched the steering wheel. The car careened around the corner, tyres screeching.

Lilly should have told him. He would have killed them both. Anthony and William. Give them a short cut to hell where they belonged.

The car swerved onto the grassy verge. A trio of coolies leapt out of the way, shouting.

He didn't care.

Rajan seethed. Where Sir James led, the boys followed. It's just that he had trusted Anthony. He had believed Anthony was a better man –

A big, lumbering lorry, laden with boxes of groceries, appeared before him. It straddled three-quarters of the road as it laboured up the hairpin bends of Haputalé pass. Rajan rammed his foot on the brakes and jerked the steering wheel to the left. He saw the shocked face of the lorry driver. The car skidded, its back swinging widely. The rear bumper thudded against the front right of the lorry. Gyrating like a rotor, the car soared clean off the road. It somersaulted down thirty metres of cliff face, shedding bits of metal.

His last thoughts were of Shiro.

She had tried to kill herself when Anthony left her. What would she do now?

Chapter 34

Shiro sat in a corner of the anatomy museum. It was the only place in the medical faculty she could be alone at this time. She knew she should be at a microbiology lecture, but she couldn't face anyone. Not right now. And she didn't want to be at home waiting for the hearse carrying her father's coffin.

She picked up a bottled pathology specimen off the shelf. She stared at the slice of cirrhotic liver. Her vision blurred and she saw her father's face. She would never see him again. The coffin would be closed. His body was too badly broken to be seen by the family. Victor had said dad had resigned, was on his way to Colombo. Something had happened in the plantation; it involved William Ashley-Cooper and the assistant Tea-maker Wright and a false accusation.

The tears she had held back at home streamed down her cheeks. Damn the Ashley-Coopers. Damn Anthony and William and the whole bloody colonial Empire. She put her forehead on the cold marble surface of the table top and sobbed.

'I know that the replacement of hepatic lobules by the fibrous tissue of cirrhosis is a sorry sight, but I have never seen it bring a young lady to tears.'

Shiro looked up at Dr Jega Jayaseelen.

'What's the matter Shiromi?' He took out a white hanky from his trouser pocket. He held it for a moment and then handed it to her. She could read the look in his eyes. He had wanted to wipe the tears off her face himself.

Shiro took the hanky from his hand. Their fingers touching as she did so. Just for a moment she had a flash of memory; a voice not too unlike Jega's saying 'tears princess?' a white linen hanky, tender loving fingers on her cheeks. Damn, damn, damn.

'Shiromi, you are missing a lecture, hiding in the anatomy museum. It's not like you. Do you want to talk about whatever is upsetting you?' Jega pulled a stool and perched on it.

Shiro scrubbed the tears off her face, blew her nose and then looked at the white hanky, now rumpled and soiled. 'Sorry.'

'Not a problem, my dear. Plenty more where that came from.'

She sat staring at an obnoxious blood-filled cyst in the liver specimen in the bottle. Her fingers trembled and the bottle slipped.

Jega reached out and took the bottle from her hands. Reaching over her, he placed it back on the shelf where it belonged.

They sat in silence, Shiro threading the hanky between her fingers, tears coursing down her cheeks, and Dr Jega watching her, his grey eyes patient and caring.

'Shiromi?'

'Sir – Jega. Why are you here?'

'I saw you come in. I know you should be at a Microbiology lecture. You looked upset.'

'Why do you care?'

'I am your lecturer, Shiromi. I can't be anything other than that till after your examinations. But after that, I would like to get to know you better.'

Shiro glanced up at him and then turned away. Damn, he reminded her of Anthony. She should go back to the psychiatry clinic. Tell them she was hallucinating.

'Shiromi, you can trust me. You are obviously distressed.'

'My father is dead.'

Jega reached out and covered her hand with his. 'Shiromi.' His voice was soft, a lingering balm on the turmoil in her heart. 'Why are you here and not with your family?'

'I can't be at home. The Ashley-Coopers killed my father and I am responsible.'

'The Ashley-Coopers?' Jega's voice carried a note of stunned surprise.

Shiro nodded on a sob. 'I hate the Ashley-Coopers.'

Jega's fingers tightened over hers.

'Who are these Ashley-Coopers, Shiromi? And why do you think you are responsible?'

Shiro stared at a specimen on the shelf. A skull with a depressed fracture. The label said 'hammer injury to parietal bone'. That's what every one of the Ashley-Cooper family should have done to them. A shudder went through her body. Her father was dead and she was contemplating murder. She was a basket case. 'You wouldn't understand. The British kings of the tea plantation, the rape of the natives, coolies, taking what they want and getting rid of anyone who gets in their way.'

Jega didn't respond. The silent seconds stretched between them. Shiro's eyes shifted to a specimen of a ruptured aortic aneurysm. Her blood pressure was probably high enough to cause that right now.

'Shiromi,' Jega said, 'look at me. Really look at me.'

She raised her eyes to his. Slate grey eyes, now filled with a deep sadness and empathy; olive skinned face framed by curly dark brown hair.

'Shiromi, I am a Eurasian. My mother was an Indian labourer.'

Shiro's eyes widened. She gasped. 'You mean you – '

'Yes,' Jega nodded, 'My father, for the want of a better term, was a British planter. His wife threw my mother out of the house when she was pregnant with me.'

'Your mother – '

The bitterness in his voice cut through Shiro's cloud of sorrow. 'Yes, Shiromi, my mother was a 'keep' to the English superintendent. That's what they called it at that time. Today we would say a sex slave.'

Shiro looked at the hand covering hers, his fingers now threaded through hers. She glanced at the square faced gold signet ring on his middle finger, the crisp linen shirt with sleeves rolled halfway up muscular arms, the monogrammed silk tie knotted at the neck of the cream linen shirt. 'But you've done okay?'

The bitterness carried through to his laugh. 'Sure. He paid for my education, set up my mother in a house. But there was no way he would recognise me as his son. He, in his own words, met his obligations. That was it.'

Shiro turned her hand over and clasped her fingers through his. He had suffered too. 'I am sorry. You must have had a horrible childhood.'

He shook his head. 'I didn't know any better. He came every week till I went to boarding school. He supported me in London, visited regularly. Guys at Queens University Medical School thought he was a benevolent mentor.' Jega's fingers tightened around hers. 'I have heard of the Ashley-Cooper family.'

'You have?'

Jega shrugged his shoulder. So like Anthony – damn.

'Wealthy, own estates in Sri Lanka and Africa –' he hesitated and then continued. 'Two sons – heirs to the plantations.'

'My father works –' a sob broke through. 'Worked for them as a Tea-maker.'

'And?'

This man would understand. He had suffered at the hands of the British. Maybe together they could make the Ashley-Coopers, William and Anthony and their father, pay for what they had done.

'I've never told anyone. Not even Lalitha knows the truth.'

Jega held her hand and waited.

'Anthony, the younger brother. I thought he was a friend. He made me love him, and then when his father gave him an ultimatum, he chose his life as an Ashley-Cooper ahead of his so-called love for me. I tried to kill myself.' Shiro shook her head. 'It makes me angry to think I was stupid enough to do that.'

'You were in love. You were rejected – it led to your depression.'

Shiro continued, 'Anthony paid my father – can you believe that? Fifty-thousand rupees for my treatment and then put more into my father's savings fund. I didn't know till later. He paid cash to appease his conscience, the bloody Judas.'

'Your father told you about the money?'

Shiro shook her head. 'Anthony's brother William sent a letter to my mother. Saying Anthony and I –' she glanced up at Jega. 'Sorry, the words he used were that we were screwing in the tea bushes.' Shiro scrunched her eyes shut. 'I have never felt so small, so worthless. And now my father –' Shiro stopped and gulped.

'William set up my father. Made it look like dad was stealing.' Shiro felt the bile rise in her throat. She swallowed a sob.

'Shiromi, you don't have to –' Jega got off the stool and put his other hand on her shoulder.

'Yes, I do, I must talk. That's what happened when Anthony left me. I didn't talk.'

He nodded and sat down, still holding her hand.

'My father handed in his resignation rather than be sacked. He is – was scrupulously honest. He would never do it. Never. My brother told us Dad said the assistant Tea-maker, Wright was involved.' She looked at Jega. Wishing again he didn't remind her so much of Anthony.

'Shiromi, you need to go home. I'll drive you.' He stood up and pulled her to her feet.

'But won't people talk?'

'You, Shiromi, have your father's integrity. Come on.'

He let go of her hand.

They walked out of the anatomy museum and climbed into his Holden sedan.

Chapter 35

Every year, the medical students travelled out of Colombo for a week long conference. This year it was to the campsite at Diyatalawa. Jega had volunteered to be chaperone for the trip.

They got into the Diyatalāwa campsite at six am and everyone decided to have a little nap before the first session. Shiro, having slept in the train, was wide awake. She slipped out of the room as soon as her roommates, Lalitha and the other two girls, were asleep. She scrambled up a little mud path above the campground to a rock ledge.

Golden rays of sunshine sneaked through grey clouds to chase away the mist that clung to the rolling green hills. She could smell the tea leaves and the eucalyptus. Strings of women in their cheap cotton saris and cane baskets tied over kumbly headdresses wound their way along the brown mud path towards the tea fields for the day's work. The bellowed commands of the kangani carried on the breeze that swirled up from the valley. She could hear the hum of the machinery in the tea factory across the valley.

It was all so familiar and yet so different.

Today she felt a stranger to this world. Was it only a few years ago that she had been part of the tea plantation life in Watakälé? The joy of life in the Tea-maker's house with her parents and brothers and her times with Anthony by the waterfall seemed a lifetime away.

It was a dream that had turned into a nightmare.

She tried to make sense of the turmoil of emotions in her heart. Bitterness, anger and a hunger for retribution bubbled to the top. If not for the Ashley-Cooper family, her father would be alive and she wouldn't feel this roiling volcano of resentment in her chest waiting to erupt. The psychiatrist advised her to let it go, to concentrate on the future. She couldn't – she had to expose the lie. The story that the assistant Tea-maker Wright and the devil incarnate, William had concocted to discredit her father had driven him out of his mind and to his death.

Then and only then, could she begin to heal.

'Good Morning Shiromi. A beautiful day isn't it? Makes you love the tea plantation.'

Shiro was wrenched out of her thoughts by Jega's voice. 'Jega! What are you doing here?'

He smiled and shrugged. 'I too grew up here, Shiromi. This is my heritage as much as yours, my dear. I love this place too.'

She shoved her hand in the pocket of her jeans, searching for a handkerchief. Giving up, she dragged her hand across her face.

'Here,' Jega handed her a clean white handkerchief. 'I've been standing here long enough to see that you are upset. And before you ask, Lalitha woke up after a nap and was worried that you were not in the room. She came to me.'

'Naturally,' Shiro mumbled. She wiped the tears off her face and looked at the handkerchief. 'But how did you find me?'

'I figured that you would want to be alone somewhere. I thought you would choose a place that looked over the Diyatalāwa valley. Then saw the marks of your shoes on the mud path.'

'Doctor and detective. Brilliant.'

Jega squatted by her side on the rock ledge. 'Shiromi, you are upset. Talk to me. What can I do to help you?'

The memories crashed back into Shiro's consciousness. Anthony by her side that awful day, the same words – *talk to me, talk to me.*

No more talk. It was time for action.

Jega's mother. She had lived all her life here in Diyatalāwa. She would help her. 'Take me to meet your mother.'

Jega recoiled like she had struck him. 'Shiromi, that wouldn't be wise. She is old and doesn't speak much English. You'd be uncomfortable with her.'

Shiro knew she had to act fast before he came up with any more excuses. She put her hand on his arm and gazed into his eyes. 'Jega, are you ashamed of me, of our friendship? Is that why you don't want to introduce me to your mother?'

Her words had the intended effect.

Jega gasped. 'How could I ever be ashamed of you? It's just that –'

Shiro jumped to her feet. 'Done, then. Let's go into town on the day we get an afternoon off. I'll ask Lalitha to come with us. That way no one's going to think we're sneaking off.' She started down the path back to the campsite.

Jega followed.

They left after lunch on Wednesday. Jega had asked the campsite owner about hiring a taxi, but instead he had offered his car and driver for the twenty-minute drive into Diyatalāwa town. They got in the car. Jega got in the front seat, his face set in a mask of grim anxiety. Lalitha slipped into the back seat with Shiro who ignored the aura of tension emanating from Jega.

The car bumped along the part sealed part mud road towards Diyatalāwa town. 'Shiro,' Lalitha whispered, 'what's happening? Why is Dr Jega looking so worried, even angry?'

'He doesn't want me to meet his mum,' Shiro whispered back.

'Then why are you doing this?'

Shiro dug Lalitha in her ribs. 'Shush. I want to ask her how I can get inside information about what happens on the tea estates. She's been around a long time.'

'Why?'

'To clear Daddy's name. Why else?'

Lalitha stared into her friend's eyes. 'Shiro, I know you. There's a lot more happening here. I don't know if I want to be a part of this.'

Shiro looked into her eyes. 'You want to help me, don't you?'

The car entered the outskirts of the town and shuddered to a stop behind an open truck. 'Aiyo sir,' the driver said. '*Pola* day, no? All the people are bringing all the things to sell. Look sir. Jak fruit and clothes.' He pointed to a stack of crudely assembled wooden crates with gaps in the sides. 'They are selling fowls and goats also.'

'A pola!' Lalitha pushed open the back door. 'Driver, let me off here. I love pola markets.'

The driver pulled to the edge of the road and Lalitha leapt out. She grabbed her purse off the back seat. 'Dr Jega,' she addressed Jega through the front window, 'I'll see you right here in two hours.' With a cheery wave to Shiro, she plunged into the crazy and colourful assortment of roadside stalls and screaming hawkers.

Jega turned to Shiro. His lips turned up in the mere hint of a smile. 'That's one girl who knows how to enjoy a couple of hours' free time. Are you sure you don't want to join her?'

Shiro shook her head. 'I want to meet your mother.'

He nodded, then pointed to a side road and directed the driver to turn into it. They stopped at the side of a little field, part grass but mostly dry mud. A few young boys in their teens were kicking an old soccer ball around.

Jega got out of the car and strode towards the edge of the field. He stood rigid and quiet. Shiro leapt out and scampered after him. She placed her fingers on his arm. The muscles tensed under her touch. 'Jega, it's all right. Let's go back. I won't ask to see your mother.'

The muscles of his arm flinched under her fingers. 'I used to come here after school. Especially on the days when my father came to visit mother. He would say hello and then give me ten rupees, tell me to go play. I would come here. They called me white boy. They laughed, asked if my mother was working.' A shudder went through him.

One of the boys kicked the ball. It sailed through the air and landed at their feet. 'Sir, sorry sir,' one of the older boys called out. Jega bent, picked up the ball and kicked it in an elegant curve directly between the makeshift goal post. 'I haven't done that since I was sixteen.'

He turned and placed his hands on Shiro's shoulders. She felt the tenseness of his fingers through the wool of her jumper. 'Shiromi, I have to talk with you before we visit my mother. It's time you knew the truth.'

'Truth?'

'You see, my mother runs a brothel.'

'A whorehouse? Why?' Shiro tried to step back. Jega's hands on her shoulders held her.

He shrugged. 'When my father's wife threw my mother out, he set her up here, bought her a little house. He came weekly to see her. He brought her gifts, clothes, expensive crockery, ornaments, even paintings. He talked to me. He said he loved her. But for all that she was his whore, nothing more.' He stopped and gazed into the distance. 'One day I went back to the house early. It was raining. I saw them.' A shudder went through his body. 'She was crying. He was handing her money.'

'Please, Jega, you don't have to tell me. Let's go back.'

He shook his head. 'When I was fifteen he paid for me to go to the St Matthias College boarding school in Colombo. Everything was paid for. I learnt later that he cut off all support to my mother from that year.'

'The bastard. How did she manage?'

He shrugged. 'That's when she decided on her business.'

'But why a brothel?'

He took his hands off Shiro's shoulders and curled his fingers around hers. 'There are many coolie girls who are raped by the British superintendents. The girls used by the superintendents are ostracised on the plantation. Sometimes they run away. When they get to the towns, all they can do is be a prostitute. There too, they are abused, beaten sometimes, die in backyard abortions. Some commit suicide.'

'I grew up in the plantation, but I had no idea it was so bad.' A memory flashed across Shiro's mind, making her head whirl. 'My best friend growing up was a coolie girl. She got pregnant.' She had always assumed the father was another coolie. But the British superintendent on Watakälé at that time was Anthony. He wouldn't? Surely? She was no longer sure.

Jega's fingers tightened around hers. 'It's possible. My mother set up the institution to provide these girls with a job. A safe place to do the only thing they can to make money.'

'But who are the clients?'

'Some are from the Diyatalāwa army camp.' He gestured to the hill over which lay the Sri Lankan Army encampment. 'Others are the very men who had brought the girls down.'

'The British superintendents?'

'Yes. My mother runs an upmarket establishment. The girls are clean, the rooms comfortable. Some of her girls even speak English. The men pay large sums for the service of these women.'

Shiro smiled at the image that came into her mind. 'So they come to your mother's place and pay big money to have sex with the very women they raped?'

Jega shrugged. 'Well, not the same one.'

'But it could happen. Dad told me that the British can't tell one coolie from the other.'

'Shiromi, there's something more I have to tell you.' He let go of her hands and placed his hands on her shoulders again. His gaze met and locked with hers. 'You have never asked for the identity of my father.'

'I didn't think it concerned me.'

'But it does, my dear. My father, the man who raped my mother and fathered me, is James Ashley-Cooper.'

'James Ashley-Cooper? As in Anthony's father?'

'Yes.'

Shiro gazed at Jega. She wasn't crazy. The resemblance was no longer imagined. 'You look like your half-brother.' She felt like a pit was open at her feet. His voice came from a distance.

'Are you all right?'

She sobbed and he reached out to hold her. But he was not Anthony. She pulled away and smiled through her tears. 'Jega, may I borrow your hanky again?'

The spell was broken. They both laughed as he handed her the clean white linen square.

They walked back to the car. 'Do you want to go back to the Pola and wait for Lalitha?'

'And not see your mother?' Shiro swung round to face him. 'Jega, she is the bravest and strongest person I have ever heard of. Please, I have to see her.'

Jega smiled as he accepted back the crushed handkerchief. 'She would be delighted to see you. I have told her about what Anthony and William have done to you, your father and the people in the plantation. Nothing the British planters do surprises her.'

Shiro stopped in her tracks as a thought struck her. 'Do William and Anthony visit your mother's establishment in Diyatalāwa?'

'She told me that William used to come regularly.'

'And Anthony?'

'No. Anthony has never been to my mother's place.'

Chapter 36

'How do you expect to get that assistant Tea-maker Wright to confess that he set up your father and that he was following William Ashley-Cooper's instructions?'

Shiro and Jega sat at a small wrought iron table in the Green Cabin Café in Bambalapitiya. Jega had offered to drive Lalitha and Shiro home after a late lecture. They had dropped Lalitha off at the little flat she shared with a couple of other girls. Shiro had asked Jega if they could talk.

Shiro stirred another spoon of sugar into her coffee. 'He's probably the Tea-maker now.' She grimaced, thinking of the Wrights in the Tea-maker's quarters. 'I've been through the documents my brother Victor brought from Dad's cabinet. Dad kept copies of the tea sales ledger entries, as well as receipts from the transport agent Hemachandra Mudalali. They matched. The entries in the ledgers in the tea factory office, however, indicated a discrepancy. It looked like Dad was pocketing the difference, cheating the plantation and Oriental Produce. Somebody fixed the ledgers in the factory office.'

'Everything I've heard about your father tells me he wouldn't have done anything dishonest.'

Shiro nodded. 'You see Jega, only two people had keys to the tea factory office cabinet where the ledgers were kept – my dad and the superintendent, your dear half-brother, William Ashley-Cooper.'

'So, you think William and that Wright guy worked together to discredit your father.'

'That's not all.' She stopped and smiled at Jega. 'I wrote to Uncle Hemachandra.'

'The transport agent in Diyatalāwa? He's supposed to be a tough businessman. Always out for a buck. You know him?'

Shiro dismissed his words with a sweep of her hand. 'Sure, since I was a baby. He loves me. Kind of like a daughter.'

'Loves you. Everyone does.' Jega mumbled under his breath.

'What did you say?'

'Forget it. What did Hemachandra tell you?'

'He was shocked at the allegations. He said there was never anything underhand in his dealings with my dad.'

Shiro stopped and looked down at the cup of tea, now cold with a film of brown milk curdling on the surface. She picked up the teaspoon and stabbed through the layer, sending drops of tea onto the table top. 'I know what you're thinking. Uncle wouldn't confess to having done it anyway. So I confirmed it.' She dropped her eyelids.

Jega reached over the table and placed his hand over hers. 'Out with it. What else did you do?'

'You see, part of the accusation made by William was that the money went into Dad's account. So I went to the bank where Dad's account is. I knew they wouldn't give me the details. So I made an appointment with the manager.' She paused and bit her lip.

'And?'

Shiro dropped her voice. 'I'm not particularly proud of this. I spun a story to him. I was the youngest; Mum says that we are almost destitute after Dad died, that there isn't money for me to go to medical school. I needed to know. My future, my career, my very life depended on it.'

'And he showed you your father's accounts?'

'Not directly, he looked at it and said that all that had gone in for the last two years was the two weekly salary payments. He did mention the large deposit into the provident fund around the time I got sick. That, of course, was Anthony's conscience payoff. Basically, the bank manager assured me that there was enough to see me through medical school and even postgraduate study.' She paused. 'I thanked him. I was a little teary.' She giggled. 'He gave me his handkerchief.'

'None of this is definitive proof that Wright and William plotted to get rid of your father.'

'I know. We need a confession.'

'And how, my dear, do you plan to get that?'

They gazed at each other across the table. Shiro's eyes brimmed with tears. Her mouth turned down at the edges. She turned her hand over and threaded her fingers with his. 'That is where you can help me.'

'You have it all plotted out, haven't you?'

She blinked away the tears. He laughed and tossed her his handkerchief. 'I think I'll buy you a box of white hankies for Christmas. Now what is your plan?'

Shiro tightened her fingers around his. 'We have our clinical placement in Nuwara-Eliya hospital next week. You'll be there with us for the two weeks. That's our opportunity to visit Watakälé and talk to Mr Wright. We get him to confess. You are the witness. Then we see William.'

'Why do this?'

'I have to clear Dad's name for my family, but also to wash out the demons in my head.' She tossed her head. 'Anyway, don't you think it's time you met your brother?'

Chapter 37

September 1969 Watakälé

'How could you do it? You allowed that awful white superintendent William to make out that Daddy was cheating.' Shiro stopped. Her lips trembled. 'He died because of it. You were his friend. He trusted you. He welcomed you into our home, yet you as good as killed Daddy that day.'

Shiro and the Tea-maker, Mr Wright, stood facing each other across the old wooden office table. On it was an open ledger.

Shiro had her hair drawn back in two tight plaits. She was dressed in a light blue cotton blouse, buttoned up to her neck. The blue pleated skirt she wore looked like it could have been part of the uniform of a missionary school which, she had told Jega that morning, it had been. She wore no makeup. Her clean, scrubbed face radiated innocence and vulnerability, the little girl of the tea plantation returning home.

Mr Wright stood looking away from Shiro. His eyes went to the locked steel cabinet and then dropped to his feet.

Jega stood with his hands stuffed in his trouser pockets. He watched a tear slip down Shiro's cheek. Mr Wright was beginning to look distressed. His hands clenched and relaxed, and his Adam's apple bobbed up and down as he swallowed.

'Shiro, child, I didn't have a choice. Your father said he was tired of being on his own here. That he wanted to apply for a job in Colombo. I thought this would just hasten his leaving. And the car, he had it fixed the day before by the mechanic. Your father was a good driver. I truly don't know what happened.'

Shiro frowned. 'You had no choice? Why? What was happening?'

Mr Wright's body trembled. He put his hands on the edge of the table. Then slumped into the chair and dropped his head into his hands.

Shiro leaned over the table. Jega moved around the table to stand close to Mr Wright. 'I was the one' he mumbled. 'I got some of the coolies to help me and the driver of the transport lorry. Hemachandra Mudalali had no idea what was happening. I regularly sent tea in the lorry to Diyatalāwa where it was picked up by my contacts. One of the coolies wanted more money. He told the superintendent William.'

Shiro leaned closer. 'So the superintendent, William Ashley-Cooper, blackmailed you? He got you to frame Dad and in exchange you get off free.'

Mr Wright nodded.

Shiro leaned even closer and spoke into his ear. 'What did you do? Tell me, please. I have to know.'

'I am sorry.' Mr Wright howled. 'I framed the man who trained me, my mentor – my friend. I did what William Ashley-Cooper asked me to do. He said he would destroy me. I have small children. I did what he wanted. I am damned. Damned!' He jumped up and ran out of the office and up the steps to the Tea-maker's house.

Shiro and Jega watched as Mr Wright ran, tripping and slipping up the muddy steps.

Shiro smiled up at Jega. 'Did you get it?'

Jega pulled his right hand out of his pocket. In it nested a tiny tape recorder. He pressed stop and then rewind. He pressed play.

'I am damned. Damned!'

'Yes, we got it.'

'Great,' Shiro grabbed Jega's hand. 'Tomorrow morning we go see the mighty William Ashley-Cooper.'

***

Appu stood with his arms outstretched, blocking the way to the steps. 'No! Chinnamma! Go back to Colombo. You must not talk to Ashley-Cooper Periadorai.'

Shiro stood with her hands on her hips. Today, she wasn't the little girl returning home to the tea plantation. She was the budding professional. The slim fitting, black linen skirt and white silk blouse with a button open at the neck were a gift from Shiro's uncle, George. They and the handmade black leather shoes had all been purchased from a boutique shop in Colombo. A silk medical-faculty-scarf, black with silver skull and crossbones, was knotted around her neck, exposing just a hint of cleavage at the neck of the blouse. With her hair drawn back in a low bun and a light sheen of makeup, she was cool and confident.

'No, Appu. I will see William Ashley-Cooper.' She growled in Tamil. 'I am not the child I was when you last saw me. And none of the Ashley-Cooper family, William, Anthony or even their almighty father, James, can threaten me anymore.'

The words were interrupted by a bout of coughing. The British accent was unmistakable. 'Who the hell is that, Appu?'

'Aiyoo. What will happen now?' Appu wailed.

Shiro tensed. She felt Jega's hand on her back, his voice a whisper in her ear. 'Hang in there. This could get nasty.'

There was no going back now. Shiro took a deep breath. Walking past Appu, she climbed the three steps to the veranda. Jega moved up behind her.

Standing closer to William Ashley-Cooper, Shiro barely controlled a gasp of surprise. He looked gaunt and unwell. The gold-flecked blonde hair was lank. His eyes seemed sunk in his eye sockets. The white linen suit and cashmere jumper hung on a frame that no longer filled it.

'Good Morning, Mr Ashley-Cooper. I hope you don't mind this early morning incursion on your time, but we need to get back to Nuwara-Eliya.'

'I damn well resent your barging into my house at this ungodly hour. Who the hell are you two, anyway?'

She tilted her head up and looked directly into William's vicious blue eyes. A shudder went through her body. Jega increased the pressure of his hand on her back.

'I am not surprised you don't remember the last time we met, Mr Ashley-Cooper, given you tried to rape me on that occasion.'

William leaned towards Shiro. His eyes narrowed, but registered no recognition. Her every instinct was to step back. Jega's hand on her back held her in place.

The silent pause on the veranda was interrupted by a female voice from the front door. 'William, why don't you invite your guests into the house? I've asked Appu to make a fresh pot of tea.'

Shiro's eyes flicked from William to the slim woman in a pale blue cotton dress and cardigan. So, William had a wife, a British one.

'They are not exactly invited guests, Janet. More like early morning intruders.'

The woman glanced from William to Shiro. She stepped closer to them and then gasped. She extended both hands to Shiro. 'Is it you, Shiro? I'm Janet, I was Janet Irvine. We were friends when my father worked here.' She stopped and glanced at William who was standing statue still. 'I'm so sorry to hear about your father.'

So he married Janet and continued to visit prostitutes in Diyatalāwa. How typical.

Shiro took the proffered hands in hers. 'Of course I remember you, Janet.

Although I wouldn't say we were exactly friends, given you didn't respond to any of my letters after you left Watakälé.'

Janet blushed and looked at her feet. 'I'm sorry. I wanted to. But my parents and my uncle –'

'Don't worry about it, Janet. All water under the bridge now.'

Shiro dropped Janet's hands and faced William. 'I understand tea plantation standards and moralities – or maybe we should say amoralities – a lot better now.' She smiled at William. 'I am Shiromi Rasiah, Mr Ashley-Cooper. The last time we met by the stream you called me some interesting names.' She cocked her head and put her fingers to her chin. 'Let me think, bit of fluff, delectable piece of flesh and even a she-devil. But you were not satisfied with discrediting your brother and breaking up our relationship, were you? You had to frame my father of theft and drive him to his death.'

Janet slipped between Shiro and William. 'Shiro, you're distraught, my dear. Your father resigned. William had nothing to do with it. It was an accident that killed him. That area is notorious.'

'You're as pathetic as your husband, Janet.' Shiro's eyes narrowed in disgust. 'You don't really believe what you are saying, do you?'

William grasped Janet by her arm and shoved her out of the way. He glared at Shiro. 'Your father,' he shifted his eyes to Jega, 'and whoever Rasiah was to you, was a useless do-gooder. My dear little brother, Anthony, your lover, pampered him to keep in your good books. Your father refused to listen to reason after I took over Watakälé.'

Shiro prayed for patience, infinitely grateful for the comfort of Jega's hand on the small of her back. 'So you decided to get rid of him. You blackmailed Mr Wright, who was the one who was actually cheating you. You made him frame my father.'

William laughed. It was a demon bray that reminded Shiro of the day by the stream. She dragged her mind back to the present.

'You are hallucinating, girl. You can't prove anything.'

Jega stepped around Shiro. He slipped the tape recorder out of his pocket. 'Actually William, we have a full confession from your collaborator, the current Tea-maker.' He switched on the tape.

Mr Wright's agonised voice came through loud and clear. 'I am sorry. I framed the man who trained me, my mentor – my friend. I did what William Ashley-Cooper asked me to do. He said he would destroy me. I have small children. I did what he wanted. I am damned. Damned!'

William continued to laugh. He broke into a fit of coughing. 'And who the hell are you?'

Shiro glanced at Jega. Jega pressed the stop button on the tape recorder, then slipped it back into his shirt pocket.

Slate grey eyes locked with blue. 'My name is Dr Jega Jayaseelen. We haven't met before, but I have heard all about you from your father and mine. You may be interested to know that he calls you a heartless bastard. For some weird reason he seems proud that he has moulded you to be like that.' He took a step closer to William. 'I am your half-brother, William. The son of the Indian woman James, your father and mine, kept here in this very house. The woman your mother, the doyen of British propriety, threw out when she came here as a bride. My mother was fifteen-years-old and pregnant when she left.'

William glared at Jega. His eyes shifted to Shiro. He guffawed. 'You two really are all into make-believe today, aren't you?'

Jega shook his head. 'I really don't care if you believe that I'm your brother or not. Frankly, given what I've learned about you and the way your brother Anthony treated Shiromi, I'd rather not claim any relationship to your family. But it's true.'

William swung back to face them. His face turned a mottled red. 'You, Anthony and that minister, Robert Kirkland, you all think you are better than me. But I always have the last laugh.' He stopped and coughed. Drops of spittle formed on his lips. The veins in his neck stood out. 'Get off my property before I get you thrown off,' William laughed again and turned away.

Shiro stepped back. Jega pushed her behind him. 'I've been to the manor, William. Your mother asked to see me. It was when I was doing my medical training at Queens University Medical School. Our father himself picked me up at Chesterfield Station in the Jaguar Phantom. It was autumn. The red gold of the ancient lime trees that line the avenue were amazing. Your father showed me your horses, I believe yours is Zeus? I met your mother in the Queen's Room. The carvings of the Tudor rose and thistle on the ceiling is truly impressive. Ask her about our meeting. We had a lovely afternoon tea. The gold rim lavender design on your mother's favourite tea service is so elegant. And the lemon tarts from the manor kitchen are divine.'

William didn't turn round.

Janet, standing at the door to the lounge, gasped. 'William, he's got to be speaking the truth. The manor is not open to the public. And your mother's tea service …'

Jega kept his eyes on William's back. 'Your mother apologised to me for what she did to mine. She told me she fully supported your father paying for my medical training. All she wanted was that he never acknowledges me as his son. A true, blue-blooded lady of the manor.'

William swung back. 'You bastard!'

Jega smiled. 'True. I am a bastard. And by tomorrow, father will have a copy of the tape and a transcript of Mr Wright's confession. It's on the way by express post. I will call him later today to fill him in. Father will know exactly what his legal firstborn son has been up to.' He stopped and shrugged. 'He probably will do nothing but he will know the truth about you.'

Jega turned to Shiro. 'Come, Shiromi. I think we are done here.' They turned and walked down the steps to the car.

William's raucous laughter stopped them both in their tracks. 'Truth? You came here for the truth? Well you can have the truth. I had the mechanic fix the brakes in your father's car the day before he died. I thought he'd go into a ditch, see it as an omen to resign. I didn't expect him to go racing off on the hairpin bends of Haputale. I guess you could say I killed him. And you know what? I am not sorry. Not one bit.' He laughed and broke into a rasping cough.

Shiro shivered. William Ashley-Cooper had murdered her father. She had her evidence, but it wouldn't bring her father back. It wouldn't change anything.

'Get in.' Jega dragged her down the steps and bundled her into the car. He leapt into the driver's seat, revved the engine and pulled away down the drive.

Shiro sat dry eyed and rigid. Jega negotiated the winding road down the hill away from the superintendent's house. 'Damn the man. I knew I shouldn't have brought you here.'

The road took a sharp turn. Shiro was silent, staring across the valley. This place, the mountains, the smells, the very air reminded her of Anthony. Across the valley was the clear bubbling stream and a small waterfall. Shiro's eyes fixed on a cluster of trees and the sentinel like rock.

'Jega, please stop the car. There is a place I have to visit.'

Jega pulled to a side of the road. 'What is it, Shiromi?'

He followed her as she pushed through the undergrowth on the now overgrown mud path. In a few minutes they came to the cluster of trees and the shield-like rock. They stood together on a ledge of rock overhanging the stream. Shiro turned to face him. 'Jega, do you love me?'

Jega stepped back. 'You are upset, my dear. It's been a stressful morning.'

She grasped his arms. 'You've been so amazing to me, Jega. I could not have done this without you. Please, I need to know. Do you care for me?'

She felt his hands in her hair. The wind blew her curls around her head, just like it had when she had stood there with Anthony. The curls coiled around Jega's fingers, just like they had Anthony's. His arms drew her close to his body. Shiro felt safe. Secure. Jega was a good man, a man she could trust with her life. He would care for her heart. Could she give it to him?

She felt his lips on her forehead. 'Shiro.' It was a whisper, almost a blessing.

Shiro wound her arms around his neck. She threaded her fingers in his hair. She heard his sharp indrawn breath. She spoke into his neck. 'Kiss me, Jega.'

She kept her eyes shut as his lips travelled over her eyes and cheek. She pushed away the memories of Anthony. She must forget. Move forward.

Jega's lips paused at the corner of hers. He slipped a hand under her chin and turned her face up to his. 'Open your eyes, Shiromi.'

Shiro blinked and looked into his kind grey eyes.

He raised a finger to wipe a tear from her cheek. 'This is where you met Anthony, isn't it? Where you finally said goodbye?'

Shiro scrunched her eyes shut and willed herself not to cry. Not trusting herself to speak, she nodded her assent.

'Shiro, you can't exorcise your memories by pretending that I am Anthony, darling. It will only bring more pain to you.' He pulled her tighter in his arms. 'And to me too.'

Shiro stepped back. Jega loosened his hold of her. 'Is that what you think I am doing, Jega? You're wrong. No, a million times, no. You are the kindest, most wonderful man I have met. I do love you.'

Jega shrugged his shoulder. Shiro flinched at the similarity of the gesture to Anthony's. 'You may not even recognise it, Shiro. You may think you love me. But you love what you see of Anthony in me. As much as I care for you, I can't accept that.'

'Please.' Shiro reached out and touched his cheek. 'I don't want that either. I want to love the wonderful person I know you are. Help me. Teach me to forget him and love you for yourself.'

'All right.' He took her hands in his and pulled her down to sit on the rock. He slipped his arm around her. She rested her head on his shoulder, pushing away the memory of sitting just this way with Anthony.

'Shiromi, you need closure. Two years ago Anthony left you. You were devastated; hurt and depressed. You have recovered physically, but you have a way to go mentally. You need to know what happened to him, where he is now, what he is doing. Then and only then, can you move on with your life.' His arm tightened around her. 'Till you do that, you will continue to live in some halfway world of hopes and dreams about Anthony.'

'There is only one person who will know what's happening with Anthony. His best friend, Bobsy.'

Jega laughed. 'Bobsy isn't a very aristocratic British name!'

'He's the minister in charge of the church in Nuwara-Eliya. He and Anthony have been friends from schooldays. I know him from when he was the assistant minister in Colombo. He married our school chaplain, Miss Grace.'

'Come on, then.' Jega jumped up and took her hand. 'Nuwara-Eliya is just a forty-five minute drive. We can be there by noon. Let's go see this Bobsy fellow and get some answers.'

Hand-in-hand, they scrambled up the path and got in the car.

Chapter 38

September 1969 Nuwara-Eliya

Jega insisted they stop for a meal in Nuwara-Eliya, and it was almost noon when they headed towards the manse.

'There it is!' Shiro pointed to the wooden sign on which the words 'Reformed Church of Scotland' were painted in black. An arrow below the words pointed to a mud road winding up and away from the township of Nuwara-Eliya. 'That's where Bobsy and Grace live.'

Jega swung the car up the road.

Shiro felt queasy. Was this the right thing to do? Did she want to know? What if Anthony was happily married in England? Had a child? Wouldn't it be better to hold on to her dream? A dream that maybe – No. Jega was right. She needed closure.

She sneaked a side glance at him. Jega smiled. Steering the car with his right hand, he covered her fingers with his left. 'It will be all right. Whatever you learn about Anthony, I'll be there. I will help you get through today.'

Shiro clung to his fingers. Yes, she could trust him.

One final turn in the mud path and they were there. The sun bathed the minister's manse and the little sandstone church on the hill. The wrought iron gate stood open. Jega drove up the muddy drive. The heady smell of roses and jasmine blossoms invaded the car.

Jega pulled up outside the manse. A slim, dark woman dressed in an ankle-length, print cotton skirt and jumper stood on the veranda looking towards the approaching car. 'Look, Shiromi,' Jega pointed, 'that's probably the maid or the nanny. Let's ask her where Reverend Kirkland is.'

'Dear God!' Shiro gasped.

Jega swung around to Shiro. 'What's the matter? Are you –'

Shiro didn't wait for Jega to park the car. She wrenched open the passenger side door and leapt out. 'Lakshmi!' Shiro screamed as she ran towards the woman on the veranda.

The woman shaded her eye against the glare and stared at Shiro's flying figure. Then with a matching scream of 'Shiro Chinnamma,' she jumped off the veranda and ran towards Shiro.

Shiro hugged Lakshmi as she sobbed. 'God, God, you have answered my prayers.'

Keeping her arm around Lakshmi, Shiro moved a half-step back. 'So this is where you have been all along. What's the big secret? Why didn't Mum want me to know? No, don't answer. It's to do with me making high class friends who are not from the plantation.' She laughed and hugged Lakshmi again. 'I'm babbling! Tell me, is your child here also? Surely Bobsy would have let you keep him? Why did you say he had to be adopted?' She hugged Lakshmi again. 'It's good to see you.'

Lakshmi smiled and disentangled herself from Shiro's arms. 'No, Chinnamma, I came here only a few days ago. I was working at Hemachandra Mudalali's till then. And yes, my son is here.'

Even as she spoke a little boy toddled down the veranda steps. 'Amma,' he called.

Shiro dropped to her knees before the boy. Lakshmi squatted by her side. 'His name is Daniel, Shiro Chinnamma.'

'My, you are a sweetie,' Shiro took the pudgy hand of the little olive skinned boy. The sun glinted on his brown-gold hair.

The boy reached out and touched her hair. 'Pretty,' he lisped.

Shiro looked into the cobalt blue eyes and felt a cold chill creep through her veins. 'Lakshmi,' she whispered, 'Daniel's father, the man who raped you.'

Daniel turned at the sound of footsteps on the veranda. He pointed. 'Da-da.'

Brown leather shoes led up to a creased pair of brown wool trousers. Still on her knees, Shiro tilted her head up. A brown leather belt, then a white shirt open at the neck and tucked into the trousers. She gazed into cobalt blue eyes the exact colour of Daniel's.

The moment froze. Shiro's breath caught in her throat. Anthony was Daniel's father. Anthony had raped Lakshmi, and not knowing that she was pregnant – or knowing and not caring – continued on to romance her by the stream. Now he had come back from England to marry Lakshmi and adopt his son. She held her breath.

She was only partly aware of Jega's hands on her shoulders. His voice, as always, was caring, concerned, 'Shiromi, are you all right?'

Daniel, sensing the tension, scuttled away to his mother. Lakshmi picked him up and stood up.

Anthony's voice. 'Shiro?'

No. She was no longer a little girl. She was not the Tea-maker's naïve daughter. She was a professional with a future. Yet the betrayal tore at her soul, ripped out that part of her that had hoped, dreamed, that maybe Anthony would come to her.

She leapt to her feet and bridged the gap between them. She raised her hand and brought her open palm down across Anthony's cheek. 'You bastard!'

Anthony caught her wrists. 'Shiro please, let me explain.'

'Explain? *You* raped Lakshmi. *You* got her pregnant and then said you loved *me*. How could you? How could you, Anthony?' She ripped her hands away from him and pummelled Anthony on his chest with her closed fists.

She could hear Lakshmi's voice in the background. 'Shiro Chinnamma, aiyoo – it is not like that.'

Anthony wrapped his arms around her. He held her tight against him. 'Please, Shiro, darling, I can explain.'

Little Daniel started wailing. Lakshmi picked him up and ran into the house.

Sobs rent Shiro's body. 'How could you? I loved you! You said –'

Jega's hands drew her away from Anthony. 'Anthony,' Jega's voice held a controlled fury. 'Haven't you and the rest of your Ashley-Cooper empire done enough to hurt Shiromi? She's doing fine without you. Let her live her life.'

Anthony dropped his arms. Shiro felt bereft, cold. She shivered.

Anthony stared at Jega. 'Who are you?'

'I'm Jega Jayaseelen'

Anthony's pupils dilated. 'Dr Jega Jayaseelen? You are –'

Shiro tried to move towards Anthony. Jega tightened his hands on her shoulders. 'Yes, Anthony. I am your father's son by his sex slave. I guess you've heard about me.' He glanced at the house. 'At least you are willing to accept legitimate fatherhood of your son!'

Shiro trembled. 'Jega.'

His hands tightened on her shoulders. He turned her away from Anthony into his arms. 'Shiro, I'm taking you back to the hospital quarters. You're trembling – going into shock. I think you've had enough for today.'

Shiro shut her eyes. Then nodded. She had been strong all day. She was now close to breaking point. Jega understood.

Jega looked at Anthony. 'We need to leave. I'll come back tomorrow morning.'

'No.' Anthony stepped towards them. 'I need to talk to her. I need to explain.'

Keeping an arm around her, Jega held out his other to stop Anthony. 'Not now, Anthony. Dammit, can't you see what this has done to her?'

He guided Shiro to the car. She went with him.

Lakshmi came running down the drive. 'Shiro Chinnamma. Wait, don't go.'

Jega shut the door of the car.

Shiro didn't look back.

***

Anthony stood on the veranda staring down the drive where Jega and Shiro had driven away the day before.

He had seen Shiro. She had grown up. Her dress, her demeanour, all spoke of the woman she was, not the girl he had held in his arms two years ago.

And just by being here, he had hurt her – again.

Jega had said he would be back. He would explain it all to him, ask him to talk to Shiro.

Lakshmi came out of the house. She placed Daniel in his arms. 'Dr Jega Jayaseelen, he is your brother?'

Anthony nodded, '*Our* brother, Lakshmi.'

'He will be back today. I am sure he will help you.'

Anthony stayed silent. What was there to say? His brother – Professor Jega Jayaseelen. He would be good for Shiro. He loved her – it was obvious. Maybe she would marry him. Anthony winced. It was good that he would be in Australia.

'Anthony,' Lakshmi continued. 'I'd like to see Shiro Chinnamma again.'

He put his hand on Lakshmi's shoulder. 'Yes, I think she would like that. Once we explain everything to Jega.'

They turned at the sound of footsteps. Jega stood before them, Hands on hips, lips turned in a sneer.

'You make a pretty picture with your Indian woman and son, Anthony. Following in your father's footsteps and *keep*ing her? Planning to get a British lass over soon? Maybe you've selected a little cottage for your mistress already?'

Anthony gasped. 'What are you talking about?'

'Don't play the innocent with me, Anthony! How could you do it? Have a child with a woman, a coolie woman, and then romance Shiromi? Seeing you has hurt her again.'

'Dear God, Jega. You've got it all wrong –'

Lakshmi took Daniel from Anthony. She put him down and pointed into the house. 'Go to Aunty Grace, Daniel.'

She turned to face Jega. 'Aiya, you don't understand. I am not Anthony's lover or keep and definitely not his wife.'

Jega swung round to her. 'Then who the hell are you to him?'

'Dr Jega, Anthony's brother raped me when I was in the estate, and –'

'William? The child is William's?'

Anthony stepped between Jega and Lakshmi. 'You know my brother, William?'

Lakshmi put a hand on Anthony's arm. 'Wait.' She turned back to Jega. 'Anthony adopted the baby. He said that Daniel deserved to grow up with the name Ashley-Cooper.'

Grey eyes and blue met and held. 'You are a better man than your father.'

Anthony smiled. 'You have father's eyes, just like –' He glanced at the woman standing by him.

Jega followed Anthony's gaze. 'You – you are another – God almighty! How many women did James Ashley-Cooper bed?'

Lakshmi took Jega's hand. 'I am Lakshmi. And I guess this means that I am your sister.'

A cough at the door leading into the house, made them all turn. Anthony turned. 'Bob, this is Dr Jega Jayaseelen.' He put his hand on Bob's shoulder. 'This is my best friend and mentor, the Reverend Robert Kirkland.'

Jega held out his hand. 'Glad to meet you, Robert. Although I must say I have heard about you from Shiro as Bobsy.'

Bob nodded and smiled. 'I'm so glad to hear that Shiro is doing so well at medical school. Her father Rajan was so proud when she got accepted. Yesterday was a real shock to her. Is she all right?'

Jega nodded. 'I made her have an early night. She's back in the wards today.'

The harsh ring of the telephone interrupted their conversation.

Grace came out onto the veranda. 'Anthony, Janet called. She couldn't talk for long – but left a message. William has had a heart attack or stroke. She wasn't clear about which. He's in hospital. She sounded distressed.'

Anthony gasped. 'Poor Janet. Did she leave a number to call back?'

Grace shook her head. 'I don't think I heard her right. She said something about Shiromi going there yesterday. Apparently William went into a rage afterwards. Accused Appu and even Janet of betraying him.'

'We were there yesterday morning. Before we came here.'

Anthony, Lakshmi and Bob turned to Jega.

Jega shrugged. 'Shiromi insisted on doing it. She had it all planned out.' He plunged his hand into his trouser pocket and produced a small tape recorder. 'I have a confession from the Tea-maker, Mr Wright, saying that he and William framed Shiromi's father. And William saying that he fixed the brakes on the car.'

Anthony frowned. 'But William wouldn't care that you know. Why was he so furious?'

'I told him I would send a copy to your father. I couriered it. It will be in Father's hands today.'

Jega turned to Grace. 'Is William in Kandy Hospital? You better get a start if you want to get there before nightfall.'

'No,' Grace shook her head. 'He was in too much pain. They rushed him to Nuwara-Eliya Base Hospital.'

Jega swung round. 'Damn! Shiromi's covering for the medical registrar there today. I need to get to her.' He raced away from them and leapt in his car. They heard the skid of tires as he screeched down the drive.

Chapter 39

Shiro put an old kettle on the stove in the hospital staff room. She spooned four teaspoons of tea into the teapot. Picking up the kettle on the first boil she filled the teapot, waited the mandatory five minutes, and poured the brew into three cups.

She turned to her two fellow medical students, Nandan and Krishna. 'Guys, get off your bottoms and drink your tea. We promised to cover the afternoon wards for the registrar, remember?' She added milk and sugar to the cups of tea and handed it to the boys.

'The one good thing about this clinical placement,' Nandan mused, 'is the fact that we get to drink the best tea in the country.'

Shiro sipped and sniffed the cup. 'True. I think this is BOP fanning.'

'Top of the class, sexy and a tea taster. No wonder old brachial plexus is mad about you.'

'He is a friend.' Shiro swiped Krishna with her stethoscope. 'Come on, boys. Let's get to the wards.'

Nandan stretched and yawned. 'Why bother? Nothing exciting happens in surgery. I've sutured a couple of coolies and cleaned a million abscesses. Can't wait to get back to Colombo General.'

Shiro slipped on her white ward coat. 'I like it here in the medical ward. The nurses treat me almost like I'm a doctor already.'

The door to the staff tea room swung open. 'Doctor, come quickl!' The nurse gestured to Shiro. Shiro rolled her eyes to the boys and followed the nurse. 'What is it, nurse?

The nurse ran down the corridor, forcing Shiro to follow.

A man was slumped over in the wheelchair, his right hand gripping the shirt over his heart. He groaned and retched into the pan the attendant held.

The profuse sweating, the pallor, the rapid staccato breath – Shiro didn't need an ECG for the diagnosis. This was a cardiac, probably a big one.

She turned to the nurse. 'Where's Dr Nirmalan?'

'He said he would be at home. To call him if we need.'

'Ring him. And get this man on a bed. Set up an ECG and get me a morphine. Also an intravenous.' Shiro picked up the admission form, then looked at the patient's face.

The hoarse whisper was a miserable echo of the arrogant tone that had ordered her and Jega off the veranda of the Watakälé superintendent's bungalow yesterday. 'What the hell are you doing here?'

Shiro took a deep breath. This was a patient. Who he was should not matter. 'I believe you are having a heart attack, Mr Ashley-Cooper.' She struggled to keep her voice calm. 'The doctor will be here shortly, but meanwhile I will give you something for the pain and set up a drip to keep you from going into shock.'

Shiro gestured to the nurse and attendant. 'One – two – three.' They shifted William on to the hospital bed. The nurse set up the ECG leads. The attendant held William's hand down. Shiro slipped on a pair of surgical gloves and picked up the intravenous needle.

'I don't want you touching me. How the hell do I know you are qualified?' William stammered.

The nurse connecting the ECG leads reached over William. 'Sir, miss is a medical student. She knows what she is doing. She is trained.'

'And,' the attendant snarled at William, 'you better be thankful that she is here to help you.'

The attendant held William's writhing body down on the bed. 'Madam, let him die,' he grumbled in guttural Indian Tamil 'He is a real devil. I know what he does on the estate.' Shiro bit her lip to keep from laughing. William would understand every word.

She concentrated on inserting the intravenous lead and injecting the morphine. She set up the saline drip, then stood up to study the ECG recording spitting out of the machine. She picked it up. A chill ran through her at the sight. A bizarre, irregular, random waveform with no clearly identifiable QRS complexes or P waves. William was in ventricular fibrillation. She picked up her stethoscope and placed it on her chest. No heart sounds.

'Nurse,' she said, 'do you have a defibrillator?'

She pulled the curtains to isolate the bed from the rest of the ward.

Ripping off William's shirt, Shiro brought her palms together over his chest. She had to try manual resuscitation. She repeated the compression.

The nurse wheeled in the defibrillator.

Shiromi glanced at the attendant. 'Look what I am doing. Can you do this while I set up the machine?'

'Madam –' he said.

'Do it,' Shiro commanded. 'Here, put your hands like this. Now push. Then release. Then push. Good. Keep doing it. '

Shiro slipped her hands into the plastic handles of the metal paddles. 'The anterior electrode is placed on the right, below the clavicle,' she said to herself. *Go on, girl. You can do this.* She threw her mind back to the demonstration she had seen. She placed the paddle in her left hand just below William's right shoulder. 'The apex electrode is applied to the left side of the patient, just below and to the left of the pectoral muscle.' Her right hand moved over to the left of his body. She pressed down on the paddles.

'Move,' she said to the attendant. 'Nurse, switch the machine on.'

The current zipped through William's body. His body jerked, then went still.

Shiromi looked at the ECG print. They were losing him.

'Damn. No change. Still fibrillating. Nurse, again.'

The jerk again.

The pointer on the ECG machine moved up, then down. Sinus rhythm. Dropping the paddles, she grabbed the stethoscope and listened to William's heart. There was a slow, laboured but normal, beat.

A sob. Janet's voice outside the curtain. 'Please can I see him? Is he dying?'

Shiro stepped away from the bed. 'Let her see him.'

Janet stepped through the curtain. 'Doctor, is he dead?'

'No Janet, he isn't dead. You can have him back, for whatever good that does you!'

'Shiro! But –'

'Save me the hysterics, Janet.' Shiro walked away and picked up the admission record. 'Nurse, stay with the patient.' She sat down at the ward desk and wrote down what she had done.

Dr Nirmalan bustled into the ward, still in casual jeans and t-shirt. 'Shiromi, I am so sorry. I was so sure nothing would happen today.'

Shiro handed him the patient notes. 'It's all right. It was an interesting challenge.'

Dr Nirmalan glanced down at her notes. 'You did manual resuscitation and defibrillation? That's impressive.'

Exhaustion caught up with her. She felt empty and drained right to the soles of her feet. 'I'm really tired, Dr Nirmalan. Would you mind if I left now?'

He nodded. 'I'll take over. Go get some rest.' He turned and walked through the curtain. 'Hello, you must be Mrs Ashley-Cooper. I am Dr Nirmalan. Sorry I was out when your husband was brought in, but Miss Rasiah has done an amazing job. Her quick thinking and action saved your husband's life.' He glanced at Janet's face. 'You should go across to surgery and get a dressing.'

Shiro slipped off the white coat and leaned on the wall outside the ward. She turned at the sound of footsteps. 'Shiromi, please, I want to thank you,'

Shiro studied Janet's face. 'Are you sure, Janet? Did you really want his life saved?' She stared at the dark shadow around Janet's bloodshot right eye, then slipped her gaze down to the cut and swollen lip. 'We should get you to emergency and get your face seen to.'

'He was upset after you and his – brother, the doctor, left. He threatened Appu, accused him of gossiping. He assaulted Appu. Appu wouldn't defend himself. I tried to stop William.' She raised her hand to her face and winced.

Shiro took a deep breath, then let it out slowly. 'Wife abuse and battery, just another link in the tale of the Ashley-Cooper Empire. Come on, let's get your face seen to.'

Leaving Janet in the hands of Nandan in Emergency, Shiro stepped out into the hospital gardens just as Jega's car screeched to a stop in the car park. He jogged across the car park to her.

'Shiromi, I went back to the manse. There was a call from William's wife. She said that William has had a heart attack and was being brought here.'

Shiro smiled at him. 'You were worried for me, Jega?'

'Of course.'

Shiro placed her hand on his arm. 'You know what I did, Jega? I saved his life! He was in ventricular fibrillation. I should have left it. Let him die. No. I couldn't, could I? Hippocratic Oath and all that. I did manual and then defib. The man who destroyed my happiness and killed my father. I saved his life!'

Jega put his hand around her shoulder.

They turned and walked towards the staff quarters.

Chapter 40

Ten days later ... September 1969 Nuwara-Eliya

'So James Ashley-Cooper is father to you, Lakshmi and Anthony? But not to William?'

Jega nodded. 'And William and Anthony are the children of his wife, Elise.'

'Then Anthony is the only child they both share?'

'Correct.'

'You, William, Anthony and Lakshmi, all children of the Ashley-Cooper Empire.'

They sat in the café next to Nuwara-Eliya Hospital. A pot of tea and a plate of cupcakes lay on the wrought iron table between them. Shiro poured out two cups of tea. She handed one to Jega.

'And the child, Daniel, is William's bastard. Typical.' Shiro shivered.

Jega reached over the table and covered her left hand with his. 'Shiromi, it's been over a week since we went to Bob Kirkland's manse and all the drama afterwards. I can perfectly understand you not wanting to see William in the ward, but you won't speak to Anthony or even Lakshmi. She's heartbroken, Shiro. We are going back to Colombo in a couple of days.'

'You've talked with them. It's right that you should. They are your family. And as for them, I can understand Lakshmi being heartbroken. And Anthony? Is he heartbroken too?' Her laugh was brittle, even to her ears.

'Maybe you should let him explain.'

She shut her eyes. 'Jega, I can see what you are trying to do. You want me to clear my head of the past so I could move forward. But Anthony betrayed me. He said he loved me, then obeyed his father and let me down. He paid off Daddy for my treatment, sent money for my uni fees. He used his wealth to assuage his conscience. I should hate him for what he did. But I can't hate him.' She opened her eyes. 'Jega, I'm scared.'

'You're scared that you will find out that you love him, not hate him.'

She shut her eyes. She couldn't let Jega see the pain.

'Shiromi, What I am going to tell you is going to rock your world even more. But I want you to listen. And I want you to make a head decision, not a heart one.'

'Okay.' She frowned, trying to read his expression and failing. 'What is this momentous news?'

'James Ashley-Cooper and his wife, Elise, are here.'

'Here?' Shiro gasped. 'As in Nuwara-Eliya? But why? To see William?'

Jega's fingers tightened over hers. 'It's complicated. James wants to work out a deal on the sale of the plantations. I believe what happened with William brought the date forward.'

'How would that affect me?'

'He would like to see you, Shiromi. He wanted me to ask you.'

Shiro shut her eyes again. She heard her dad's voice. *White bastards think they can do what they want.* Yes, she would meet him. Show him that she and her people in Sri Lanka didn't need to kow-tow to the white Raj. He could take his money and shove it. She smiled.

'You're amused. That's a good sign. Does that mean you'll talk to him?'

Shiro nodded. 'You think I should?'

'Yes. He said he'll ring you at the doctor's quarters this evening.'

She grabbed his hand in both of hers. 'I'll do it. I'll show him what we Sri Lankans are made of. I'll do it for my parents, your mother – all the natives and coolies.'

Chapter 41

'Miss Rasiah, this is James Ashley-Cooper.' Who would believe that the high and mighty head of Oriental Produce could sound nervous! But he did, just a teeny little bit. Shiro took a deep breath and exhaled slowly.

'Good evening, Mr Ashley-Cooper.'

'Firstly, my dear, my wife and I would like to thank you for saving William's life. We talked to doctor Nirmalan. He told us that William would have died if you hadn't acted as you did.'

'Thank you, Mr Ashley-Cooper.' So he spoke of William by name, not as 'our son'. 'Dr Nirmalan is very kind to say so. I only did my duty.' *And*, she thought, *when did I become your 'dear'?*

Now he sounded hesitant. 'But the real reason I called you was to invite you to have lunch with my wife and me tomorrow.'

Shiro cradled the phone in her hand. An invitation to lunch with James Ashley-Cooper and his wife. *Okay, Daddy. This is for you.*

'I would be delighted to meet you both at lunch.' She drew her intonation from the elocution classes and tea time conversations with Miss Grace Rowling.

'Thank you, Miss Rasiah,' He sounded relieved. He must have expected her to refuse. 'I'll send the company car for you. It's a white Rolls Royce. You will recognise it by the Oriental Produce crest on the door – silver, two leaves and a bud. Would eleven-thirty be a convenient time for the chauffeur to pick you up?'

Shiro bit her lip to keep from laughing. Like she needed to have the Oriental Produce crest to identify the car. Did these people think the car park in Nuwara-Eliya Hospital was full of Rolls Royce and Wolseleys at visiting time?

'That would be nice, thank you.'

'We are having lunch at the Royal Hotel.'

'The Royal Hotel?'

'Yes, my dear, I am inviting you to have lunch with us at the Royal Hotel. And just in case you are concerned, I have informed them that I will be entertaining a guest for lunch tomorrow. Trust me, there will be no problems.'

He is either testing me or letting me know that he doesn't care about the proprieties of the whites only policy in the Royal Hotel. Okay. I can play along.

'Thank you, I'll be ready at eleven-thirty.'

'I look forward to seeing you tomorrow, Miss Rasiah.'

***

Shiro slipped on the slim fitting, black linen skirt and looked through her blouses. 'Not white today.' Picking out a pure silk, clotted cream blouse and beige cashmere jacket, she slipped her feet into a pair of heeled black leather shoes.

'Okay,' she said to her reflection in the mirror, 'let's go face the master and commander of the empire!'

The chauffeur, dressed in a white, long sleeved suit and peaked cap, stood by the white Rolls Royce. He reached out and opened the back door for her. 'Your carriage, princess.'

Shiro jerked back and looked into the chauffeur's face. Only her childhood friends and family called her princess.

'Elmo! I didn't know you worked as a driver for Oriental Produce.'

Elmo, eldest son of the apothecary in Watakälé, pulled his cap off. 'I work as a chief clerk in the Colombo office, but the boss wanted someone who knew the hill-country roads.' He swept his hand towards the car. 'Who would pass up the opportunity to drive this beauty?'

Shiro walked around the car to the front passenger seat. Elmo held the back door open. 'No way, Shiro. You will arrive in style. Remember this is the Royal Hotel we're driving to.'

He had a point. Shiro slipped into the plush comfort of the black leather upholstered seat. 'Thanks, Elmo.'

As the car turned onto the main road, Elmo caught her eye in the rearview mirror. 'The Boss and the Mrs aren't too bad. They've been nice to me. One of the first things he did was tell me not call him sir. No colonial bunkum, he said.'

'I don't trust them, Elmo.'

'You remember when we were kids, Shiro? You were always the brave one with the big dreams and plans. Trust your instincts on this meeting.'

The car turned into the drive of the Royal Hotel.

A couple stood side by side at the entrance to the hotel. He stood tall and straight, dressed in a charcoal grey suit and white silk shirt. His greying, blond hair lent an air of distinction. In contract the woman was a delicate porcelain figurine in a pale mauve, ankle length woollen dress. Her hair formed a pale blonde frame for her delicate features.

Elmo drove up to the front of the hotel. He jumped out and opened the door for her. 'Shiro,' he said in an undertone. 'Dad told us about what happened between you and young Ashley-Cooper. Keep your chin up. I'll be driving you back after lunch. We can talk then.'

Shiro slid out of the car and smiled at Elmo. 'Thank you.'

***

The obligatory pre-lunch drinks of iced tea with a twist of fresh lemon was followed by dishes of spicy mixed seafood salad. The conversation followed a predictable track. A repeat of thanks for saving William's life, followed by questions about medical school and life in Colombo. The health of her mother. Her brothers careers.

The waiter cleared the salad plates.

It was time to move this conversation forward. Shiro smiled to take the edge off her words. 'Mr Ashley-Cooper, why exactly did you want to see me?'

He smiled. 'Miss Rasiah – may I call you Shiromi?'

Shiro nodded her assent.

'There are some things I want to say to you that need a face-to-face conversation. Some of what I say may make you annoyed, even angry. I ask you to please hear me out. Can you do that?'

Shiro nodded again.

'Firstly, I want you to know that I knew and trusted your father. I can state categorically that I would never have accused him of any dishonest dealings.' He glanced at his wife. 'I had no idea what William was up to. I am not proud to say that. I should have kept an eye on him, but under the circumstances, I let it slip.'

Shiro looked into the slate grey eyes. So like Jega's. 'Thank you for your words about my father. I guess by circumstances you mean the impending nationalisation of the plantations. But you do know now what William did?'

'My dear,' he leant over towards her, 'it was diabolical.'

'Shiromi, it's amazing that you saved his life especially when you knew what he had done. You truly are an exceptional young woman.' Elise Ashley-Cooper's cultured tone was in keeping with her gentle bearing.

Shiro looked from one to the other. 'He was a patient. I did what any health professional would do under the circumstances.'

James and his wife exchanged glances.

'There's another reason I wanted to see you, Shiromi. Jega tells me that you know the family history. I am not proud of all of it, but it is what it is. What I do know is that *my* three biological children all love you very much.'

Shiro kept a smile pasted on her face. Where was this conversation going?

'What I am trying to say is that Elise and I would be happy to see you continue your relationship with any of them.'

It took all her control to keep quiet.

The waiter came back with their main course. Grilled salmon on vegetable couscous.

Shiro kept her eyes down on her plate.

Slim manicured fingers fluttered over Shiro's hand. 'Shiromi, we will not object to a relationship between you and either Jega or Anthony.'

Shiro picked up a piece of salmon on her fork. She forced herself to swallow. She took a deep breath. *Calm down, girl.* 'Jega is a good friend, Mrs Ashley-Cooper. And I haven't had any contact with Anthony since –' She put her fork down and looked direct at James Ashley-Cooper. 'Since you forced him to stop his friendship with me and leave Watakälé for England.'

Black eyes and grey met. 'Jega told me that you are beautiful and brilliant. Janet said that you were an avenging angel when you took on William. And Anthony – well you know what Anthony feels for you.'

The waiter placed a dessert menu before them. 'No, thank you.' Shiro smiled at the waiter. 'I'll have a cup of tea. Black with no sugar.' It gave her the time to collect her thoughts.

'Mr Ashley-Cooper, when Anthony and I were friends, I was a schoolgirl. I am now on my way to being a doctor. And he is moving to Australia with his son.'

The waiter placed the tea service on the table. Elise Ashley-Cooper picked up the silver teapot and poured the tea. She added milk to hers, then passed the other two cups to Shiro and her husband. Her voice was soft, almost a whisper. 'But you still care for him.'

Shiro put her cup on the saucer. She wouldn't let them see her pain. 'Anthony was the first man I cared for. But I will move on. I have my medical career here. I am finished with plantation life.' She blinked her eyes. No tears. There would be time enough for that later.

Elise's fingertips brushed Shiro's hand. 'We talked about that with Jega. He tells us that the study you have done here in Sri Lanka can be transferred to a medical school in Australia.'

Shiro looked from one to the other. 'Why would I want to do that?'

James Ashley-Cooper cleared his throat. What now?

'Shiromi, you are upset. I understand. But there is one more thing you need to know and I hope it will help you to bring the closure you need. Will you hear me out?'

Shiro shrugged.

'Anthony and I spent a lot of time together after he left the plantation. It started off with my desire to make him understand why I needed to get him away from it –'

'And from me.'

He winced. 'Yes, that too. But in the time we spent together, I realised that Anthony's plan for the plantation and the people was more than just a fly-by-night dream. I realised that it made sound economic sense.'

Shiro raised her eyes to meet his. She might as well be frank. There was nothing to lose now. 'My father and Anthony both talked to me about it. They saw it as their moral duty to help the staff and labour. It was not just about money.'

He nodded. 'Oh, Anthony made that very clear to me. In the end, it was his passion that won me over.'

'You agree with their plans for staff and labour wages and savings?'

'Yes Shiromi. That is why I am here.' He glanced across the table at his wife. 'We plan to spend the next three years implementing Anthony's reforms and negotiating a clean handover to the government.'

'*You* will do it?'

'Elise and I will live in Watakälé. We are in contact with the other plantation owners. The plantations will be handed over to the government of Ceylon – well, Sri Lanka, with the staff and labour rights already in place.'

'So the government will not be able to renege on it after the takeover?'

'Once set, the Sri Lankan government cannot go back on it.'

Shiro smiled. 'It is what Anthony and my father dreamed of. But Daddy is dead and Anthony will be in Australia.'

'Anthony will make a trip to Australia to negotiate the deal with the vineyards. But he will come back and spend six months here helping me. There is no way I could do it all without him.'

'And William?'

'He is too ill to continue. Janet and he will go back to England as soon as he is able to travel.'

'Anthony must be ecstatic.' She looked away from them, at the red roses in the hotel garden. Anthony back in Watakälé. In her dreams she would be with him. But that was all it was – a dream. It was time for her to move on. She pushed her chair back and stood up. 'I need to get back. Thank you for lunch. And thank you for sharing your plans for the plantations. It will be appreciated by the staff and labourers.'

She shook hands with them both. James Ashley-Cooper's hand was firm and warm. Elise held Shiro's hand in both of hers. 'Anthony talked about you to me, Shiromi. You are all he said and more.'

They walked her to the car. James Ashley-Cooper didn't wait for the driver to get out, instead he walked down the steps and held the car door open for her.

'I have asked the driver to be available to drive you to Watakälé. It will help you get the closure you so desire. You said you wouldn't be back to the plantations. Maybe this is a chance to say goodbye?'

Why not? What better way to rid herself of the demons than to return to where it all started in the Oriental Produce silver-embossed chariot. She smiled at them both. 'Thank you. That is kind of you.'

James Ashley-Cooper nodded and moved to the driver. 'Madam would like to visit Watakälé. You can take your time. We are in no hurry for the car.'

Shiro slid into the back and sank back in the seat. The car slid forward.

'Elmo, I'm glad you are driving me back. I've just about had enough of the mighty British Empire.' She groaned. 'Invitation for lunch, indeed. What were they doing? It was like – thanks for saving the life of one of our progeny. Would you like one of the others as a reward! And she has the audacity to ask me if I *cared* for Anthony. Cared –' Shiro laughed. 'I wonder how they would have responded if I had said that I loved him and love him still!'

She dropped her head in her hands. 'Then he tells me that he's staying for three years. Setting up the payment and savings plan for staff and labour. He plans to hand it all to the Sri Lankan government as a fait accompli! Anthony gets to see his dreams come true.'

The car purred along the main road.

She felt a sob build in her throat. 'This is all so stupid. Elmo, please take me back to the hospital. Watakälé was a bad idea.'

The car slowed, then pulled off the main road towards the lake. 'Okay Elmo. I'm a basket case.' she sighed. 'Let's walk by the lake and talk about the good old days when we were children.'

The driver got out and opened her door. He flicked off his cap and held his hand out to her. 'No, Shiro. Let's talk about the future.'

She looked up at the gold hair and blue eyes that filled her dream and her heart. 'Anthony, how –?'

He reached into the car and drew her out. He held on to her hand. 'Because my dreams cannot come true without you. Because you are avoiding me and because you have just said that you love me.'

'You cheated.'

'Sure. But it worked, didn't it? You wouldn't return my calls, Shiro. And Jega said it wouldn't be wise for me to come to the hospital quarters. Not good for your professional reputation.'

'And today?'

'My parents realised quickly that I was unhappy in England. Things have changed, darling. The era of the white British Raj is over. My parents realise that. They also know that you, princess, are my love, my heart.' He tilted her face to his. 'I was terrified when I saw how close you are to Jega. He is a good man. So worthy of you. But I wanted to tear you away from him.'

Shiro smiled up at him, watching the shades of anxiety and fear cloud his eyes. 'And just now you said that you loved *me*.'

She pouted. 'I thought I was talking to Elmo.'

He drew her into her arms. She went to him. She felt his fingers in her hair. The clips dropped off. Her hair blew around her face onto his. She heard his indrawn breath. 'Shiro darling, please give me a chance to show you how much I love you.'

Anthony teased his knuckle down her cheek and cupped her chin in his hand. 'Lakshmi told me about a dream you and she shared as children. One where you would be together, your children playing. The dream can come true, princess. Our children.' He smiled and touched her lip with his finger. 'Yes, yours and mine will play with Lakshmi's Daniel, except it will be in a vineyard in Australia and not a tea plantation in Sri Lanka.'

Shiro shook her head. 'Your parents and Jega helped you plan this meeting didn't they? That's why your mother said I could get credit for my courses in an Australian medical school.'

'Jega cares for you deeply, Shiro. He knows now that I encouraged you to follow your dreams of medical study and would never ask you to give it up. He contacted the Adelaide Medical School. And my parents, they realise that you are my future. Marry me, princess. Come with me to Australia.' Anthony reached into his pocket and pulled out a small velvet covered box. He flicked it open.

The blue sapphire absorbed the sparkle of the diamonds that surrounded it. 'It's the Ashley-Cooper engagement ring. My grandfather had it made. It was meant to represent the Ashley-Cooper Empire. The Sri Lankan sapphire surrounded by South African diamonds. The wife of the firstborn wore it. I wondered why my parents didn't give it to William. Now I know.' He picked up her hand and slipped it onto her finger.

She glanced down at the ring and then into Anthony's eyes. In the clear blue depth she saw his love – and her future.

'I think I like the sound of Dr Shiromi Ashley-Cooper.'

Anthony's arms tightened around her. He bent his head to kiss her.

Shiromi giggled.

Anthony raised his head. 'I'm not sure I like that twinkle in your eyes, princess.'

Shiro placed her hands on either side of his face. She stood on tip-toe to whisper in his ear, 'I can't wait to show our children the letters Ann Ashley-Cooper wrote to me!'

Glossary

Acca: (Tamil) older sister.

Achchi: (Tamil) grandmother.

Aiya: (Tamil) used as term of respect, like 'sir', although it literally means brother.

Aiyoo: polite exclamation. Akin to saying 'Oh dear'.

Amma: mother. Also used as a term of respect, akin to madam, as in 'Malar Amma'.

Aney: casual exclamation, in this context it is expressing delight.

Angé pore: (Tamil) move over there.

Annai: (Tamil) older brother. Sometimes used as a term of respect to an older male.

Appa: (Tamil) father. A wife didn't address her husband by name. She would call him 'Appa' which means father.

Appu: the cook and housekeeper to British superintendents.

Arak: home brewed alcoholic beverage from the coconut palm.

Ayubowan: (Sinhalese) salutation wishing the recipient a long life, typically as a greeting or a goodbye.

Baila: lively dance music introduced to Sri Lanka by the Portuguese.

Betel: the leaf of the vine piper betel chewed with areca nut and slaked lime paste. It is a mild stimulant.

Chenthamil: (Tamil) the native Sri Lankans from the north of the country believe that they speak a pure unadulterated dialect of the language.

Chinnamma: (Tamil) young miss. Lakshmi addresses Shiro as Chinnamma out of respect. The word 'amma' means mother, but is also used as a sign of respect, akin to madam.

Coolie: indentured Indian labour working in the tea plantation.

Egg Hopper: made from a fermented batter of rice flour, coconut milk and sometimes a dash of palm toddy. Cooked with an egg in the centre.

Ganja: marijuana.

Hodhi: a light gravy of coconut milk, turmeric and spices.

Ingé pore: (Tamil) come over here.

Jaffna Tamil: Tamils who trace their heritage to the north of Sri Lanka.

*Kadala*i: boiled and tempered pulse with coconut and hot chili.

Kade: small corner store.

Kaluthai: donkey.

*Kangan*i: (Tamil) Indian labour supervisor.

Kavanam: (Tamil) be careful.

Kiribath: rice porridge cooked with coconut milk.

Kohled: eyes outlined and painted in black eyeliner like paint.

Mahal: (Tamil) daughter.

Nandri illatha kaluthai: (Tamil) ungrateful donkey.

Nohuthu: (Tamil) a cry of excruciating pain.

Palaharams: (Tamil) A generic term for snacks sweet and savoury.

Palayang yako: (Sinhalese) go away, you idiot.

Parvati: Hindu Goddess considered as the supreme Divine Mother. She is considered her as the ultimate Divine Shakti — the embodiment of the total energy of the universe. She was homemaker and the protector of her husband (Shiva).

Pasikithu: (Tamil) I am hungry.

Periadorai: (Tamil) the senior superintendent of the tea plantation.

Periamma: (Tamil) madam. Amma is mother. However when the prefix 'Peria' or 'big' is added it means madam.

Pittu: steamed cylinders of ground rice paste layered with coconut.

Podeher Aiya: (Tamil) the minister in church.

Rambuttan: small red fruits about the size of golf balls. The fruit flesh is translucent, whitish or very pale pink, with a sweet, mildly acidic flavour

Roti: griddle cakes made with flour, water and grated coconut.

Seenisambol: A dish made with chopped onions, chillie powder that is sweet and hot.

Soonyam: a curse or charm meant to induce the demons to bring illness or death on a person.

Stringhoppers: a form of steamed rice noodles. A traditional Sri Lankan breakfast dish.

Swami: a holy man with supposed supernatural powers.

Thambili: juice of the young coconut.

Thosai: savoury pancake originating in South India.

Thovil: thovil or 'devil-dancing' is a ritualistic healing ceremony that primarily belongs to folk religion. The dancers dress up to represent demons.

Uderata Maniké: (Sinhalese) upcountry girl. The name given to the locomotive taking the train up to the hill country.

Vadai: Indian-style savoury fritters made with variety of pulses and fried.

Vallukum: (Tamil) you may slip, it is slippery.

Vayapothu: (Tamil) shut up.

Veedu: (Tamil) house.

Veeté poungé: (Tamil) go home.

Vellala: A high caste Tamil.

Vesak lanterns: colourful lanterns of paper and bamboo sticks lit to celebrate the commemoration of Buddha and his Enlightenment.

About the author

Patricia Weerakoon is a medical doctor cum academic turned Sexologist and Writer. She retired in 2012 from a career as director of an internationally renowned graduate program in sexual health at the University of Sydney to pursue her passion for writing and public speaking. Her novels bring together her international experience in sexual health and her passion for her homeland of Sri Lanka.

As a Sexologist she has translated her passion to bring good holistic sexual health to all people into practical sex education, sex research and sex therapy. Patricia has a recognised media presence and is a popular public speaker and social commentator in Australia.

Follow Patricia Weerakoon and find out more about *Empire's Children* at her blog: patriciaweerakoon.com/empireschildren